# Also by Andy Remic

*Spiral*
*Quake*
*Warhead*
*War Machine*
*Biohell*
*Kell's Legend*

A COMBAT-K NOVEL

# HARDCORE

## ANDY REMIC

SOLARIS

First published 2009 by Solaris
an imprint of Rebellion Publishing Ltd,
Riverside House, Osney Mead,
Oxford, OX1 0ES, UK

*www.solarisbooks.com*

ISBN: 978 1 84416 792 0

10 9 8 7 6 5 4 3 2 1

A CIP catalogue record for this book is available from the
British Library.

Designed & typeset by Rebellion Publishing

Printed in the US

*This one's for Sonia, and she alone.*
*For inspiring the hardcore... but definitely not the*
*nurses.*

# JUNKED

THEY CALLED HER Kotinevitch. Vitch... Vitch the Bitch. She didn't mind. She kind of agreed. She certainly lived up to the image of fucked-up aggravated psycho with hardcore in-your-face kick-ass violence. She was First General of Quad-Gal Military's Prime Fleet.

General Kotinevitch stood on the bridge of the FRAG Bulk Fighter, *The Indestructible,* as around her marble lights glittered, laser-traces humming hydrogen songs in secondary ears, and her staff rushed about urgent business. She stared into space; deep space, velvet, endless, uninviting, her face bleak as she listened to the bustle of battle *coordination.*

*This is it*, she thought. The moment she'd been waiting for all her life. The battle she knew, from inception into the military, had to come. The utmost test of all military minds. Galaxy-wide *War*.

*It is a deterrent. But if we must go to war, then we will go to war. If there must be bloodshed, then it will be terrible.* She remembered all too clearly her naive words. It seemed millennia since she uttered those childlike sentiments; now, she appreciated the irony. Threat of war was no longer a deterrent. It was real. Big. Bloody. Fucked-up. Violent. And very, very real.

Vitch's War Machine must *live*.

Around her, space seemed to *glow* black. The System of Xylag was small, and sparsely populated. Googan, its singular star, was old. No, *old*. Fat, bloated, a sickly crimson casting eerie glows of wrinkled patronage across spinning wards. The four planets under Googan's watchful gaze were Tuton, a black and red veined dwarf planet with a thin crust and consisting of almost permanent seismic and volcanic upheaval; Jekyll, a Jovian planet, mammoth, green, a gas giant with twin rings of heavy-metal infused silicates and selenium; YYK, a small warm terrestrial which would have been perfect for human life if its atmosphere didn't entirely consist of cyanide and nitrogen; and the fourth, Outermost, was a minor, consisting of a body of gas, purple and orange, with twin ruby moons.

Kotinevitch had moored her FRAG Fighter close to Jekyll, aware that magnetic interference would be greatest here and thus potentially disrupt the enemy scanners and communication. She was also aware of the *need* she felt within. As if Jekyll protected her WarFleet with its huge bulge, its glowing rings; its sheer bloody mass.

She had picked the perfect ambush spot. The junks were coming. It was pivotal Vitch hit them hard.

" Permission for de-LS."

" Permission granted. Begin the relay."

Kotinevitch watched the scanners with a practised eye. The blackness of space seemed to *distort*, and the arriving machines decelerated at an incredible rate. First BULK Attack Crafts, fifty of them, slamming from nowhere to hang suspended in the crimson glow of the bloated Googan star. These vehicles were mammoth, and stocked from port to aft with military-grade weapons. Their single purpose was to destroy. Using Halo Missiles, they had been known to take out entire *planets*.

Watching the fifty vessels stabilise on purple jets, and despite herself, Kotinevitch allowed a cold, brittle smile to crease her face. Then her features hardened like frozen hydrogen. She had awesome firepower at her fingertips. *Terrible* power.

This time, Quad-Gal outnumbered the enemy, eight-to-one.

As a politician, Vitch knew they needed a swift end to this expanding, accelerating upstart Empire. The junks were invading, decimating, polluting worlds in their escalating path across the Sinax Cluster. Now it was time for payback...

Engines howled in silent agony as three thousand Piranha Fighters in a protective D7 Transport shield shimmered from 0.9LS, and banked like a shoal of glittering fish around the manoeuvring, shifting BULKs. In comparison, they were lithe, swift and piloted with consummate skill. Vitch felt pride swell in her breast. She stemmed it harshly. Now was not the time for such matters. The junks would be there in less than an hour. Her preparations had to be *perfect*. Her *ambush* had to be precise.

"I need the magnetic resonance shields online, Kade."

"Charging now, Lady. Detonation in five, four, three, two..." a huge rumbling emanated from the gas giant Jekyll as Kotinevitch hijacked magnetic resonance from the planet's rings in order to mask her fleet.

A pulse of serenity surged through the fleet...

"We are invisible to the enemy," said Kade, voice steady, eyes locked on scanners. "When the junks arrive, they won't know what hit them." He eyed General Kotinevitch squarely. "They'll be canon fodder. Easy-meat spaghetti for our High-Tensile Slayers."

"Good. They asked for it." Vitch's voice betrayed no emotion.

She watched as more of her WarFleet arrived,

Alligator Mobile Dead-Guns, D5 Transports, the new D9 Transports with Land-Stellar dropLines, swarms of K5 Lancasters, B2 Spitfires and G7 Hurricanes howling through the harsh no-go zones of DeadSpace, to emerge...

Here.

Like an artist, Kotinevitch sculpted her craft. Like a writer, she arranged every letter, every word, every perfect stroke of punctuation. Like a musician, she composed; her ships were her notes and she directed them with infinitesimal care in a broad, sweeping arc, with three layers of reserves, one of which nestled on the opposite shores of Jekyll.

There would be no mistakes.

They would crush the enemy.

"Ten minutes. Incoming," said Kade.

Vitch nodded, nerves starting to nag her psyche. What had she missed? What strategy was overlooked? There had to be *something*. But there wasn't. The junks were ambling like a fat pig into a trap of spears. Thirty thousand ships. Fifteen million *workers* of the junk army. It would have been messy, if not for the pure-fire detonation.

"They're like ants," Vitch told herself. "They feel nothing. Have no emotions. We are cleansing the Quad-Galaxies of an aggressive pollutant. A toxic scourge. It's that simple."

*Fifteen million lives...*

"Game on," . said Kade, glancing over to

Kotinevitch. She could sense his tension, but knew he would not crack. Kade was a professional, and she'd seen him rise through the ranks with consummate ease. He wouldn't crumble.

Like processed code, perfect to the binary digit, the junks were cruising across the Xylag System, their armada laid out in a classic spearhead. Kotinevitch found her mouth had gone... dry. She blinked. Felt a tick twitch the corner of her eye.

The enemy force was *big*. "I hope to all that's holy we're still invisible," she whispered.

"We are." Kade's voice was confident, smooth, slick. "Shit," he said. "This is gonna be one huge fucking fry-up. We'll pop up on their visuals in three minutes. General, shall I give the order to attack?"

Vitch nodded. "Yes. I want twin-layer twenty-five round Krater-Bursts from arrayed FRAGs, with fifteen hundred Piranhas in streamer-formation down both flanks to mop up anything not decimated therein. We'll keep the Lancasters in reserve, I don't trust these bastards as far as I can..."

"Lady." It was something about the tone of Kade's voice that froze Kotinevitch mid-speech and sent her mind spinning through a billion spirals of uncertainty as she analysed stratagems perfected hour after hour after hour, not just by her, but by all the great strategists of QGM, including the legendary General Steinhauer.

"What is it?" Her voice was cold. But she needed no answer. She could see for herself, on scanners and through *real* space. The junks had slammed into a sudden halt, huge wings of fighters arcing out like horns from the central core of troop transporters.

*They know we're here*, hissed an internal voice. *Now we'll have a real fight on our hands...*

"They see us," snapped Kade.

"Deploy the FRAGs." Her mouth was a desert. They were still out of range. The ambush relied on their magnetic invisibility thanks to Jekyll's generous rings of heavy-metal infused silicates and selenium. Their fleet was supposed to magnetically blend...

Vitch watched the mammoth FRAGs lurch forward, with twin arcs of supporting Piranha Fighters swaying to either side in formation. But she realised immediately something was wrong –

The junks had halted. They seemed to be waiting... for something. But what?

"Are we still clear system-wide?" snapped Vitch.

"All clear," said Kade.

"Something's wrong."

"What are they waiting for?"

"Fire when in range."

"Four, three, two, one..."

Kotinevitch could not hear the build-up of energy, but knew inside the FRAGs their ears would be bleeding. She watched the external coils *glow* and waited for the *thump* of awesome firepower – which never came.

"What the hell is *that?*" hissed Kade.

Kotinevitch's head snapped right. Her eyes narrowed. Then her mouth dropped open in total, awe-struck horror.

In a blur, Jekyll's titanic rings, each 150,000 miles across and five miles thick, spun on their axes and *streamed* towards Kotinevitch and her vast, encamped War Machine... A trillion trillion tonnes of rock and metal flowed from the gas giant's twisting, eye-beguiling rings as they flowed and powered and sheared and slammed towards the Quad-Gal WarFleet –

"Sound the retreat!" screamed Kotinevitch but it was too late and it happened so fast Kade didn't even have time to smack the signal. Jekyll's vast rings flowed and *consumed* the FRAG Bulk Fighters in an instant and sudden flares of fire and detonation signified their immediate destruction, their total annihilation. Vitch turned, to the left, catching a glimpse of the waiting, watching junk ships and felt sour bitterness, and hatred, and cold, cold fury fill her brain and body and soul as she realised with brittle clarity that the junks hadn't wandered into her trap; she had wandered into theirs.

Jekyll's solar rings ate the WarFleet.

Explosions roared in a rapid machine-gun concussion which pulsed through the entire system, and out beyond, into the Void, on the screams of a million dead...

In the blink of an eye, the entire Quad-Galaxy navy was destroyed.

COMBAT K: EFFICIENT in infiltration, assassination and detonation. Combat K, unsung heroes of the Quad-Galaxy, soldiers of fortune, the Special Forces elite squad who always got the job done. With only one drawback... they hated one another. But now, a directive: from General Steinhauer, of the Quad-Gal Military.

"Combat K will carry out missions for QGM. All three of you *will* co-operate, because you have been implanted with spinal logic cubes. If you do not work together, then you die. If one of you kills another, then again, all three die. Horribly. You have no say in this matter. You will work for QGM, you will help bring about the end of the junk invasion, the junk acceleration. Or you will die in the process."

"I'd rather fucking die," snarled Pippa.

Steinhauer smiled. "Die, then," he said.

THE BLIP, A semi-sentient Monitor-Drone, watched Combat-K uneasily as they cruised through a seemingly endless state of REM sleep. It was a long haul from The City in a cold, cargo-storage SLAM Freighter. In half-stasis pods, Combat K dreamed, and the Blip watched their dreams on linked nerve-spine monitors, searching for... inconsistencies.

Pippa dreamed of a young girl with her hair in

flames. Pippa twitched, crying for her mummy, and was chased by a group of savage snarling children, screaming at her, hurling matches, yelling, "Burn the witch, burn the witch, burn the witch." Tears rolled down her face as she curled into a ball; and her sorrow lasted an eternity.

Franco, as usual, was dreaming about sex. Only this time it was a forced infection, and he awoke, cold and grey, vomiting and scratching, the *beat* of the rhythm through his veins carrying strange alien toxins which made his flesh bloat, his internal organs die, and he awoke screaming screaming screaming... into *another* dream, which simply repeated his frustration, his infestation, his raw and painful agony, of both body and soul.

And Keenan dreamed of his girls, his young dead girls, and they were beautiful and radiant and they stretched out for him, pleading in their eyes, in their cries, "Come with us, daddy," they said. "Be with us, daddy. We *miss you.*" And Keenan fumbled with his Techrim 11mm, cold shivering hands placing the barrel in his mouth and pulling the trigger. There was a muffled *blam* and the rear of his skull detonated, skull shards and liquid mashed brain ejecting in slow-mo spirals and he blinked, was normal again, alive again and he dreamed of his girls, his young dead girls, and they were beautiful and radiant and they stretched out for him, pleading...

All life is a cycle, thought the Blip.

And all death a fitting end.

PART I

# SICK WORLD

# CHAPTER ONE

# PARTY BOY

IT WAITED IN the slime, playing with its peroxide-blonde hair, twirling tight curls and bobs between fingers with lacquered, polished nails, and enjoying the feel of oozing mud and rotting vegetation. Cherry-red lips pulled back over crooked yellow teeth as the creature *grinned*, and it knew, *knew* fresh meat was coming. It could *smell* it. And if it waited for long enough, fresh meat always arrived, fresh and plump and wriggling and tasty. Screaming, yes, but that was an inconsequence easy enough to handle. What took *real* skill was keeping the meat alive. Helping the meat repair. Nursing the meat in getting *better*. That was the real skill.

* * *

THE TITAN PLEASURE Cruiser *Razzle* was sixty kilometres long, half a klick wide, a missile-ship crafted from Plutonium Dakkra and humming 0.7LS through hydrogen, methane and vast pockets of carbenes. It was a long dacromet needle piercing the most remote reaches of the Quad-Galaxy... a needle, threading an invisible galactic eye.

Originally built for the thousand-year Helix War, the Pleasure Cruiser's original objective had been infantry and vehicle transport – on a *vast* scale. After the Helix War was brought to a violent, bloody and sudden conclusion by the Quad-Gal Peace Unification Army, so the Titan was retired from active military service and forwarded to a tacky pleasure travel outfit named *Whoral Pleasure* based on the hedonistic corporate hive of The City, and specialising in two-year Sinax Pleasure Cruise deals, with machine sex thrown in for free.

Now, however, after a recent spate of attacks by the expanding and flowering army of toxic aliens known as junks, Quad-Gal Military – or QGM – had requisitioned the ship as fast transport through Quad-Gal on a very select group of missions. Carrying a vast array of Combat-K and reg. army squads, even as QGM Generals formulated missions and directives, so the craft delivered troops, teams, even whole armies in a vast machine-gun volley of proactive and, unfortunately, *reactive* missions. Reactive was bad. Reactive meant the enemy had the tactical advantage.

One of eighty such stellar onslaughts, the *Razzle* was governed by the recently crippled figure of General Steinhauer, the originator of QGM Combat-K teams and currently in a state of high anxiety. As the Pleasure Cruiser hummed around him, and the orange and black glow of his suite gave him a pounding migraine, so the General pushed himself back from his desk and for the millionth time glanced down at his severance.

Steinhauer bobbed on the HoverChair, then gritted his teeth in a caricature of a smile. Bastard, he thought. *Bastard*. Even with sub-atomic nanotechnology, for reasons apparently unknown to medical science, Steinhauer could neither rebuild nor graft legs in place onto his disabled and savagely severed anatomy. According to top military surgeons, Steinhauer's own body violently rejected any attempt to rebuild his legs, and after the recent horrors of Biohell, the media nickname tagged to the deviant horrorshow that went on down on The City at the hands of corrupted hardware manufacturer NanoTek and its governing AI alien-grown GreenSource Mainframe instigator, so people no longer trusted biomod improvement nanotechnology – in case a person woke as a different damn *species*.

"You OK?" came a soothing, female voice. It was the HoverChair's inbuilt Psychosis Monitor. Her name was Jemma.

"Yes," snapped Steinhauer, irate for no reason.

He grimaced again. Actually, he did have a reason. He had no legs. And no genius of science could replace that which he'd taken so much for granted. "Stop asking me the same damn questions over and over again. In fact, stop analysing my mental health – because at this current moment in time, I haven't got any mental fucking health!"

Steinhauer dropped back to his pit of depression. And thought gloomily about the junks.

KEENAN WENT TO step through the doorway to his shared quarters, when Franco dropped his shoulder and barged his way in. Scowling, Keenan followed and watched Franco drop his pack, put his hands on his hips, and beam around the narrow combined recreation and sleeping quarters. The decor was art nouveau, all twisted alloy and bubble-filled glass. The floor was a new type of spongy jewel. Even the sinks gleamed, with swan-head taps. The toilet was a contemporary aero-suck titanium-III model. Advanced.

"I'm bunking here!" Franco landed on the bed, and bounced a few times. A spring popped. Franco beamed. "It's all right this, ain't it Keenan? I mean, getting ferried to our next mission on a damn *pleasure cruiser!*" His eyes gleamed, and he licked his lips.

"I wouldn't pay to stay here," said Keenan, dropping his own pack to his bed and eyeing Franco warily. "It's a little bit too… *tacky* for my liking."

"Tacky? Tacky! Keenan, your middle name should be *Moaning-Old-Goat*."

"You're the guy with a magpie eye for every plastic glitter bauble you can get your paws on. Now listen, we've got forty-eight hours until our DropShip leaves for Sick World. In that time we have to undergo medicals, get kitted out, check vehicles and weapons, and have upgrade implants. I don't want you heading out on the piss."

"Moi? Piss?" Franco spread his hands. "Why would you possibly think I might do that?"

"I know you, dickhead. So, no women, no beer, you understand? I need you switched on when we hit the ground."

"Hey," said Franco, "have you *ever* known a mere ten pints of Guinness stop me performing?" He scratched his ginger goatee beard, and frowned. "Or even twenty, for that matter? I am a veritable *party animal*, Keenan. You *have* to let me out to play."

"No."

"Aww, go on Keenan, don't be such a stick in a bucket of turd."

Keenan pulled free a battered Techrim 11mm pistol, and weighed it thoughtfully. "I'm not a... a *stick* in a bucket of turd, idiot." His words were tight. Controlled. But his eyes shone. "I'm just helping you to help yourself."

Franco slumped to his bed, and kicked his sandals forlornly. "Fine words coming from a damned Jataxa alcoholic."

"I don't drink anymore," said Keenan. "Not after Biohell. Not after the GreenSource Mainframe." He shivered, just a little, and remembered the cold clarity of alien thoughts flowing through his veins, acidic, cold, like hydrogen through an engine.

"Well, I believe I deserve a drink. I've, um, had some recent bad news. Needs a bit of cheering up, I do."

"You do? Why?"

Franco twisted uncomfortably. "Weeee*eelll,* do you remember how I got married to my sweet Melanie? My liddle chipmunk? My little pocket of furry honey delight?"

"You mean your eight-foot tall twisted deviated fiancée? Yeah, I remember it all too clear. You're a fucking braver man than me, Franco." Keenan shivered.

During the horrific events which had overtaken The City, an entire planet dedicated to pleasure and hedonism, and whereby anybody planet-side who'd taken a vanity biomod human or alien upgrade *transmogrified* into mutated, zombie-like creatures, Franco's new-found true-love, a tax-inspector by the name of Melanie, had changed quite horrifically into an eight-foot tall quivering mottled genetic super-soldier. Despite their best efforts to find Mel medical help, and get her changed back to a form considered more human, they had been unsuccessful. Apparently, NanoTek, the organic engineering butchers who created Mel's unfortunate biological modification, had made this particular model a *one way process*. Franco, however, being a man of his word, a soldier of iron principles, and with a constitution greater than any hardcore barroom brawler, had gone through with his ultimate promise. That of marriage to what was, effectively, a zombie.

It had been an interesting ceremony.

And an interesting wedding night.

"Well," Franco puffed out his chest, watching Keenan unpacking his kit, "I'll come right out and say it. We've had a bit of a lovers' tiff. There." He looked about in a shifty manner.

Keenan stopped, holding a pair of chemical-socks. He stared at Franco. "You had a lovers' tiff with an eight-foot mutation?"

"Aye."

"Did she bite off your head?"

"Very funny. No. It would appear we had very differing standards about how to conduct marital life."

"Meaning?"

Franco shook his head. "It was disgusting!"

"You mean her jellied vagina? The pus which continually leaked from her nipples? Or maybe the way her distended jaw continually drooled what could only be described as vomitus?"

"No, no, no, none of that." He waved his hand. "The damn woman expected me *to do my own ironing!* She wanted me to *wash the fucking dishes!* And, and this was the worse thing mate, like, I just can't believe she even *thought* this was a rational request..."

"Go on."

"Mel expected me to *shave off my beard.*"

"The horror," grinned Keenan, unloading several Techrim mags from his pack which *clacked* as he tossed them on the bed. "I expect she wanted you to pluck your nostrils, too. You never were one for a neatly-trimmed nasal bush."

Franco stared at the floor, looking sheepish. "Yeah, well, she filed for a divorce."

"*What?*"

Franco looked at Keenan. There was a hint of pain nestling deep in Franco's blue orbs. He sniffed. "Yeah. She filed for a divorce. I signed the paperwork yesterday. I'm officially a free agent."

Keenan scratched his head, and pointed at Franco. "So, let me get this straight, you're telling me *you were divorced* by an eight-foot mottled dribbling pus-drooling genetic mutation?"

"That's one way of putting it," mumbled Franco. He looked up. And brightened. "But look at it this way! At least I'm the *Party Boy* again! I like women! I like all kinds of women! But most of all, I like women I don't *know* very well!"

"You've not been listening, Franco."

"Eh?"

"No beer. No women. We have a briefing in..."

he checked his implanted plutonium watch. "Five minutes. Hangar 57. So sort out your shit, change your sandals, grab your PAD and follow me." Grumbling, Franco followed Keenan from the quarters and they headed for the mission barracks.

HANGAR 57 WAS packed with perhaps three thousand operatives, ranging from normal reg. soldiers up to Combat-K special forces. There was a dour, serious mood in the air as Keenan and Franco filtered through the ranks of men and women, some seated and many standing in groups, huddled and talking softly. Franco spotted Pippa, waved, and headed off before Keenan could stop him. Cursing, Keenan followed, and watched Franco slump down next to the lithe, athletic woman with bobbed brown hair and cold, grey eyes. She smiled up at Keenan, and he kicked Franco on the ankle as he squeezed past and took the only available seat – beside the woman he'd once swore he would kill.

"Ouch!" Franco rubbed his ankle. "Well, look at this! The original and the best Combat-K squad, back together again!"

"You make us sound like a breakfast cereal," said Pippa, running a hand through her hair. She turned to Keenan, and was about to speak when General Steinhauer floated in on his HoverChair and bobbed before the podium. A hush fell across the gathered soldiers.

"Welcome, all," began Steinhauer, face lined with pain from his recent dual amputation. Despite powerful drugs, the doctors could never quite remove the agony which burned him – both physically and mentally. "You are aware you have been hand-picked as those at the top of your particular fields. Recent events have shown we have underestimated the junks, and by association, Leviathan. The junks are three steps ahead of us, both in terms of numbers, weaponry, tactics, and technology. Two days ago, they destroyed General Kotinevitch's WarFleet."

Steinhauer paused, allowing that to sink in. Several gasps could be heard through the ranks.

Steinhauer continued. "Not only was the WarFleet crushed and decimated. It was done so with consummate ease. Arrogance. A disregard for the Quad-Galaxy's might, so long unchallenged after the brutality of the Helix War. Now, as you know, our mission here is one of intelligence gathering. The junks originated somewhere relatively local – and we need clues as to their origins, the source of their technology and, most importantly, how we can take the war to them. You have all been assigned to small squads, carefully picked by my Under-Generals in order to complement one another's specific talents. In a few moments, data will be transcribed to PADs and call-signs initiated. I want you to team up with your new squad mates, and from thence specific instructions will be streamed, and myself and Under-Generals will circulate in order to answer specific questions. Understood?"

"YES SIR!" thundered Hanger 57.

"One last thing, soldiers of the Quad-Gal. If we'd spoken two days ago, well, I had a different speech planned. The recent annihilation of Kotinevitch's WarFleet has put a new spin on events. The junks are accelerating their war effort, my friends. We need something, something special, in order to stop them. Only you can do this. Dismissed!"

Keenan's PAD buzzed, and he glanced down, then across to Franco. "Well done, Big Man, you've been promoted."

"Eh?" Franco was busy watching the arse of a lithe but powerful woman with long, jagged-cut red hair, who had just risen from her seat.

"It says here that our Combat-K gang are going to Sick World, but not alone. We're all Squad Captains. Franco, Pippa, you'll take a team of three down to the surface of Sick World; from there we'll split, carry out specific intelligence gathering and search several flagged archaeological sites, then reconvene after five days to plan the next step. If we think we have intel on the junks, we report and delve deeper. If not, we skip planet and head for the next designated target on the list."

"I'm a Squad Captain!" beamed Franco. He stood, and puffed out his chest. "Wow! That means, yeah, that means I have a team! We can do team building! Appraisals! I can give advice! Hell and damnation, I hope they're all pretty."

"Hello? Captain Haggis?"

Franco whirled, giving a full-teeth grin. The athletic woman with jagged red hair was smiling down at him, head tilted as she looked at her new boss and realised his eyes had strayed disconcertingly towards her cleavage.

"Hello there!" Franco saluted, a sloppy salute which had seen him, during his military career, clean an inordinate number of industrial bean-bins. He eyed the woman up and down with a lustful leer, noting the two swords sheathed, criss-cross, on her back. "Well well well, what have we got here, pretty one?"

Keenan choked. Pippa shook her head, sighing a sigh which said, *Jesus, Franco, some things will never change.*

The red-haired woman stared at him. Hard. "My name is Fizzy. And you can wipe that filthy look off your face for a start. It's going to be a long mission and the last thing me and the girls need is some leering pervert as a Squad Captain."

"The girls?" swooned Franco.

Fizzy nodded, to where two more tall, athletic women were weaving their way through the bustling throng of military activity. She introduced them. "This is Shazza." Shazza was tall, voluptuous, brunette. "And Candy." Candy was tall, voluptuous and blonde. All three women eyed

Franco with worrying distaste.

Franco, eyes popping from his skull, looked up towards the roof of the Pleasure Cruiser. He licked red, gleaming lips. Grinned. And said, "Yes. There is a god of the Quad-Galaxy! Girls? Follow me, and allow me to begin your education."

Franco moved away, hips swaying, and the three female squaddies followed uncertainly. Pippa fell against Keenan, laughing, and Keenan could not keep the grin from his battered face.

"He's got so much to learn if he thinks he has a chance in Seven Hells of getting near one of those femme fatales," said Pippa.

"Yeah, but the way he sees it, he has the Jonny Allen Syndrome. Try it with every fish, and sooner or later, one bites the bait." Allen had been an old Combat-K squaddie renowned for his amorous attentions, to robots as well as women. He used to have his bedpost notched for each sexual encounter. When asked about alien conquests, he'd tap his nose conspiratorially and lick gleaming lips and say, "But that's my little secret."

"Wonder where my squad is?" mused Pippa, looking about.

"Mine's here," said Keenan, and gave an internal groan. Who picked this ragtag bunch of mercenary detonation-heads? he thought, sourly, whilst forcing a smile to his face and shaking the hands of the three unkempt individuals who shuffled before him.

The first man was small, wiry, his army shirt cut off at the shoulders showing iron muscles like cord around poles. His arms were heavily tattooed. In fact, his chest, neck, cheeks, arms, hands and knuckles were all heavily tattooed. If there was bare flesh, the man had tattooed it. He shook Keenan's hand with the sort of gold-toothed grin that had Keenan checking his wallet.

"Ed," he said, voice a low growl. "I've heard a lot about you, Keenan. We should work well together. You're a man who gets the job done."

Keenan nodded, lips tight, teeth clenched. "I hope so."

The second man was, on first impressions, normal. Normal height, normal build, no discerning features. His brown hair was of average length, his features almost mild in their façade. It was his eyes that gave him away. One was orange, the other violet. And they told of a man not entirely there in the mentalist department. Keenan should know: he d spent enough hours around Franco Haggis.

"Maximux," he said, smiling with crooked teeth. "This should be a fun gig down on the Sick World. A sick world for a sick mind, I always say."

"Yeah, fun if you're a psycho," said Keenan, voice low, aware that Maximux was not breaking his handshake.

The grin widened. "I try my best."

And the third was quite obviously the leader. Last to introduce himself. Leading from the back

– that way, you got better odds. And taking his time to weigh Keenan up, time to observe Keenan's strengths and weaknesses, even as Keenan returned the favour. He was tall, powerfully built, had long, curly black hair, and an eye-patch. Keenan bit off the urge to crack jokes about pirates and parrots. This wasn't the sort of man you made jokes with.

"Nice to meet you, Keenan."

"And you would be?"

"Snake."

"I've heard of you."

"Only bad things, I hope?"

Keenan smiled easily. "Yeah, mate. Only bad things."

Pippa slapped Keenan on the back, drawing the attention of the three men. She grinned, eyes locked to Keenan's. "Well fellas, I'll leave you to play cricket. Don't play rough now!" She ambled away, laughing to herself. She'd seen the light of anger and annoyance in Keenan's eyes. Here was a squad you could do without, the sort of group you had to watch, and watch closely lest they prize the gold teeth from your jaws.

Pippa moved to the rendezvous on her PAD. And stared at Mel. "You've got to be joking. Shit. It's Franco's missus!"

Franco's ex-wife stood a little over eight feet tall. She was slim and wiry, skin a dark mottled brown, spotted, corrugated, and slick with grease. Her body was a mockery of a human female body, with long, quivering, dangling breasts reaching almost to the monster's waist, and with nipples like plums oozing grey pus. She had a long curved neck, and a small head which shone, round and hairless. Her lower jaw staggered out from a nightmare face in a staccato jump, the nose two pin-pricks, the ears flaps against pus-oozing orifices. Melanie's neck crackled with plates of armour as she moved her head, and her legs were thick, short, powerful. She growled at Pippa, who blinked.

"Who let you in?"

"Einhauer. Ed I id erling ervice."

"And now you're on our team?" Pippa considered this. She had to concede, Melanie was a tough cookie, and was a damn sight more powerful and efficient than ninety-nine percent of the Quad-Gal military she'd met on ops. Pippa reached out, took Mel's heavy claw, and shook the distended zombie appendage. "Glad to have you onboard."

"Elcome."

The next to arrive was a huge woman, as wide as she was squat, her jowls wobbling as she walked with her bulk compressed in the largest XXXXXXXL size uniform the QGM could administer. Her hair was tied back in a tight black bun, her face was oval, friendly, and yet her eyes and jaw were strong. Her breasts were huge, like badly-inflated comedy balloons, and her legs like shapeless, hairy tree-trunks.

"Olga. Nice to see you again," said Pippa,

weakly. She glanced across to Keenan, who was listening to his squad speak but with a curious, detached look on his face. They weren't the kind of men to turn your back on.

Whereas she... she seemed to have acquired the Combat-K Reject Squad. All she needed now was a Slab Mud Wrestler, or perhaps a sadistic, humourless SIM. In the end, it was worse even than that.

He was squat and powerful, broad-shouldered, with a shaved head and small, black, shark-eyes. His face was a bad example of Frankenstein-stitching from an event involving an industrial bone-stapler and an irate ginger squaddie one ace short of a pack. Once a spook for Combat K, and leader of a rebel outfit on The City during "The Zombie Troubles", the soldier was a washed-up burned-out hopeless senile delinquent.

"Betezh." Pippa smiled a tight smile. "Nice."

Betezh beamed. It was the sort of smile a shark gave before chewing off your legs. "Hiya Pippa! Isn't this incredible? I can't believe I've been assigned to your squad! I think somebody important has been pulling a few strings."

Pippa glanced over to Franco, in animated conversation with his bored looking team, and he grinned at her, and she *knew*. Money had changed hands. Franco did have that sort of sense of humour. Franco beamed, and gave her a dual thumbs up. Pippa gave him the finger.

"Yeah, it looks that way," agreed Pippa, eyeing Mel, Olga and Betezh with one horrific sweep of her gaze. Still, she thought. It could have been worse. She could have been landed with Keenan's dodgy back-stabbing mercenary team. At least these deviants she could *trust*. At least she'd seen them in operation; and that way, to some extent, knew what they were capable of.

"Ou OK?" asked Mel, looming over Pippa and making the combat woman jump.

"Yeah, Mel. I'm fine. Thank fuck we're not dropping into a fast-roll combat situation, that's all I can say."

KEENAN AND FRANCO stopped outside their quarters. Franco grinned at Keenan, who tilted his head, watching his little ginger friend.

"This is a *great* gig, ain't it Keenan?" beamed Franco.

"What do you mean?"

"What a doss! A skive! A fucking *party*, bro! Five days on a planet already scanned by DropBots. No enemies. No alien life forms. No trouble. Just you, me, Pippa, and a horde of sexy vixen team members. Did you see their legs, Keenan? Did you? And their breasts, mate? I tell you, I'd die a happy man if I could get my face between a few of those plump sweet pairs of peaches."

"Franco, you got *divorced* only a few days ago!"

"Aye?" He looked confused. "And?"

Keenan sighed. "Listen. We've a lot to do before DropTime. I want you on the ball, kit sorted, ready to move. I've got a meeting with Steinhauer – he's requested, shall we say, a *special* chat."

"So you want me polishing my boots?"

"And your guns."

"But Keenan!"

"What do you mean, 'But Keenan'?" Keenan's voice held toxic daggers.

"We're on a Pleasure Cruiser, baby! In my book, that's an open invitation to at least sample the finer pleasures of what our unwitting hosts have decided to place on the platter of pleasure." He beamed.

"No."

"But *Keenan?*"

"Confined to quarters. And, just to make sure you stay there, *Cam* is going to keep an eye on your ass."

Cam buzzed into view, his battered black shell scratched and dented. Small, about the size of a tennis ball, Cam was Keenan's personal Security PopBot. In reality, he had proved himself a lot more efficient and intuitive than his original directive implied.

"Oh no," said Franco, lifting his hands before him. "Not you!"

"Yes. Me." Cam sounded smug. "If he tries to leave, Keenan, do I have permission to sting him?"

"Definitely," growled Keenan, and stalked off

down the corridor, a modern-day Grendel in a steel-ship cavern.

Franco and Cam glared at one another in the corridor. Well, Franco glared at Cam. Cam simply spun, displaying tiny, glittering yellow lights. Yellow was smug in PopBot displaymatics. That much Franco knew.

Franco ran for the door opening. There was a brief struggle as Franco tried to squeeze through the portal and close it before Cam entered, but the PopBot's strength belied his tiny alloy size, and the door slammed shut, nearly trapping Franco's fingers.

"You little shit!"

"You ginger moron!"

"Alloy testicle."

"Bearded idiot."

Franco glared at the PopBot. He pointed with a stubby finger. "Listen, Keenan might have told you to confine me to quarters, but I'm going for a shit, reet, and I want my damn and bloody privacy. Alreet?"

"OK, OK. But don't get any ideas, midget. Last time, you punched me to the floor and volleyed me down the corridor. Don't think it's going to be so easy this time! I'm a GradeA+1 Security Mechanism with advanced SynthAI and a Machine Intelligence Rating (MIR) of 3450. I have integral weapon inserts, a quad-core military database, and Put Down™ War Technology. Nowadays, I don't get punched that easy, baby."

Franco grinned an all-teeth grin, grabbed the nearest alien pornography magazine, and headed for the loo.

"We'll see," he mumbled irascibly.

FROM HIS EMERGENCY belt toolkit, Franco extracted a Size 15 and stared at the four bolts which clamped the TitaniumIII toilet to the floor. He got down on his knees, poked his head around the base of the toilet, then attached the tool. There came four short *bzzzts* and Franco grinned at the toilet, as if savouring a private joke. With a hefty grunt, he hoisted it to one side where it made a *clang*.

"What are you doing in there?" came Cam's nasal whine.

"I'm taking a dump. Now fuck off."

"No, no, you're up to something in there, you little ferret."

"Get back to oogling Gonad Monthly."

Franco peered down into the sewage corridor beneath the toilet. A thick blue gunk was flowing in a stream of effluence, merrily on its long journey to the Pleasure Cruiser's Fuel-Compact. On a no-waste pro-eco journey, even shit had its uses.

Will he believe it? thought Franco, eyes gleaming at the prospect of a pint of Guinness and wobbling breasts. Yeah, of course he'll believe it. He's a moron! And, let's be honest, Franco premeditated, it's just a downright unfair and tasty poison dragging a hedonist like me onto a ship like this, then expecting me to sit like a Billy-No-Mates in his quarters whilst every other bugger is out partying and jigging! Jus' not on. Jus' blummin' disgrace. An' everything.

Franco poked his head into the fast-flowing corridor and screamed, "Aiiie." The noise echoed metallically.

"Hey!" came Cam's voice from outside the bathroom. "Franco? Franco? What you doing, lad?"

Franco eased himself to the corner of the bathroom, and crept behind the mercury shower curtain which shimmered liquid silver.

"Franco! I'm warning you! Naked arse or not, if you don't reply in three seconds then I'm coming in!"

Franco chuckled to himself.

The door squeaked open, and Cam spun warily into the chamber. His sensors took in the abused toilet, the flow of effluence in the sewage corridor, and the simple obvious fact that Franco would fit. "I don't believe it," snapped the little PopBot. "The lengths that deviant will go to for a beer and a romp with a prostidroid. The sneaky bastard!"

Cam lifted on a stream of ions and dropped below the toilet. Sensors scanning, he sped along the corridor, faster than the gushing charge of blue gunk. It was only when *another* clang reached his sensors, followed by four short *bzzzts* that he realised he'd been had. Conned. Duped. Bamboozled! Hornswoggled! By a ginger-bearded squaddie of indeterminate sexual hygiene.

"I don't believe it!" Cam slammed back along the sewage-drain and stopped, bobbing beneath the now replaced toilet. "Franco!" he shouted, voice echoing up and down the shit-chute. "Franco Haggis, you let me out this minute!"

"Suck it, sea urchin!" shouted Franco. Then he grinned at himself. "There is no charge for awesomeness!" he said. There came the slam of an alloy door, and the receding patter of sandals.

Cam shot upwards, and bounced from the underside of the TitaniumIII toilet. It was tougher than it looked.

"Bugger," he said.


THE TITAN PLEASURE Cruiser *Razzle* had its fair share of elitist wine bars, upmarket proxer demijoles, fine ZubZub cuisine restaurants, and thousands of high-class sophisticated drinking depots where one could mix with all manner of sophisticates. Franco avoided these like a particularly nasty plague-pit full of toxic corpses, and instead found himself a Lower-Deck bad-joint replete with unwashed blood-sticky floors and heavy drug-smoke haze. *The Winchester* was a drinker's drinking den, a gambler's gambling pit, not just a pub or a bar, but a *joint*, baby, *a joint*.

Franco strode in, chest puffed out, and peered

through the crowds of ne'er-do-wells. If there was a squaddie or remaining citizen on the Titan Pleasure Cruiser *Razzle* who had something to hide, he hid it here. If there was any form of criminal activity to be found, it was here. Franco breathed in corruption like oxygen, and gave a big sigh of relaxation. "Mamma. Daddy's home." He strode purposefully to the bar, scrambled onto the high stool on the third attempt, and thumped both fists on the smeared and oily bar-top.

A barmaid approached. She was tall, gangly, with a plethora of tattoos running up and down her arms and her black hair piled atop her head in one of the latest fashions. "What'll it be, cock?" she said.

Franco blinked. "Did you just call me cock?"

"Aye, cock."

"Hey baby, I *love* this place!"

"What're you drinking, cock?"

Franco gave a broad, beaming smile. He eyed the glittering Aladdin's cave behind the bar. He licked his too-long desert-dry lips.

"*Everything,*" he said.

IT HADN'T TAKEN long. But then, these things never did. And it had to be said, without recourse to hyperbole, and with all due consideration to the laws of slander, that Franco was well and truly *fucked*.

He sat at a corner table in a low-slung digital

bum-stool, folded almost in half and surrounded by a gaggle of dirty, leering, half-caked grotty individuals. Some were reg soldiers out for a good time and to hell with military prison. Some were Ship Dwellers, again out for a good time, and to hell with any sort of prison. All were listening, enthralled, as Franco regaled them with one of his drunken tales.

"Yeah, guys, and gals, sorry, s'not meaning to be sexist, after all, I like women, I do, I'm the Party Boy after all..." he took a long experimental drink from his fizzing pink lager, "but whem..." his voice dropped to a hushed whisper, and the group shuffled in a little closer, "whem you've been in a top-secret hush-hush clandestine Combat-K squad for as long as I have," he tapped his nose conspiratorially, missing on the third stroke, "them they send you on the best of best of top secret mishons. Oh yes. You wait and see what *I've got lined up.*"

"What have you got lined up, Franco?" asked a young blonde woman, with a disconcertingly innocent face that wasn't lost on Franco. Innocent was good. Innocent was open to Franco abuse. He beamed her a smile, and winked. "'S top secret, love."

"Aww. Guwon."

Franco slurped his pink lager, frothing a considerable amount down his shirt. "Right then. Shh! And all that. But me and the guys, and Pippa, she's a gal, we're heading down to Krakken IV, otherwise known as Sick World! We've got a very important mishon to find out whether the junks used to live there. Or not. But it's totally, totally top secret, reet, and nobody is to know outside of this table."

"Or this room?" said the blonde.

"Aye, aye, maybe even the whole *Winchester*. But the point is, they picked *me*," he puffed out his chest, quite a feat from the confines of the digital bum-stool, "to lead the whole expedition! And if there is dem dirty junks, why, why I'll smash them!" He beamed again, as if he'd just penned a particularly impressive sonnet, or finished composing a symphony.

"And what of the crown?" whispered the blonde.

"Crown? What crown?" Franco frowned. "Whaddya mean?"

"The fabled *treasure* down there on Sick World. Surely you've heard of it?"

"Treashure, you say?" Franco's ears perked up. Through an alcoholic smog, tiny little valves started to spark and step.

"Yeah, Krakken IV is rumoured to have the fabled and immeasurably valuable treasure of Iskander's Crown! Carved from sub-PlutoniumIII, it's supposed to be very dangerous. Loads of treasure-seekers have died trying to locate it."

"And where would I find such a treashure?" slurred Franco.

"Oh, they sell maps at the bar, just ask for Apple Annie. She'll smuggle you one. Fifteen Ship Creds."

"Think I might just do that!" He eyed the group, which had grown to perhaps twenty now, many of whom you wouldn't trust with your newskube, never mind your top secret mission statement.

The blonde lady leaned forward. She placed both hands on Franco's knees. She stared into his eyes. Franco drooled a bit, an umbilical connecting chin to chest.

"Listen," she said. "I was wondering if you fancied coming back to my room? If you're feeling a bit energetic? I have some fine… music, we can play, we can dance. That sort of thing." If Franco had looked closely, at this point, through his alcoholic haze, he might have noticed tiny slanted gills on the blonde woman's neck.

"Hey! Don't mind if I do," beamed Franco.

"Thing is… well… I'm not human."

"Tha' OK," beamed Franco.

"My name's Amil. I'm a Prakku."

"'S great, love. Which way we going?"

She stood, took his hand, as her gills hissed in oxygen intake. She smiled, and to Franco, looked quite beautiful, quite the most angelic thing he'd ever witnessed. Which is good, he reasoned, because my last bird was an eight-foot zombie deviant. This *had* to be an improvement! Reet?

Franco failed to notice the way she walked. What, with her fish-scaled legs and webbed feet slapping the tiles, Franco also didn't quite notice the smell of *fish*. After all, the Prakku were an alien *aquatic* race that spent 85% of their time either beneath the sea, or on a ship like this, in huge saltwater marine tanks.

Finally, and perhaps most importantly, Franco failed to notice the man in the dark corner of The Winchester. A man sporting an eye-patch and long, dark, curled hair. A man who'd been watching Franco all night.

CHAPTER TWO

# DROPSIDE ZERO

"WHERE IS HE?" growled Keenan.

"Be patient," soothed Pippa. "He'll be here."

"Well, the little fucker didn't come back last night, nor this morning. And it took me half an hour to free Cam from the blue sludge shit-canal beneath the toilet! The levels rose, soaked the poor little mite in ship-wide effluence. It's played hell with his electrics."

"Well," said Pippa, "I had noticed his ego getting the better of him. Maybe Franco did the little PopBot a favour?"

"Yeah, right. You're too forgiving."

Pippa's eyes were cold, and her humour dissipated. "I'm trying, Keenan. Trying real hard."

The long queue of Combat-K and regular

army squaddies were waiting for their pre-Drop medicals. It was also the time for Combat-K to visit the Upgrades Department – also affectionately referred to as The Splicers.

Keenan checked his PAD, grinding his teeth. "Well, the bastard better get here soon, or he'll miss his injections. God only knows what he'll catch down on Sick World if he doesn't get inoculated. The place used to be a colony for all manner of alien leprosies, biological experiments and a search for cures to all manner of rare human-alien symbiotic diseases."

"You read your INFO PACK as well, did you?"

Keenan nodded, and smiled. "I'm a good boy."

"We're assured by the DropBot scans it's now OK," said Pippa, as the queue shuffled forward towards an ominous military green door which opened and closed with deep metallic *clangs*. "After all, all that Sick World stuff was a thousand years ago. Then they withdrew funding, and the research projects were closed down. There's nothing there now, just a planet left to its own devices for ten centuries."

"No," said Keenan, dropping his voice. "That's not quite what happened."

Pippa frowned. "You know something I don't?"

Keenan nodded. "I'll tell you later. In private. Let's just say the history books, once again, are far from accurate. What's that line from *th3 m1ss1ng*'s song? '*Let us celebrate, my friends, with rewritten histories and a fictional past*'."

The queue moved on, and Pippa nodded. "Like that, eh? Well, Franco's gonna be in a world of shit if he misses today. Although I've got to admit, he's had some pretty savage diseases and survived. We used to call him the Viking of VD back on *The Bombay Blast*."

"Yeah," growled Keenan. "Well, if he doesn't show, then he's a risk to the mission. I'll give him a bullet myself. Sharp end first."

FRANCO MOANED. HE groaned. He whined. He whinged. He croaked. He coughed. He spat. He pushed himself up on elbows, eyes still sleep-glued shut, then slumped back again because it was just too much damn effort. "Urgh," he said. He ran his tongue over dry lips and wondered who was beating his head with a lump-hammer. Slowly, he realised nobody was beating his head with a lump-hammer, but it was, in fact, a hangover.

One eye unglued. Fixed on a tangle of auburn hair on the pillow next to him. Then it closed again.

*Girl?* he thought.

*What girl? What did I do? And more importantly, what have I caught?*

He peered under the bed covers at his inert and considerably shrunken willy, but could see nothing untoward. But that didn't mean he hadn't contracted some lethal alien cock-virus, did it? Eh?

He emerged from under the covers like a snail creeping from a stolen shell. He eyed the hair again.

The body next to him, curiously angular beneath the covers, shuddered. It made a metallic snoring sound. Something went *ticker ticker ticker*, almost like… clockwork. The body shuddered again.

"Um. Hullo?" said Franco.

The head rotated 180° and stared at him. It was a robot dog.

"Aiiee!" screamed Franco, leaping backwards from the bed and standing, hands on hips, eyes wide open, staring at the metallic mutt. "What the hell are you doing in my bed? Eh? Eh? You dirty damn bloody mutt! And, more importantly," he stared around, "where is my bed? Where's this? Where am I?" He scratched his bollocks. The dog's brown eyes followed his fingers with a curious feral glittering.

"Get out!" screamed Franco, and idly, the robot dog, with various clanks and whirrs, clambered from the twisted bedcovers and leapt down to the threadbare greasy carpet. It sat down. Its doggy head, angular, silver, alloy, lifted and regarded Franco with something akin to wonderment.

"Ruff," it said.

"OK, OK, listen up you weird and wacky metal mange-maestro. I don't know what the hell you're doing here, in fact, I have no bloody idea what *I'm* doing here, but I want to get one thing straight. I'm not into any funny robot-fetish canine doggy business, OK? You're a dog. A robot. Whatever. And I'm a man!" He puffed out his hairy chest.

'"Got that, dog-meat breath?"

"Ruff," said the dog, and stood. It whirred over to Franco, legs kicking, and sat down again. A small drawer in the dog's chest slid out on neat hydraulics. There was a slim metal pamphlet. Franco eyed the pamphlet warily, having been the victim of junk mail before. Slowly, reaching forward, he snatched the slim volume and eyed the robot dog with a scowl. He read the front cover:

> *Congratulations!* on your purchase of the DumbMutt v1.2 special robotic friend. This little special friend will be your friend. A friend for life!! Please find enclosed the instruction manual and ownership deed in a variety of Quad-Gal languages, Braille and scent-sensorship.

> Thank you, Franco Haggis, Quad-Gal resident DNA number 6753675347645-3764575324652. As you read this, a genetic sample has been taken from your fingertips and relayed digitally to the DumbMutt's brain. He is now yours. He will never leave your side. He is forthwith electronically registered to your DNA and as such will follow you to the ends of whatever planet you inhabit [insert here]. If you lose your DumbMutt v1.2 special

robotic friend, do not fret, because he *will* eventually find you. If you vacate the planet, he has emergency funds to book passage on a Shuttle to anywhere within the Quad-Gal bubble. In effect, your DumbMutt special friend will follow you to the ends of the Galaxy. Well done in this, the Smart Choice.

We do hope you enjoy your DumbMutt v1.2 special robotic friend. He will be a very special robotic friend. For life. Your special friend DumbMutt v1.2 comes with many exciting innovations and technical upgrades over the previous DumbMutt v1.1, which tended to burst into flame and kill the owner. Don't worry! That doesn't happen anymore! Not often, anyway [please read legal addendum].

Your friendly special friend DumbMutt v1.2 is called [Sax].
  Please be kind to it. And remember. A robot dog is for *life* not just for [insert applicable religious festival].

Franco eyed the dog, which panted mechanically. Somewhere deep inside, a heavy flywheel went *clunk*.

"So, you're Sax, eh lad?"

"Ruff."

"Why did they give you that weird quiff?" He eyed the straggled auburn tangle, sitting atop the dog's alloy head like a mop atop a dustbin; a toupee on a mannequin. Franco sighed, and hunted for his clothes. "Hey, have you seen my pants, boy?"

"Ruff." Sax padded over to a chair, where Franco's clothes had been neatly folded, and nudged them with his damp metal nose.

"Good boy." Before he could help himself, Franco patted the mop of hair – and shuddered. Sax wagged its stumpy tail. "Anyway," he shrugged, "I'm not quite sure I understand all this business. After all, I didn't *buy* you. You're not *mine*. What indeed was all that nonsense about a deed? Haha. Ha.'

There came a *ticker ticker ticker* sound. Sax opened his mouth, and a long stream of punched foil paper ejected. Franco took the paper, and read in letters made up of pin-prick holes:

**Please take good care of your DumbMutt v1.2 [Sax]-model. Your DNA has now been registered with the MMI central core database. Your deed will last: <u>999 years</u>. Thank you for your custom.**

©hv3801 Metal Mongrels Inc.
QGSMA Quad-Gal Safety Mark Assured
(pending).

Franco crouched down, face to muzzle. "Ach. Right. Well. You see, Sax, mate, buddy, faithful fellow, the thing is, I'm a bit of a special man you see, I work covert ops for a Combat-K squad and I'm kind of going on a mission, so I kind of don't need a dog. Sor*ree*."

He stood.

Sax gave a whine.

Franco dressed, and walked to the door. Sax's sad brown eyes followed Franco. Franco opened the door. He frowned. "Look," he said. "I... I give you to yourself. There. Self-ownership. Your deed has been returned. So go on, bugger off, go and do whatever it is that little metal robot dogs do."

Franco closed the door and stared at the peeling wallpaper of an unfamiliar non-memory. Shit. Where am I? More importantly, who was I with? Even more importantly, why don't I remember her tits? And even *more* importantly, what's that fish smell?

There was a *crash*. A splintering, rending of timber kind of sound.

Slowly, Franco turned. Sax was sat, surrounded by shards of door, looking sheepishly at the floor.

"Ruff?" it said.

"Bad doggie!"

Sax wagged its tail.

"No! Bad doggie!" Franco waved a stern finger.

"Ruff."

"Hell, dog, can't you say anything other than 'ruff'? I thought you AIs had bloody technically advanced minds, or something?"

Sax seemed to think for a while, angular metal dog head on one side. Then it ventured, "Sax?"

"So that's it? You've been programmed with *two whole words?*"

"Borrocks?"

"Sax, and borrocks," said Franco. "That's it?"

"Ruff." Sax nodded forlornly.

"Jeez," hissed Franco, and started down the steep stairs. He stepped into a teeming alloy lane, which he dimly remembered as being Pleasure Cruise Central, that happy core artery from which all hedonism stemmed. Franco glanced around. He had a nagging feeling he was late for something. Ah yes! *Medical! Covert ops! Mission! Sick World!* He grinned, and checked his watch. But his watch had gone. Stolen!

"Damn and bloody blast!"

He checked his pants. His wallet had gone as well.

"Triple damn and hot ring cheese bloody buggering!"

"Ruff."

Franco clenched his teeth. "Look! Sax! Will you *fuck off?*"

"Ruff." Sax ambled over to Franco, lifted its head, and started licking Franco's groin.

Franco leapt back. "Ahh! Geddoff! Dirty dumb mutt!"

"Sax. Borrocks. Ruff."

"Great," scowled Franco, and set off at a lope through the heaving throng. *That's all I need. A hangover. No memory of last night's sex. All my cred and non-poor slots are gone, nay stolen! And now I've to chaperone a bloody robot dog. Well, we'll see what happens when I get to the internal quadrant barriers, yeah? Staff squaddies there'll fry his robot dog-ass! Let's see him say borrocks to that!*

A few paces behind, like night follows day, like salmon swimming upstream, like birds flying south for winter, on sheer instinct Sax trustingly followed its new master at a steady, solid, rolling pace. The sort of pace it could keep up for, ooh, centuries.

KEENAN AND PIPPA were emerging from their medicals when at the far end of the corridor a door opened, somewhat sheepishly, and there was a major kerfuffle. Franco barged his way in, red in the face and looking distinctly hung-over. Close behind followed a large robot dog, fashioned from silver and black alloy (and apparently beaten into shape with a hammer), which seemed to be wearing a wig. Franco was arguing with the wigged dog as he stormed past the patient queue and pushed in at the front, ignoring a range of sarcastic comments and evil glares.

The dog sat down with a clang, a few feet from the squaddie. "Borrocks," it said.

"You OK mate?" said Keenan, head tilted.

Franco beamed suddenly. "Hi Kee! Hi Pippa! Yep. Never better."

"Where did you get to last night?" Keenan, although smiling, had a face set in steel. His teeth were just a little too bared. His jaw line just a little too tense. Muscles in Keenan's jaw flexed, and Pippa placed a restraining hand on Keenan's arm and hushed him.

"Apparently, Franco," said Pippa, "Keenan's PopBot ran into a bit of trouble last night. Got trapped in the sewage canal which runs beneath the living quarters."

"Ha!" said Franco. "That'll teach him to sniff the toilet seats in the ladies quarters! Damn freaky little robot pervert."

"Franco!" Keenan's voice was far beyond warning.

"OK! OK! It's a fair cop guv'nor. But before you bust me back down to private just think of the horrific night I've had, and be thankful I'm here at all. *And* I've got to put up with that metal heap of shit! It just won't leave me alone! Tell it, Keenan, go on, tell it!"

"Tell it what?"

"Tell it to go away!"

"Why?"

"It's latched onto me. Is like a bloody parasite. A leech sucking on my testicules."

Keenan grinned. "Well, it's not the first dog to do that."

"Oh har har, don't start mate, I ain't in the mood."

"How was she? Did you get to party?"

The interruption came from a young soldier, in front of which Franco had so inelegantly pushed.

"Eh?"

The soldier smiled, and it was a smile filled with superior knowledge. "The alien you took home last night. You were going for a dance, and stuff. How was she?"

Franco's face had formed a painful rictus of pain. "*What* alien?"

"The one we tried to warn you about. Franco mate, you were *so out of it* you just waved away our advice like annoying drug smoke. She was called Amil. She was a Prakku."

"A whattu?"

"A Prakku. They're a marine-based alien lifeform."

A disconcerting image flashed into Franco's mind. He instinctively grabbed his groin. "Um?" he said.

"I've heard of them," said Pippa, eyeing Franco carefully. "Said to be human on top, but..."

"But what?"

"Kind of *fishy* down below."

"What do you mean, fishy?"

The door clanged open. "NEXT!" bawled a hefty female sergeant with biceps like slabs of ham and a No.1 shaved head.

Franco was dragged into the cubicle. The door clanged shut, but they could still hear the exchange.

"Drop 'em."

"But... I'm not wearing any underwear!"

There came a big sigh. "Why not?"

"It's a long story. About fish, apparently."

"Gods, there's always one, isn't there?"


THE RAPID OFFENCE SLAM Cruiser *Rearward Entry* howled down the docking hole and hit space in glorious... silence. Like fleas on a dog, it carried three precious DropShips attached to its underbelly as it left a trail of purple carbide pollution in its fast curve from the Titan Pleasure Cruiser *Razzle* towards the glowing ball that was Sick World...

Krakken IV.

The Planet of the Damned.

Once a glistening jewel in Quad-Gal's crown, the Sick World had originally been at the pinnacle forefront of medical exploration and research into the hybrid crossover diseases which mutated when humankind and alienkind finally *clicked*. Man, being predominantly a creature of fluid, had a weaker organic chassis than he originally anticipated and proceeded to collect and transmit a variety of interesting, challenging and downright *dangerous* diseases the minute he began his cosmological integration.

And so, as Man spread enthusiastically across the Quad-Gal, eyes wide like a newborn kitten, he developed new diseases, ailments, organic oddities and deviations. As Man fucked and fought, bonked and bled his way across a new set of galaxies so the interesting mix of organics led to some really *weird* shit. Sick World was born, brainchild of Professor Malkus Malkovitch, original creator of The Great Malkovitch University down on The City. On Krakken IV, Malkovitch gathered together the greatest medical minds of the age, and the planet was divided into discrete sections across the weirdly shaped landmass of the three major stable land continents.

Around the equator, the major, desert-like, rocky barren continent of Second Djio was given over to the exploration, research, quarantine and cure of rare conditions and diseases. South of the equator was nothing but deep green sea circumventing the globe, but north, on the verdant and lush mid-latitude continent of Kludek, populated by rich forests, lakes and beautiful thrusting purple mountains, were built the finest medical and surgical care and rehabilitation suites the mind could dream. And finally, far north, as the snow and ice began to eat the land, was the continent of Yax, a freezing wilderness given over to research, experimentation and confinement for those cases that were... not quite so simple.

To all intents and purposes, the entirety of the planet Krakken IV *became* Sick World: the premier planet for curing mankind's and alienkind's ills. And, just a few hundred years after inception, as glittering alloy hospitals lay scattered across the planet like diamonds on velvet, it was mooted that no sickness would go uncured, no disease could not be tamed, nothing broken that could not be fixed.

Sick World became Paradise for the Plague Crowd.

Until...

Something went wrong. No history refers to the incident, a thousand years past. No text books, no vid, no kubes, no stacks, nothing had specific *detail* on Sick World and the reason five million people pulled out. And they pulled out *fast* on giant TEC; Titan Emergency Craft. In the space of a single day...

All that *was* known was Krakken IV was *quarantined* Quad-Gal wide.

For a thousand years.

And since then, officially, nobody had ever been back.

KEENAN STEPPED INTO the cockpit with a smoke dangling from his lips, and froze. There was a man, seated, in a blue and white pinstriped shirt, dark trousers and polished shoes. He smiled in a strained but friendly fashion down the barrel-eye of Keenan's Techrim 11mm.

"Hello, my name is Professor Miller," said the man, and gave a broad smile. His teeth gleamed white in a face so tanned it was orange. He ran a hand through the grey square-cut hair of a politician, and watched uneasily as the gun tracked him.

"Keenan!" Pippa slammed into the cockpit, and gently lowered his arm. "Shit, Keenan. I'm sorry. I meant to say, this fucker was allowed on board at the last moment. Steinhauer's instructions."

Keenan, cigarette between his lips, smoke making him squint, holstered his weapon. "What the fuck," he said, staring hard at Miller, "are you doing on my ship?"

"Quad-Gal's ship," said the man, curtly. He stood, and Keenan glanced down at the polished leather briefcase. With twin clicks the man opened the briefcase, and produced a sheaf of papers. He sat down again. Looked up at Keenan. "If you'd like to be seated."

"I'll stand."

"This is Miller, Chief Health and Safety Officer for QGM."

"*What?*"

"Chief Health and Safety Officer." Pippa forced her face to remain straight, and stared hard into Keenan's eyes. "It's orders, Keenan. Orders. I've seen the paperwork. Triple-stamped. All official. You can't mess with army bureaucracy, you of all men know that irrefutable truth."

"I thought we'd left that shit behind."

"You never leave that shit behind," said Pippa, a hand on his arm. "Just hear the guy out."

"Yeah, then throw him out," muttered Keenan. He sighed, eyed Professor Miller, then took a seat opposite the neat, prim, fastidious bureaucrat. "Go on. Hit me with it. What the hell do you want? And don't even *try* and tell me you're coming down to Sick World…"

"I have been commissioned by the Quad-Gal Military Authorities to carry out certain, shall we say, official surveys of combat practice in the field. You will find my authority comes not just from Steinhauer, but from his superiors and *their* superiors. Right the way to the top of the ziggurat." He eyed Keenan coolly, and Keenan suddenly saw *beyond* the bad tan, neat-clipped hair and expensive shirt. Miller had ego. He was a pedant. He had a damn *agenda*.

"Shit."

Miller gave a tombstone smile. "Yes, I will be accompanying your outfit down to Kraken IV. And I will require certain paperwork tasks to be completed before, during, and after all said missions in the vicinity."

"What kind of paperwork tasks?"

"Could I ask you to put out the cigarette?"

"No."

"I insist."

"So do I."

Miller coughed, staring hard at Keenan. "I can see we are going to have some initial problems, as I see you have issue with authority."

"Only when it's on *my* fucking ship."

"Amusing, Keenan." He handed over a slim metal volume. "Before we land on Krakken IV, I need each member of military personnel to fill in this questionnaire."

"Why?"

"For my records."

"What is it?"

"A risk assessment."

"A fucking *what?*"

"A risk assessment." Professor Miller bristled, and a shadow of arrogance sleeted his features. "It is a bureaucratic necessity to carry out certain distinct levels of assessment pertaining to the nature of risk in specific situations."

"We're entering a possible combat zone," said Keenan, voice low. "Of course there's gonna be a risk. The whole damn place was evacuated a thousand years ago! And despite DropBot scans, nobody *really* knows what's down there."

"As you readily admit there to be risk present, we therefore need to assess the probability of given situations throwing up foreseeable threat to the safety and health of those men, and women –"

"And deviants."

Miller paused, then continued, "– and *deviants* under your command."

Keenan flicked through the slim volume, and picked out a question at random. "'In the eventuality that you may come under enemy fire, please list three ways in which you should attempt to minimise being shot, as per Minimising Being Shot Regulations, hv3717.'" Keenan eyed Miller thoughtfully, and turned to another page. "'When working with dangerous explosives, you first need to familiarise yourself with the Working Safely With Dangerous Life-Threatening Explosives Regulations, hv3721, and list five precautions you might take in order to help save lives and not cause damage or vandalism to property not belonging to yourself.'" Keenan removed his cigarette, scratched his forehead, then put the weed back between his lips. "You ain't joking, are you?"

"No, Mr. Keenan. Health and Safety is no place for comedy."

"Damn right. Listen to this one, "'When engaging an enemy combatant, first you must take time to assess the situation and answer the following simple three-stage question: a] Before firing your weapon, is the enemy combatant a direct threat to you at this precise moment in time? b] Before firing on an enemy combatant, can you be *absolutely sure* he (she/it) is insistent on causing you harm beyond reasonable doubt? c] If possible, ask the enemy combatant to fill in a Risk Assessment Co-combatant Strategy Assessment form in order for both combatants to properly understand the seriousness of their situation, and thus decide on the best course of action for the future [as per Working Safely with the Enemy Regulations, hv3719].'"

"I don't need to listen to this, Mr. Keenan. I wrote it."

"The whole book?"

"The whole book."

Keenan stood, and drew out his Techrim. He toyed with the weapon thoughtfully, and flicked free the safety. Professor Miller paled, despite his deviant tan. Keenan smiled. "When it comes to risk assessment, Mr. Miller, I want you to consider one thing."

"Which is?" Miller bristled.

"Did *you* carry out a risk assessment prior to entering this situation? Because, if you did, and if you know me, then you're putting your sorry skinny arse on the line, my friend. I suggest you take your self-published pamphlet and *fuck off* out of my face before my bullet carries out an intimate Risk Assessment of your Fucking Skull Interior."

Miller hurriedly packed his things in his briefcase, and tripped on his way to the door. He turned at the portal.

"You will regret this, Mr. Keenan."

"I doubt it, mate," said Keenan, lighting another cigarette. "I very much doubt it."

KEENAN CLICKED OFF the kube and rubbed his eyes. "What makes Sick World so damn safe now, then?"

Cam, hovering near the ceiling, apparently analysing the alloy roof tiles of the Rapid Offence SLAM Cruiser, buzzed down low with a glittering of orange lights. "Quad-Gal Military have been steadily compiling a database of worlds during the past few years. Using swarms of AnalysisBots and DropBots, they snap down to the surface, take samples, search for life using the most advanced equipment imaginable, and re-post back to the military Core DB. Sick World has been scanned, Keenan. It's dead as a dead duck."

"Hmm." Keenan rubbed his stubble, as around him the SLAM hummed. Built for speed, it was far from a refined cruise. It would have them in orbit around Sick World in thirty-six hours, arcing past and detaching its three DropShip cargo which, in turn, would separate and head down to the planet's surface.

"It's an easy mission," said Cam. "We head in, search the surroundings, take samples of soil, rock, minerals, that sort of shit. There have been a few ancient edifices flagged up for exploration; we prove the junks had nothing to do with Sick World then we hot-tail it out of there." Cam seemed to beam, which was hard to understand, being a small, alloy PopBot with no discernible features. "What can go wrong?"

"I don't buy it. Nothing in life is that easy."

A door slid open, and Pippa emerged. She looked annoyed as she slumped into the Comfort Bay's SquashCouch.

"You OK?"

"No. Betezh and Olga are at each other's throats. He keeps calling her a whale of blubber, she keeps calling him Frankenstein's Reject. They're doing my damn head in, Keenan. And to top it all, I've had Franco sniffing around me again. You'd think he would have learned his bloody lesson!"

The door slid open, and Franco sidled in, peering at his back-trail with obvious suspicion, like a spy being followed. He saw his Combat-K comrades, straightened, and smiled a beaming smile. The door hissed shut.

"Hi!"

"You OK, Franco? You look a bit twitchy?"

The SLAM rocked violently, engines screaming, and settled down gradually. Outside, rocks bounced from the hull and shattered into billions of fragments.

"Damn that pilot!"

"There isn't one," snorted Pippa. "The SLAM's automated! Weren't you paying attention at the briefing?"

"Yeah! Of course!" He snorted in derision.

"They don't call me Franco 'Academic Arse' Haggis for nothing, you know! Every little detail has been sucked in, stored and precisely filed in the nanomodular computational memory bank that is my brain." He grinned. "Anyone for a sausage?" He moved towards the InfinityChef™.

"'Memory bank'," mocked Pippa. "Yeah, about 1K, I reckon." She watched Franco extract a long greasy sausage from the alloy machine, slap it on a plate, and smother it in fiery horseradish sauce. "Franco, even for you, that looks disgusting."

"I'm a growing lad."

"You'll end up looking like Olga!"

"Nothing wrong with meat on a lass," said Franco, taking a huge slimy bite. As he chewed, he eyed Pippa thoughtfully. "Hey, would you..."

"No."

"But you don't know what I was going to say!"

"The answer's still no."

"Hrmph."

"The answer's still no, dickhead."

Franco chewed for a while. Then said, quickly, as if afraid she might cut him off, "I was only going to ask if you wanted a chew on my sausage." He grinned. Cubes of fat were caught between his teeth.

"You're just utterly revolting."

"I try my best."

"Listen," said Keenan, "when you two lovebirds have finished the banter, are you both happy with your squads?"

"No," said Pippa.

"Yes!" beamed Franco. "Never before have I seen such healthy vibrant vixens!"

"I meant in a militaristic context," said Keenan.

"So did I." Franco winked.

"We touch down in thirty-six hours. How did the Upgrades go?"

"Good," said Pippa. "We all had Pearl comms implanted in our earlobes. Franco went for some extras, though."

"Extras?" Keenan raised his eyebrows. "What you been up to, Franco?"

Franco looked suddenly shifty. "Nuffink."

"What do you mean 'Nuffink'? I need to know how you're tooled. If you had one of those crazy-arse heart-neutronium bombs implanted, you could jeopardise the entire mission. So come on, spill the beans."

Franco stuck out his lower lip. "It was supposed to be a surprise!" He glared at Pippa. "Until a certain person went flapping her big flapping lips. OK, I had my wisdom teeth done."

"And that means?"

"They're WiTs," said Pippa, slumping down with a coffee and rolling her neck to ease tension. "Dickhead over there had three of his teeth replaced with WiTs – tiny removable bombs. I'm sure only a lunatic would have bombs implanted in his fucking *head*."

"Hey!" snapped Franco. "Less of the

implanted. They're a temporary fixation. I also had EZooms."

"The digital eyeball zoom enhancers?"

"Yar," said Franco, chewing.

"I fancied those myself, until I saw what the micro-surgery entailed. Scalpels inside your eyeballs? I think I'll stick with my own Nature-made units, thanks. Go on mate, what else? False pectorals? A penis enlargement? Some kind of bowel sluice?"

"No-*oooo*." It was the way he said it. Keenan and Pippa exchanged a glance.

"Spill it," said Pippa.

"Well, I wouldn't like to say..."

"We need to know," growled Keenan. "Any more implied insanity you inadvertently add to a mission, well, hell, we need to know about it. Yeah?"

"OK. I, um, I had a Temple Pill. Injected." He grinned.

"A Temple Pill? You mean one of those crazy damn onboard religious nutters? Helps you find enlightenment? Or so the marketing shit goes, anyway. Franco, no way is that sort of cheap Jaiwanese crap available from Quad-Gal military. It's outlawed. It's fucking *dangerous,* mate."

"Can you remove it?" said Pippa.

Franco shook his head. "Not here. Not now. Well, not without a big scalpel..."

"Tempting," mused Keenan.

"Where did they inject it?" said Pippa, sipping her coffee.

"Where else?" said Franco. He tapped the side of his head. "In my temple."

"Oh, ho ho," said Pippa. "Religious nutters with a sense of humour. How droll."

"It's the best place from which Father Callaghan can communicate. It's a place that has, shall we say, *soul*."

"Father Callaghan?" Pippa nearly choked on her coffee. "Franco, mate, you're insane enough without a bloody religious implant. You're a certifiable *dick*. And talking of dicks, have you shook off that dumb dog yet? It keeps pissing in the corridors. Surely a machine shouldn't do that? Well, it damn well stinks."

"Ha! Sax is a robot! It can't piss!"

Cam made a buzzing sound of annoyance. "Franco, that would be the DumbMutt's supposed air freshener."

"An air freshener?" said Keenan, reclining and pulling free his Techrim. He started to clean and oil the weapon. "Why the hell would a robot dog want an air freshener?"

"To freshen the place up," said Franco. "Obviously."

"Obviously my arse," snapped Pippa.

"Interesting you should say that," said Cam, green lights flickering on his battered black casing. "It's actually called an Actuating Rear-tube Sphincter

Ejection-unit. The DumbMutt is supposed to be a house-pet for bored househusbands. It's supposed to, you know," Cam coughed a metallic cough, "help with the housework."

Keenan barked a laugh. "An Actuating Rear-tube... you mean his ARSE? Very amusing. Only Franco could buy himself a robot with an ARSE."

"Hey, I didn't buy it. Him. It. Sax. He was a gift."

"From the alien? For robbing your wallet?"

Pippa stared hard at Franco. "Franco, how *does* your life get so complicated?"

"I'm just a victim of circumstance," said Franco in a small voice, and having finished his sausage, headed for the sliding hatch. "I'm off to check on my vixens. I left them lubing their weapons and checking out their collection of g-string camouflage gear."

"Are you serious?" said Pippa.

"I'm always damn serious!" snapped Franco.

"I want you back here in an hour, with your squad," said Keenan, eyes steely, jaw a grim line. "The time for games is over. We've got a mission, and I want it pulling off smoothly. God only knows what we'll find down there."

"Ach!" said Franco. "This is a piss gig, man. We'll cruise in, doss and toss about, then cruise out again. No drama. No aggro. Sweet as a honeycake. Succulent as a pussy." He smiled, showing his missing tooth. Or *tuff*, as he called it.

"I'll believe that when I see it," growled Keenan, voice low.

"You should be more like me!" beamed Franco. "The world's a much happier place." He stepped through the hatch and, licking sausage grease from his beard, went indeed to check on his squad. And, in the narrow, alloy corridor, a voice in his head said, "*Don't you worry none, my Son. They could never understand your internal complexity.*"

"That's all right, Father Callaghan. They're good friends really. I'm not upset, not at all." His eyes gleamed, as he pictured vixens oiling oily thighs. He was sure Candy, Fizzy and Shazza would be getting down to the *real* interesting bits soon...

"*Well I'm glad about that, my Son. The road to Enlightenment is up a steep and winding hill. You will have to suffer all manner of rocks and sharp objects thrown – nay! hurled – at you, and they shall be, and yet you may never reach the summit of your steep and manful climb! But it is the journey to Enlightenment that will fill your heart with joy, my Son, as you suffer the impurity of Eternal Pain and Suffering, and Struggling, and Agony. Amen.*"

"Amen," mumbled Franco, miserably.

THEY SAT AROUND the table of the Ship Lounge, staring at one another and sipping coffee and battlestim juice – an energy drink endorsed by QGM Military EnergyDrinks™. Keenan entered, and cast a slow pan across the group, assessing each individual and wondering who he could trust. First there was his own team. Snake was reclining on the rear two legs of his chair, one leg folded over the opposite knee as he rooted in the tracks of his army boot with a fork, prizing free something solid and black. He glanced up at Keenan, his one good eye appraising the squad leader. Snake smiled, and it was not a very nice smile. Still, thought Keenan, Snake's official QGM report was good. Exceptional, even. He was certainly an efficient man in a fire-fight, and had pulled off a number of missions solo; a manner which Keenan himself preferred. If you went in alone, it was safe – because everybody was the enemy... and it made targeting that much easier.

Ed and Maximux were sat close, in quiet conversation, hunched over steaming coffee mugs. Both had shifty eyes and glanced up, watching Keenan warily. Keenan turned, observing a low-key growling argument between Olga and Betezh, his eyes taking in Olga's huge spade-shaped hands and their clenching and unclenching knuckles. Keenan smiled inside; Betezh better be careful, or he was going to get his head kicked in.

Mel sat at the far end of the table, a deviant apart, her small black eyes staring at the ceiling. Occasionally she shifted, and her natural pus-creamed armour crackled. Pippa met Keenan's gaze and gave him an uncertain smile.

Finally, Keenan watched the body language of Franco's squad. Fizzy and Shazza were sat, bodies turned slightly *away* from an excited and over-eager Franco, who was showing them how to strip down a Kekra quad-barrel machine pistol and oil the important parts. His hands glistened with gun-oil. Candy had been pulled by Steinhauer at the last moment for a separate Combat-K infil, to make space for Miller accompanying the outfit. This suited Keenan fine. The fewer women to distract Franco from the job in hand, the better. Indeed, the fewer people who accompanied Combat K, the better. He couldn't help but feel he'd been lumbered with a party bucket of idiots.

"OK," said Keenan, moving to the head of the table. All eyes turned on him. "You all know why we're here. We have five days on Sick World to try and find evidence of the junks; nothing, however, points to this being their home-world, so I want three discrete slick missions; in, analysis, rendezvous, then we'll get the fuck out and reconvene at a central location I've sent to your PADs. Everybody got that?"

The squads nodded, and Snake lit a cigarette, his cold blue eye regarding Keenan with intellect.

"Each squad member has been assigned a Permatex electronic WarSuit, except for Olga and Mel, who have Permatex WarPanels in the hold. We've all got digitally linked RealTime Tuff-Maps™ which will show every squad member and their location. You've also been given tins of mini RollerMines which are good for booby-trapping an area and carry electronic signatures linked to QGM forces and your individual spinal implants. Each DropShip has three InfinityChefs, SleepCells, and comes equipped with an off-road 6X6 Armoured Giga-Buggy and four KTM Dirt-Spaz motocross bikes, for reaching those inaccessible places." He smiled. "Any questions?"

"When do we get paid?" said Snake, and blew a plume of smoke.

"When the job's done," said Keenan, without blinking.

"Any bonus for finding evidence of these bastard junks?"

"No."

Snake shrugged, his eye never leaving Keenan. Keenan held the glittering gaze for a few moments, then glanced over at Franco's Angels. "You OK, ladies? I mean, having been stiffed with a certified insane pervert as your squad leader?"

"We're used to it, Keenan," smiled Fizzy, the fiery redhead. Her eyes flashed like diamonds. "And trust me, we have ways of dealing with miscreants."

"I object," said Franco, haughtily, "to being spoken about as if I'm not in the room."

"Franco, when you've had a rainbow pill, you really aren't in the room."

"Acknowledged, but that was a long time ago, when I was," he twitched, "a guest in the pleasure hotel known as Mount Pleasant." He scowled at Betezh, but the scarred ex-Combat K man didn't take him on. Franco hoisted a perfectly functioning Kekra. "Anyway. I'm a lot better now." He stared longingly at Fizzy's robust breasts, pert above the line of her WarSuit.

What seemed many moons ago, Franco had been incarcerated at The Mount Pleasant Hilltop Institution, the "nice and caring and friendly home for the mentally challenged" under the watchful supervision of a certain Dr Betezh... but that had been over a year ago, now. Betezh had been an implant from a powerful politician, put in place to keep tabs on Franco during his time there. Betezh was an ex-spook, QGM secret service, and in an act of revenge Franco, once he'd escaped Mount Pleasant and the tables had been turned, repaid Betezh's former electrical torture by stapling the man's face with an industrial bone stapler. It had all become a bit of a mess, but they laughed about it now. Sometimes. When they were drunk.

Keenan checked his watch, and lifted his PAD. "OK. Let's synchronise our systems. I'm sending a signal in three, two, one..."

They spent ten minutes checking PADs and earlobe communications, all the while Franco muttering and moaning about the indignity of wearing pretty earrings. When they were done, Keenan watched them filing from the room until only he, Franco and Pippa were left.

"Pippa?"

"Yeah, boss?"

"Keep an eye on Olga and Betezh. There was friction there." Olga and Betezh had a history of argument, from their tense time together down on the decimated world of The City during the outbreak of Biohell.

"I noticed," said Pippa, smiling softly, but without humour. "Hey, have you noticed the way Snake watches you?"

"Indeed."

"You gonna be OK?"

Keenan stared at Pippa, at her beautiful oval face, pure white skin, her neat, bobbed hair. *God, he thought, you are so beautiful. But you are the murderer of my family. How can you stand there before me, breathing, smiling, looking so fucking casual?*

He took a deep breath, his hate a distant, glowing ember, just waiting for the right injection of oxygen to re-ignite. Keenan ground his teeth. No. There were wider, more important issues at stake. Like saving millions of people from the expanding and invading junk armies.

His petty, minor, pathetic personal revenge would come later.

Much later.

"I'll be just fine," he breathed.

Franco ambled out, fiddling with his Kekra and leaving Keenan alone with Pippa. She moved to him, cat-like, graceful, and stopped, close, and he could smell her natural perfume, the aroma of the woman he had once loved. And hell, he thought. Say it. He still loved her. She was a narcotic, permanent, running through his veins. He would never be free of Pippa's addiction.

"Can I ask you a question?" she said.

"Ask away."

"If we weren't locked together, in this squad, in this mission, and," she gave a sardonic smile, "by spinal logic-cubes that would detonate our spines if we dared to go against one another... damn Quad-Gal Military's sense of humour, right?"

"Yeah?"

"If things were different, would you still try to kill me?"

Keenan moved closer. They were inches apart.

"Yes," he said.

Pippa's eyes closed, long lashes dark against pale translucent skin. They opened. Her grey eyes stared up into Keenan's. She licked her lips, leaned forward, and kissed him gently. For a long moment he allowed the kiss, then pulled back.

"I cannot."

"Nor I."

He stared at her. "I... cannot forgive. I am not a great enough man."

"I still love you, Keenan."

Keenan turned, and strode from the Ship Lounge.

FRANCO CLOSED THE door of his SleepCell and sat on his bed. It was a narrow alloy affair, with crumpled covers and a blue alloy headboard. Franco glanced around despite the room being only eight feet by six and, happy he was alone, reached behind the headboard and pulled free a small, crumpled sheet of paper. It was thin, flimsy, not like the RealTime Tuff-Maps™ used by the squaddies. With trembling fingers Franco unrolled the parchment on his bed, and stared at the rough outlines of the three continents of Sick World.

Franco grinned to himself, finger drawing a line which traced a jittery trail across the map. Franco double-tapped the flimsy material and organo-paper hummed and zoomed in. Again he tapped, and again it zoomed... until it registered a building, and within, a marker.

"Treasure," muttered Franco, his eyes wide, mouth open, lips wet. If nothing else, he thought, I'm going to come away from this lame mission a rich man! Soil analysis? Pah! Rock gathering? Pah! Searching ancient ruins? Humbug! Why couldn't QGM find me a real damn mission? Shooting things! Or, more importantly – his eyes gleamed – *blowing things up!*

It had to be said, Franco was an expert with explosions, detonations, and indeed any form of high-powered violent particle acceleration. His main job before Combat-K had been that of demolitions expert in quarrying the White Tooth Range at Reinhart and Seckberg Quarries Ltd, and his sole responsibility that of engineering and structuring explosions in order for miners and quarrymen to reach precious lodes. Franco could smell HighJ from a thousand paces, and tell exactly what type and quantity of explosive had been used – just by the roar of detonation. It had been commented that he was an obsessive; he'd be the first to agree.

Now, he stared at the map.

He thought about pitiful, meaningless, pointless, futile damn missions.

And how, in the boredom-filled interim, he might make himself a very rich man...

THE RAPID OFFENCE SLAM Cruiser *Rearward Entry* howled at the zenith of its still accelerating arc, and below, spinning into view, loomed the colourful and slightly ovoid planet, Krakken IV. Sick World. The Hospital Planet. The Continent of the Cursed.

Touching a few metres from orbit there came three heavy-duty *clangs*, and the military DropShips detached with a roar of stabilising motors and spread, like petals from a flower stem, and slammed down towards the spinning panorama below...

In a blink, the SLAM Cruiser was gone.

Combat K and their teams were on their own.

The three teams had separated into personal DropShip vehicles, and each team watched through vertical-drop windscreens as Sick World enlarged at a horrifying rate. Colours and gases swirled and coalesced, and the planet became a panorama, became continents and oceans. Sunlight gleamed across the Sick World and Franco, in his own DropShip, gasped as he piloted the fast descending vehicle.

"Beautiful, ain't she?" said Shazza.

"Impressive," agreed Fizzy.

"OK, checking earlobe comms," said Pippa from her own craft. "Are we all plugged in?"

One by one each squad member confirmed, and Pippa ran through PAD integration and Tuff-Map bandwidth.

Through the higher reaches of the atmosphere the three streaking ships left arcing trails of vapour, gently curving away from one another as they began descent and flight-path programming to individual locations. Only then, did Keenan's low growl come over the monitors.

"I've got a problem."

Snake leapt forward, his eye analysing the DropShip's scanners and readouts; he glanced at Keenan, whose knuckles had gone tight on the control rods. "We're dropping fast, Keenan. What's up?"

"Something's locked the ailerons. I can't bring us out of the dive…"

"What is it?"

"The scanners are saying a physical obstruction."

"I'll go and look," snapped Snake, turning.

"No," said Keenan. "You take the controls. I'll check it out."

"Ed," said Snake, "go with Keenan, see if you can help."

Ed nodded, and followed Keenan up the DropShip's internal gyroscopic ramp. Keenan reached the cargo doors and heard engines screaming as Snake applied extra backward thrust, beginning to slow their descent... but he knew, knew they were going too fast in their violent drop. If they didn't level out, they'd plough a furrow in the landscape deep enough to plant a city.

Keenan peered out of the portal, but couldn't quite see the ailerons. The DropShip had started to shudder. He hit a palm-pad which read his ident, confirmed, and with a *hiss* the door slid open a few inches allowing an insane, buffeting wildness to enter the DropShip interior.

"What's going on, Keenan?" came Pippa over the earlobe comm.

"We're about to become pizza."

Keenan edged towards the buffeting gap, and Ed came up close behind. Keenan glanced back at the wiry, tattooed man, who gave a grin of encouragement which reminded Keenan of a shark encouraging a goldfish into its jaws.

OK, he thought. This is where I explore my trust issues!

"You hold on tight, now, won't you?"

"I'll do my best, Keenan," said Ed, grabbing the larger man's belt.

Keenan peered out into the buffeting insanity. The wind nearly took his head clean off, and he could smell a fresh, bright scent, the purity of air without heavy industrial tox. It reminded him of home. Galhari. A home now ravaged, abused, invaded, a home nothing more than a junk-infested, toxic wasteland...

Eyes streaming tears, Keenan peered out. But could see nothing.

"We have two minutes!" screamed Snake down the corridor. "I can't guide her, Keenan! We'll end up in the sea!"

Keenan dragged his head back in, took a deep breath, and stared hard at Ed. "I'm gonna have to go out."

"You'll be crushed by the pressure, man," said Ed.

"No. The Permatex will protect me; I just need you to keep an eye on the straps and reel me in when I'm done." He ran across the corridor, slamming open a locker to pull free a long coil of TitaniumIII cable on a reel. Back at the door, he clicked and locked the reel in place, and snapped two locks to his own belt.

Then he moved to the edge, and the howling, screaming wind.

Keenan glanced at Ed; their eyes met. Ed gave a single nod.

Keenan stepped out into the buffeting wind, hands like clamp-claws on the recessed holds down the DropShip flanks. The world was a bright expanse. It was like God had peeled the top off the world and let the sunlight in.

*This is insane*, his mind rebelled, as pressure slammed him like an axe blow.

*I am going to die*, he thought.

*I'm going to be sucked free and smashed into the fucking engines...*

*Shit.*

Slowly, inch by painful inch, Keenan forced himself along the wall of the screaming, rocking DropShip...

CHAPTER THREE

# SICK WORLD I: KLUDEK

IT WAITED IN the slime, playing with its peroxide-blonde hair, twirling tight curls and bobs between fingers with lacquered, polished nails and enjoying the feel of oozing mud and rotting vegetation on pale and pasty skin. A distant roar infiltrated the heavens, and the creature looked up, a quick, insect-like movement. Blue eyes narrowed in a fat slug-face, and cherry lips pulled back over crooked yellow teeth as the nurse *grinned,* lips peeling right back over a distended jaw bone as a tongue fought at teeth cage bars and finally pushed free on a bed of saliva, unrolling and unrolling right down to the nurse's plump, generous waist, where it thrashed and twisted, like a caught eel.

"Come – to – me," croaked the nurse, levering her arms back and jacking her body up from the slime, where it was revealed she had no legs, just two rounded stumps with stalks of bone protruding like wood from tattered skin. The nurse smiled, and it was a friendly smile; the sort of smile an inmate gives to the warden. "I want to make you better again," she said, in all innocence.

ONCE, DURING A stint as an engineer on a Class III Cruiser whilst training for Combat K, Keenan had slipped and fallen into a pressure vat. His protective SuckSuck rubber clothing saved him, but even after the *suck and hiss* of the blink-response inflatable, the experience had been incredibly painful, a continued pummelling of pressure waves, rolling him and crushing him, as if beaten eternally by plate-sized fists. Now, clinging to the side of the DropShip, Keenan felt a twinge of memory – only this time he was thousands of feet above the ground, and one wrong slip, one twist, one fall, and he'd be sucked away and broken on rocks far below; or worse, ground like minced beef-substitute through the vibrating, howling engine ports.

Keenan edged along the wall, fingers locking to recess after recess. Cloud streamers hissed past his face. Water trickled down the neck of his WarSuit. The world was a howling cacophony, every sense slammed and battered, every moment a perpetuity of pounding. Teeth grinding, boots slipping and kicking, Keenan edged and edged, and more on instinct than a realisation of where he was, glanced up, the engine ports closer now, as were stubby wings and aerofoils used to guide the DropShip. Keenan's eyes narrowed. There, halfway down the aerofoil flap, was a black alloy box – effectively, a wedge. Shit. The ship's been sabotaged, he thought, mind a whirl of sour cream. He eased out his Techrim, itself a battered animal of combat, and with the whole world juddering and pounding around him, his ears whistling, piercing him with pain, he levelled the weapon which vibrated under pressure and fired off a shot. The *crack* was lost, and the bullet missed. Keenan fired again, and a spark ricocheted from the wedge, but the alien artefact remained securely in place. Eyes streaming tears, Keenan released a long, easy breath and focused. He squeezed the trigger, and the alloy wedge flicked, and was gone. Immediately the aerofoil started responding, and Keenan put his gun away and eased himself back along the flank of the DropShip. The machine groaned, and dropped suddenly, and through tears Keenan could see the ground rising awesomely fast.

*Snake, what are you doing?* he thought.

*Snake! Pull the bastard up...*

Engines howled, a deep reverberating drone beginning past the edges of hearing and rising fast in pitch. The DropShip's nose lifted, levelled, and started to gain height. Keenan caught a glimpse of violent jagged rocky peaks, rimed with ice, flashing beneath his boots and the belly of the DropShip. He licked dry lips, and the thoughts which flickered fast though his mind were far from complimentary.

Reaching the door, he reached in and Ed grabbed him, wrist to wrist in the warrior's grip. Ed grinned. "You did it, mate."

"We were sabotaged. The aerofoil was wedged."

Ed hauled Keenan in, and the battered Combat-K veteran slumped to the floor, his muscles screaming at him, his eyes full of dirt and mouth full of fumes. He breathed, and lethargically unhooked the clips from his belt. Then he glanced up at Ed and grinned. "Thanks for not letting go."

Ed's head tilted. "I've as much desire for life as you, Keenan. Whoever booby-trapped the ship certainly isn't on board. Or…" Their eyes met.

Keenan shook his head. "Don't worry about it. Whoever is playing games, well, it'll come out in the wash." He gave a full-teeth grin, and checked his Techrim, sliding free the magazine, then slamming it home with a precision *clack*. "You see if it doesn't."

"You OK Kee?" came Pippa's voice on the comm.

"Yeah, babe," he breathed. Then his teeth clamped shut. *Babe?* Shit. A close encounter with death and he'd suddenly gone and forgotten her savagery, ruthlessness and downright *evil*. The female of the species? More deadly than the male? Damn fucking right.

"We see what you did," came Pippa's voice. "Well done. Tough gig."

Keenan watched Ed head for the cockpit, leaving him alone. He coiled his cable back on the reel, and dumped it in a locker. Voice low, he said, "Listen. Somebody wanted us *down* and out of the game. I think it's an inside job."

"Why's that?" said Pippa, voice a purr.

"Because I checked the DropShips myself; the only people who've been near after my surveillance are the squads."

"So we've a mole?"

"Aye, and a bad one. One who's out to see us all dead."

"But it can't have been anybody on your ship."

"Why not? As long as he, or she, had good crash protection equipment stashed. It's amazing what you can survive in these technologically advanced times; remember Ket? We should have been cat meat."

"I remember. Listen, I'll speak when we meet at the LZ."

"Out." Keenan's eyes glistened in the gloom. *When I find you*, he thought, *you're going to eat a bullet.*

JETS ROARING WITH green fire, the three DropShips banked, swooping low over an undulating sandy coastline. They howled over thick cross-organic jungle, hazy through early morning steam, and the screams of monkey-trees echoed up at the deafening noise of the three infiltration class infantry ships.

Pippa, her keen eye on the scanners, pulled imperceptibly ahead as they flashed over trees, a swathe of white beach, and blue and pink coral that reared from the sea like corrugated fingers, leading the other DropShips in a sudden rush towards their destination...

Behind her, Mel was snoring, strapped into a modified CrashCouch, and Betezh and Olga had ceased their squabbling and fallen into an uneasy silence, eyes watching the flash of green, white, turquoise and blue through the FlexGlass windshield. Pippa thought to herself they looked like sulky schoolchildren, and the image of both in ties and blazers made her grin, her reflection in the FlexGlass a ghost grinning back.

"Game on," she said, lifting the nose of the DropShip. Motors whirred, and engines howled in response to her precise commands as the vehicle slowed over a massive stretch of sand, a hiatus in the jungle where the beach had spread outwards, consuming the land, usurping the thrones of many mighty hardwoods. Like a lake of sand, a yellow plateau, the kilometre-wide oval ate into the landscape and, with scanners spitting numbers across her HUD, Pippa checked stability readings and brought the DropShip down, unfolding landing gear neatly, and just in time. Engines died, and clicks and hisses echoed out across the beach.

Pippa moved to the ramp, stomped down the corrugated alloy, and stepped out into the heat.

It hit her, a wave of humidity, a hammer-blow of temperature. Pippa loosened the straps of her WarSuit and jumped into the sand, which covered the toes of her boots in an undulating wave. Behind, the other DropShips rotated, jets howling, and lowered, fusing circles of sand into glass, which crackled and *pinged* as engines died and it cooled.

Pippa shaded her eyes, gazing off at the shoreline. White breakers crashed against the beach. The sea shimmered, flecked with silver. Too much like Molkrush Fed, she thought. *Way* too much like Molkrush Fed. But at least on this mission, she wouldn't be left alone with Keenan. The temptation was… too great.

Betezh stumbled down the ramp behind her, followed by Olga, grumbling and hoisting at her barely restrained WarBra. Mel stayed back, in the shade of the ship. She blinked lazily, jaws drooling zombie-pus.

"Wow," said Betezh. "This is a beautiful place."

"Just make sure you don't look in any of ze rock pools, ya?" said Olga.

"Why?" Betezh raised an eyebrow.

"Because you scare yourself away! Har har!"

"Bitch."

"Bastard."

"Fatty."

"Frankenstein."

"Frankenstein was the *creator,* not the monster, you bolshy rubber-ring idiot."

"Ha! You combine ze worst of both!"

"Kids, kids," said Pippa, holding up both hands. "Shut it, now, or I'll have you on a charge. I'll confine you to the ship. I'll hold back your lolly pop rations – whatever it takes to make you behave like adults."

"S'not me," sulked Betezh, face a frown, scars forming strange patterns against his broad flat skull. "She started it."

"Ze did not!"

"Did."

Pippa cocked an MPK and held the barrel under Betezh's nose. "Need any more persuasion, motherfucker?"

"OK, boss."

Pippa watched the ramps of the other ships descend, and she strode across sand, meeting Keenan, Franco and Cam at the centre of the LZ. They nodded to each other, and Franco patted Keenan on the back.

"Well done up there, compadre."

"I won't rest until I find out who dicked with our ships."

"I'm sure they'll make their presence known, soon enough." Franco hoisted his Kekra quad-barrel machine pistol. "And when they do – fooie!"

"Keep taking your pills, mate."

"I am, mate."

Franco threw a long glance to where Mel hovered, just inside the DropShip. Their eyes met. Mel turned, and disappeared. Franco sighed, then he sighed again, he lifted his shoulders, then slumped, and sighed for a third time.

Keenan grinned. "I thought you said it was an amicable divorce?"

"It was. It is. I mean, we're splitting everything fifty-fifty."

"But you haven't *got* anything," pointed out Pippa.

"Yeah," said Franco, showing the black hole of his missing tooth. "But she's got plenty."

"So you're going to clean the poor lass out?"

"Hey, *she's* divorcing me! I figure the least I'm owed, after, after... after *sleeping* with her, with *it,* with a bloody zombie, is a bit of, y'know," he twitched, and rubbed at his reddening neck, "compensation."

Keenan eyed Franco warily. "I'd forgotten what a money-grabbing little bastard you could be, Franco."

"Hey, can I help it if I was born poor? Can I help it if I try to make my honest way through the world and people step on my financial toes? No. No. I can't bloody well buggering hell help it, can I?"

"But your mother left you a small *fortune,*" said Keenan.

"Gambled it."

"And your uncle left you a fucking *star base.*"

"Sold it. Drank it. Y'know how it is."

"No, I don't think I do."

Keenan took a deep breath, and looked to Pippa instead. "However." He took another deep breath, not quite believing Franco was in charge of a squad. "All the DropShip scanners are giving readouts which confirm the original data. No intelligent sentient life on the planet, ergo, no threat. This, hopefully, should be a pretty straightforward foray into our designated regions. And we meet back at this LZ in five days. Are we all clear what we have to do?"

Franco pulled free a thick pack from inside his WarSuit. Papers fluttered free, and were snatched by a cool breeze rolling off the sea and carried high, like fluttering white doves, before disappearing off over the jungle.

"Sorry," he said, snatching at fluttering sheaves, "what was our mission again?"

"You've not read the docs?" said Pippa, aghast.

"Hey, I was going to check them out on the final jag here." He pulled a face. "Not all of us are swots, you know."

"Swots?" snapped Pippa. "I'm a swot now, am I, you total dickhead? I bet you don't even know what damn continent you're travelling to. Do you?"

Franco grinned, and held out a hand, palm up. "Chill pill, sister." He gazed around. "Looking at this fine continent, you'll be happy to understand

I've packed plenty of combat shorts, plenty of UV50, and a massive stash of sausage. And if that doesn't see me right through this frankly comedy mission, I don't know what will."

Pippa leant close to Franco. When she spoke, her words were a low growl. "Maybe snow shoes should have been on your list, *idiot.*"

"Wah?"

"You're going to Yax," said Keenan, slipping on a pair of square-cut Oakley *Solaris* shades. "It's just by the north pole. It's snow, ice, crevasses, the full gamut of raging arctic conditions." He showed his teeth, although it was far from a smile. "Why did you think Fizzy and Shazza brought their skis?"

"Optimism?" ventured Franco.

Pippa tutted, eyed Keenan, and said, "All comms are up. I'll see you back here in five. And you?"

"Yeah?" beamed Franco.

"Don't get killed."

"Aye aye, Cap'n."

Pippa stalked off, and herded a newly squabbling Betezh and Olga back into the DropShip. Pippa could be seen directing a grumbling crew in carrying huge, rectangular alloy cases.

"Better be off," beamed Franco, holding out his hand to Keenan. "I'm sure one of the gals will lend me a jacket."

"I'm sure they will," agreed Keenan, shaking Franco's hand. "And Pippa was right. Don't get killed. And don't get into any trouble. And if you *do* get into trouble, use your kube, comms, even your linked Tuff-Map. You got all that?"

"Yeah." Franco turned, and waved to the female soldiers lounging like lizards in the shadow of the DropShip.

"And Franco?"

"Yeah mate?"

"I have a question."

"Shoot."

"It's about, well, I'm just curious, it's just that, when you said that, I mean, when you got married, right, and you and Mel, well, when you made it back to the hotel room, what I wanted to ask, was, well, did you, y'know, and, well...

What was it like?"

Franco stared, stonily, ahead. He coughed. Turned. And without a word, strode back towards his DropShip.

Keenan shrugged. "That bad, eh?" he muttered, and lit a cigarette.


"CHANGE OF PLAN," said Pippa, hoisting her weapons and her pack. Franco, who had been poking suspiciously in his own pack as the teams made final preparations to separate and begin their search and analysis of Sick World, glanced up. He smiled, a broad smile, and produced a long, evil-looking, purple sausage. It was slick with grease, and smelt of death.

"Found it!" Triumph.

"What the hell," said Pippa, "is that?"

"It's a sausage, muppet. A Slim Jim." He bit it, with a crunching sound, and began to chew. It sounded like cogs in a blender.

"This is the score, and I've cleared it with Keenan so no bloody moaning. Because Candy was pulled for another mission at the last minute, and you're a team member down, we're transferring Olga to you."

Franco pointed at Pippa with the purple bratwurst. "No."

"It's orders. Betezh and Olga are fighting like cat and dog, so it'll immediately alleviate that problem. I'll take Miller with me, because the moaning, whining son-of-a-bitch will have a harder time trying to talk when I pierce both his cheeks with my yukana. Franco, this situation is not up for negotiation."

Franco, about to speak, waggled his sausage… and there came a *shring*, a blur of movement, and six slices of meat tumbled to the soil. Franco focused on the end of the decimated weiner, grimaced, then extended his focus beyond to a poised and quivering Pippa, sword raised above one shoulder, her stance that of a formidable ancient sword-fighting warrior queen.

Franco popped the last of the sausage into his mouth and chewed thoughtfully. "I'd get that blade oiled, love. Looking a bit battered, a bit the worse for wear." He shook his head, face showing regret.

"A shame, to let a fine weapon like that rot."

Pippa clucked in annoyance, and sheathed her blade. She stepped in close, an embodiment of menace. Voice low, she muttered, "be careful where you wave your next sausage, *dick*head. It might just get the same treatment."

"What?" Franco beamed. "So you're offering up your services as a bona fide sausage chopper from now until the end of time? You're such a girl. Such a lass. Such a –" he leered speculatively, "*fine specimen of a woman.*"

Pippa stalked off, furious despite herself, stomping past Keenan who walked to Franco, tightening straps and pulling on his desert EBH despite the heat. "You ready?"

"As ever, bro."

"No shit, right? No drinking, no shagging. You're on mission, on task, and I'll bust you down to toilet inspector if you fuck with me on this one."

"OK, OK, why's everybody on Franco's bloody case this morning, eh? Answer me that? Eh? Just answer it?"

"Because you're a fucking liability, mate."

Keenan stalked away. Franco mumbled something sulkily, and rooted in his pack for another Slim Jim.

IN-SHIP, PIPPA CO-ORDINATED a final communications check, and when happy everybody could talk to everybody else, and all equipment was ready to go, the three DropShips lifted into the sky, jets turning areas of the beach to crinkling, crackling glass, and veered off in three discrete directions, Keenan to Second Djio, the equatorial desert region and Franco to Yax, a northern ice continent where once the doctors of Sick World had carried out RECs, namely research, experimentation and confinements. She, Pippa, as she grasped controls and climbed the DropShip into thinner reaches of atmosphere so that a luxurious rich verdant world fell away beneath and spread out, a vast and colourful vibrancy, a tapestry of silks and wools, thrumming with depth and colour and vivid contrasts, realised with a start that Sick World, the so-called abandoned Sick World, was a truly stunning and beautiful place.

Distantly, Keenan and Franco's ships disappeared in opposite directions. Pippa glanced back, to where Mel was gnawing on a bone, Betezh was oiling his MPK morbidly, and Miller sat, arms folded, grey eyes stoic as he observed every single minute action (presumably with a nod to health and safety implications). Pippa noted Miller had no safety harness fastened, contravening his own regulations. She snorted, smiled at the irony, and forced the DropShip into what it did best: a Target Drop.

It took three hours for Miller to regain consciousness.

"Stick that in your risk assessment," she muttered.

* * *

"IT'S GORGEOUS!" BEAMED Betezh, gazing from the cockpit.

"Yeah," said Pippa.

"Grwll," added Mel, conversationally, her head tilting above Pippa and a long spool of drool descending to land on Pippa's WarSuit. Pippa returned her gaze to the lush, vibrant scenery, and frowned.

Before the cooling, clicking DropShip, which perched on a mountain plateau, sat a valley of unsurpassable beauty. Grey and purple rock faces curved away, gently scooped, through a scattering of tall noble trees, swaying gently, to a distant lake which shimmered, silver, catching the afternoon sun.

"It's perfect," gabbled Betezh.

Pippa threw him a glance. "I didn't think scenery would be your sort of thing."

"Hey, just 'cos I look like a reject from a horror movie prop bin, doesn't mean I don't appreciate nature. I like to stroll through trees, feel the breeze in my hair – well, on my scalp – and swim in cool fresh waters just like the next man." He seemed to squirm, suddenly prim and proper.

Miller, whom Mel had strapped into a MedBag, mumbled incoherently. The lump on his head, from his flailing and accelerating connection with the cockpit interior, was the size of an egg from a hormone-fuelled uber-chicken.

Pippa opened the door, and a ramp slid to the rocky ground on hydraulic hisses. She strode down and a cool mountain breeze nudged her shoulder-length brown hair. Pippa placed a hand against the DropShip's hull, as if steadying herself, closed her eyes, and took a deep breath. She remained, poised, as Betezh poked out his head.

Hands on hips, he strode forward and gazed about. "It's wondrous! Mel, are you coming out? Come on girl, get some fresh air, I feel like a caged chicken after being cooped up in that shit-hole for so long."

Tentatively, Mel, stooping due to her considerable height, clomped down the ramp and stood with head bobbing at the end of her corrugated, armoured zombie neck. Mel, it had to be said, had a long and interesting history, which she recalled in infintesimal personal detail in her semi-autobiographical semi-autobiography, *BIOHELL – The Story of a Zombie Super Soldier*, available from all good bookshops Quad-Galaxy wide.

Betezh strode to a ledge and leapt up with surprising agility. He surveyed the uninhabited expanse before him. "It's a whole world! With no people! Or zombies…" he half turned, "no offence meant, love. There's nothing to pollute the natural calm! Nothing to destroy the equilibrium! It's bloody superb! I think I might just move here…"

"It's wrong," said Pippa. She stood still, eyes closed, hand on ship hull.

"Huh?"

Pippa's eyes clicked open. "This place. It's wrong. It feels wrong."

"What do you mean it feels wrong, you crazy daft wee girl? Just look about you! We are in Eden! Paradise! It's a Farashko painting made real, a De'zano sculpture animated by the gods!" Betezh took a deep, exaggerated breath. "And by God, it smells damn fine."

Pippa moved forward, mouth a thin line, brows knitted. She dropped her pack, glanced around, and gave a little shake of her head. "There's something bad here," she muttered, rubbed at tired eyes, and turned, lifting her remote. "OK. We'll set up BaseCamp here. Now stand back." She smiled. "After all, in the name of Health and Safety, I wouldn't like anybody to get squashed."

Pippa keyed in a nine-digit code, and flicked a switch. With a groan, huge cubes slid from the DropShip's rear quarters and suddenly the whole ship reared up, as if on legs, sections moving, sliding, realigning to a symphony of disjointed metallic cracks. Whirrs and hisses filled the mountain plateau as the DropShip transformed into a cubic shelter, a base, an analysis station from which Combat-K could begin their admittedly simple mission.

Clicks and hisses finally died away.

Betezh grinned and rubbed his hands together. "Let's get a brew on," he said.

* * *

MEL AND PIPPA patrolled the perimeter, weapons drawn, faces tight. They picked their way across alien rocks, pushing through huge ferns and bowing trees, the scent of summer high on the breeze and the world feeling empty, serene, and perfect.

"It's too nice," snarled a sweat-streaked Pippa, as they completed a three-klick circuit and appeared back at the DropShip BaseCamp. "Just too perfect. As fake as a wedding cake. As painful as twenty-year marital sex."

Mel growled.

"No offence meant. And anyway, you're divorced now, right?"

Betezh had lit a fire, and was boiling a pan of water on the flames. Insane, in reality, because a CoffeeChef™ would provide any hot beverage of choice, as long as you wanted gritty tar-shit in a gritty shit-cup.

Pippa strode across the rocky clearing, boots clumping, and kicked the pan free. Water spiralled. She stomped the flames, until dead. Betezh, still holding a forlorn spoon, looked up at her with questions.

"No fires. No smoke. We could be seen for miles."

"The planet's uninhabited," said Betezh, quietly.

"Says who?"

"The reports. The DropBots. The AnalysisBots. That's who."

"To hell with the DropBots. An empty world? I'll believe it when I see it."

"You mean you can't see it?" He caught her eye, and shut up. Trust me to get lumbered with the Dull Party, he thought.

Grunting, Betezh stomped up the BaseCamp's ramp and, grumbling, ignited the CoffeeChef™.

Pippa stared at Mel. "Any problems?"

Mel, eight-foot transmogrification that she was, shook her head. "Rwwll."

"Good girl."

Pippa moved to the lip of rock which overlooked the valley, and leapt lightly atop the precipice poised over a three-thousand foot drop. Her eyes followed jagged contours of rock on the violent descent down, then spread, encompassing the picturesque valley. She snorted. "Yeah. Right."

Betezh appeared, peering warily over the edge. He carried a cup, which he passed up to Pippa. "Long way down."

"Don't be such a pussy."

Betezh stared long and hard at Pippa. "Is there anything I can say, anything at all, to which your retort will not in some way offend? I mean, you're so masculine it's damned scary."

"Masculine?" Danger.

"Yeah." Betezh sipped his machine tar, and grimaced. "All you do is wave your sword, or guns, and shoot things and kill things. Franco told me, about way back on the Dead World, when I was unconscious. Apparently, you wanted to shoot me there and then." He gave a nasty grin.

"That's right." Pippa's gaze was a challenging one.

"Don't you think that attitude is a little bit... wrong? To shoot a man whilst he's on the deck?"

"No."

"Don't you have any compassion?"

"No."

"Not for anyone?"

"No. Now fuck off and fix the CoffeeChef™. This shit tastes like... shit."

Grumbling, Betezh retreated, and Pippa turned back, staring over the valley. She sipped the warm gritty brew. Tears stained her cheeks.


"So this is Kludek, hey?"

"Grwll."

"Wait here."

Betezh, mouth open, hand outstretched with a new cup of coffee, watched in amazement as Pippa moved nimbly across the treacherous rocks and began to climb a nearby rock face. Sword and guns sheathed, she ascended a steep rocky wall in seconds and was gone. Betezh turned to Mel, whose head bobbed. He shrugged. "She must have something in mind. You want this coffee? No?" He sighed. "Suppose I better drink it." He drank it. Choked a little. "S'funny really.

They should rename the damn machine... call it a CoffeeShit. With a ™ of course."

Mel stared at Betezh, her MPK machine gun held loose but strangely threatening. Betezh eyed the weapon, wary for a moment, his eyes straying to survey the corrugations of Mel's deformed body. She stretched and he watched her pus-dribbling breasts wobble. Then her eyes, small and black, locked to his, and he blushed suddenly.

"Grwwll grwl grl."

"What? What do you mean, I'm staring at your tits?"

"Grwwll." Mel shook her head, and blew a pile of snot onto the ground. Betezh's eyes followed the trajectory of mucus, which collected and formed a neat pyramid pile and sat there, green, glistening, wobbling.

Betezh looked deep into Mel's eyes. He cleared his throat. "So then," he began, and with flapping lips, and widening eyes, searched his limited mental filing cabinet desperately for a topic with which to converse with a zombie-mutated female ex-tax inspector. "Did you enjoy being married to Franco, or what?"

Mel turned her back on Betezh. She let off a long, evil, sour fart, and moved back to the DropShip BaseCamp, wide hips wiggling.

Betezh shrugged, and gazed off uneasily across the beautiful valley.

Maybe Pippa was right. It was too stunning. Too perfect.

Betezh lit a KJ cigarette and puffed the spark-filled orange smoke.

PIPPA CLIMBED, SWEAT rolling down her face, her limbs revelling in the violent exercise which for so long had been denied her. Up she flung herself, fingers searching out ridges of rock, boots finding lips and edges, pushing her ever upwards. Quickly she climbed, confidently, sweat glistening on her brow and turning her hair lank. Her muscles sang, and her fingertips burned, scratches soon appearing on her palms and the backs of her hands, her fingernails battered and scratched, her skin scuffed. She paused, halfway up a teetering tower of rock-wall and, reaching behind in her pack, pulled out thin gloves. She examined her fingernails. "Bollocks." She pulled the gloves on, gazed up the vertical ascent, sweat running back down to drip from her hair, then hoisted herself up with a grunt and accelerated once more into a rapid, steep climb.

Pippa climbed for minutes, which lengthened into a good half hour of fast-paced scrabbling, swinging, grunting and heaving. Finally, her breathing laboured, her WarSuit soaked within and humming softly to dissipate sweat, the Combat-K assassin hauled herself over the final lip and slumped onto her back, eyes closed, face scrunched, allowing her panting to fast recover. She sat up, sunlight blinding her for a moment, a cool breeze kissing her deliciously, then climbed to her knees on the ragged pinnacle of rock. She was on top of the mountain. For a brief moment of glorious joy, she felt on top of the world...

Kludek spread out in a glorious 360° panorama. Forests followed the contours of the land, leading to huge shimmering lakes and more distant, purple-sided mountains. On the surface, it was entrancing, emotive, and totally absorbing. Pippa pulled out miniBinos and clipped them to her nose. They clicked and buzzed, aligning with her eyes and hot-wiring to her brain using WhizzWaves. Hands on hips, Pippa scanned a seventy kilometre area, taking her time, moving through the trees, examining the surfaces of lakes, looking for

What are you looking for? she thought, and gave a tiny internal shrug. Something. Anything. Not just signs of life, but... evidence of previous junk existence. Maybe even current junk existence. But then, how could that be even remotely possible? The junks were toxic, contagious, they poisoned and destroyed everything they came into contact with. They were natural born killers. A scourge on the living. To the junks, life was simply something born to die.

Pippa's gaze swept the glorious land.

There!

Her gaze moved back, more carefully this time. It was screened by forest, but it was there, a klick from a large oval lake. It was a building. A large building, mammoth in fact, constructed from grim grey concrete. There were barred windows, and it reminded her sourly of a prison complex. Pippa had spent her fair share of time in prison.

Adjusting the brain focus, she moved in closer and saw the edges of walls were crumbling and streaked with the detritus of millennia. Understanding dawned. This was an old hospital complex, from the days of Sick World's operational past. And yet... why hadn't the forest reclaimed the building? Surely, after a thousand years, Nature's awesome might should have taken the hospital and pulverised it into base fragments?

A puzzle, then.

And a place to be explored... Steinhauer wanted samples, soil, rock, and exploration of anything out of the ordinary. Well, this was out of the ordinary. Pippa locked the location, removed the microBinos, and clambered to the rim of the precipice. A near five-thousand-foot drop loomed, sheer, foreboding, but it held no fear for Pippa. She wiped free sweat. Nothing held fear for Pippa; she'd seen too much, done too much. Fear was just a pointless emotion that happened to other people.

She dropped into the abyss, towards the toy BaseCamp below.

BETEZH WAS WAITING with the KTM Dirt-Spaz motocross bikes fuelled and primed. Pippa had comm'd him during her rapid descent. As her boots hit dirt, Betezh looked into a face lined with tiredness but with cold grey eyes; solid, stone, unrelenting and iron.

Betezh scanned the sky. "It's getting late."

"We have time."

"Wouldn't like to get caught out in unexplored terrain after dark."

"What are you?" sneered Pippa, "Combat K or Combat Chicken Soup? Get your shit together. We're moving out. Mel, you stay here and keep an eye on the 'Camp. And that bastard Miller. Wouldn't like him sniffing around our personal effects. Betezh, you good to go?"

"Yes." Betezh watched Pippa stomp to the bikes. His voice dropped to a whisper. "Whatever you say, boss."

Pippa slung her leg over the KTM and fired the engine, which rumbled into life, vibrating the big bubble tyres. Pippa gestured, and Betezh mounted his own ride, strapping his MPK machine gun to his back and grabbing the high bars with a grimace. "I'm not comfortable on a bike."

Pippa tutted, and opened the throttle, easing around the BaseCamp and heading out across a natural rocky trail. Betezh followed, huge tyres swallowing smaller rocks and ejecting them in his wake with little *phrips*. He was muttering, but clamped his teeth tight under threat of more Pippa mockery. Betezh never had been comfortable around women. That, and his Frankenstein stitching, was probably why he was still single.

Pippa led the way, first down rocky trails, then to wide natural avenues between sweeping hillsides of forest. Scents bombarded the two Combat-K soldiers, and they powered along at a modest pace, bike suspension thudding, tyres churning grass, until Pippa finally called a halt. Betezh pulled up alongside her.

"Everything OK?"

"It's up ahead."

"And you think it's an old hospital building?"

"Yeah. Either that, or a prison."

"Why would they need prisons on a Sick World?"

Pippa looked sidelong at Betezh, her mouth hinting at a smile. "You never read your background stuff, did you Betezh? You're a man in the same mould as the Franco Haggises of this world, you know that?"

Betezh beamed, taking this as a compliment. "So? Go on, spill the beans."

"There were people here, and aliens here. Sick people. Sick aliens. So far, so normal. But then, the sickness wasn't just a cough and a cold, wasn't just a broken leg. They had the criminally insane here, as well."

"Criminally insane?"

"The nutcases, the sex offenders, the murderers. Imagine a gross genetic blending of human and alien, taking, say, a Triklon for the sake of argument; now, those armoured fuckers were tough as hell, but mentally stable. Mix the two, add a few weird proto-virus strands, and God only knows what some of those doctors witnessed down on this diseased ball of sputum."

Betezh shivered. "I thought this was, y'know, just for illness. And stuff."

"Yeah Betezh. And stuff." She blipped the throttle, and her KTM gave a savage roar, returning to fast idle. "Just make sure you've got your gun primed."

"The DropBots said the place was clear."

"Maybe so. But I don't trust nothing. Only myself. My gun. My instincts. And baby, now they're screaming..."

"Bah! You're just being paranoid. Too much combat, too many army drugs in unwilling veins. You're talking a big load of shit, Pippa, and its spewing from you like a sewage-run overflow." Betezh stumbled into silence. He remembered to whom he was speaking.

Pippa stared at him for a long, hard moment, then shot off on her bike. Cursing, Betezh followed and they sped down a slippery moss-covered hill towards the outskirts of the hospital complex.

Betezh gazed up. And up. And pulled up beside Pippa with a small skid. He noted she'd killed her engine, and Betezh did the same.

"It's big," he observed, without necessity.

Pippa nodded. "Look around. At the mud pools."

Betezh noticed for the first time they'd travelled through a massive field of glooping pools. They bubbled softly, bubbles occasionally expanding and popping on the murky grey-brown surface.

"You smell sulphur?"

Pippa nodded. "I was more concerned about the tracks."

Betezh's eyes followed several long, slithering trails to the edge of the pools. "Ahh, that could be caused by simple erosion. Y'know, rain coming down off the hillside. Or something."

"It's the 'something' I'm worried about."

Pippa dismounted, and her KTM crackled, engine cooling. She pulled free a D5 shotgun and strapped it to her back, then checked her twin yukana swords which glinted with a hint of green.

Green?

Pippa and Betezh glanced up at the same time, where the edge of the horizon was glowing a fiery green.

"What the hell's that?" snapped Betezh, jumpy now.

"Night's falling. Sick World's moon, Jangla, reflects a green radiance. It's a kind of reverse sunset; we're seeing it now."

"So… soon it'll be dark?"

Pippa nodded, and re-sheathed her swords. "Sure looks that way."

"Maybe we should head back to BaseCamp? Y'know, explore in the morning, sort of thing?"

Pippa gave Betezh a withering look, then touched her earlobe comms. "Mel, you receiving? Good. Is everything OK there? Good. Listen, we've found the hospital complex I saw from the mountain top. We're heading in now, to explore…"

"Ow!" snapped Betezh, and slapped at his neck. Pippa frowned at him, and continued to speak to Mel.

Logging out, she moved forward and examined a small, red welt on the big man's tanned, dark skin. "What is it?"

"Felt like a bite."

"But there's no life down here," said Pippa, with a smile. "Come on."

They moved forward, stepping gingerly over a drag-trail perhaps two feet in width. Pippa knelt, examining the ground. "Whatever it was, it came from in there." She nodded up ahead, at the ancient hospital.

"Ouch!" Betezh slapped the back of his hand. He scowled. "Something bit me, Pippa. I ain't happy about this, because I'm the sort of man who attracts all manner of nasties and bugs and flying bastards. Look, you've not been bitten!"

"Maybe I have purer blood."

Betezh followed Pippa, and they came to the towering walls, crumbling grey, pockmarked with centuries of erosion. Wire cores stood out from several fallen sections, and the air was musty, not just with trace elements of sulphur from the nearby bubbling pools, but from a kind of inherent, locked decay on a slow-time half-life release.

Betezh stared at the sky. "It's definitely getting dark."

"Don't be a pussy." Pippa stepped across the threshold, between twisted, mangled, rusted gates which had been folded back as if by an angry giant's hands. There was a huge yard beyond, leading from the perimeter walls to the main building complex, and it was littered with rubble and debris, steel wires and huge chunks of old masonry.

"Why are there no weeds? No trees? No plants in cracks and crevices?"

Pippa shrugged. "Maybe it's the sulphur," she said, softly.

"Nothing wrong with *my* crack," giggled Betezh.

Pippa stared at him, then moved forward between piles of rubble. The main hospital complex ahead was a huge, cubic structure. Barred windows graced only the upper reaches, all small black holes, like missing teeth, hinting at nothing within. The only entrance Pippa could see consisted of large double doors; large enough, she presumed, to accept a big alien on a stretcher-trolley from a blue-lit turbo-ambulance.

"Ouch!"

Pippa turned. "Are you making this up, dickhead?"

Betezh stared at her, and relaxed into a lazy smile. "No girl, of course I'm not. Hey, you know, when we get back to BaseCamp we should crack open a few beers, y'know, tell some funny stories. I bet Mel has some crackers, y'know, about life as a zombie, and what it's like on your wedding night." Betezh stepped forward, swaggering a little, and poked Pippa in the upper arm. She slapped away his hand.

"What are you doing?"

"What do you mean, what am I doing, chickpea?"

"*Chickpea?* Betezh, have you been *drinking?*"

"No! Of course not! That would be so unfopressional."

"Unfopressional?"

Betezh frowned. "Unfopressional! Pippa, babe, girl, chick, chipmunk, have *you* been drinking?"

Pippa gave a quick look to the double doors, which were gleaming with green light from Sick World's rising moon as shadows lengthened from the fast setting sun, then pulled free her PAD. "This might hurt," she said, and slammed the PAD extension cable into Betezh's neck. It gave a blip, as it analysed his blood. Pippa pulled free the PAD with a *slup* and analysed the readouts. She frowned… as something *nipped* her neck.

"Ow!"

"Y'see!" Betezh started to giggle, and suddenly fell back on his arse in a manner of drunken comedy slapstick. He started to roar with laughter, and slapped both his knees. "This is just *great*, don't you think? In fact, this looks like a good place to sleep." He started to curl into a ball and close his eyes...

"Shit." Pippa knelt by him, and slapped him, hard, a brutal stinging slap to his heavily-scarred cheek. "Listen! There's morphine in your blood. You're feeling euphoric." Something buzzed by Pippa's face and she twitched, an incredibly fast movement. The something *blurred* past her vision, then hovered, a foot before her. It was a tiny insect, a tiny metal insect, and Pippa's eyes narrowed as she saw instead of a face, it seemed to have –

A diminutive, almost microscopic, hypodermic needle.

Pippa's arm moved fast, still enclosed around the PAD which gave a chime, and snapped the insect from the air, imprisoning it. The PAD started to buzz as it analysed its trapped specimen and Pippa looked around, wary now. She drew her sword. Betezh giggled again. "Wha' you gonna do with that, chicken? Slice the little buglies in half?"

Something buzzed, and Pippa slammed the yukana. There came a tiny *flash* as the insect disintegrated. "Yeah," she snarled and, grabbing Betezh's collar, hissed, "Move your arse, soldier, we need to get inside the building. I've got a nasty feeling these little fuckers are gonna come in a swarm..."

"Then we'll get high!" chuckled Betezh.

"No. Then we get dead, then we get *eaten*. Move yourself!"

Betezh scrambled across the yard, almost on all fours as Pippa's eyes, narrowing through the half-light of the day/night transition, picked out more flying bugs. And the frightening thing was... she'd been right.

They rose from the bubbling pools, moonlight glinting green from the many insects' silvered carapaces, and buzzed in a tiny storm across the yard towards the scrambling duo... Pippa dragged Betezh with all her might, grunting and cursing and screaming at his giggling and general laid-back euphoria as they sprinted now for the abandoned hospital building and slammed against doors, which rattled in a heart-sinking *I'm locked* kind of fashion.

"Bastards!" screamed Pippa.

"Just press the button," slurred Betezh, grinning inanely.

"What fucking button?"

"That big red OPEN button, there." He pointed with a drooping scarecrow arm.

Pippa slammed her palm against the button. There was a *buzz*, and the doors opened easily allowing the two Combat-K squaddies to fall into a large, well-lit reception area. Outside, a *swarm* of insects sped towards the opening and the warm, fresh meat sprawled inside, sweating and stinking nicely. Pippa kicked at the doors, which lazily, languorously, started their juddering procedure of closure.

"Ch, ch, ch," said Betezh, and roared with incredibly boisterous laughter from his rolling, scrabbling position.

Several insects buzzed in, and Pippa's sword slammed left and right, sending tiny flashes sparking against a backdrop of darkening night sky. The doors closed with a *click*. Pippa whirled, eyes searching, and one final insect landed atop her head and stung her. She dropped, whirled, and her yukana killed the tiny thing with an actinic spark.

"Dit get you?" slurred Betezh.

Pippa rubbed her head. "Yeah. The little bastard."

Slowly, one of her knees buckled, and Pippa toppled to the sterile, cream-tiled floor. She watched the strip-lights overhead, and noted that in the corner, one was flickering, on off, on off, on off, in an annoying fashion. Something crept through her pleasure-filled brain with the lethargy of a steam-train grinding through an uphill tunnel. Who services the lights? Light bulbs don't last for a thousand years. Her eyes dropped, following ancient copper pipe-work, green and furred, which disappeared through the wall... and her last vision was of Betezh's leering, grinning, morphing face as she slipped unwillingly into unconsciousness.

SHE COULD SMELL them. They smelled of warm meat, sweat, salt, fear and sexual fluids. The nurse licked her lips. She liked salt. It made her tingle. And she liked sex juice. It made her writhe. She crept to the edge of the darkness beneath the stroboscopic strip-light and watched the tall woman, the dangerous one with the sword, watched her fall and the nurse's long tongue lolled out, dragging on the floor and leaving a trail of ichor. The nurse dragged herself forward a little, stumps scraping the tiles like wood on stone, and she rubbed at her mouth as drool eased free, smudging her cherry-red lipstick, so carefully applied, reapplied, and reapplied continually for the past several hundred years. After all... she wanted to look pretty. Her eyes fixed on the big fat man, big and fat, yes, but plenty, plenty meat. He rolled about, laughing, infected by the Morphs and their euphoria liquor and the nurse knew, knew as clear as Jangla followed the sun, chasing her like a rabid lover destined never to catch, that the fat man would succumb to the juice and would lie down and sleep and there would be no fight in him, no more, and her job, her *joy* would be so very much easier.

CHAPTER FOUR

# SICK WORLD II: YAX

FRANCO SKILFULLY PILOTED the DropShip towards the Yax co-ordinates with a big sloppy grin on his chops. This is going to be so ace, he thought cheerfully, picturing in his mind's eye the huge crate of seventy-two bottles of AssHole Vodka he'd packed, the crate of tinned Nuclear Chilli, a second crate of irradiated Curry Cream Cakes (*Yummy, Yummy In My Tummy, Graaargh*!) and the raison d'être of Franco's culinary machinations, a third and final crate of Puker's SuperFire Horseradish (guaranteed to put you on the bog for a month, or your money back!!!!!!!!!). Franco loved horseradish. It was his favourite food in the world, and he smeared it on anything and everything that couldn't crawl off his plate; and maybe a few things that could.

As he piloted, one hand nonchalantly draped over the steering yoke, he eyed the rear-view mirror. There was Fizzy, red-headed and fiery, high cheekbones, dazzling green eyes, haughty and proud and rebellious and *right up Franco's particular fantasy back alley*. And there was Shazza, brunette, shorter and a bit more plumped out than Fizzy but hey hey hey Franco certainly loved a chick with a bit of meat on her, a bit of ham on that rump ass, so to speak, a bit of wobble to the chicken breast department... and certainly *right up Franco's particular fantasy back alley*. And then, there was –

"Shit and bugger and hot damn curried frogs."

*There* was Olga, huge and hairy, arms like a German shot-putter, head like a bulldog's only without the charm, and a powerful suffocating headlock that guaranteed she got a regular shot of "ze sexual intercourse" she so liked. Olga was staring into the mirror, ergo, into Franco's wandering eyes.

"Har har har!" boomed Olga, her voice drowning out the sultry chatter of the two uber-vixens seated just behind Franco and strategically positioned so that with a certain little *twist* of the mirror, he could peer down their buxom bosoms. "I see you there little Franco Haggis, all shy and sexy, and giving Olga ze eye in ze mirror you have cleverly positioned to watch your favourite oxen gal. Yar?"

It should be explained that Olga, prior to joining

Combat-K as an honorary appointed veteran, had been instrumental in Franco, Keenan and Pippa's escape from beneath the violent lava-filled depths of the GreenSource Mainframe on the Biohell infected, well, *hell,* of The City only months earlier. During the mission, Olga had developed a serious crush on Franco and wasn't about to let something like his complete lack of reciprocation get in the way of using and abusing his muscular (if somewhat short and stumpy) body. Without Olga, Franco would surely be dead, and there were few moments that went by without her reminding him of the God-awful truth, and thus her need for some kind of payback, preferably in a grotesque sexual manner. Pippa had commented that Olga was the female sexually deviated version of Franco, himself a sexual deviant extraordinaire. Franco had been far, far from amused, and refused to acknowledge she was, in fact, correct.

"Um, actually…" began Franco, in retaliation to this most slanderous of slanders, but his voice petered out as he caught a glimpse of the rapidly changing landscape beneath. Glorious trees and lakes and mountains had gradually dropped, panning out into ocean, and then the ocean filled with chunks of ice. Now, as they cleared a towering black mountain range of jagged dragon's teeth, Franco saw a wilderness of ice and snow unfold before him. There were mountains, yes, but high jagged-bastard mountains filled with the kind of ice that crushed men for breakfast, ate women for dinner, and burped out their bones as a party trick.

"What the hell is this?" he boomed, leaning forward, his languorous slouch suddenly dead and buried. "What's all this snow? And ice? And damn and buggering icy mountains? Eh? I said, eh?"

Fizzy leant forward, red hair a sultry tangle. "You mean you didn't read up on Yax? And you thought Pippa was joking?"

"Eh? I mean, of course I read about it." Franco preened. "It's just, I thought this was some kind of hot desert wilderness, filled with lakes and forests and we could go fishing and dancing, and fishing and loving, and get up to some deep-forest tomfoolery." He coughed. "All I've packed is shorts and t-shirts."

"Honey," said Shazza, running a hand through her hair (replete with Combat-K combat hair-clips), "it's damn near -40°C out there. In a T-shirt you'd last about twenty-five seconds before you went blue, maybe five minutes until death. Why the hell did you think we all brought hi-tech winter kit? Ice axes? Laser-guided grapplers? The finest in heated WarSuits?"

"Um..." Franco scratched his ginger goatee beard. "I thought the axes, were, y'know, weapons. For fighting with. To kind of, go, alongside, your, guns." He faltered. Then brightened. "There must be some winter kit in the hold of this here DropShip, after all..."

"No," interjected Fizzy. "We checked. After take-off, when we realised you were so foolishly and unprofessionally under-equipped. You're like one of those dumb-fucks who dies on the mountain, wandering around without Gore-Tex, no map, no compass, completely underestimating the savage murdering brutality of *Nature*. She's a bitch, ain't she?" Fizzy grinned, a big-teeth grin which didn't allow Franco much opportunity for humorous camaraderie.

Olga's hand descended, slapping Franco's shoulder so hard he nearly pitched under the cockpit console. He grunted, coughing, and saw the gleam in Olga's eye.

"No."

"What do you mean 'no' Little Franco?"

"Just, no."

"But you not know what Olga suggest."

Franco stared at her huge flat face, her small, pig-like eyes. They seemed full of… concern. Like a mother's concern for a particularly retarded son.

"Go on," said Franco, warily.

"Olga is big lass, yes? Well, she sure her clothes will fit Franco absolutely no problem lubberly jubberly. That way, Franco not freeze his skinny-arse off in ze freezing wastes of Yax. Sound like a good plan?" She roared with laughter, and slapped Franco again. "Of course is ze good plan."

"OK," said Franco, voice slow, and still imbued with a terrible wary suspicion. "Suppose I was to say yes…"

"Let's go, then, to Olga's bed chamber and help you struggle from your little pants and T-shirt and standing all naked in Olga's bedchamber so you can then try on some of Olga's underwear, did I say ze underwear, silly me Olga was meaning ze clothes for ze winter mission of course." She beamed.

"Yes, go on Franco," said Fizzy, grinning at him. "Go and entertain Olga for a while. She's gagging for a bit of *hero* company like what you have to offer. I'm sure she'll grab your…" ·

"Borrocks," said Sax, choosing that moment to look up from his basket, wig slightly askew. Something inside him went *clonk*.

"Yeah, don't be such a wet fish," chimed in Shazza. "Go on. Olga's a lass who loves a good time, doncha gal?"

Franco deflated. In a small voice, he said, "I suppose I might pop along in a little while to have a look at your, um, wardrobe." His eyes narrowed. "But don't be getting any bloody damn and bloody ideas, alreet?"

"Ideas?" Olga fluttered her eyelashes. It had the same effect as a bear fluttering its eyelashes prior to pulling your head clean off. "I would ze never dream of it, sweetie."

* * *

YAX WAS A savage harsh land of ice-storms, ice-hail, ice-sheets and snow. Much of the year was spent in darkness, and when there was a hint of daylight the sun hung low, a bloated red orb slung over the horizon like a zombie corpse over the back of a saddle. The DropShip howled, banking, jets turning ice-hail to water and lowering slowly, a wary predator, between walls of jagged, ice-encased mountain and lower yet, into a broad valley split by a sluggish, ice-bobbing river. Occasionally, sparkles of red fire blossomed amidst the ice, then hissed and were extinguished, leaving trails of frozen magma and ash from the underground volcanic fault which kept this river fluid amidst a -40ºC summer.

The DropShip cooled swiftly with several alarming clangs and bangs. Landing struts, sunk deep in snow and ice, quickly assimilated a sheen of ice webs.

Creaking, the hold ramp lowered and Franco stood, hands on hips, beaming. He wore knife-cut army combats and a Guinness t-shirt. His face glowed instantly red from frost-nip, and his broad smile, showing his single missing tooth, was nothing if not a platter of massive fake humour.

"Ach, it's not that bad!" he bellowed, and strode down the ramp, hands still on hips, like some perverse and deviant catwalk model. The wind whipped him with cat-o'-nine-tails lashes of pain. Snow stuck instantly to his ginger beard, forming long curled icicles. He turned, surveying the three huddled figures in the doorway, wrapped in heavy furs and the most advanced military Gore-Tex

Combat-K would and could provide. "It's just, y'know, refreshing. Like a dip in a cold bath after a sauna. That sort of thing. Makes a man of ye, so it does."

The three females stared at him. Warily, they emerged, and slid worryingly down the ramp. Fizzy poked Franco in the chest. "You've gone blue, dickhead."

"Ate some bad cheese."

"You've ice in your beard!"

"Must have been that ice-pop I had after lunch."

"Mate, you're shivering worse than a blue-peanut junkie during a gun-turkey withdrawal."

"Yeah, well," he grinned, "suppose I need a voddie. The chill affects me like that, sometimes."

"Franco," Fizzy looked deep into his eyes, "you are one stubborn son-of-a-bitch."

"Hey, I never said I was perfect. Never said I was Mr. Franco 'Perfect Pecs' Haggis, never said I was some kind of incredible macho hunky superhero, although now I think about it, I am. Come on, let's get this show onna road, this ship launched, this sperm ejaculated from the barrel. It's gonna be a long, hard gig of," he sniggered, holding his belly with one scarred hand, "collecting damn soil samples." The team of four stepped away from the DropShip, and Sax appeared, groggily, just as Franco hit the TRANS key. The DropShip growled, motors whirring as panels clanked and slid, hydraulics hissed and the whole vehicle stood up and transformed into a DropShip BaseCamp. With a strangled *"Borrocks"* Sax tumbled back into the interior, and they could hear him banging and clanking around, bounced and tossed as walls rearranged themselves and Sax was bounced around like a spanner in a tumble drier, like a bone between slurping jaws.

Steam hissed, melting more snow and ice. The wind howled mournfully. Franco slapped his blue thigh, and strode up the new ramp towards the gleaming interior. Once inside, away from the storm which crackled around air-vents like an electric banshee, Franco scowled at his team. They stared back at him, only moderately disbelieving. Being part of a Franco Haggis combat squad was a bit like being committed.

"OK team. This is how it works. Today, we'll establish a rearward leisure-time comfort-zone with our main priority being that of spa-works, imbibing pleasure-sense altering substances and with the possibility of loquacious arousal on the imminent horizon if I'm not very too much mistaken."

"Yah," beamed Olga, beaming.

Franco frowned. He coughed. "Um. Right. Then, tomorrow, Fizzy, you can be in charge of soil samples. Shazza, you're on rock samples. And Olga can collect ice samples. And Sax can do the housework, with or without his wig. I think that superb plan has covered all the bases, so it has."

"And what will you do?" said Fizzy.

"I am the Team Leader. I will Lead the Team."

"Yeah, but what will you actually *do?*"

Franco leered at her suggestively. "I'll have both my hands full, don't you worry you none."

"Tsch," tutted Fizzy. "Damn Ruperts."

"I can see you're the feisty one in the crew!" said Franco, slowly, brain working hard. "And that's why I want to do *your* staff appraisal first! I'll see you in my quarters in half an hour. With or *without* your uniform."

Franco winked. Fizzy stared at him, face stone.

IT WAS LATER. Much later. BaseCamp was established. Sax was downloading upgrades, although Franco was damned if he could work out what possible benefits a mute DumbMutt could garner from any kind of possible digital download. Maybe they were upgrading his brain, ha ha?

"At last! Is ready!" Olga swirled her giant fork in the giant pan, and held up a cube of quivering meat on the end of three long prongs. The other members of the team sat around an alloy table, knives and forks clasped in hands, plates empty, staring at the wobbling cube. Olga's eyes widened. "Is good, ya?"

"What," said Shazza, placing her knife and fork fastidiously by her plate, "is that?"

"Meat stew."

"What kind of meat?"

"Is meat."

"Beef? Pork? Dog? Rat? Za-beeber bug? Krustalanious Snake Burger? What?"

"Is meat, innit?" Olga tossed the cube, and Franco caught it expertly, popped it in his mouth, and chewed.

"Mmm. It's good, sweetheart." Franco coughed, frowned, remembered himself. "Quite tasty. I'll have me a pan of that."

Olga dished out huge ladles of quivering meat stew, and the team ate in considered silence for a while. Franco was the first to finish and, belching heartily, he pushed his plate away and patted his fat and, some would say, nicely rotund, belly. "Great meat stew, Olga. You're a fine cook."

"Ach, thank you Franco. I make ze special effort, just for you."

Franco coughed, and turned his attention to Shazza. She was picking wordlessly through the meal, focused as if working on the latest world-saving mission. Franco coughed again. Shazza looked up. "Yes?"

"Wondered if you, like, fancied coming round for a game of Monopoly afterwards. You'd be amazed what this smart-uniformed squaddie can do with the Old Boot."

"Err, no. Anyway, what about your wife?"

Franco's eyes glazed over. "Wife?"

"Yeah, you're wife. Mel. Just a few hundred klicks south-west of this very position. Would she be happy, you soliciting affection via a dodgy game of Monopoly like this?"

"Solicito whatting?"

"Look," Shazza nudged Fizzy, "I'll tell you what we can do, seeing as you've pulled rank and instead of collecting samples for the QGM we seem to be having a day of relaxing, or as you call it, a rearward leisure-time comfort-zone. Considering we're doing *fuck all* to aid the war effort, why don't you nip over, visit your zombie chick. Give her a good seeing to." She winked, coquettishly.

"Do *what?*" snapped Franco. "Now – now listen here! Me and Mel, well, we got divorced."

"So, you're single?" asked Fizzy, running a hand through glossy red locks.

"Yeah, baby," growled Franco.

Fizzy turned a sideways glance to Olga. "See. I told you. Now the playing field is well and truly open. Go for it, girl. Especially one with your, ahh, culinary skills. A man like Franco should be biting your hand off for a second chance at wedded bliss."

Olga beamed.

Franco stood, a little woodenly. "Actually, girls, whilst you're here relaxing, I've decided to take the Giga-Buggy out and do a spot of scouting, secure the area, check the perimeters, you know, that sort of brave solitary hero sort of thing."

"I'll come with you," said Olga immediately.

"No, no, I'd rather work alone on this one."

"How long will you be?" said Fizzy.

"Not sure, y'know, as long as it takes." Franco grinned. "I tell you what, Olga, get yourself back in that kitchen and make me a fine sausage stew for when I get back. How's that sound?"

"I'll stew your sausage," muttered Olga, licking her lips.

"Eh?"

"Nothing, Team Leader Captain Franco." She beamed, showing missing teeth, gold teeth, and a tongue and lips arrangement that could suck a tennis ball through a straw.

Franco shuddered, expressing a field of goosebumps, and made his way from the canteen, heading on a mission for the hold.

THE 6X6 ARMOURED Giga-Buggy was a serious piece of off-road kit. Armed with stowable eight-barrel MiniGuns using sixteen different types of interchangeable ammunition, it also packed K52 Dragon SAMs and armour-piercing 52mm canons. It could operate fully submerged in water, quicksand, even magma for a short period of time, and was rated a 10.2 on the anti-NBC filtration channels. It was, as Franco succinctly put it, an *awesome* piece of battle shit.

Franco clambered through to the cockpit, his belly scraping on hull struts, and sat ensconced in the most high-tech military-grade digital equipment found this side of a Quad-Gal Future Battlefield.

Franco squinted at the controls, then looked around conspiratorially, as if someone might have snuck inside the cockpit without him seeing. He eased a rolled-up document from the inner pockets of his recently acquired combat jacket (recently acquired from Shazza's locker when she was sat on the toilet), and unrolled it on the Giga-Buggy's cockpit controls. He focused. His finger traced a line, and mouthed co-ordinates, then he stared up and *out* of the Giga-Buggy's screen. A storm howled. The Buggy's readouts said it was getting worse.

"Ach, I'll be all right," he muttered. "After all, it's not every day a squaddie has the chance to get his paws on a fabled treasure carved from sub-PlutoniumIII! Iskander's Crown, hey, here I come!"

He gunned the engines, with a series of crunches engaged twin gearboxes, then nosed the vehicle out of the BaseCamp's protective shelter…

Out, into the storm.

HOURS HAD PASSED. Franco's earlobe comm buzzed. It was Keenan.

"Everything OK your end, Haggis?"

"Aye, boss," said Franco, easing up on the Buggy's ascent of what he considered a quite treacherous rocky, ice-strewn trail, criss-crossed by several narrow but threateningly deep crevasses. As the Buggy stopped, ice creaked, ominously. "Nothing to report from here except snow, more snow, a bit more snow, and possibly a touch of snow. Is everything OK up your end? No horrible monsters or zombie deviants or anything?" He cackled quietly at this Big Joke. After all, the planet had been cleared by the DropBots, had it not? It was as safe as safe could be. Safe as butter. Safe as daffodils.

"Yes." Keenan's voice was cool. Controlled. But Franco had known Keenan long enough to detect a hint of something; if not worry, exactly, there was an element there, a suspicion maybe, a hunch.

"But something's not right?"

"No," said Keenan. "I've patched this through just to you. I'll talk with Pippa in a while. I'm not on a Global Channel. After all," Franco could almost *hear* the grin, "wouldn't like Snake and his buddies to listen in on our little love messages, would I?"

"You don't trust them?"

"About as far as I can throw them, and they're hefty blokes."

"Well, keep me informed," said Franco.

"You too. Where are you now?"

Franco stared at the icy mountains, and down at his treasure map and the glowing trails of dots. "Um, just doing a recce, y'know, checking the place is safe from... from..."

"Ice zombies?"

"Aye, them's the fellas."

"Well, have a good one."

"You too, Keenan. Out."

The comm died and Franco sat, listening to the ice beyond the walls of the Giga-Buggy. If I find the treasure, he said to himself, grinding his teeth a little, then I'll be sure to share it with Keenan. And with Pippa. Obviously, with Pippa.

He tried hard to convince himself. He didn't do a very good job.

THE GIGA-BUGGY ROARED through ice and snow, six huge bubble wheels churning a mush and ejecting spikes and chains to deal with the harder slides; up slopes the Buggy snarled, belching out toxic black fumes, down narrow valleys, through frozen forests of white icing, across solid rivers of ice with depth monitors *blipping* at Franco, who paid little attention, so focused was he on the treasure map and thoughts of wealth, cash, dosh, loot, and Iskander's Crown in particular. Some sly research had told him the Crown was indeed a deeply valuable artefact sought by a thousand museums Quad-Gal wide. Franco's research had also revealed the Crown lived in an underground ice palace filled to the brim with fist-sized diamonds, rubies, kreegers and splaffs. That's why Franco had brought the Buggy. There was lots of boot space for stash.

"Hmm."

Franco jabbed brakes, and the Buggy slid sideways before coming to a halt scant metres before a four-thousand foot precipice. Wind howled up, blowing snow like confetti. It reminded Franco of his wedding day to Mel. The zombie. He grunted. It did little to put him in a good mood.

"Bloody shite missions," he muttered. "I deserves to be a rich man! Splaffs like my fist? I'll have me some of that treasure."

The wind howled a song between mountain peaks. Trees rustled around the throbbing Buggy. Franco squinted at his map, then at the Buggy's screen. He tapped in fresh co-ordinates.

NOT RECOGNISED Ø   flashed the console.

"Huh?"

He tapped in the co-ords again, slower this time, aware he had five thumbs and fat fingers porked up on a diet of fat, fat, sausage fat, cheese fat and fat-filled fatty horseradish.

NON-EXISTENT Ø flashed the console this time, more urgently. Outside, the wind sang as huge bruised iron clouds gathered and made threatening growls of planet-sized menace. To Franco, none of this existed. There was only The Moment. And The Moment was searching for The Treasure.

For a third time he input data, and the console made a rude sound at him, halfway between buzz and fart. Franco thumped it, because that sort of thing always seemed to work for him, a deviant symbiosis of the flesh and the mechanical; then, in annoyance he slammed open the cockpit and stood up, radiant in one of Olga's huge billowing hand-knitted orange and green striped cardigans, which blended quite naturally with his combat camouflage, or so he thought.

The console remained obstinately silent. GET STUFFED, it seemed to be saying. YOU ARE AN IDIOT.

He punched a key. It farted at him.

GET FUCKED, implied the Buggy.

Franco sighed. "OK. Have it that way. I'll navigate manually, you fat porky pig in shit." Back in the Buggy, brushing snow from the shoulders of his fetching cardie, he moved the Buggy slowly up the slope and across a narrow, fragile ice bridge – which he only recognised as such when it crumbled noisily behind him. Roars boomed distantly as snow and ice picked up velocity and violence. In rear scanners Franco watched ten-thousand tonnes of ice tumble into a planet-sized gorge. Franco scratched his beard. "Damn and bloody bollocks," he said, recognising that he now had what could be considered a serious problem vis-à-vis returning to BaseCamp. Still, the treasure beckoned in the way only treasure can, and Franco *knew* he'd always find a way round the problem. He always did. That's why they called him Franco "Lucky Scrotum" Haggis. He had a history of non-impregnation.

Avalanches boomed in the valleys below, like a spastic bass drum rhythm.

Franco crawled his six-wheeled Giga-Buggy

onwards and upwards towards that which he was promised.

Well, in his own head, anyway.

Franco halted, and tyres crunched on packed ice. Franco gazed up. The sky was darkening, fast, rimed at the edges by hints of green ice. Soon be night, he thought, mood turning saturnine. Franco hated the night. The dark. The cold. Give him bikini-clad machine gun toting dancing tequila-swigging party girls on a sunny alien beach any day! Preferably, and he acknowledged this was a distended fantasy, each with three breasts. *Makes me wish I had three hands!* he grinned, replaying an old squad joke.

Something glinted. In the ice. Buried.

Franco squinted.

"Wassat?" He scratched his beard, and killed the Buggy's engine. Silence fell in like a tumbling of worlds. He opened the cockpit, and the outside environs were curiously still, perfectly calm, a plateau of the idyll. Franco climbed clumsily up, clumped across corrugated steel, and *thumped* into the snow up to his knees.

He started to move forward. "Blast. Bugger. Damn." The snow impeded every movement, every little action, making every exploit ten times harder. Wading forward, Franco was soon red in the face and acknowledging in that secret place every sausage-eater holds in his heart that he really, obviously, most definitely should give up dodgy meat.

Franco halted. Everything was Christmas still. He squinted again, altered direction, and waded forward like a whale in quicksand.

"Ah har!" Franco stopped, and poked at the glinting thing. It was a sign. A metal sign. Franco brushed away loose snow and scratched his nose. The sign read: **REC CENTRE**. Franco prodded it. "Eh?" he said. "What's that supposed to mean?"

And then, with a subtle shifting of focus, a *different* world swam into view. Franco blinked, lower jaw dropping open like a slack primate on discovering a stash of bananas. There, as if formed from ice and glass, was a building; low walled, gleaming, refracting, a prism in its entirety and so placed as to be almost invisible from any angle amidst its snowy domain.

"Wow," said Franco. "This must be it. The Treasure Temple! The place where I gets to fill my pockets!" He licked ice-rimed lips, and rubbed vigorously at his ruddy cheeks. He blew into frosted hands. His eyes gleamed like jewels. "Man," he chuckled, "I'm gonna be *so* fucking rich!"

Franco moved forward, pushing through snow towards the obvious entrance...

IT COULD NOT believe its luck. Meat. Warm meat. Breathing, sweating, stinking, ripe with salt. It heaved itself onto its haunches, tensed its massively powerful muscles, brushed free a recent fall of snow, and bellowed like an exploding sun...

* * *

THE HAPE CHARGED at Franco, who stood, stunned, mouth agape, arse reciting a sonnet. It was big, eight or nine feet in height, covered in a thick, shaggy, matted fur, its eyes blood red, its fangs a dirty yellow and pulled back over jaws and teeth and tongue which reminded him so very much of a human –

"Rrrshcriek!" screamed the Hape, pounding snow, claws leaving long grooves, head pushing obscenely forward on muscles as thick as Franco's waist in its eagerness to rip and tear and rend and feed –

Franco fought with his pack, and dragged at his D5 shotgun. Ice-numbed fingers fumbled and tugged at straps as the huge, *huge*, grinning, screaming monstrosity, a kind of long-armed ape with a skinless human face and bobbing, curled white hair and blue, blue eyes slammed towards him with sickening speed. The D5 came free, swung around. Snarls smashed the crisp air and the creature faltered, stumbling a little, but still came on. Fangs stretched for Franco. He could seem himself reflected, distorted, in their glistening slime... The D5 boomed in his hands again, shells screaming into the mass of fur and muscle, but still the beast came on, and Franco started to stumble back, worry etched into his features as he pumped the weapon, fired again and again, each shot slamming the huge beast, slowing it a fraction in its erratic hate-fuelled charge but not actually dropping it...

"Wah!" screamed Franco, pumping shot after shot into the beast, and as it finally faltered, stumbling, feet-like claws skidding and gouging the snow, it slammed him, taking him in a huge furry embrace that sent his D5 skittering lost in the snow and sent him rolling, rolling in an embrace like lovers through powdered white as they whirled round and round. Franco could smell hot fur and meat and bad breath and blood and the thing had him, encircled, ensnared, clasped like a horny drunk fat bird as they pulverised through the snow and eventually and finally rolled to a halt.

Franco waited to see if anything else horrible might happen.

Finally, he opened a beady eye.

A seven-thousand foot drop met his gaze, only inches from his nose. It was quite possibly awesome.

With a grunt, Franco reached up and lifted a mammoth, heavily muscled arm from his chest. It flopped uselessly to one side, and Franco scrambled from the Hape's death-grip. Franco stared down at the human face, the ape body, and nodded to himself. Yeah, he thought. Hape is a good name. A *human ape*. He shuddered. What sort of weird messed-up deviant experiments have been going on here? He stood up. Hot damn and damn bloody chickenballs. Franco shuddered, then stamped his sandal in the snow.

"Goddamn!" he shouted. "What's going on? The damn DropBots scanned this place! They said it was deserted! No life! Lifeless! Safe! And then this here big bastard of a human ape monster thing comes charging and spitting and snarling at me from the snow!" He stamped his foot again, sheer indignation overwhelming his fear.

Franco stared hard at the grey-white fur. The humanesque face was oval, quite pretty. And now, quite dead.

"Bugger."

Franco cast about for his D5, aware he stood on the edge of a precipice. "There! Aha!" He crunched toward the edge of the drop, and reached for his D5. There came a distant, second-hand creaking of snow. Franco froze like an idiot in a spotlight.

Somewhere, in a distant cage of memory, a key turned in a lock with a tiny *click*.

What was the word? he thought.

Cornice?

Hell, he thought. Isn't that when snow builds up on the edge of a ridge, or overhang, or summat, and then some fool and damn blast idiot goes wandering over it not realising that all they're actually standing on is raw snow, and not that good hard solid hard rock beneath?

Franco gazed down. His fingers flexed.

The cornice creaked, and Franco fancied his

boots slid a little deeper into the treacherous overhang.

He twitched.

From the corner of one eye he watched at least a dozen of these newly christened *Hapes* awake from slumber in deep snow-holes and rise, like mighty fur-bedecked leviathans, shaking off snow from shaggy matted hides and turning blue-eyed, oval-faced *intelligent* gazes on this little sandalled man stretching for his gun beside the recently felled corpse of one of their ilk *who also was conveniently lending a good six-hundred pounds of excess baggage* to the creaking, and now *sliding and collapsing* cornice...

Franco grabbed his D5 and pounded through the snow, sliding and kicking as behind him the snow floor *disintegrated* and the dead Hape's body slid, arms akimbo, spinning around as it moved and then disappeared into valley oblivion below and Franco found himself pounding through snow and sprinting against a sucking avalanche intent on dragging him like sand through an hourglass.

The awakened Hapes howled, pounding chests with fists the size of shovels.

And as Franco slid and fought the sucking ground, like a squadron of fighter bombers, the Hapes spread out and charged.

"IT's GETTING LATE," said Fizzy, watching the sun sink over the horizon from the ramp of the

BaseCamp. "He should have been back now."

"Ach," snapped Olga, scratching her mighty bosom, "Franco's a big boy, bigger than most," she winked, "and he can look after himself." Her eyes misted in reminiscence. "Did I ever tell you about ze zombies? When I was shot, and the horde was rampaging in on me, and Franco, bravely, heroically, powerfully, waded in and shot ze zombies from their feet and rescued me from that baying horde! Har har har. He was a sight to behold!"

"I'll bet he was," sniggered Shazza.

"No!" snapped Olga, pointing with her large wooden spoon which now dripped sausage stew. "You mock! You should not mock. Yes, he wears flapping sandals and has a beer belly you can balance your dinner on, and yes, he appears a loud, uncouth, misogynistic psychopath with an insane streak only held in check by rainbow pills. But there is more to ze Franco than meets ze eye."

"Such as?" Fizzy was cleaning her weapon, a Meckler & Seburg 11mm machine-pistol with fire-thrower attachments. Green light from the rising moon played over the matt black weapon, giving it an eerie, ghostly look.

"He has a noble heart, he is a man of courage and great bravado, he is true to his friends, and he believes in a fair fight. Ha, Fizzy and Shazza, I challenge you to find another such man in this depraved and sexually deviant day and age."

Shazza coughed. "Have you read his Poop Sheet? Franco Haggis is the biggest sexual deviant this side of the Seven Rings! Pippa, as part of the same Combat-K squad, filed no less than seventy-two complaints of sexual harassment, and shot him. Twice."

"Ach, that was only her being playful. I spoke with Pippa. She enjoyed the attention."

"She enjoyed the…" Shazza stared hard at Olga, at her huge flat head, her flat features, her gold teeth, her body like a mud wrestler and biceps nearly as thick as her own voluptuous waist. Shazza shook her head. "You're a crazy fool, Olga. A chick with an obsession, and I hasten to add that I use the term 'chick' in its broadest possible capacity. A bit like your arse."

Olga scowled. "I'll have you know, you skinny little tart tits, that…"

A sudden howl rent the air, a screeching, warbling, multi-layered wail of such tortured proportions, such strangled angst and pain-filled despair that all conversation died and the three women stared at one other, aghast. Fizzy cocked her M&S with a hollow clack.

"What," said Shazza, "was that?"

"I thought the DropBots reported this planet uninhabited?"

"It would seem they were wrong," snapped Olga, and disappeared, reappearing with a D5 shotgun clasped in her big hands. It seemed tiny, like a liquorice lollipop in the hands of a child. Olga's face was gargoyle stone: solid, unbending, grim.

It came, scuttling across the snow in the green light of the rising moon. It was small, like a fist-sized spider, but even in the green light it was quite clearly –

"A head!" snapped Olga. "It's a head! With legs!"

The head – small, shrunken, skin wrinkled like a prune – sported four spidery black legs erupting from points on the topside of the skull, and carrying the head almost like a fruit in a basket. Tiny insectile claws made a skittering sound as they gripped the ice, propelling the head forward with surprising speed and agility. Long blonde hair trailed behind the voodoo visage, and the most frightening aspect of the entire vision wasn't the tiny black emotionless shark eyes, but the bright red lipstick smeared liberally on shrunken prune-lips...

The head leapt straight at Olga, who jerked as if tugged on a line. So entranced was she by the vision it hadn't occurred to her it might be hostile. The screech came again and tiny lips opened revealing razor teeth, lipstick tinged, snapping for Olga's throat –

Her D5 boomed, and the head was punched back into the air, a reverse trajectory. Olga aimed down the short stocky weapon, and sent another volley of quad-shells which exploded the head, spattering the snow with thick black-oil blood and tangles of back-combed blonde tufts.

"Ugh," said Olga.

"Good shot," said Shazza.

"Cheers."

"What the hell was it?"

"A Head?" offered Olga, eyes scanning the nearby rocky ground and distant screen of thick conifer forest. "A genetically mutated Head? Hey, I seen much worse with ze zombies. Did I tell you about..."

Another came, scuttling hurriedly across the ice. The three women watched it dispassionately.

"This is gonna get tiresome real fast," said Fizzy, priming her flame thrower. The Head scuttled, shrieking, and leapt, a huge stream of fluid ejecting from its screaming mouth and slapping up the wall of the BaseCamp where it hissed, fizzing, as some form of concentrated acid. Fizzy squawked, ducking the stream, and flames billowed from her weapon, catching the Head in the blast and roasting it, still screaming, punching it back blackened and crisped. Flames flickered down, leaving scorched hair brittle on the snow. The Head warbled, and finally rattled into silence. Flames died to embers, a smell of roast pork filled the clearing.

Olga nudged Shazza. "See that? It was a Piss Head, har har."

Shazza scowled. "This is hardly a time for jokes."

Olga nodded ahead towards the distant tree line. "I quite agree," she said, voice a low husky growl, hands tightening on the D5.

From beneath the trees came five, ten, twenty… fifty of the Heads, scuttling out in a small dark horde, each face smeared with lipstick, each trailing bright peroxide-blonde hair, each shrunken little head fixing dead black eyes on the three women on the acid-scorched ramp. Their legs jiggled up and down like badly-controlled puppets. Their shriek, when it came, rose in pitch and volume to a terrible degree of rage and had the three women stumbling back up the ramp, stamping free snow as the Heads charged and leapt, jumping in bounds of perhaps ten or twenty feet at a time like leaping fleas on a dead dog's carcass. Olga slammed the ramp button, but it gave a buzz. Olga stared at Shazza. She slammed the button again. Again, it gave an obstinate, middle-finger screw-you-bitch buzz.

"It's been locked on the cockpit console!" shouted Fizzy.

"Better go unlock it, then," growled Olga, and levelled her D5. Quad-shells howled across the clearing, disintegrating two Heads into black-tar splatters. More streamed past, and the *mass* seethed, surged, and leapt towards the base of the ramp as Fizzy disappeared and Shazza lowered her own M&S weapon. Bullets cackled through the scampering Heads…

"Better start praying," said Shazza grimly as the first Head landed on the ramp, and Olga blasted it into shards of infinity.

"I did that the day I was born," said Olga, and pumped her weapon.

FRANCO SPRINTED, BUT with each powerful scamper his legs were sucked away and he was dragged backwards towards the fast approaching precipice. The howling Hapes had spread out, teeth glinting, rabies dripping like nectar from bent and crooked fangs in freakishly calm human faces. It unnerved Franco more than any venereal disease ever could, and that was saying something. The Hapes, now in a crescent horn formation, charged to within a few feet of Franco who screamed like a woman, throwing up his arms shamelessly to protect his face (not the face, not the face!) as he tried to aim his D5 amidst desperate scrambling...

A Hape leapt, snow hissed, and it was spun away, howling. The others leapt and Franco, spinning now in the sucking falling snow, was spared a horrible death at the teeth of the Hapes as they all went over the edge amidst a seething roaring pounding booming fall of deafening tumbling snow chunks and ice blocks and general avalanche...

Franco, arms above his head, wailed for his mother.

Franco's sandalled feet, toes blue, pedalled hopelessly as the snow and ice roared around him and in the melee he jostled and bumped against equally panic-stricken Hapes whose only misfortune in life now was to a possess a hunger that far outweighed their intelligence.

Suddenly, the snow and ice were gone.

Franco swung, his mouth open like a guppy fish, wondering what the hell had happened. Below, he watched the avalanche, replete with snarling, thrashing Hapes, descend into oblivion. Noise diminished, slowly, like thunder from a vanishing storm.

Franco swung, a fish on a hook.

"Huh?"

He glanced back, and saw some kind of Titanium line attached to his pack. He scratched at his beard. He contemplated what had just happened, and the only conclusion he could come to was that someone, or something, had rescued him.

Franco stared down at seven thousand feet of sheer, steep, ice-cliff. Wind slapped him like an irate girlfriend. Franco swung, idly, aware with growing irritation that that was all he could do.

There came a *jerk* on the line.

Slowly, Franco started to ascend.

Sourly, he realised his D5 had gone. "Bugger bugger bugger." With a series of jerks and tugs, he finally broached the edge of the cliff, devoid of its overhanging and very treacherous cornice. His hands gripped claw-like in snow and he dragged himself up a low slope, panting, red in the face, sweat stinging his eyes and tickling through his short ginger goatee beard. And, into view, came...

Sax. Sax the DumbMutt. All v1.2 of it.

"Bollocks," said Franco, not quite believing what he was seeing.

"Borrocks," agreed Sax, and padded forward, panting, a faithful metal hound, a true friend and rescuer for this, its fallen master. The DumbMutt stopped, and a long metal tongue, plated with scales in the manner of a snake, lolled out and licked Franco's face, leaving an oily residue, smelling like old tuna.

"Get the fuck off!" he snapped, slapping the tongue away.

"Ruff," said Sax.

Franco scrambled to his knees, and followed the trail of cable back to the Giga-Buggy. Quickly, his mind worked out the series of events.

"So you stowed away in the Buggy with me?"

"Ruff."

"And kept your head low until we stopped?"

"Ruff."

"Then you saw me in trouble, and launched the Buggy's Compact Cable as I went over the edge, thus stopping me from falling to an untimely but much deserved death?"

"Ruff. *Borrocks*."

"Yeah yeah, well." He gritted his teeth. Took a deep breath. It was going to hurt him to do it. Torture his soul. But, he recognised: he must. "OK then. Sax. Thanks. Thanks for saving my life. Good dog. Good boy."

"Ruff." Sax wagged its tail.

"Now, get back in the damn Buggy. Before I catch fleas."

Sax padded off, and clambered into whatever rearward orifice had ejected him like a long slick metal turd.

Franco fought with the cable for a good few minutes, finally managing to disengage himself. He stood, ruffled, pride injured, but alive. Saved by a metal DumbMutt. "The bastard," he muttered, realising that sometimes, possibly, it was better to be dead. He strode back to the sign, looking warily about for more of the Hapes.

What were they? From whence had they come? Were they defending the weird glass building? The REC, whatever that was? Or maybe, yeah, maybe they were mystic guardians defending the treasure within!

Franco nodded to himself and, moving to the Giga-Buggy, re-armed himself with another D5 shotgun, and an MPK machine gun. Might get rough, he thought, and added a few grenades to his belt.

Bravely, Franco strode through the snow, images of Iskander's Crown and the gleam of sub-PlutoniumIII clear in his money-addled mind. He strode with long loping strides towards the REC Centre's entrance far below...

Behind, Sax stood in the snow panting oil-mist. The metal dog shuffled woodenly over to the sign and regarded it for a while, head tilted to one side, unconvincing hair flopping in its eyes.

Sax reached out, and licked the sign. Under its heated oil tongue, a thin film of snow and ice melted. **REC CENTRE**. Sax licked some more, and below the acronym three words were revealed.

### RESEARCH. EXPERIMENTATION. CONFINEMENT.

Sax trotted back to the Giga-Buggy, curled up, farted a sour-oil fart, and promptly went for a recharge.

WIND BLEW LOOSE snow through the green-tinged night. Franco halted at what he presumed were gates, and reached out, touching their slick, glass-like substance. The whole place looked modern. Too modern. Out of synch with the idea that this place had been abandoned a thousand years previously.

"Hmm." Franco scratched his chin, and stepped forward across the threshold. Winter flowers, white and blue, lay scattered randomly about, the only sign that what was once a kind of exercise yard for patients was now given over to the elements and raw cruelty of nature. No longer was the guiding hand of Sick World's doctors and nurses in charge of ordering chaos.

Franco edged forward, his new D5 weaving a slow figure of eight as he searched for howling Hapes. Reaching the double doors, again of steel and dark glass, there was that sign again. **REC CENTRE**. Franco pushed open the doors and stepped inside.

It was cool, and dark, but emergency lights picked out silhouettes down a long, wide corridor. *Emergency lights?* Was it feasible they'd been on, and working, since the mass evacuation of the planet a thousand years ago? Franco, despite being quite mad, found it improbable.

So, he mused, that meant somebody was changing the light bulbs. But why? Some kind of mad hermit left behind? Or a family of hermits? A whole clan of hermits? And why the hell did he think it might be hermits?

Striding forward through barely lit gloom, Franco started to hum to himself, a tune that went *de dum de dum de dum de dum, da dumly dum de dum...* and as he gained more confidence, and the corridor stretched off before him, wide, and inviting, long, and seemingly never-ending, so his impending happiness at finding the impending treasure of Iskander's Crown broke through his caution and he burst into song:

> The Son of God goes forth to war,
> A kingly crown to gain;
> His blood red banner streams afar:
> Who follows in His train?

Franco's words echoed and bounced down the sterile medical corridor, growing louder, more boisterous with every passing syllable. Will *I* be a king when I find this crown? he thought, eyes wide, gun weaving. Am I, he supposed, the man who would be king?

His song stopped, and so did his sandals. His words boomed ahead, bouncing from wall to wall to wall, then echoing back from the tomb-world-lit gloom like a fish on a piece of elastic.

Franco twitched. He whirled, suddenly, D5 pumping, eyes squinting. "What was that? Who's there? Show yourself!"

Nothing. Nothing moved. Not a whisper of breeze stirred the wide sterile corridor.

A feeling crept over Franco like the repeating chilli remnants of last night's curry. A feeling stirred deep in his bowels, again, the symptoms of a particularly bad vindaloo. It was quietly nauseating.

Distantly, something flickered. A blue sparkle, which reminded Franco of long-gone childhood days on Quad-Gal Bonfire Night, celebrating the attempted detonation of the Quad-Gal UN Parliament, a little ginger Franco with mad afro, eyes wide, nose cold, holding a blue fizzing sparkler in stumpy fingers.

Franco moved forward, silent now, cursing himself for his boisterous singing and acutely aware that during a treasure hunt one shouldn't perhaps be singing about the treasure one was hunting for. Just in case, y'know, you alerted any possible guardians, denizens, or other Bad Monsters.

Franco headed towards the place where he'd seen the blue sparkle. Nothing. Nada. Deserted. Just an abandoned steel trolley, listing slightly because it had a missing wheel. Franco's eyes roved over the walls, ceiling and floor, his unease growing exponentially, but unaware exactly why.

He coughed. Puffed out his chest. "Right then," he said, scratching his beard. "OK then. So, this recce went well, didn't it? Maybe I'll just, y'know, head back to Fizzy and Shazza and Olga, check out that sausage stew they's cooking up, maybe pop back tomorrow to try and find this here treasure."

He stopped. Realisation dawned, and he turned back, staring at the trolley. There were straps. And bare wires. And... electrodes. Patches. Clamps. *Testicle* clamps. The trolley was just like the one they'd used to restrain Franco Haggis at The Mount Pleasant Hilltop Institution, the "nice and caring and friendly home for the mentally challenged".

Which could, possibly, mean… Franco's eyes went wide. That *this* REC Centre had in fact once been a mental hospital!

Shivers wracked Franco's body.

Goosebumps wandered liberally over his arms and neck, and, whilst once he would have savoured this faintly sexual experience, here, and now, in this horrible terrible place, the feeling left him nauseated. "Bugger."

Franco started to run, his spine tingling, his hair standing on end, and then a curious thing happened. Static discharged through his beard, crackling and sparking and sending bright stars flashing before his eyes.

"Ow! Ow ow!" he stopped, skidding to a halt, rubbing frantically at his smoking beard. "What was that? What magic is this? What the buggery happened?"

Blue light sparkled at the end of the corridor, and Franco noted it was the place where he had originally entered the REC Centre. Then the light started to grow, a tiny, sparkling ball of blue fire which separated into twin balls of sparkling blue fire as it grew closer and closer and Franco heard a rushing sound and in panic he fired his D5 with quad snarls but the light jigged, down and left, then back on course, and crashed into him with sudden violent ferocity sending a shock through his chest and head which slammed him backwards, D5 skittering away, and delivered a few hundred volts direct to his system –

Franco lay, stunned. He could taste copper. Smell ozone. His fingers tingled.

Groaning, he started to sit up but something landed atop him, pinning him down. His eyes adjusted, past the sparkling blue lights which were... which were *hands*, long-fingered hands filled with sparks of electricity dancing and swirling and discharging constantly. Even now he could hear a faint *hum* of restrained power. Franco coughed. Beyond the lights he saw a man, naked, thin-limbed, taut and muscular, with a huge blobby head and thick electric cables running on and out of the skin on his arms and chest and neck. The man was bald or, at least, what remained of his hair was charred, blackened spider-hair in tiny smoking clumps. His eyes were wild, truly wild, spinning like a scoreboard on a pinball machine. He opened his mouth to smile, and Franco squinted – there was a black box trailing a cable like an umbilical. It took a few moments for Franco to realise it was a battery pack.

Fear slammed Franco. A weird, mind-expanding fear. He bucked, attempting to struggle and the man with the battery pack in his mouth clapped his hands in a shower of fizzing, crackling sparks, and slammed both fists down on Franco's head. Electricity shrieked, Franco went rigid in electric-shock spasm, and all his lights went out.

* * *

THE PAIN WAS intense, even in a pit of unconsciousness. Like a drowning man struggling for the surface, Franco swam from depths and surfaced into darkness. He blinked a few times, mouth full of metal, tongue an electric eel, skin scorched and tingling and burning. "Urgh," he muttered, and turning his head slightly, spat a desert dry spit which achieved nothing. "What hit me?"

"I expect you met one of our Convulsers," said a soft, gentle, female voice. It was a voice filled with caring, a voice filled with understanding, a voice that said to Franco *I am a nice person who will not cause you any pain* and *I belong to a creature who is a beautiful angel and might, if you're really lucky, give you a snog.*

Franco forced himself not to turn. He had learned by bitter experience it was far too easy to break his illusions.

"What," he said, experimenting with the shape of his tongue and lips and teeth, which all felt metallic and covered in fur after his savage electrocution, "is a Convulser?"

"They run wild around the REC. They charge themselves up and electrocute anything that crosses their path. We keep stingers to deal with them; sends them squealing and spitting batteries back to whatever hell it is from which they squirm."

"Was I right in thinking it had ECT pads for its hands?"

"Yes," said the sanguine voice that, with each passing second, filled Franco with a growing confidence that he'd been rescued from a fate worse than death. "They've taken the Electro Convulsive Treatment machines that were once used on patients, and absorbed the machine into their flesh; it's quite horrible and bizarre, if you ask me."

"I agree!" agreed Franco.

"By the way, my name is Sabrina."

Franco bit his tongue, and turned his head. She was sat by his bed, his hospital bed, and Franco's eyes immediately fell on her generous cleavage. Sabrina's bosom quivered like ripe, vibrating melons, filling, or rather, *over-spilling*, a skin-tight nurse uniform which required little, if at all any, imagination. Sabrina coughed, and Franco's eyes lifted from this simple visual pleasure to her face which, if anything, was even more beautiful. She had perfect, flawless, almost translucent skin. Her features were framed by a shock of bright blonde hair, and she wore a very sexy and very inviting succulent red lipstick.

"Are you a nurse, or an angel?" said Franco.

Sabrina laughed coquettishly. "Oh, you do flatter me, Franco."

"You know my name?"

"We went through your pack. Please excuse us, but you were unconscious for hours and we wanted to check your blood group and allergies before administering any treatment."

"You administered treatment?" Franco was suddenly suspicious. Franco was always suspicious. It came from suffering eternal and continuous bad luck.

"Just a muscle relaxant, to combat the shock given by the Convulser. And some burn cream applied to your chest. You were scorched by the impact." Franco relaxed a little, and released a large sigh. "There's nothing to worry about here, Franco, we're all friendly nurses. *Very* friendly nurses. And you've been such a brave, brave little boy."

I'm in bloody heaven, thought Franco, suddenly.

Thank you, God. Thank you for delivering me from evil! *And* for delivering me into the bosom did I say bosom ha ha I meant *hands* of this buxom lovely nurse wench. Franco beamed, his beam an all-teeth beam.

"So," edged Franco, careful now, precise, for he didn't want to ruin this illusion which had saturated many a fantasy on long, lonely evenings with only his right hand for company. "So... let me get this straight. You're a nurse, there's lots of other nurses, and you're here in this hospital in the middle of nowhere..." he glanced about, noting the plethora of empty beds, "and with no patients to satiate your lust did I say lust ha ha I *meant* professional medical need to help people and make people better. Would you say that's a fair appraisal of the situation?"

Sabrina leant a little closer. Her eyes sparkled, as if filled with angel dust, and Franco could see she was gently amused by him, no, not gently amused, more than that, she was *dazzled* by him.

"You, little Franco Wanco, are our only liddle biddy patient. And you're being such a good boy, such a brave soldier, such a grown up liddle policeman, so you are."

"I am?"

"Yes." She was closer now. Her breath was sweet, like flowers. "You are. And do you know what happens to brave little soldiers on this particular ward filled with generously proportioned and *sexually deprived* nurses?"

"Something nice?" ventured Franco.

"Oh yes, baby, something nice," she crooned, and lifted her arm, resting her chin on her hand. Only, she didn't. Because she didn't actually have an arm, or a hand on which to balance her beautiful and flawless chin.

Franco stared. And he stared damn hard.

"What's that?" he ventured, eventually.

Sabrina fluttered her eyelashes. "What do you mean, *sexy?*"

"Um. That thing. There. Where your arm should be?"

"That? Why, that's my No. 3 Syringe."

"But... but... it's your *arm*, woman!"

"Yes, I had it genetically hot-wired to my stump after the amputation."

"The amputation?"

"Yes. The multiple-amputation. During the War of the Doctors."

Sabrina stood suddenly, a fast, fluid motion, her limbs unfolding as if she were some kind of mechanical spider. Both her arms were huge, steel hypodermic needles, each hand a needle like a finger of sharpened razor steel. She had a bosom, yes, a sexy bosom, no doubt, a charged and wobbling Franco-wet-dream of a bosom, certainly, but below her waist her legs weren't legs at all, for each limb had been replaced, bone-grafted, with a crude steel and plastic crutch, little holes peppering each alloy length in order to adjust her height. Sabrina took several steps back, her crutch-legs clacking on the tiled floor. Only then did Franco notice the smell. The medical smell. The stench of sterile swabs, of iodine-cleansed instruments. The perfume of the autoclave machine.

"Is something wrong?"

"Gah," said Franco, and sat up. Although he didn't. This seemed to be a day of things *not* happening.

Franco realised he was strapped, very firmly, and with wide leather straps, to the bed. "Bugger," he said, eyeing Sabrina with the sort of look a donkey reserves for a carrot when the pesky vegetable is tugged away.

Sabrina clacked forward, generous bosom bouncing. "Sorry about the straps, Mr. Haggis.

But this *is* a sanatorium. And we see from your records that you were once a patient at The Mount Pleasant Hilltop Institution, the 'nice and caring and friendly home for the mentally challenged'. Well, we'd be happy to continue with your therapy at *no extra cost.*" She smiled. It was a dazzlingly beautiful smile. "We're nice like that, around here."

"No," croaked Franco. "Wait! I was discharged…"

"You escaped."

"I was wrongly incarcerated! It was a set-up! After the days in the Combat Squad…"

"Ahh yes, the Combat Squad. Combat K. Another figment of your mad and overused imagination. Shame on you, Franco, for coming up with such a psychologically weak scenario in which you perpetuate your super-hero combat-soldier narcissistic wank-fantasy little boy chickenhawk longings."

"I'm not mad, I tell you!" snarled Franco, yanking against the straps with all his strength. The bed jumped a little, metal legs clattering.

"Now now," said Sabrina. "Time for you to calm down, little man. After all, there's a whole host of nurses here with, shall we say, *very special requirements* of you. After all, we haven't seen a male specimen of your *masculinity,* your *calibre,* for, oooh, about a thousand years."

Franco squinted. Behind Sabrina, from the gloom

of the emergency lighting, emerged at least another five or six nurses. Each one, in their day, must have been a stunner, but now they were a sick and maudlin collection of medical experimentations gone wrong. One woman had scalpels for arms. Another's upper torso had been organically welded to a wheelchair, and her stumped arms had tiny grippers with which to grasp the rubber wheels. A third – Franco blinked in horror – had a colostomy bag for a head, her little blue brain swirling around in some kind of murky brown liquid, along with her eyes, which bounced around like energetic goldfish. Another nurse had some kind of weird stainless-steel integrated head and neck brace, metal scaffolding rising from her shoulders and encompassing her face. Big metal teeth protruded roughly from her jaw and fake teeth clacked together with tiny, tinny sounds. This eager nurse came forward, metal teeth clacking almost uncontrollably, as if in a frenzy of excitement, or – *the horror* – sexual arousal.

"This is Ginger," said Sabrina, smiling kindly and calmly down at Franco's prostrate body. "She has a *very* special request." Sabrina gazed at Franco's groin.

"Oh no, no way, you can just all get to buggery, you bloody mad rampant deviant nurse bitches from hell!"

"Buggery?" said Sabrina, with a narrow smile. Ginger produced a long, slightly banana shaped metal object from beneath her tight-fitting uniform, allowing her buxom breasts to bounce back into place. The object gleamed, as if well polished, or at least, well used. Franco paled. It was a C1 Three-Blade Sigmoidoscope Anorectal Retractor, 140mm. Ouch. "If that's what you want, Mr. Haggis, we can certainly entertain. After all, we are here, simply, to please." She smiled, waving the Anorectal Retractor.

"No!" screamed Franco, "No no no!" He thrashed and jerked and pulled and struggled at the leather straps, but they were old, and well-designed, designed, in fact, to stop people escaping. "You'll not get away with this! I'm a man! I have my, my morals! I'm not…" he fluttered his eyelids, "some kind of tart."

"You must calm down," said Sabrina, eyes glinting. "It hurts less that way." She advanced, lifting one hypodermic arm. Franco saw clear fluid sloshing around inside the chamber. She gave it a little squirt, and fluid spurted from the tip, a premature ejaculation. "Here," she leant close, smiling broadly, her perfume engulfing Franco with a heady fragrance that made him swoon. "Let me give you a bit of help.'

CHAPTER FIVE

# SICK WORLD III: SECOND DJIO

KEENAN STOOD ON the ramp, shielding his eyes from glaring equatorial sun and breathing in a hot, arid air which made him want to choke. The heat shimmered on the desert. From the DropShip ramp spread a hostile dry wilderness of sand and rocks, thousands upon thousands of large, rounded boulders, and several remote outcroppings of staggered ancient cliffs, sheer and orange and distantly threatening. Keenan moved down the ramp and rolled himself a cigarette using Widow Maker tobacco.

"Pretty hot," said Snake, leaning against the rim of the doorway and staring down at Keenan, his one beady eye squinting in bright light after the gloomy interior.

"Aye." Keenan lit the weed, and took a deep, deep drag.

"You roll one of those for me, soldier?"

"You'll be asking to share my bunk, next."

Snake laughed, a low, easy, rolling laugh, and strode down the ramp, slapping Keenan on the back. "I think we got off to a bad start, me and thee. I think you have a very low opinion of the work I've done."

"Cam?"

"Yeah boss?" Cam spun into view, silent, stealthy. Snake whirled, fast, gun *clacking* gently against Cam's case. Cam flickered a fast series of coloured lights, which Keenan read and gave a single nod.

"Should watch where you're poking that thing," said Cam. "Somebody might take it and shove it up your arse."

"You're a tad tetchy for a little PopBot," said Snake, holstering the 11mm with a whisper of leather. He smiled, but it was a cold smile, an imitation of humour, and Keenan could see the message in Snake's eye. He'd been close to pulling the trigger; and he didn't like Cam... or maybe just PopBots in general. Keenan filed this for another day.

"Cam, sort out the DropShip. We're gonna take the Buggy, do some scouting." He looked sideways at Snake. "That OK with you, Big Man?"

Snake smiled easily, his dark eye unreadable. "Whatever you say, Keenan. You're in charge."

"I just wouldn't like to step on your toes," said Keenan, and handed Snake the cigarette.

Snake took a long drag, and blew a cloud of tox over Cam, who backed away, motors whirring. "I'm a snake, pal," he said. "No toes to step on."

WHILST CAM FINE-TUNED the DropShip into a BaseCamp, Keenan, Snake and Ed headed off in the Giga-Buggy to secure the area, and make sure there were no nasty surprises waiting out in the sand. Cam busied himself with the BaseCamp's computer, whistling happily to himself as he tweaked emissions, regulated aircon, sampled the immediate sand around the BaseCamp using CampGrippers (which brought to mind several rude jokes via a comedy subroutine), and generally checked that all was working and well; especially necessary after the initial apparent sabotage during descent.

There came a tiny *click,* and Cam spun fast. Maximux was stood, stripped to the waist, his body wiry and taut, tendons standing out like cables under chicken-skin. A light sheen of sweat bathed him, and he wore long combat trousers and high black boots, strapped with the latest TitaniumIV digital garrotte laces. His head was down as he fiddled with a tiny metal mechanism.

Cam bobbed for a moment, watching Max suspiciously, then he chided himself. They were all Combat-K now, and despite being on what was widely regarded as an easy gig, they still had a job to do, and would do it to the best of their ability. After all, were they not consummate professionals?

"What are you thinking?" came Max's drawl, and his head lifted, eyes staring at Cam. His hands went still.

"Um," said Cam. "I was just considering our position. That we're all Combat K, and we'll get the job done to the best of our ability."

"Yeah." Maximux grinned, and his face contorted, looking *not quite right* against a human head. Cam's lights flickered. He felt uneasy, which was a rare feat, for he had no glands or chemicals with which to feel such an emotion. It was the nearest machine code equivalent. "We'll certainly do that, boy."

"Um. Actually," said Cam, ever the pedant, "I'm not a boy, I'm a GradeA+1 Security Mechanism with advanced SynthAI and a Machine Intelligence Rating (MIR) of 3450. I have integral weapon inserts, a quad-core military database, and Put Down™ War Technology. I am," if he'd had a mouth, he would have beamed a smile, "quite a prize. The Prodigal Son. The light that burns twice as bright."

Maximux took a step forward, then stopped again, fiddling with the tiny, intricate metallic contraption in his hands. "What the hell is Put Down™ War Technology, if you don't mind me asking?"

"It's a war technology that allows me to put you down."

"Very droll, tinner."

"Tinner?" Cam's voice was aghast. Tinner was pre-war slang, very, very old. It was used in the Bad Old Days when bots were introduced with poor slung-back AI, riddled with codebugs and datagremlins, and bots got a reputation for the mass-slaughter of their physically inferior human makers. Millions had used the term tinner to refer to bots which had been sentenced to die for crimes against organity. To a PopBot, there could be no greater curse, no greater prejudice, no better form of slavery insult. It was "nigger" for the machine digital age. "I…" Cam considered his words very carefully, and focused a core on the metallic object which Maximux carried, but it registered as 0% threat, "I haven't heard that *word* in a long time."

"Yeah, well." Max stopped his fiddling. Fixed Cam with those dark, crazy eyes again, reminding Cam to do a quick file.folder recce and convince himself that Maximux, despite current submissive demeanour, was a raving psychotic paranoid lunatic. Too many drugs and too much battle. He'd murdered his own grandmother over a loaf of bread. Slaughtered his own sister due to drug paranoia and a transferral of his own faults and shortcomings onto her innocent psyche. Max was, to all intents and purposes, a top class Grade A genocidal fuck-up. "The thing is, Cam, PopBot,

War T and M treknology bastard SynthArseache MIP fucking rusty old oil-stinking *tinner,* the thing is, I don't fucking *like you.*"

Cam considered this. "Maybe that's a good thing?"

"It's not a fucking good thing!" screamed Max suddenly, eyes popping forward, veins standing out on his neck. "How can it fucking be a fucking good thing, you fucking rusty little bag of colostomy spuke? You insult my intelligence, you insult my bravado, you better be careful tinner or we'll have to take this outside."

Cam contemplated this. He was, obviously, dealing with a madman. He backed off a little, displaying calming blue lights, and buzzing as he armed his many internal weapon systems. Cam might have looked like a battered metal testicle, he may have emitted the odd sour-oil and ozone smell and had little or no élan when it came to conversing with psychotic members of the crew, but he *was* dangerous in his own little way. He'd fought, bettered, and killed superior models of PopBot, and many a nutcase alien, without a backward glance at the slippery blood trail. A pussy, he was not.

"OK, OK, calm down," said Cam. "This is like one of those pub-fight things, isn't it, where the bad guy slicks his way into the taverna and starts to pick a fight with the good guy, dressed all in silver and white, and there's no way the good guy can actually wriggle out of the situation, and a fight is inevitable but obviously the good guy always wins."

"No," said Max, lifting up his hand with the metal object, "the good guy does not always win. In my experience," he smiled, showing several blackened teeth, or McGowans as they were known, "I usually fuck him over and buy myself a drink."

"Oh." Cam scanned the object again. It was some kind of tiny projectile weapon, completely harmless to a PopBot who could move far faster than any metal projectile weapon ever invented. "What *are* you doing with that?"

"Putting you down?"

Cam snorted a laugh. "I think it's time I called this in to Keenan..."

Maximux fired, an object spun, stopped a metre from the barrel of the PopBot, flicked open a series of directional panels, like the petals of some tiny flower unfurling, and hit Cam with a concentrated blast of Nitrogen-funnelled EEMP.

Cam clattered to the deck, jiggling.

Max moved forward, knelt, and poked Cam. Cam buzzed. Max poked him again. Cam buzzed again, but was unable to speak. Max moved close, grinning. "It's an Enhanced Electro Magnetic Pulse. But you couldn't see it, it's invisible to your scanners because it's purely mechanical. Uses and distorts a planet's natural magnetic field for the pulse, thus it needs to carry no charge. We used to use them on Pulleekon, hunting down the rogue tinners there. But then, you don't know that. The missions were illegals. Nothing's recorded. And this machine doesn't officially exist."

Max stood, stretched, his spine popping like castanets. Then he walked out, returning with a lead-lined AI CageBox. He dropped it to the floor, and tiny legs sprouted. It walked over to Cam, and using retractable claws ushered the disabled PopBot into its interior.

"The thing is," said Max, to Cam, who could hear every word but not respond, "we're gonna fuck your good buddy Keenan up. We're gonna take over this fine equipment. And we're gonna make us some pretty pennies. And I know what you're thinking, tinner, you're thinking that there's a war going down, and the junks are spreading, and invading, toxing and killing all those innocent people and aliens an' all that, and yeah, that's bad," he grinned again, a very wide and humour-filled visage, "but like I always said, there's money to be made in war." He paused, contemplating Cam in the AI CageBox. "This war's gonna make some people very, very rich. And I like being rich. Better go get my guns ready. I believe this Keenan's a feisty one."

THEY SLAMMED ACROSS the desert, Keenan leaning on the wheel to avoid huge boulders which littered the ground at regular intervals. Dust plumed behind, a trailing cloak of sand, filling the sky like yellow mist.

"Hey, Keenan," said Snake from the back seat. His long hair whipped in the wind created by speed, and his skin had a gritted texture from sand sticking to sweaty flesh. "You know that Pippa lady, do you think she's kinda pretty?"

Keenan glanced over his shoulder, and there was a *clang* from beneath the 6X6 Buggy. Keenan focused back to the desert, revving hard as they climbed a high series of dunes, leaping from the tops and powering down opposite slopes, engine growling, huge tyres digging in and paddling great sweeps of desert into their wake. "Kinda pretty? Snake, my man, have you got a death wish?"

"What's that supposed to mean?"

"She's a dangerous lady."

"I'm a dangerous type of guy," he swaggered.

"No, I mean, sword-in-the-back-of-your-neck-whilst-you're-asleep type of dangerous. You can't fuck with her."

"I don't *want* to fuck with her," grinned Snake. "Just fuck her."

Ed sniggered, leaning back to Snake and lighting the mercenary's cigarette. Snake blew plumes of smoke, hair whipping, one eye fixed on the back of Keenan's head. "So what do you say?" he half-shouted, over the roar of the engine, words exhaled on plumes of smoke. "Can you fix it for me? A date, I mean."

"No."

"Come on Keenan, you know her better than most."

"No."

"Why's that? Trying a keep a slice of that sweet tasting pussy pie for yourself?"

Keenan slammed the Giga-Buggy's brakes, and they slewed sideways down a towering sand dune, all six wheels spinning, engine roaring, until they juddered to a halt. Keenan turned in his seat, demeanour cool but eyes burning. "I'll give you one piece of advice, Snake, and I'll say it only once. Don't talk to me about Pippa. Not if you don't want to pick your teeth from the sand with broken fingers."

"Ooh," said Ed, "bit touchy on that subject, are we?" He rubbed sand from his tattooed face, and drank from his canteen, dribbling a goodly amount down his white vest.

"It's a... long story. Something I'm not willing to discuss. Let's just say she's damaged goods, off limits for discussion, and Snake can try and tease her with his snake all he likes, but if he's not careful, she'll bite the damn thing off." His eyes transferred to something over Ed's shoulder, and his expression changed from annoyance to awe. "Shit, will you look at that!"

From the sand rose a squat tower of rock, searing, jagged, rougher than a redneck and a deep crimson in colour, skein-threaded with silver and blue webs of mineral deposits that caught the light and glittered solemnly. But the most incredible feature was the *carvings*, etched with minute precision across the monolith's surface in entirety, some images large and sweeping, full battle scenes, others tiny pictures, either of creatures, animals, or simply scenes from daily life. Together, the montage formed a whole – the image of a planet, circular, black, rugged.

"That's *awesome,*" enthused Ed, jumping out of the Buggy and standing, hands on hips, staring at the edifice. It powered up, perhaps three or four hundred feet in height and sheltered from the wind, from the desert, by an almost protective circle of high sand dunes. The dunes also hid the structure behind folds of sand, allowing it near invisibility from the planes above.

Keenan stood up in his seat, eyes scanning, then he glanced back at Snake, who shrugged his shoulders.

"I thought this place was extinct," he said, rubbing his eye-patch.

"Yeah, but we're looking for *remains,* archaeology pointing to this being the cradle of birth for the junks. Doesn't mean anything has to exist here now."

"You want to explore?"

"We need to take a look." Keenan rubbed his chin.

"I think we should go back for Max and Cam. Get some more specific equipment; the more hands we have on this, the better."

Keenan checked his watch. "We have time, and equipment enough. I stocked up the Buggy before we left, although I didn't expect anything this... drastic." Keenan jumped into the sand and approached the edifice, which he realised was not simply a geological feature, but had become a totem, a monument from a time long past. His eyes scanned across the images, piecing together battle scenes and wars, all described pictorially in elegant and finely-carved detail. And yet... curiously, it made no sense. There was something disturbing about what he could see, something a touch out of synch with reality. The creatures represented were human, and human-like, and quite beautiful. But there was something wrong with the carvings. Keenan could feel it in his bones...

Now the Buggy's engine was dead, a great silence fell upon the three men. Occasionally, the wind would hook a howl from the monument's summit, long, mournful, drawn out like intestines from a quartered victim; but then silence would fall again, interspersed by the occasional hiss of sand over sand, and the panting of three rapidly over-heating squaddies.

They circled the monument, searching with care, and found one opening leading steeply down. They stood, looking down into the black pit.

"I ain't going down that," said Ed, staring with undisguised horror. "Nobody said anything about crawling around in caves. There could be anything down there; snakes, scorpions, kleeklags, bloody anything."

"Your bravery astounds me," snapped Snake. "I'll go."

"You sure?" said Keenan.

Snake grinned. "There's nothing down there nastier than me."

Keenan locked a Leech to the monument's face, ran it through a loop on his own belt, and attached the G-Ring to Snake's belt. Snake pulled free his gun and checked the magazine, then nodded to Keenan. He stepped back, feet against the frighteningly steep decline and, lowering his head, squeezed down into the aperture. Within seconds, he was gone, swallowed by the monument's mouth.

THE SUN BEAT down on Keenan like a hammer on an anvil. Sweat coursed down him, and Snake's weight was a heavy burden, torturing his hands and back and making him realise he was getting far too old to continue without the genetic surgery so fashionable in the military these days. After a while, the line went limp and Ed, seated in the sand, glanced at Keenan.

"Wonder what's down there?"

"Something spectacular," said Keenan, and lit

a cigarette. Smoke stung his eyes, but he did not care. He craved the fix.

After a few moments, Keenan felt twin tugs on the line, the signal for him to start hauling Snake out of the pit. Keenan braced himself, his smoke dangling between sun-baked lips, and as he took up the strain something, some sixth sense, warned him with a screeching of alarm bells ripping his brain out through his ears and he spun to see Ed, the needle by Keenan's neck and dripping bright blue fluid, as his arms slammed up and grabbed Ed's arms and the two men grappled, thudding to the ground, Ed atop Keenan, Keenan holding the needle millimetres from his throat. They grunted, shifting around, but Ed was heavy, heavier than he looked, and his sweat dripped into Keenan's eyes.

"What you doing, fucker?" snarled Keenan.

Ed did not reply.

"You're being a stupid arsehole. Get off me!"

Ed did something, a *flick* of the wrist, and the needle spat from the syringe and stabbed Keenan's throat. Blue liquor injected, and Keenan's vision swam. He laughed, then, a gurgling of honey as darkness fast-swamped him and the merry-go-round of the world stopped, allowing him to step neatly off.

THE WORLD TASTED sour, in his mouth and in his brain. Betrayed, that taste told him. The bastards stabbed him in the back. In the balls. For a long time Keenan dreamt of his two girls, his Rachel and Ally, and he remembered the fine times, the good times, the best times, before they died, before they were murdered. It almost made it worthwhile to be poisoned, or drugged, or whatever his mentally diseased accomplices had done to him.

Groggily, Keenan came round, and he could *feel* something slick, something sluggish surging through his veins in rhythmical spurts which matched his own heartbeat. He sat up, in darkness, feeling rock beneath his hands. Realisation hit him, and he groaned. The bastards had thrown him down the pit.

Keenan sat for a moment, orientating himself, pain slamming through his left hand. He could not believe, just could not damn well believe the bastards had turned on him. And for what? What possible reason, what possible motive could they have for betrayal?

Keenan tried his earlobe comms. "Pippa? Franco? You copy?"

Dead. Great.

All at once a score of bruises, aches and pains rushed him and he groaned again, cradling his hand, realising he'd broken two fingers. Methodically he searched himself, checking for other broken bones or torn muscles or ligaments, anything that would impede his function, as pain from the long fall, the battering of the fast rocky descent, thumped him in the brain. Keenan gritted his teeth, and as he pulled free a med-strip and neighbour-bound his broken fingers, wincing and taking deep breaths, he amused himself with what he'd do to Snake and Ed if he managed to get free and catch up with them.

As his eyes adjusted, so the most gentle of ambient lights was made available. It emerged from the silver skeins flowing through the monument, and although it was barely enough to see by, it at least illuminated the vague outline of the chamber in which he sat, huddled with his own pain, riddled with a hot agony.

As far as Keenan could make out, the chamber was small, with tunnels leading away. Some objects on the ground told him all he needed to know; they were bones, old bones that crumbled under his fingers when he tried to lift them, but bones all the same. This had been, or was, the home of a predator.

Keenan reached for his pack, but it was gone. As was his array of weapons. At least he still had his WarSuit and, reaching down, Keenan tapped both boots. Each revealed a tiny, triangular blade and Keenan pulled them free. Each blade was only an inch long, but incredibly sharp and very, very tough. Hardly weapons at all, more survival tools, but at least Keenan had something to work with.

Keenan stood, and whacked his head on the roof. He dropped to his knees again, reaching above himself until he found the shaft down which he'd slid and tumbled in an unconscious mess. Mouth a grim line, he stood again, rising into the hole, and his fingers probed the edges around the rim. It was smooth. Too smooth. Too smooth to climb, at least...

Above, there came a distant sound. Like thunder, but instead of petering out it went on, and on, and on, an ominous pounding which made Keenan, alone in his tiny rock cell, shiver. What's going on up there? Murder?

He grinned. I fucking hope so.

For a few experimental moments he attempted to climb using his daggers, but there simply weren't enough holds in the rock, so he crouched again and peered about, nose twitching at the cool breeze. A breeze meant airflow through the tunnels, which in turn meant an exit. Lowering himself, Keenan moved about the confines of the chamber, and found five possible exits. Great, he thought. A maze. Which way? Which way out? Confusingly, all tunnels blew with a cool flow of air, and Keenan licked desert-dry lips and wondered how that was possible.

"You're a long way from home," said a soft, female voice, so quiet for a moment Keenan thought it was simply the moaning of the wind.

Keenan blinked rapidly, backing away, both daggers before him.

"Put your knives away, little man. You won't need them with me."

"I'll be the judge of that," snapped Keenan, spinning around, unable to pinpoint the direction of the voice. "Where are you?" He pictured the bones in his mind. "And *what* are you?"

There came a laugh; deep, rich, genuine humour. And then he could see her, hunched in the mouth of a tunnel, an eerie glow of silver surrounding her from deposits in the rock. She moved, and there were several metallic crackles, almost insect-like, but not quite, and curiously disturbing. She moved forward, unfolding from her crouch and crossing her arms in a very human gesture.

"I am Elana. This is my Cathedral."

"Elana. You're human?" Keenan squinted. In the poor light she was thin, and wearing what looked like silks which floated around her in the breeze. She had long dark hair, but everything else was obscured.

"Not... quite."

"Well, what are you?"

"Is this a philosophical question, Mr. Keenan? Or maybe a scientific examination? Perhaps you'd wish to study my place in the social hierarchy? What am I? Parasite? Deviant? Do I fit the normal template for your particular bastardised and twisted evolution? After all, humanity was given a mighty helping hand in their galactic soup and quest for knowledge." She paused, seemed to smile. Her silks floated ypnotically around her. "Come with me Mr. Keenan. I want to show you my Cathedral."

Keenan relaxed back, the knives still in his hands. He released a breath. "Is there a way out?"

"There is always a way out. But come; first, let me show you some hospitality. After all, you've taken a nasty tumble. How are your fingers? But I get ahead of myself, and in reality it is for your own benefit they pushed you down to my Haven."

"How so?"

"Listen."

Keenan could still hear distant thunder. A gloomy, threatening noise like a collision of worlds. "What is it?"

"It's the Rockfall, Mr. Keenan, and very, very dangerous."

"Rockfall?"

"Come with me. Everything will be explained."

Keenan rocked to his feet and approached Elana, catching a glimpse of great beauty at the same time as the stench of putrefaction. Elana turned and, stooping, led Keenan into a long, narrow corridor of smooth rock.

"You have been here a long time?" said Keenan.

"Longer than you could ever dream."

"Years? Is this a prison?"

"No, this is the Cathedral. My Haven. I stay here lest VOLOS spy my movements and decide he has tired of my petty intrusion. I don't like to remind him that I exist, for if I remind him I exist then I seek to further his wrath."

"VOLOS?"

"I forget. You are not of this place. Still, I should not speak the name." She laughed. "It is not a wise move to anger your gods, especially when they are as evil as He."

Keenan remained silent, following Elana, breathing the bad smell, almost sulphuric, certainly choking, and wondering if it came from this hinted-at pretty creature before him or the surrounding rock.

As they moved, so the light changed, grew brighter, became more diffused. Colours started to filter through the air, like laser beams of fuzzy iridescence. And then... then Keenan's jaw dropped open and he stopped as the interior of the monument opened into what Elana had quite rightfully described as a Cathedral...

The interior space was *massive*, a canyon hollowed from the inside of the rock, a huge, jagged mountain leading up through shafts of colour to a distant, distant pinnacle. Keenan stared in wonder at the dazzling colours unrolling lazily through the thick-lit air, like lasers through honey. The whole world felt sleepy, as if tumbling through slow motion, and Keenan realised he stood on a ledge, very high up; and below, far below, was a lake of light, collected, merged, spooled skeins of rainbow swirling and coalescing as if caught in some strange magnetic field.

"That's impressive," said Keenan, forcing words between slow-mo lazy lips.

Elana turned, and smiled, and she smiled with the face of a junk.

Keenan's hands lashed up, but Elana struck out with awesome speed, knocking both knives from Keenan's hands. He watched his blades spin away over the colourful abyss, then fall fall fall into a rainbow infinity.

"I am not your enemy," said Elana. Her face, well shaped, well proportioned, damn, thought Keenan, say it, although the word burned him worse than any toxic poison. Elana *was* pretty, in that her face was finely sculpted, high cheekbones, thick black hair swept back and tied high, her well-endowed figure hung with floating silks that did nothing to hide her athletic, voluptuous, and – to a human at least – exciting physique. But her face, her face was that of the junk, a once beautiful and proud and intelligent race, long ago deviated, polluted, made toxic and turned out into a cold hydrogen-infused galaxy with only one motivation: to kill. Keenan stared at Elana, looked into her blood-red eyes, observed her skin, like pitted, old, corroded iron, her nose a small nub, her mouth very narrowly rimed with lips. She smiled, spreading her hands apart, offering no threat, and Keenan was a coiled spring tensed ready to attack and maim and murder for these *junks,* this *pestilence* had attacked his home-world and brought slaughter and desolation to millions of innocents...

"Wait," said Elana, words soft, thrumming, cutting through the thick colours which swirled down from above. As she spoke, Keenan could see the silver interior of her mouth, the tiny triangular teeth and the small, black, forked tongue.

"I should kill you," snarled Keenan.

"But you won't."

"Oh yeah?"

"Because I have looked into your heart, looked into your soul, and I have read that which Emerald gave you. You are no longer a simple human entity: you have been changed, you have been genetically altered, you have been given a *gift*. Look into my heart, Keenan. Search me for evil. And if you find any there, please, feel free to kick me from the brink."

Keenan blinked. And using his alien-given powers, an ability which curled like a snake in his chest, tail in mouth encircling his heart, asleep, dormant, so Keenan allowed the flow of *green energy* freedom and he reached into Elana, reached into the junk, searching for evil and corruption, putrefaction and the taint of tox. But she was clean. She was good. She was pure. And, almost with disappointment, Keenan withdrew; for Keenan was a killer, and at this moment in time, he had a lot of reason to kill.

"You helped Emerald," said Elana, words a lullaby, mouth flashing silver, "and in return she entered you and left a residue of what the Kahirrim call kurr. You have the Dark Flame seed in your heart, Keenan. You are no longer wholly human. But then, you know that, you accept that, and you use it."

Keenan found his eyes were closed. He was reliving that merging with the alien, Emerald, on a different world, in a different time. It seemed so long ago, so incredibly distant. But she had given him something; aside from the gift, she had given him the will to carry on with life, to clutch at sheer existence, unadulterated life-force. Without the gift Keenan would have long ago become radioactive dust.

"You're a junk, anathema to life in the Four Galaxies," said Keenan.

Elana nodded. "It is so. And yet, I am different, Keenan. I am a purity, a distillation. Maybe I was so evil I simply came out the other side? Or maybe I wasn't fully corrupted when the Junkala fell from grace."

"Junkala? How *old* are you?"

Elana's expression was distant, and there, in her Cathedral, with light tumbling down as if from a billion different stained-glass panes, Keenan realised that she *was* beautiful, a strange deformed beauty, a beauty of soul and character and age and existence. Not simply aesthetics. Something much more deep.

"The Junkala lived in utopia. We were masters of art, literature, genetics, the building of new civilisations, the guiding of races from egg to travel. We sought gateways, stepped like gods into different planes of reality. Until we found Him."

"Him?"

"Leviathan. He followed us, pursued our arrogance, and here on this world he created VOLOS to watch over us, to nurture us, to deviate us to his template. Yes, Keenan." She looked at him then, into his eyes with her own blood-red orbs that Keenan found dangerously disturbing. "Leviathan was here. Leviathan created the junks, from the Junkala. He corrupted us. Twisted us. And your quest, on this," she laughed, a tinkling of chimes, "this *Sick World,* well, you have taken the first step. You are in the right place."

"I seek answers."

"To questions? How to stop the junks? Leviathan? I do not have such answers. I was an artist, Keenan. Never a warrior, never a warlord. But... I can point you in the right direction. I can set you on a path to – answers. To salvation."

"For me, or you?"

"For both, I feel." She grasped him, her hands on his shoulders, a movement so sudden Keenan gasped. "Keenan. I am filled with a shame so deep you could never comprehend. The junks, you despise them, every organic form in the Life Bubble despise them for they are the scourge, a pestilence, the bringers of death. And yet we were not always so. I would seek to make amends. I would seek..."

Keenan reached up, touched her pitted, metallic hand. "Redemption?"

"I want to help put things right."

"The Quad-Gal Military seek to exterminate the junks. Annihilation. Extinction."

"That may be what it takes."

Keenan sighed, and looked beyond this curious anomaly, out into the swirling colours. "I am tired of death."

"It is a natural cycle; the way of things. And yet, what the junks impose is far from natural. However." Elana composed herself, removing her hands and smoothing down her silks. "You must come with me. I have something to show you."

"With regards Leviathan?"

"No. First you must seek VOLOS."

"And what do you want?"

Elana tilted her head. "In return for my help?" She laughed again. "I want nothing, Keenan. Just to feel like I helped, before VOLOS rediscovers me and obliterates my puny Junkala shell from existence."

"Is he really that powerful?"

Elana waved her arm, summoning a platform of swirling colours. It eased towards the ledge, and bumped gently, nudging the rocky lip. She fixed Keenan with a stare he could not read, her emotions lost to him on that subtly-skewed alien face.

"He is Hardcore," she said, simply.

* * *

"WE ARE THE fucking smart party!" howled Ed, and gave a high five to Maximux from the back seat of the 6X6 Giga-Buggy as they roared across the desert. Snake was watching a blip on the scanner. It was Franco's exact location. And Franco was on the move.

"OK, we're locked on to him," said Snake. "You two need to stop congratulating one another like amateur homosexual bank robbers, and get the guns ready. Right?"

Max stared hard at Snake, then smiled a wide smile, and Snake knew what that smile meant. Maximux would wait until they had the money, then make his move. Snake, however, would be waiting.

They ploughed on, engine roaring, sand billowing in their wake. Above, thunder rumbled in the heavens, a deep and urgent grumbling.

Snake glanced up, then back at his two companions. "Thunder?" he said. "In the desert? I thought it never rained here?"

"It doesn't," said Ed, frowning.

Snake slowed the Buggy, warily. He hadn't lived so long, and retained his single eye, without being cautious. Thunder rumbled again. Now, the green-tinged night sky was lit by a flicker of lightning. It was green, and cracked the distant horizon apart. And yet, and yet –

"There's no rain," said Snake, eyes narrowing.

"What kind of thunderstorm has no rain?" said Ed, uneasily.

Snake stamped the brakes, and the Buggy slid to a stop. All around, the desert was silent. Black, rimed with green, an eldritch night scene.

Distantly, there came a pattering sound.

"Ach!" breathed Ed, "here comes the rain. Thank buggery for that! I was starting to get worried."

"Wait," said Snake, a quiet word on an exhalation of mistrust.

"For what, Big Man? Christmas?" This brought a snigger from Maximux, ever one to share in a bit of sarcasm.

The pattering got louder. More violent. And ahead, sweeping towards them, they saw a storm of –

"*Rocks?*" hissed Ed.

"It's the fucking Rockfall," screamed Snake, slamming the Buggy into gear and spinning sand in a panic of acceleration. The Buggy slewed around, spitting out a streamer of sand, and ploughed off down a steep sand dune, swerving to avoid rocks.

"What's a Rockfall?" asked Maximux, patting Snake on the shoulder.

"It's a storm that pisses rocks all over your head," screamed Snake. "Now let me fucking drive!" His boot slammed the floor, and they howled across packed desert, jigging left and right, whamming past long-fallen rocks, skidding around outcrops of jagged granite, and all the while, behind, a sweep of rocks tumbling from the enraged heavens followed at speed, filling the horizon with a sheet of granite from edge to edge, and, more importantly, more worryingly, it was slowly gaining...

"We can't outrun it!" came Ed's shrill cry.

But they tried. They had no other option.

The thundering was louder, green lightning crackled, and the rain of rocks came slamming towards the Buggy like a granite tsunami, a solid blurred teeming wall of merciless death...

And then it was over them. They drove, as if in tune, in a perfect equilibrium, rocks smashing and thudding all around as they powered along.

"You're doing it!" hissed Ed, patting Snake on the shoulder.

The rock hit the bonnet of the Buggy with such force, it broke the vehicle in two, flipping it up into the air from nose to arse, wheels spinning skywards with a grinding screech of metal. Sparks filled the area and the Buggy tumbled over and over and over. In its falling trajectory more rocks struck the Giga-Buggy, knocking it left, then right, bashing it and pulverising armoured steel as it was spat across the desert like a pinball in a machine, to finally come to rest on its roof, clicking.

Rocks thudded all around, some as large as a house.

The three men climbed from the Buggy, took one ragged look at each other, and with arms over their heads – as if that would make a difference – ran for it.

Sourly, Snake thought, it's gonna be a long, hard, bastard night.

THEY DRIFTED DOWN, for what seemed days. Keenan fell into a state of standing catalepsy, unmoving, suffused by the magic of the Cathedral's tumbling colours. "It is so beautiful," he said at last, as coils of red, green and amber lassoed his body and then gently spun away, entwining like snakes in oil.

"Do not underestimate the Colours. It is my Cathedral's defence mechanism. There is a high-density magnetic field charged with elenium-particles; the colours drift, ensnare, but at my command can become rigid. I can rip you into a billion atoms at the flick of the wrist," she said. And smiled.

"And yet, you still fear VOLOS?"

"And so should you. I have a nasty suspicion he will shortly become aware of your intrusion and seek to stamp you from the planet. As he did when the place was colonised, for the purposes of Sick World."

"So it was VOLOS who chased away all the medical staff? A thousand years ago?"

"Chased away?" Elana shook her head. "No. It is worse than that. Let us say he is millennia bored, and enjoys his little games."

"I feel like a child," said Keenan. "There is so much I don't understand."

"All will be revealed. If you search in the right places."

Within minutes the small pad drifted down and bumped against a rocky floor. Keenan jumped off, glad to have something solid beneath battered boots, and then glanced up. The world above was colour, constantly shifting, bright and ethereal, like a billion coils of entrapped rainbow. He had never seen anything quite like it.

"Where are we going?"

"I said I was an artist. After the fall of the Junkala, I appointed myself protector of that which I could save."

"You want to show me paintings?"

Elana smiled again, on that curious pitted face, and Keenan realised the facial gesture was for his benefit. To try and put him at ease. Shit, he thought. What I would give for a solid MPK machine gun right now. Gritting his teeth, and limping a little, he followed Elana across the rocky floor and into a side-cavern; here the colours began to dissipate, and the air felt cleaner, more pure, and Keenan suddenly felt almost abused. As if he'd been breathing some toxic agent. He coughed, and rubbed at his chest with broken fingers, realising his lungs were burning.

The cavern was lined with paintings, some large, some small, some twisting out from canvas and paper and bark and glass and metal, erupting in colourful splendour from a 2D background into resplendent 3D, all in paint, without any form of structural support. Keenan, ignorant to art by choice, walked across the rocky ground, eyes scanning the thousands upon thousands of pieces of work. He realised Elana had stopped and, turning, he gave her a questioning look. "What am I searching for?"

"You contain the Dark Flame. Use that which resides in your soul."

Keenan shrugged, and strode along row upon row of paintings on glass using metal inks. Then something seemed to stab him in the throat, pain flaring, and he turned, focusing on a tiny image no larger than five or six inches. He walked towards the painting, boots scuffing on rock, and had to crouch to see the picture clearly.

Keenan stared – and with a start, he realised the picture stared back.

It showed a metal face, simple, with round eyes and a mouth spewing cables. "Welcome, Keenan," said the painting.

"How can you know me?"

"I have been waiting for you."

"I don't understand."

"I knew you would come. Down the millennia. I have waited for you."

"But you're just a painting?"

"No. I'm a timeline, an umbilical between one moment and another, two static points of space and time locked and held in place by powerful machines created by the Spinners."

"So, you're alive?"

"In my present, yes, but it is many thousands of years before you even exist. You must listen, for time is short, and VOLOS awakes even as we speak. VOLOS is a Machine God, this is his planet, his world; it has always been his world. Once the Junkala ruled VOLOS with powerful engines, bending him, twisting him, forcing him into subservience in the name of Culture. After centuries of imprisonment, VOLOS broke free of his chains, and his retribution was terrible. He slaughtered, maimed, and helped deviate the Junkala..." Suddenly the metal face calmed. The junk, for Keenan suddenly realised, this was what he perceived, relaxed and exhaled with eyes tight shut. Then the orbs flashed open, swirling dark crimson, and the face said, "Keenan. You must find VOLOS. You must destroy VOLOS. He helped Leviathan create the junks. He controls the junk armies. They are his plaything. He is bored, millennia bored, and cannot be bargained with."

"Where will I find VOLOS?" Keenan's voice was cracked, like desert-dry timber.

"Seek the Silver River."

"Who are you?" whispered Keenan.

"I am the Junkala King. I am He who ruled VOLOS. I am He who corrupted VOLOS," he smiled sadly, eyes downcast, "thus bringing about the downfall of my species. He's coming, VOLOS is coming..." Suddenly the face screamed, such a high-pitched terrible screaming as Keenan had ever heard and his hands slammed over his ears as he reeled backwards, hairs on his neck standing tall, skin crawling in horror. Before him, the metal face in the painting disintegrated, became liquid, and flowed like mercury on oil spreading into a faceless, amorphous, shimmering pool.

Shaking, Keenan turned to Elana.

"He just died?"

"Yes. You witnessed the Breach of VOLOS. It is part of junk History. The One Lesson."

"But... I saw it happen? Right now?"

"Yes." Elana nodded. "Only the Spinners could explain. They were experts at manipulating Time." She looked around, and Keenan suddenly realised the whole cavern was trembling. Elana hissed, crouching, and snapped, "This is no Rockfall! VOLOS has followed the signal from the Junkala King, VOLOS has tracked you down through millennia to here at this point, this time, and he's *coming* for you, Keenan!"

A roaring filled the cavern, and the vibrating rose in mammoth leaps until the whole world felt as if it were being ripped apart, and Keenan stood at the epicentre of the largest and most violent earthquake he'd ever encountered. Huge rocks fell from above, tumbling and crashing around Keenan, who sprinted, slamming his back against a wall as the top of the Cathedral was physically *ripped free,* as if by some awesome storm.

"What can I do?" screamed Keenan; panic, a rarity, welling in his soul.

Elana turned fear-filled eyes on him, and she was crying. She was crying blood from red junk eyes. "Run!" she screamed. "Run for your life! Find VOLOS! Destroy him if you can, and you will stop the spread of the junk armies!"

A rock, larger than a house, slammed down from above and obliterated Elana from existence. Keenan blinked. A sickness surged through him, and he leant against the vibrating walls as blood ran in trickles from the edges of the huge boulder.

"Keenan," came the impossible words of VOLOS, from above. They weren't spoken words, or any form of communication Keenan had ever experienced. They were just there, digitally transcribed at the forefront of his brain in a deafening, roaring cacophony of anger and rage and pure white hatred. There was a choking noise, and Keenan realised, in horror, that the terrific, deafening sound was laughter. "I have waited such a long time for you, Keenan! Come to me. Come to me, little man!'

# PART II

# WAR OF THE WARDS

# CHAPTER SIX

# ACCELERAPER

PIPPA DREAMED, AND in the dream she walked barefoot through sand and sun shone on her glowing skin and the world felt fine. Somebody approached at a fast run from behind, feet padding sand, and Pippa fought down the urge to draw her yukana and slice off his head as hands grabbed her, hoisting her into the air, squealing and kicking, her wet hair snapping round as she was pulled into a tight embrace and she looked down into his face, the face of her dream lover, once real, now gone. "I love you," she murmured, nuzzling him and kissing him, and knowing deep down inside that it was this love, this nurturing, this *connection* which killed the violence in her soul, turned her from monster to human, from killer to sane. He kissed her back, tasting sweet, and lowered her gently to the ground, bearing her to the sand, his hands stroking her wet hair, and her eyes were closed and she was lost in the ultimate pleasure of the moment, welling deep down within, radiating outwards as she felt the pleasure building, building, escalating and rising to consume her –

Her eyes clicked open.

It was dark. She knew immediately something was wrong and tried to move, to sit up, to glance about, but found she was strapped tight to a metal trolley. Her mouth tasted bad, like a skunk had sprayed it, and her head pounded with a three-bottle punch. Above, strip-lights lay in metal darkness. There was a humming sound, bass and deep, and the air felt fuzzy, strange, almost unreal. It reminded her of something. Something *bad*.

She remembered the ecstasy of her dream. It had been a false pleasure. A drug orgasm.

"Shit."

She turned left, saw only a whitewashed wall containing... oxygen tubes, and a set of strange metal pipes running up into the ceiling. She glanced right, and blinked. Betezh lay, strapped to an alloy trolley, his shirt and suit ripped open and a large red circle drawn on his chest. Pippa glanced down. She, too, had her WarSuit open revealing her pale breasts and flat belly. From her sternum to lower abdomen, somebody had drawn a large, red circle.

"That's not good," she muttered. "Betezh?" She raised her voice a little. "Betezh!"

"Urh."

"Wake up, dickhead!"

"Urh. What did I drink? I feel like a drank an ocean of bad whisky."

"No, you were injected by tiny flying insects. What needs to worry you *right now*, is that we seem to be in an operating theatre with our shirts open and large red circles drawn on our bodies. So open your bloody eyes and help me think of a way to escape."

Betezh licked his lips several times, and tried to sit up, struggled for a moment, then lay still. "Ahh," he said. "Ahh. It's like that, is it?"

"Yes. What can you see to your right?"

Betezh glanced. "It's a trolley. Full of, um, nice shiny medical equipment."

"Like scalpel-type shiny medical equipment?"

"Yeah. And those hooks they use to pulls things out, and forceps to keeps things open, and long thick needles for injecting." There came a long, long silence. "You don't think they're going to use them on us, do you, Pippa?"

"Well, let me think for a moment now. Of course I fucking do! Can you reach something sharp? Something we can attack these straps with?"

Betezh strained. "No."

"Damn. Can you move *anything?*"

"No Pippa. Not even a testicle."

"Not funny, Betezh. This situation is starting to make me sweat."

"Ahh yes," said a voice, from beyond both soldiers' field of vision. "That could possibly be because we are about to remove your internal organs."

There came a period of contemplative silence.

Betezh coughed. "Did you just say that, Pippa? In that kind of comedy educated voice that only posh people on TV use?"

"No," said Pippa gently, eyes glinting, "I think it came from our captor."

"Yes, that would be correct. Forgive my lack of manners, and allow me to introduce myself." A figure moved into their line of sight, standing between the two trolleys and resting a hand reassuringly against both patients' feet. "I am Dr. Bleasedale." A face smiled, and Pippa squinted, unsure whether the figure was a man or a woman.

There was a *clang,* and the buzzing sound increased. Intense triple-halogen theatre lights sprang into life, filling the operating theatre with a brightness that dazzled Pippa and Betezh. They squinted, and slowly watched Bleasedale swim into focus.

She was modestly small, with short curly brown hair and a large purple burn scar covering half her face in a wide crescent. Her eyes twinkled, like a mischievous child. She wore a starched white doctor's uniform, a small white peaked cap, and high black leather boots. She carried a short black stick in one hand. She seemed a curious mix of scarred doctor and Nazi imitator.

"Why," said Pippa, speaking slowly and moistening her lips, partly because of the expired drugs, partly due to a fast-growing avalanche of fear, "why would you want to remove our internal organs?"

"I thought that concept would be obvious, daarling," said Dr. Bleasedale.

"Not to me," said Pippa, in a small voice.

"Because," said Bleasedale, twitching her stick so that it struck Pippa's lower leg, "we have a shortage of internal organs here at the Kludek Institute, ya?"

"The Kludek Institute?" said Pippa.

"Ya. Here, we pride ourselves with the finest of medical and surgical procedures, stringent aftercare, and the rehabilitation of patients in need of generous rest and respite. It's all in our policy documents and aftercare procedures. They're quite extensive. I wrote them, daarling. You should see the Health and Safety Policy! It's full of health. Lots of health. And lots of safety." She smiled.

Betezh gave a moan. "I kind of like my internal organs," he said, close to tears. "I mean, I like, I kinda need, I kinda *want* them. They're mine. They're what, you know, keeps me alive and digesting food and all that stuff."

"Mere formalities," snapped Dr. Bleasedale

impatiently. "You will be recompensed for your loss, and given temporary replacements." She smiled then, and her androgynous scarred face split into nothing less than an Evil Dictator Grin, the sort of arrogant smile found on all high-ranking individuals who abuse their positions of power and are not afraid to trample on the Little People in their stampede for more. More of what? Hell, more of *everything*.

"Don't we have to sign a consent form, or something?" muttered Betezh.

"Already signed and sealed. Whilst you were unconscious. Don't worry yourself about such trivialities. Soon, you'll be the proud owners of Hecker and Guttenberg Ersatz Mechanical Organs, the finest in the business!"

Dr. Bleasedale's stick rested on Pippa's leg, close to her right hand. If *she could just stretch a little bit, just manage to...* Pippa lunged for the stick, but Bleasedale was surprisingly quick. The stick moved, swept back, and slammed across Pippa's cheek with a *snap* that made her gasp, and left a long welting mark against her fair skin.

Pippa, whose head had dropped with the blow, lifted her chin, and in her eyes shone a dark light of murder. Her eyes watered, but they weren't tears of pain or fear, it was an outburst of sheer rage-filled animal frustration.

"I'm going to fuck you up," snarled Pippa.

"Unlikely, daarling," said Dr. Bleasedale, turning

her back on the two captives and moving towards the trolley filled with instruments. She started to busy herself, readying tiny machines and trailing wires to the two Combat-K squaddies. She attached pads to faces and chests, and soon the operating theatre was filled with *blips* and *beeps* signalling blood pressure, respiration, heart rate and brain activity.

Dr. Bleasedale turned back and, with a smile, placed her stick on the trolley. She pulled on a pair of rubber gloves, and they were quite the most ominous pair of rubber gloves either Pippa or Betezh had ever seen.

"Now lie back," said Bleasedale. "You won't feel a thing."

She smiled grimly.

"Actually," she said, "you will feel quite a lot. All of it, in fact. We call it *open cavity surgery*, aha. Ha ha. But then, that's what the Great VOLOS would want. It's all part of the Sacrifice, and it's the Sacrifice that counts."

"Wait!" squealed Betezh like a pig with a spear up its arse. "Don't do this! Kill her, her over there, the pretty lady with the funny bob."

"Betezh!" hissed Pippa, eyes wide.

"I'll do anything, tell you anything, just don't kill me, please!"

There followed a long, embarrassed silence.

"Dickhead," spat Pippa.

Dr. Bleasedale held up her stick. In her other

rubber-gloved appendage, she held a syringe. "Betezh. Thanks to your whining, your pleading, and your willingness to sell out your fellow Combat-K operative, I am willing to change my plans for you."

"Thank *you*," breathed Betezh, going limp against his straps.

"Bring out the decapus!" shouted Bleasedale. Almost instantly, double doors were whammed open and a trolley wheeled in by shuffling zombified nurses. Their skin was green, hanging off their bones, and each visible orifice – and there were many – oozed a treacly brown pus. The trolley contained a decapus. It was big, caged, and had a bulbous rubberised black body, with ten tentacles curling and whipping from its core in obvious agitation, if not downright enraged hostility. There came a steady *clang* as a limb bounced off the bars. Occasionally, one would curl between the bars and wave madly around, as if seeking an enemy. Amidst the black blubbery flesh, somewhere deep within folds, were many tiny black eyes and a yellow beak. In all, it was a seafaring monstrosity that would have probably benefited from being left in the sea.

"What," said Betezh, "are you going to do with that?"

Even as he spoke, a tentacle curled out, caught one of the green-flesh nurses (still peroxide-blonde, still cherry lipped), and started to repeatedly bang her against the cage bars, first dislocating limbs with crunches of stressed bone, then ripping her (it?) limb from limb in a scatter of rancid putrefied flesh. Betezh nearly gagged. Pippa smiled grimly.

Bleasedale seemed oblivious to the carnage going on behind her jackboots. She smiled down at Betezh with her best Nazi leer, and said, "This, daarling, is my decapus. I have been searching for subjects for some time, in order to experiment with transplant surgery."

"Transplant surgery?" queried Betezh, in a toddler voice.

"Ya, we cut off your arms and legs, and transplant the decapus tentacles in an attempt at cross-surgery and combined genetic misplacement." She had moved closer, was leaning against Pippa's trolley. Pippa's eye fell to the syringe, which dripped a clear, viscous fluid with a slow, steady *tick*.

"I don't want bloody octopus limbs!" howled Betezh.

"Decapus," corrected Bleasedale, pedantically.

Pippa's boot suddenly lashed out, catching the syringe and flicking it upwards. It spun, and landed in Pippa's outstretched hand. She smiled grimly, and Bleasedale, taking several steps back, shrugged. "You think that will do you some good, ya daarling? It is a pain enhancer, simply injected to enable you to suffer *all the more*."

"Good," snapped Pippa, and with unerring accuracy, flicked the hypodermic at Bleasedale who moved, too late. The long thin needle embedded in her eyeball and she gave a shriek multiplied by ten as the pain enhancer went immediately to work, injecto-brain. Clawing at her dart-stuck face, Bleasedale staggered back – straight into the tentacles of the decapus, which picked her up like a flopping ragdoll and starting waving the doctor around, squealing and wailing, before tossing her with awesome force against the wall, where she crunched, crumpled, and hit the ground.

"Great," snapped Betezh. "And how does that help our situation exactly?"

"Oh please don't hurt me nasty wasty doctor lady, I'm just sooo afraid of dying," mocked Pippa as she struggled with her bonds. "You fucking back-stabbing little Judas."

"Hey, Pippa, girl, chick, it was all a ruse, right? I was just buying us some time until you found a way for us to escape…"

Pippa cursed. Somehow, she had made her bonds tighter. "I'm wrapped tighter than Franco's bondage gag. Can you get out of your straps, Betezh?"

"Oh yeah," hissed Betezh, "like I didn't think of that one before, oh no, I thought I'd just lie here during the whole crazy crazy peepshow and not even, like, get a hand free and grab a scalpel and attack the bitch, or something."

"Betezh, shut up."

At that moment, there came a terrible bone-crumbling roar, and the decapus opened the bars of its cage like a key opening a sardine can. Pippa and Betezh glanced at one another as the decapus crawled free, and extended its black blubbery body, brushing the ceiling a good fifteen feet above, tentacles whirling like tensioned steel cables as they whipped and snapped about.

"Um, I don't think our situation has improved," said Betezh.

"Shut up!" Pippa struggled with the ferocity of her nature.

The decapus picked up the two remaining green-flesh nurses, and tossed them aside with contempt. One struck a wall, crumbling into a ball of compressed rotten flesh; the other struck the medical utensil trolley, splitting in half with a *crunch* so that two body sections spun away in different directions and toppled the trolley. There came a church-bell series of chimes as implements scattered across the floor.

The decapus roared again, and fixed its many beady eyes on the two patients strapped to their trolleys. Its beak clacked, and to Pippa's panicked mind, it seemed as if the creature was laughing.

"Oh no!" squeaked Betezh, as the decapus pulled its tentacles together and in a strange, accelerated, crab-like whirling dervish of betentacled squidgy motion, charged at the helpless Combat-K victims...

\* \* \*

MUSIC SLURRED, A mix of sax and piano, languorous and sleazy, but classy at the same time. Franco leant on the doorbell, and as the door opened he hitched his thumbs in his belt and grinned, showing his missing tuff.

"Hey baby," he said, "I'm here to fix your Indigo5000 Super Deluxe Helix Washing Machine. I've brought all my tools."

The woman who'd answered had yellow-scaled skin, long black panther hair, and was looking kinda sexy. She wore a skimpy see-through negligee, her breasts were cupped in silver pointed containers (with tassels), and her horned one-toed feet poked from furry slippers.

"Hi handsome," she said, purring, "There's only one tool you'll be needing in my hot bitch kitchen." She grabbed Franco's dungarees and pulled him inside, her mouth clamping limp-like to his, her tongue probing into his mouth and searching his many chrome fillings with slurping desire.

Franco pulled away for a moment. "Wait! I *do* have to fix the washing machine, love."

"Well," growled the Fedrax alien female, "let me put it on a high vibrating spin as I watch you work!" Growling, and with hips swaying, she led Franco through to the kitchen with its 360° panoramic forest scene, scents included (at no extra cost!) and began to undress Franco, tugging at his workman's dungarees and stroking at his throbbing member.

"Oh baby," said Franco, growling himself.

"Oh darling," purred the alien.

"Oh baby, yes," said Franco as he sprang free.

"Mnmnmnmf," muffled the alien, affixing her mouth to his tackle.

"Oh baby go for it! This is my dream! This is my dream!"

It was the smell that made Franco suddenly aware that he *was* dreaming. It was a kind of sterile hospital smell, the stench of an antiseptic ward, the aroma of medicinally-cleaned corridors, the underlying sweet acid hint of gentle putrefaction. He opened his eyes to see something, *something*, attached to his tackle down below. "Aiiiee!" he screamed, as the colostomy-bag-headed nurse pulled away with a tiny *slupper* sound as her plastic-bag-integrated-orifice-impeller disengaged from Franco's fast-shrinking member. "What are you doing?" he screamed, yanking at the straps on the table. "Just what the hell do you think you're doing? Can't an honest guy have a peaceful sleep without being... being... being *molested* by some –" he stared hard at the mutated and deformed multiple-amputee, his eyes following the nurse's freefall eyes as they slopped around inside the makeshift colostomy-bag skull-sack, "um, freaky shit-bag headed nurse! After all, what have you got in there? Shit for brains? Hell. So you have."

Franco sputtered to a halt. He realised he had been physically *moved*.

"Whoa!" he said, gazing around hurriedly, neck-tendons bulging as he strained pointlessly at his straps. "Just wait a chicken stock minute! What the bloody hell bollocks is going on here, then?" Distant, like a fuzzy Velcro train easing through a treacle-filled tunnel, memories of events trickled a return. Franco visibly paled. He rallied, focused, then realised what he was seeing before him, and slumped back feeling suddenly nauseous and weak.

"Cut! Cut, I said!" came a gargled echoing voice from inside a bedpan. Franco blinked. The nurse had replaced her decapitated head with a stainless steel silver bedpan, complete with polished wooden handle to one side. Her eyes peered through tiny circular holes in the steel, or indeed, were maybe even attached to it. If she turned quickly, nurses nearby had to duck lest the bedpan handle caught them a *thwack* on the skull.

"What's going on?" said Franco, weakly. He suddenly felt weaker than a kitten. More vulnerable than fish on a plate.

"Ach, you ruin my film!" said the bedpan nurse. "All this kerfuffle and all ve vant is a simple rumpy pumpy oral scene. Have you people got no sophistication, timing, or eye for the finer celluloid delicacies? Hey? Hey?" Her voice echoed, tinny, as if, encased within a bedpan. Which it was.

"Film?" said Franco, voice shrinking quicker than a Poodle's bravado when faced with a rage-filled Rottweiler.

"Ya! Ve making porno film! *Franco and the Nurses*, ve vas going to call it, but now ve settle for *Franco and the Sick Nurses*." She laughed. All the other nurses laughed, and Franco's deranged eyes twitched rapidly about the room. There must have been twenty of them, all standing around, naked. However, where once twenty naked nurses would have filled Franco with a lust so brain-consuming he would have *popped* out of sheer primal excitement, now, here, faced by these nurses *merged with medical explosion and mutation,* Franco simply wanted to die a quick and painless death.

Hell, he thought, fuck it, make it a painful death. Anything's got to be better than what's about to come!

"Now then, girls," he said, eyes skipping nervously from one deformed nurse to the next to the next to the next. Never had he seen so much peroxide-blonde hair and cherry-red lipstick. Except for those with surrogate skulls.

The director, whom Franco had mentally christened Bedpan Head, came close to him, breasts dangling and pierced with... *Ye Gods,* thought Franco, *they're pierced with Brinkerhoff Rectal Speculums! Oh, sweet Mother of Mary!* Franco knew this because he'd spent a considerable time in and around hospitals, and had had his fair share of rectal examinations with a fair number of Brinkerhoff Rectal Speculums.

This was fast turning out to be Franco's worst nightmare. And he'd had a few.

"Get away!" he screeched.

"Listen, sweet Franco," said Bedpan Head, "ve have here a movie to make, your very own little pornographic keepsake, so stop moaning because you're holding up veekly production and ve have *so many more movie to make!* Ya."

"No!" screeched Franco, "let me out let me free let me go, it's not bloody fair, I don't want to play anymore!" He struggled, pounding against his bonds whilst the deformed nurses stood around, several clinking metal-grafted limbs on floors and walls as they waited for him to burn himself out.

*What's that?* he thought. *Is that the right-hand leather strap about to give way?* He pulled and pulled and pulled.

*Wow!* he thought. *It hasn't given way.*

He slumped back, finally, exhausted, and stared down at his shame. They had stripped him to his BWAUs. His Big White ASDA Underpants. Franco's lower lip came out. He sulked. "This is not befitting a Combat-K operative," he muttered.

"Roll the cameras!" shouted Bedpan Head, and coming in close, hands clenching and unclenching as if she was about to enjoy something, she grinned down at Franco (or so he imagined, from inside her stainless steel cage of exo-skeletal skull) and hissed, voice low and filled with the sort of vehemence one did – not – mess – with – "You listen up Franco, and listen good for ve von't stand for you vasting our time and messing up our film! You perform, ya? Your life depends on it!"

"Ya," said Franco miserably, and watched twenty naked deformed nurses, several with Bowman Lacrimal Probes pierced through noses and lower lips turning faces into a parody of punk piercing, a merged mask of metal, a cage from which even they could not escape, descend on his mostly naked sacrificial beer-bellied body with grunts, squeaks, dribbles and moans of impending pleasure and ecstasy.

IT WAS LATER. Much later.

*This can't be happening to me*, thought Franco. But it was. This used to be my fantasy, he thought. And he was right. It used to be. But now it had turned into a nightmare. By a long stretch of deviant imagination.

Darkness had fallen. The nurses, after doing unspeakable acts to Franco's unspeakable body, had left, somewhat unspeakably. He was alone, covered in baby oil, his ASDA underpants sticky and molten, his raw lips whimpering softly. He was also rubbed red raw in several places, and stinging sorely in several others. I never knew I had so many orifices, he thought miserably.

Suddenly, a thought occurred to him. His Pearl earlobe comm! He could summon help! Get rescue! If nothing else, summon a gun and start eking out some kind of revenge, gunslinger style. He grinned, a nasty grin, in the dark. He'd show them nurses a thing or two with a slick weapon in his hands. He shuddered, and his smile fell. They had managed to kill his love of double entendre. The bastards. And that was a crime worse than any genocide.

"Pippa?" he hissed, activating the Pearl.

Nothing.

"Come in, Pippa. Or Keenan? You there, buddy?"

Nothing.

"Cam? Shazza? Mel? Fizzy? Olga?"

Nothing.

"Holy shit. What about you Betezh? You there, you freakish face-mangled bastard?"

Nothing.

And Franco realised. Either the earlobe comm was dead. Or he was alone.

Totally alone.

TIME SLIPPED INTO a meaningless slurry. Like a torture victim deprived of external sensory stimulus, Franco became attuned simply to The Moment. Like a child, he regressed into a form of simplicity, losing his sense of history, time, worth, dignity. After a while, there were only scenes. Scenes in the movie, the porn movie, that had become his existence.

*   *   *

IN WHITE UNDERPANTS, he hung by leather bound wrist-straps, swinging gently as a dwarf nurse with external metal hips oiled him over in long, lunging motions, making him swing like a butcher's slab of beef in a breeze. Franco, chin out, eyes ahead, said nothing, did nothing, but as she reached his underpants she smiled at him from behind her CPR facemask, breathing in and out, in and out, in and out, and her hands slimed oil over his tackle. Franco focused. He chewed his tongue. He set his mind wandering to bad things. But still, there came a reaction. A large one.

"Good," crooned the nurse, applying more oil.

"Bollocks," said Franco.

GAGGED, AND BOUND, and strapped face down on an alloy bench, with cameras rolling, the nurses massaged Franco's bulging shoulder muscles. They crooned, and chattered, and moaned as they rubbed at him. No no no, said Franco's mind. This is bad. This is dirty. Filthy. Abuse. Molestation. I am nothing more than a sexual object being used for their damn and bloody intense personal gratification, and I *will not* play ball. Through a hole in the alloy bench hung his distended genitalia, like a chicken hung by its neck, and the nurses with their slick tongues and tracheotomy pipes found their way to him. The camera zoomed in. And despite himself, Franco grew a goodly few inches.

"Good," crooned the nurse, affixing callipers.

"Bollocks," scowled Franco.

THEY POURED BLOOD from O Neg bags over his head, and body, and massaged him. They pissed on him, metal crutch legs clacking on alloy benches as streams streamed rivers across his skin. Cry me a river, he thought. Yeah, right. Franco gagged, and the camera got a close up of his face, beard contorted in rage, eyes rolling. They stabbed him with hypodermics, trailing them up and down his flesh, scratching him, stabbing him and he gave little "yowls" on demand. With pads of pus-filled bandages they teased him, stuffing them into his mouth and watching him choke and vomit. Nothing was too much for these demented creatures, as they stroked him with incontinence pads and whispered sweet nothings in his ears, metal teeth clacking, huge external dental braces shining eerily in the fake glow of halogen lighting. Some wore orthodontic buccal tubes, some monolock self-litigating ceramic brackets, some matrix bands, half hollenbachs and spoon excavators. It was all quite disturbing and Franco hummed to himself, cursing his foolish treasure hunt, and wondering how much treasure could be worth all this aggravation. None. He'd rather die a poor man.

I should have stayed back in BaseCamp, he realised after a long, long time.

Not gone running off and buggering about looking for some mythical bloody crown that probably doesn't even bloody well exist.

I should have chatted up Shazza instead. He considered this. I was in there, he thought.

"You're so macho," crooned one nurse, wiggling her forcep-clamped breasts in his face. They clanged against Franco's teeth. "You're big and strong, enough to turn me on, with big blue eyes and able to satisfy, baby, you're big and strong, *more* than enough to turn me on, a man to dominate, to love and protect me and take care of my every need, know what I mean macho man?"

"Come here," said Franco.

"Ooh yeah baby!"

She swung her breasts close, and in a fit of insane hatred Franco grabbed one compressed ripe melon in his teeth and shook his head like a dog with a bone, as the nurse started to screech and blood spewed and flowed and sprayed and Franco wouldn't let go, oh no, this was it; they'd pushed him around and took him for a fool and used and abused and mistreated and molested him and he was fucking *mad* and totally had enough and was getting some tasty juicy needful payback...

The nurse broke free, leaving a tit hanging in Franco's jaws.

He spat it out.

"Get me a gun!" he screamed. "I'll execute every last motherfucking one of you!"

Sabrina approached, from the darkened shadows of the "film set". She was smiling. She waved her hypodermic arms in a slow weave, and they caught Franco's frenzied eyes, calmed his frothing mouth, and she moved close and a long needle slid into his chest and the injection was like a long smooth draught of liquor.

"Relax," said Sabrina.

Franco's head nodded down. His chin touched his chest.

"I've had enough," he mumbled.

"That's OK," whispered Sabrina, cherry lips brushing Franco's ear and tickling him. "Because the next movie is terminal."

FRANCO DREAMED. HE sat in a valley amidst tall black mountains, enclosed, ensnared, seated before a fire opposite Father Callaghan, who wore rough brown robes and a serene look of placid gratitude, as if he'd just eaten the world's greatest hotdog.

"What you grinning at?"

"Be calm, my son."

"Calm? But they're gonna kill me!"

"Hmm." Father Callaghan placed his chin on his fist, and nodded, thoughtfully, gazing into the fire. "That's interesting. Tell me more."

Franco scowled. "What more do you need to know?"

"Well, I've been programmed with a trillion separate response arcs."

"Ha! You're nothing but a damn chip."

"Still, I'm here to help."

"By doing what?"

"By calming you in your hour of need. By making you *think*."

"I don't *need* to think, I *need* a machine gun."

"No no no. First, use your mind. Then, your fists."

"I can't do anything. They keep drugging me, just like at Mount Pleasant, and they they they keep me strapped up tight. I've tried to escape, but they just keep oiling me up like some huge fish, and and and *and* it's just not damn bloody *fair*."

"You know what I'd do?"

"Hmm?" Franco was staring into the flames now. He was considering jumping in them. "Go on, bloody Father bloody Callaghan, religious extraordinaire with so much good advice to give. Go on!"

"Oh, to mock! Franco, 'tis simple. You need to play dead."

"Easy for you to say! You are dead."

"No, I am non-living. AI. Still, think about it."

"Ha! Bloody useless damn Temple Pill. I want my damn $19.99 back."

Father Callaghan, the fire, the dark mountains, all started to fade in pixellated blocks, like a low resolution computer game or bad video decoding.

"Think about it," whispered Callaghan.

* * *

FRANCO OPENED HIS eyes. The darkness receded. Lights came up, to reveal no less than forty nurses in various states of dismemberment and dress, forming a huge circle around his bound and hanging body. Franco glanced up, at the leather straps which tied his hands tight to a large, rusted, iron hook. Franco swung, gently, like a dead dog on a washing line. He blinked a few times, and gradually became aware of... the silence.

"Father bloody Callaghan," he muttered. And realised the nurses, all of them, with their peroxide-blonde hair and red lipstick, with their rubber-ring bellies and strapping calf muscles, their genetically grafted medical implements and strong, black, sturdy, comfy shoes; all of them, it dawned on Franco's diseased and whirling mind, all of them carried –

A weapon.

"Ha ha ha," said Franco. "Now listen here, girls."

The circle started to close.

"Now, just hold on a moment, ladies."

One nurse gave an experimental *swish* of a giant scalpel attached to the end of a pole. It reminded Franco disturbingly of the Grim Reaper, albeit with curly blonde wig and a succulent choice of lipstick hues.

"We really do need to talk about this." Franco stared up, wiggled his hands, flexed his numbed fingers, and breathed the pervading medical stink of sterile utensils. He started to struggle. Infuriatingly, the nurses did not increase their pace.

They knew when they'd cornered a rat. When it had nowhere left to run.

And when it was ready to *die*...

THE HEADS LEAPT towards the BaseCamp's hull doors, and Olga's D5 boomed and clattered alongside Shazza, pale and green-tinged in the moonlight. Their guns roared, fire flaring from barrels, and then Fizzy was back, panting, face sweat-streaked.

"Stand back!" she screamed, and holding a Nape firethrower, she pushed between her two comrades and as the Heads converged and leapt as a pack, so flames roared out to meet the unholy alliance of spider and nurse, engulfing the mass and spitting them backwards, black and flaming, chittering and stamping little burning legs.

The three female squaddies stumbled back, and as Fizzy slammed shut the BaseCamp's door they caught a glimpse of hundreds more advancing from the night. Within seconds, there came *thuds* and *bangs* and *clangs*. Dents quickly appeared in the thick steel, like bulges in a balloon, and the three women stared at one another.

"This can't be happening," growled Fizzy, face lit in an eerie manner by the glow of the Nape's flickering nozzle.

Olga gestured to the BaseCamp's five-inch plate-armoured door. "It not just happening. It getting worse!"

They could hear a *fizzing hissing* sound. Even as they watched, droplets of acid-molten alloy rolled down the interior and started to melt through the floor.

"We need to get the hell out of here," snapped Shazza.

"What about Franco?" said Olga, eyes hard. "He's out there. Somewhere. On ze other side of those *things.*"

"He chose to leave," hissed Shazza. "The dickhead."

"We have to reach him!"

"No."

"Yes."

"No."

"Yes!" There came a crunch. Fizzy and Shazza stared at where Olga's hand had crushed tiny finger-shaped dents in her D5 shotgun. They glanced at each other.

"Let's get off the ground first," snapped Shazza. "Then, if we're still alive, we can get a lock on the ginger midget."

They ran down narrow alloy corridors, thumping them shut in retreat. BANG BANG BANG went the doors, sealing the three women further and further in the belly of the metal tomb. Olga had fished out her PAD, eyes scanning millions of frequencies. And even as she ran, pounding along, girth squeezing through narrow apertures, bosom wobbling frighteningly, she was intent on the task of locating Franco which *technically* should have been very, very easy. She cycled through comms. Everything was dead. Franco had, digitally at least, vanished.

"Bugger," said Olga.

"Strap yourselves in," cried Shazza, pulling at her harness as they reached the cockpit. "It's going to be a wild ride when the BaseCamp turns back into a DropShip! It was never designed to do it carrying human cargo. We're *supposed* to be outside. This is *supposed* to be a simple, non-threatening mission!"

She slammed the keys, and the BaseCamp vibrated savagely.

On the screen before Shazza symbols flashed in blue. Then red.

Behind, down the metal corridors, they could hear doors being wrenched apart. The Heads, well, what they lacked in size and stature, they made up for with ferocity.

"There's only two doors left," whispered Fizzy.

"The BaseCamp won't change back," snapped Shazza. "Something has to be damaged."

"We must get out of here!" roared Olga, eyeing the door warily. Her hands were sweat-slippery, panic writhing on her fat face like the contortions of a stroke victim. More clangs echoed from the BaseCamp's interior.

"There's a trapdoor. Down to the Giga-Buggy." Shazza pulled out of her harness, hair sticking to her sweating brow, and dropped to her knees. She hoisted open the trapdoor, peered into the gloomy subterranean space, then dropped lithely through. Fizzy followed, with louder clangs ringing in her ears, and Olga stared at the space, then down at her enormous belly blubber. "Bugger," she muttered, threw down her shotgun, and jumped, wedging tight in the trapdoor space and grunting, locked in position, her legs kicking below, arms flapping above. Wedged.

She felt Shazza and Fizzy grab her legs and start to heave. Her belly squidged and slopped, but overhung the trapdoor square by many inches and for the first time in her life Olga wondered about the wisdom of a diet.

"I'm stuck!" she bellowed.

Muffles came from below. Again, her friends tugged on her, leaving claw imprints in her fat leg flesh.

There came a *clump*. Olga lifted her head, little eyes fixing on the final door. She licked nervous lips, and suddenly realised her position. She'd thrown down her weapon, leaving herself unarmed.

There was more tugging, but Olga's eyes remained on the alloy door. Then there came a thump and a dent appeared. With a hissing sound, acid started to eat through the portal and Olga started to scream and bellow, struggling and wiggling, twisting and pushing as below hands pulled at her sturdy calves and wobbling thighs.

"They're getting through!" she screamed. They would eat her. Eat her face, her eyes, her head. Olga shuddered. Nobody should have to die like that. She cracked her knuckles, and with a grim scowl, thought to herself, *Well, I will take zem with me!*

Below, there came the roar of an engine. Olga increased her frantic struggling, eyes growing wide as she realised with a bitter taste on her tongue that Fizzy and Shazza were abandoning her. Leaving her to die. Leaving her to be eaten by those terrible, genetic mutations...

I cannot believe it, she thought sourly.

I can't believe they'd run away...

Saying nothing, Olga continued her frantic silent struggle, eyes locked morbidly on the door. Long streaks had burned through with acid. The alloy portal quickly resembled silver confetti streamers. Beyond, filling the corridor like an explosion in a mannequin factory, were hundreds of bouncing spitting wild-eyed scraggy-haired nurse Heads. They bounced and charged and sprang and leapt. The doorway groaned. Olga had only a few seconds left...

Olga heard the spinning of tyres, could smell a hint of exhaust fumes; and she knew.

Knew now, that she was all alone.

She was going to die, alone.

\* \* \*

IT WAS RAINING boulders, a storm of jagged rock, a torrent of giant stalactites tumbling and crashing around him, obliterating everything into pulverised stone shards. Keenan could see Elana's blood, leaking from beneath the large boulder which had crushed her, and his mouth was dry, his brain bitter, and his eyes narrowed as anger coursed his veins. He was sick. Sick of being used. Sick of being bullied. Keenan gritted his teeth, and, glancing up, stepped out. *Fuck it*, he thought. So what if I die? So what if I am crushed? I will get to join my dead girls, be with them for all eternity. What care I for the problems of Quad-Gal?

He laughed then, a sound verging on the manic, and with head held high he walked across the crumbling hall. Rocks and boulders slammed all around him, but like a man blessed, a man with an intuitive gift, he passed through the crumbling Cathedral untouched.

Standing on the platform, he sailed up through colours and he could feel a mammoth animosity, bearing down on him... Keenan blinked, the alien substances in his veins surging and roaring through his mind. And he could see, and he could feel, and the Dark Flame burned in his heart and Keenan could see VOLOS for the first time and knew, knew his life was strange and odd and *old*, as old as Leviathan. And with a certainty, and surety, as clear as night follows day, death follows life,

Keenan *knew* VOLOS could not see him, he was invisible, and more, Keenan knew that VOLOS feared him.

Up soared Keenan, his hands outstretched through the swirling colours and mist, and all around him the world roared and Keenan, flying blind, trusting to Fate, landed at a random platform and walked along a narrow tunnel, and out into the dark fresh night...

Outside, the Rockfall was stuttering now, dying, the rocks from the sky becoming fewer, more staggered, smaller in size and ferocity. And then the holocaust from the heavens abated, and everything was still except for a pall of desert dust hanging above the beaten ground. Keenan climbed a nearby dune, and turned.

Around him spread a sea of dust, swirling, disturbed, and Keenan watched the Cathedral, now Elana's tomb, crumble and crack, toppling in on itself. Eventually the rumblings and violence subsided, until an eerie silence rolled across the desert. Keenan scratched his chin, and considered his position.

What had happened in there? Had he been guided?

He looked at the backs of his hands, criss-crossed with tiny scars from a thousand different battles, a myriad of ancient wars. Never had Keenan been so reckless; never had he given in to intuition, to another sense, so readily and with such little care for his own self-preservation.

*I should have died*, he realised.

But you did not.

I should be buried in that tomb of rock.

But you are not.

His eyes played across the desert, and with a click of his tongue, he stood in a quick, fluid motion. Energy surged through him. He felt young again, whole again, awash with a strength which had gradually bleached away over the years. Keenan felt more powerful than he'd ever felt. It was a feeling he liked, and he revelled in the dark energies whipping through his veins, heart and mind.

He turned. Orientated. Snake. Ed. Maximux. Keenan grimaced, and clenched his fist, cracking a few knuckles. Those back-stabbing treacherous whores. When Keenan had finished with them, well. His eyes shone dark in the desert gloom.

Well, thought Keenan. They'd be better off dead.


KEENAN CROUCHED IN the sand, fingertips stretching out, resting lightly on the cold, rough surface. The dust had nearly settled, sand clouds drifting to rest in a shroud over the newly-fallen rocks. Keenan smiled grimly, watching the BaseCamp, now nothing more than a battered, smashed wreckage. So, he thought, that's the way we're going to play this game. He glanced up at the sky, and shook his head. Rocks from above! Rock rain! God did have a wicked sense of humour, didn't he?

The BaseCamp was in complete darkness, a twisted, spectral, skeletal husk under the glow from the green moon. Wary, Keenan made his way down from the rocky dunes and stopped, hand resting lightly against bashed hull, his head lifting, eyes casting over the unrecognisable BaseCamp. Would they have survived the Rockfall if they'd been inside? Unlikely.

Keenan crouched, creeping through a skewed doorway and into a corridor of broken panels. He made his way to the armoury, which had been smashed to hell. Burn marks had scorched the walls from detonating ammunition. Keenan rummaged around for a while, and found a few serviceable Babe Grenades, and one of his stash of Techrim 11mm pistols. He shoved this in his belt, and found a pack, filling it with ammunition.

Again Keenan tried comms, but there was nothing. He shook his head again.

Some fucker's playing games, he thought, and for an instant glanced up, through the mangled BaseCamp ceiling, up towards distant stars. Quad-Gal Military? Steinhauer? He better pray he's not set me up like a goon, came Keenan's internal snarl. Because I'm getting tired of this shit. Something dark, slime-snared and brooding curled around his heart like cancer. A leprosy of attitude flooded his veins.

Real tired.

He walked awkwardly down a buckled corridor, and blinked. There, lying amidst shattered debris, even abandoned by the weird organic cage, was Cam. Keenan dropped to one knee and, with both hands, lifted the little PopBot. "Cam? You hear me, Cam?"

Nothing. No lights. No artificial life. Nothing.

Cam was heavy, despite his tiny tennis-ball size, and Keenan carried the PopBot outside into the cool desert night. Sitting cross-legged, and placing his Techrim by his side on the chilled sand, eyes glancing warily about, Keenan eased open Cam's primary access panel. He instigated a power re-route, then a hardware diagnostic check and full software reboot. Sluggishly, Cam's lights flickered into life. With a gradual acceleration, Cam came back online and lifted gently, motors humming, from Keenan's hands to hover in the air.

"You OK?"

"That bastard."

"Which one?"

"Maximux. I'm scanning now."

"How did he bring the Great and Mighty Cam down?"

"Nitrogen-funnelled EEMP. Don't mock. I'm going to pull his arsehole out through his ears."

"I thought you were a pacifist?"

"Whatever gave you that idea?"

"You did."

"Only when it suits me," growled Cam. "There.

Found them. They're currently three klicks away, immobile."

"Camping out?"

"Hard to say. I can scout ahead…"

"Oh no. You're all I've got at the moment, and the whole world seems to be crumbling into rat-shit. I can't get any comms. See if you can establish some form of contact with Pippa and Franco; hell, any of the others. Something very weird is going on down on this planet."

Cam bobbed for a moment, lights flickering on his battered casing. "What happened out there, Keenan? You seem… different."

Keenan grinned. "Let's just say I found God."


"I CAN'T FIGURE it out," said Cam.

"I thought you were a GradeA+1 Security Mechanism with advanced SynthAI and a Machine Intelligence Rating (MIR) of 3450. Surely a simplistic communications problem *shouldn't* be a problem."

"Hey, listen, buster," snapped Cam, "there are a billion possible reasons why the comms might not work. From simple degradation of components to the interference of RSPs, random solar particles. So shut up and let me focus on finding people."

Keenan lit a cigarette, and headed back into the damaged BaseCamp to see what he could salvage. The remaining vehicles were all battered out of recognition, except maybe for some compressed oval wheels. With a cigarette dangling between his lips, Keenan dragged at wreckage, and tried to fire an engine half-heartedly. There came a whine of starter, but no fire, no energy, no life. "Shit."

He rummaged around in the stores, discovering the InfinityChef™ was battered to hell and would only spew out a thin, gruel-like soup. Instead, Keenan found the emergency rations crates. There were ten identical crates of PreCheese. "I'll bloody kill Franco," he growled, shaking his head, not quite believing that somebody allowed the little ginger squaddie to be in charge of emergency rations. With a love of cheese, sausage, horseradish, and little else, it was the kiss of culinary death to allow the little bugger anywhere near any kind of food stores.

Stocking up on a few tins, Keenan at least found coffee and sugar, and moved back to the lockers. He kicked the lock off Snake's, and rummaged around the offal inside. Then he pulled free a tiny cube. "Hello sunshine. What've we got here, then?"

Keenan crawled back through the wreckage, and tossed the cube to Cam, who ingested the storage device. "Found that in Snake's locker. Give it a scan, see what you find."

"It's a Bug."

"Yeah, I know what it is."

"Preliminary surface reading shows dialogue. Fast scanning… it's Franco."

"Franco? Why the hell would Snake bug Franco?

Into a bit of eavesdropping on perverts, is he? Likes the sound of simulated flesh on flesh?"

"No. Listen to this. '*But me and the guys, and Pippa, she's a gal, we're heading down to Krakken IV, otherwise known as the Sick World! We've got a very important mishon to find out whether the junks used to live there. Or not. But it's totally, totally top secret, reet, and nobody is to know outside of this table. / Or this room? / Aye, aye, maybe even the whole Winchester. But the point is, they picked me to lead the whole expedition! And if there is dem dirty junks, why, why I'll smash them! / And what of the crown? / Crown? What crown? Whaddya mean? / The fabled treasure down there on Sick World? Surely you've heard of it? / Treashure, you say? / Yeah, Krakken IV is rumoured to have the fabled and immeasurably valuable treasure of Iskander's Crown! Carved from sub-PlutoniumIII, it's supposed to be very dangerous. Loads of treasure-seekers have died trying to locate it. / And where would I find such a treashure? / Oh, they sell maps at the bar, just ask for Apple Annie. She'll smuggle you one. Fifteen Ship Creds. / Think I might just do that!*'"

Cam stopped. Keenan's eyes were burning, and he was grasping his Techrim in a manner that worried Cam so much that a rainbow of uncertain lights flickered across his casing.

"You OK?"

"No," snarled Keenan. "If it wasn't bad enough

that our dickhead Franco friend fell for a crock of bullshit like that, it's even worse that fucking morons like Snake follow and believe. So I got dumped in a pit to die because of fucking *treasure*? Is that it?"

"What happened out there?" said Cam, voice soft.

"Ha! Stabbed in the back. Injured pride. But the one thing I despise worse than treachery is treachery for money. Fucking blood suckers. Fucking scumcheese mercenaries." He spat, eyes gleaming. "Have you found Franco yet?"

"Not yet."

"But you've locked onto Snake and his merry band. Are they moving yet?"

"No. They're still. Probably got hammered by the Rockfall."

"Good. Get your shit together, Cam. It's time we paid Snake a visit."

KEENAN RAN THROUGH the cool hours of the night, boots ploughing sand, shoulder strap from his pack digging his flesh and making his scowl lengthen. Despite the early hours and the chill, sweat poured from Keenan and his muscles and tendons screamed at him.

"Come on," he muttered. "You're supposed to be Combat K."

He pushed on through pain, through discomfort, and Cam buzzed along beside him, saying nothing, aware they were heading for battle and considering the part he had to play. On the one hand, he could understand Keenan's anger, especially at being betrayed for cold hard currency, but on the other – well, Snake, Ed and Max were still Combat K. They were all under Steinhauer's orders. Now that a war was on, Cam was Quad-Gal military property, and this gave him a serious conflict of interests.

He sighed in binary. Swore in machine code.

Keenan crouched at the top of a rise, wiping sweat from his face, his short hair slicked back and eyes cold. Cam noticed the Techrim, and despite Keenan's panting, the robot-steady hand. Cam had seen this before. Keenan was in attack mode. Keenan was ready to kill.

The Giga-Buggy 6X6 squatted below, currently on its roof. Snake stood to one side, smoking a cigarette, as Ed and Maximux heaved and pushed, attempting to get the vehicle upright.

"They've no chance," muttered Cam. "It'd take twenty men."

Keenan nodded, and slowly exhaled. He glanced at the sky. "Dawn soon."

"Yes."

"Any chance of more Rockfalls?"

"I'm not sure. I haven't yet worked out what causes this phenomenon."

"Try and figure it out, there's a good lad. I can do without getting crushed in the desert. It's bad for morale."

With sunlight streamers touching the horizon, Keenan marched through the sand towards the struggling men. Ed was the first to notice him, and shaded his eyes, squinting. He went for his shotgun, but Keenan's Techrim slammed his fist, a single bullet smashing the stock of Ed's gun and sending it spinning to the dirt. Ed sucked his damaged fingers, as Snake turned with an easy smile, smoke drifting from his nostrils. Maximux scowled at Keenan, his manic eyes hooded, his lips writhing as he mouthed the involuntary curses of the mad, with twitching fingers straying towards his guns...

"Touch them, and I'll blow your damn head off."

"Keenan, old boy!" beamed Snake. "What brings you out here?"

"Surprised, dickhead?"

"Not at all," said Snake, voice smooth, glancing to Ed, who gave an almost imperceptible nod which did not go unnoticed by Keenan. "I know Ed gave you the jab, but it was for your own good. Your own safety, compadre. We were just looking out for you, because if we didn't..."

"You'd lose a lot of money?"

Snake shook his head. "What you talking about?"

"The treasure. The crown."

"Ach, that treasure." Snake grinned, and moved fast, gun coming out as Ed dived for his shotgun and Maximux charged Keenan. Keenan squeezed off three rounds, gun level, head cool, and the second shot went through Snake's wrist with a crunch of bones and a spurt of fluid flesh. The third buzzed from Snake's WarSuit, as Ed fired his shotgun and Keenan dropped to one knee, teeth grim, Techrim in both hands, and returned fire. Bullets howled across the desert. Ed was punched back, three rounds in his WarSuit as Maximux hit Keenan full on, and Keenan rolled back, coming up fast, a right hook slamming into Max's face, a left straight breaking his nose, and a front kick lifting Maximux from his feet and depositing him five feet away on his arse. Gun gone, with a scream Keenan charged, fury swamping him, all reason dissipated like early morning mist, and he slammed into Ed who was rising with his shotgun, WarSuit buzzing and sparking after Keenan's bullets, and the two men hit the ground. Ed head-butted Keenan, stunning him, but Keenan's fist found the tattooed man's jaw and knocked him back. Max leapt on Keenan's back, and Keenan slammed his head back and dropped one shoulder, and his right elbow powered into Maximux's throat to the accompaniment of choking sounds. Keenan's fist hit Ed between the eyes, a second blow cracked the man's cheekbone, and a third laid the tattooed man out cold. "That's for the injection," snarled Keenan through a mouth of blood. He whirled, kicking up sand, but Snake was nursing his blasted hand and Maximux had gained his feet, circling Keenan, a short gold blade in his hand.

"I'm going to gut you like a fish," said Maximux, and Keenan could read the light of madness in the man's eyes. But then, he'd kind of known that from the start.

Max leapt forward, the knife slashing for Keenan's throat and Keenan swayed back, dropping a shoulder, moving fast. Again Max leapt, and Keenan kicked sand in his face, dodging back from the random sway of the flashing blade.

"We should have killed you back at the monument."

"Stop talking, and show me," snapped Keenan.

"I'm going to cut out your eyes."

"Why, you need four, dickhead?"

Maximux cursed.

The blade flashed for Keenan's throat and he ducked, rolling, coming up fast and giving a single shake of his head to Cam. *No. I want this one*, he was saying. I want this fight. I need to feel the surge. I need to prove I am still Combat K. Still a soldier. Still a man.

They circled in the sand.

"You scared, Keenan?"

"What, of a piss-stinking twitching lunatic like you?"

"You bastard."

"Better a bastard than have my brain dribble like jelly from my ears."

Maximux screamed something unintelligible and charged Keenan, who sidestepped, slamming a punch to Max's temple. He stumbled, knife slashing out, and whirled – into Keenan's boots. Max stumbled back, coughing. Keenan leapt again, both boots aiming for Max's head, but Max grabbed his attacker's legs and they went down in a tumble. They wrestled for the knife, punches a blur, and suddenly everything went still. Keenan stared down into Maximux's eyes, and there was a connection there. For an instant Keenan saw the light of madness fade, and Max was as sane as the next man. Then he gurgled, his chest heaved, and blood came out of his mouth and ran down his chin giving him a crimson beard. Keenan's gaze lowered. The blade protruded from Maximux's throat, angled steeply, cutting down through the man's lungs.

Maximux tried to speak. Keenan gritted his teeth, felt Max convulse beneath him. Max closed his eyes, and died.

"Don't move, dickhead." Keenan froze, the barrels of a D5 caressing the back of his skull. The voice was Snake's. All humour, all slickness, all gentle camaraderie; all had gone. "Get to your feet. Slowly. And tell the PopBot if it so much as *farts* I'll let you have all four barrels. I don't believe the little bastard can move *that* fast."

Keenan caught Cam's attention, and the PopBot lowered towards the ground, resting on the sand, submissive, like a dog rolling over to reveal its belly. The last thing Cam wanted was to provoke an emotionally-high trigger-happy psychopath like Snake.

"Seems like we have a problem," said Snake.

"Yeah. It's hard to get blood off a fine dagger like that."

"You absolute bastard."

The D5's stock slammed Keenan's head, and he went down on one knee, blood drooling from his jaws. Stars spun in his head, mental confetti, and he waited for his mind to clear, fists pounding on the inside of his skull like an enraged beast trying to escape the cage.

"What do you think?" Snake was talking to Ed, who was nursing his battered face, wincing at his cracked and swollen cheek.

"Kill him," said Ed, voice emotionless. "Kill the Combat-K bastard."

Keenan turned, eyes meeting Snake's singular orb. Snake gave a little shrug, as if to say, *hey, what the hell, I only work here.* His fingers tightened on the triggers, and the D5 gave a terrible, fire-screaming roar...

# CHAPTER SEVEN
# CONFRONTATION

MILLER, HEALTH AND Safety Officer, wasn't feeling very well. He sat on an alloy bench in the BaseCamp, staring at Mel, with her slick and scaled skin, pus oozing from orifices, fetid breath filling the room with fetidness. Miller rubbed at the lump on his head, at the bruises on his arms under his (now torn) shirt, and stared down at the neat form balanced on his knees. At the top, he scratched with a precise and fine-nibbed pen:

Accident Report.

He glanced up again, and noted that Mel was watching him. He wondered how long it would take to catch an infection from the mutated woman, indeed, the *zombie,* and made a mental note to file a report about the problems of travelling with a zombie deviant, just as soon as he'd finished the report on the circumstances that had led to his now *several* accidents aboard the DropShip/BaseCamp combo.

Victim: Professor Chris Miller, GIOSH, GEBOSH, GREBOSH, GUBBOSH.

Attending Officer: Professor Chris Miller, GIOSH, GEBOSH, GREBOSH, GUBBOSH.

Report filed by: Professor Chris Miller, GIOSH, GEBOSH, GREBOSH, GUBBOSH.

"Grwwwwl," said Mel. It was a long, low, drawn out kind of growl. The kind of growl a panther makes a nanosecond before pouncing on prey. The kind of growl a bear makes when it comes upon a starving human emptying its carefully hoarded winter stash. This was not a growl for the faint-hearted. This was not a growl, for example, that instilled happiness.

"Yes?" Miller raised his eyebrows, like tufts of chewed taffeta against the bright orange of his ersatz suntan.

"Ippa een oo ong," said Mel, forcing words between her twisted jaws in a close approximation of human speech, but not for one second allowing the recipient to forget she was an eight-foot deviant zombie monster who could quite easily (and quite readily) bite off and chew an entire human head.

"Excuse me?"

"Ippa. And Etezh. Een oo ong."

"Pardon me?"

"Ippa and Etezh een oo ong!!"

"Say again?"

Mel stood, and her head scraped the ceiling of the BaseCamp. Miller noted this, and clocked the fact he would suggest slightly higher ceilings for travelling mutants for safety purposes, re: the bumping of heads, despite the fact it would cost trillions of QG dollars for this pointless work; after all, Mel was one-of-a-kind...

Mel moved close, stooped, and pushed her face close to Miller's. Her breath rolled over him like sewage, and he gave a little cough. There was a *snap* as he broke the nib of his pen. "Ippa!" spat Mel. "One oo ong! Ot come ack! Eed go ook for em."

Mel reached out, and picked Miller up by his shirt-front. Turning, she propelled him to the ramp and tossed him outside, where he rolled in the night dirt and lay for a moment, staring at a green-tinged sky.

Mel leapt out, and picked Miller up. He stared around. "You want to go and look for them? Why didn't you say? All I need to do first, Melanie, is ask you to fill in a request – in triplicate – asking your onboard superior – that's *me* – for permission to leave the BaseCamp. Then I can submit forms F5 and EGH7.2 to QGM for various permissions and grants, and we can reconvene, ooh, say 9.30am to discuss how we can best go about a search and... and... and..." He stared at Mel. She pulled out an

MPK machine gun. It looked *very* small in her long brutal talons.

"Ollow me."

"Where?" Miller's voice was small, like a child's.

"Ee ake uggy."

"But I can't drive it! I haven't filled in the correct paperwork, nor requested an Off-World Driving Permit! I couldn't possibly..." He stopped. Mel was growling at him again, her breasts wobbling and dribbling ooze from the rotten, plum-like nipples. Miller swallowed, and decided he maybe could keep his mouth shut on this one occasion. Nothing like a zombie for teaching someone to overlook pedantry.

"I rive! Oron."

Within minutes they were in the Giga-Buggy, Mel scrunched in, head pressed against the roof. She fired the engines, talons clumsy on controls, and Miller scowled at his zombie pilot. "I don't think it's actually very safe, actually," he whined. Mel revved the engine. "You're too big. And clumsy. And, um, have you applied for your Provisional Zombie License? I'm sure you're *not allowed* to drive unless you have one, along with a P5 Medical Certificate." The way he said *not allowed* made Mel, even in her mutated state, think of the class swot. And she hated those guys.

Mel revved the Buggy again, and slammed forward over dirt-track, wheels pounding rocks and suspension sending Miller ploughing into the padded ceiling of the vehicle. When he emerged, red-faced, blood trickling from his nose, he scrabbled and strapped himself in, pulled out his pen, and started to write a letter of complaint.

THE BUGGY CRUNCHED stones. Mel peered outside the cockpit, head tilting, eyes scanning. It's too quiet, she thought, eyeing the hospital building, its crumbling grey walls, high windows like opaque black eyes. She glanced back at Miller, still filling in his damn forms, and released the doors with a *hiss*.

"Did you do a Possible Hazardous Air Check? Did you?"

"Grwll."

"What about a Hostile Environment Risk Assessment?"

Mel slapped Professor Miller, a lazy, backhanded motion that flung him across the Buggy's interior and left him gasping beneath shaggy eyebrow tufts. She moved, body squirming and leaving trails of pus on the walls and, dragging him behind her, threw him outside. He landed in mud, ruining his fine clothes further, and Mel dropped out. She cocked her MPK, and pulled a D4 shotgun out, proffering the weapon to Miller.

"I'm a pacifist," he said.

She offered the weapon again, with a jerk.

"No, I couldn't possibly. I am merely here in an observatory capacity."

Mel growled, and offered the weapon a third time. It was the sort of growl that said *take the weapon motherfucker before I shove it all the way up your arse*. Miller took the gun, gingerly, and peered down the quad barrels.

Mel moved ahead, wary, head on her long neck weaving as she scanned the undergrowth. The moonlight was fading and a curious twilight had suffused the landscape, making everything grey-green and blotched, as if the world was drawn in chalk. Mel moved to the two abandoned bikes, propped on side-stands, and stopped, head coming up, then gazing at the distant double doors of the hospital.

Pippa and Betezh are in there, she thought.

Mel smiled, a zombie smile, and led a whining, complaining, moaning Miller towards the double portal.

PIPPA STRUGGLED WITH all her might as the decapus charged, its thick limbs a whirling spaghetti mess, and slammed the two occupied trolleys with its bulk, limbs curling around Betezh's trolley where the man screamed and whined and moaned and begged, lifting him and the trolley in a swift sweeping motion, and sending him spinning across the operating theatre. In the charge, Pippa's trolley was flung onto its side, where it spun across the floor, spitting sparks.

Betezh hit the floor and compacted into his trolley. He screamed like a girl. Pippa, face scrunched, rode out the spinning until she came to a skittering, juddering halt. One wheel on her trolley rotated slowly, squeaking.

The decapus roared, tentacles coming up, beady eyes squinting, beak clacking. Pippa's eyes fell on a stray scalpel. She urged her fallen trolley to the scattered implement, and her questing fingers stretched as the decapus moved, bulk weaving as it stared first at Betezh, then towards Pippa.

"Go for Betezh, go for Betezh," muttered Pippa as her fingers found the scalpel, and twisted, playing with the blade, manoeuvring it slowly into a position where she could attack her binding straps.

The decapus charged at Pippa, clacking and howling...

"Bastard bastard bastard." The scalpel sheared the straps and, with the huge blubbery creature bearing down on her, Pippa sat up, twisted awkwardly, and slashed the bindings on her ankles. The decapus was feet away. Inches. A tentacle limb the width of Pippa's waist swept towards her, and Pippa was up, swaying, and back-flipped three times out of the limb's trajectory. She landed lightly, scalpel still held, and her head snapped right to Betezh. The decapus turned on him, a limb lashing out towards the stunned soldier's head...

Pippa's arm came back, and slammed the air. At the end of her fist was the scalpel. It flew, straight into the eye-cluster of the decapus. The beast suddenly howled, all ten limbs lifting high in the air where it beat the ceiling in agony and black blood gushed from the small wound of popped eyes.

Pippa ran to Betezh, scooping another medical implement, what looked like a small saw, from the floor. She skidded on knees to his position, and cut the four straps holding him to the mangled alloy trolley.

Panting, Betezh knelt beside Pippa and they both stared at the decapus, which had lolloped off across the theatre, stopped, and was swirling its tentacles in apparent pain.

"What now?" panted Betezh.

"We kill it."

"What with? They took our guns..."

"I need my pack."

"That psycho Bleasedale put them over there, in that locker in the corner... I watched one of the nurses rummaging through it."

"That one, there? The one on the other side of the monster?"

"That'd be the one," said Betezh, with a dark grin. "You never thought it'd be easy, did you?"

Pippa snorted, and unrolled smoothly to her feet. She waved her arms, and the decapus seemed to calm, rotating with squelches to face her. "Get over to Bleasedale," muttered Pippa. "Stop the beast from killing her."

"Why?" snorted Betezh. "The jackbooted freak would be better off dead."

"Because I want to *question* her," said Pippa, and charged at the decapus which reared up, massive, ten thick limbs whirling like a basket of snakes. Five rushed out to meet Pippa, but she leapt, somersaulting above the creature, and spreading into an athletic roll and dive which took her to the lockers. Confused, the decapus whirled about, and focused on Betezh. It roared, and the floor shook.

"Not me! Not me!" screeched Betezh, and covered his head with his arms.

Pippa slammed into the lockers, opened a thin metal door rimed in rust, and grabbed her pack. Because, combined with her pack, were her –

Swords.

Twin *shrings* chimed the air. Confidence, strength, calm, all flooded Pippa and she turned, her eyes narrowing as the decapus towered over Betezh and the beast prepared to slowly cave in his head.

"Hey, you, you fish-stinking heap of gelatinous shite!"

The decapus paused, its blubbery body undulating around, beady eyes fixing on Pippa. She leapt, twin yukanas whirring in blurs of dark steel. Tentacles came up in defence, but a yukana was forged from a single molecule, and could cut hull steel. They slammed through blubbery tentacles, which parted pumping tar-ooze and slapped to the sterile tiled floor, writhing as if they had a life of their own.

Pippa ducked a tentacle strike that would have

clean removed her head, rolled right, and in three strokes cut another tentacle into separate chunks, which thudded to the ground, twitching and filling the air with a stench like woodsmoke and fish.

Betezh, who had finished cowering, began scooping up medical implements. These, he launched at the decapus, many embedding in its thick hide as it screeched and roared, beak clacking, and tried to turn Pippa into psycho paté.

The rest of the battle was short, sharp and vicious. Removing most of the other tentacles, Pippa stepped in close, looked up into beady eyes, and rammed a yukana through the decapus up to the hilt. The beast quivered, and slowly sank down into a spreading blob. Its limbs went still. Silence fell like fallout.

Betezh stood, and puffed out his chest. "Did you see that? Did you see how brave I was?"

"*What?*"

"All them scalpels and stuff, look, they're all stuck in its hide. I'm a damn fine shot, even though I say so myself."

Pippa stared hard at Betezh, and shook her head. "Wake that bitch up. We need to get out of here."

After reclaiming his pack, Betezh slapped Dr. Bleasedale across the face until, blurry-eyed, she coughed and became animate. She blinked, confused, then stared morosely at the decapus. "You killed him?" she said, voice low.

Pippa nodded. "Ya, daarling. Come on, on your

feet. You're going to show us the way out of this shit-hole."

"You can't possibly leave yet," said Bleasedale. "The fun was just beginning! I have operations to perform! Transplants to, er, transplant. I am a *professional*, and you are fools to turn down my medical attention. I will make you live forever!"

Pippa's yukana snaked out, the tip of the gore-covered blade touching just under Bleasedale's chin. Using the tip, Pippa lifted Bleasedale's eyes until she could look long and hard into the depraved surgeon's gaze.

"You're going to give me some answers," said Pippa. "Or I might just carry out surgery of my own. What did you do with our guns?"

"They were taken to the weapon stores."

"Why the hell has a hospital got weapon stores?"

Bleasedale went suddenly quiet, her eyes shifting from left to right.

Pippa's sword moved up Bleasedale's cheek, and pressed. Blood welled at the tip, and ran down the depraved doctor's chin, dripping onto floor tiles.

"Pippa." Betezh's voice was low.

"What?" she snapped, turning, eyes narrowing.

"Don't," he said.

"Don't what? This bitch was about to carve us into pieces."

"Yeah, but, don't."

Pippa gave a short, nasty laugh. "You're all so fucking weak," she snarled, as Bleasedale moved suddenly, fast, much faster than Pippa had anticipated; a boot slammed Pippa's groin, and a fist cracked her sternum. Bleasedale sprinted for the double doors, and was gone in a second, leaving the doors swinging to smear chunks of nurse zombie flesh in wide dark arcs.

Pippa wheezed, gave Betezh an evil look, and snapped, "Don't just stand there. Chase after her!"

Betezh leading, they ran to the doors, pushing them open to reveal a wide, polished corridor. Strip-lights illuminated the spotless tiles and walls of the corridor. Ahead, signs informed visitors of different wards and departments.

There was no sign of Bleasedale.

"Where did she go?" snapped Pippa.

Betezh shrugged. "You bloody well let her escape!"

"If *you* hadn't been whining about me cutting her up, we could have got some answers. Come on." Pippa jogged forward, a sword in each hand, face grim, WarSuit speckled with decapus gore.

Betezh followed at a distance, fighting with the straps of his pack.

The corridor was long, wide, and had perhaps forty doors leading off what appeared to be the main hospital artery. It was eerily quiet. Pippa led the way, further down the artery, swords at the ready, head swinging left and right, listening.

Betezh's boots started to squeak on the polished floor.

"Betezh!"

"What?"

"Stop squeaking."

"I can't help it! It's me boots!"

"Gods, why do I always get the idiots?"

She halted again, listening carefully, and spun with swords at the ready as a door back down the corridor opened revealing Mel, with an unhappy and muddy Miller in tow. Pippa relaxed, allowing the tension to ease from her body.

"That's our way out," she said, smiling, then louder, "Mel! Down here. What took you?"

"Ick ead."

Pippa nodded, and felt a little bit of confidence returning. Mel and Miller both had weapons and, sheathing a blade, she took the D4 shotgun from the unprotesting Health and Safety Officer. She pumped it, and grinned.

"You see any trouble on the way in?"

Mel shook her head, which brushed against a hospital sign, making it sway gently, squeaking. It read: REHABILITATION UNIT THIS WAY >.

"Nothing? No deformed nurses with no legs? No mad doctors in black leather boots? No little bitchy insects that sting you and put you to sleep?"

Again, Mel shook her brown-scaled head, saliva drooling from jaws to ruin the perfectly clean and highly-polished floors.

"I think," said Betezh, "that Mel can lead us out. Ain't that right, girl? You used your sense of sniff, didn't you girl? Tracked us that way, ain't that right girl? Just like a sniffer dog aha ha ha."

Mel pulled out her PAD, and shook her head, scowling with zombie deviant brows at Betezh. Her long talons punched in digits, and the PAD displayed Pippa's location.

"It's the spinal logic-cubes," said Pippa, voice low. "The PAD picks up their digital signature. Steinhauer may have signed our eventual death warrants, but on this occasion he did us a favour." Pippa smiled at Mel. "It's good to see you, Mel." She breathed deeply, genuinely pleased. "It's good to have a bit of backup. Thanks for coming."

Mel gave a purr.

"This way?" Betezh, eager as ever to get away from imminent danger, was edging along the corridor.

"Wait." Pippa was rubbing at her head, frowning. "We have to investigate. Right?"

"Oh no," said Betezh. "We nearly got carved up in there by a mad surgeon and a decapus sea-monster. What do you mean, we need to investigate? Look around you! There could be hundreds of these deviant nurses and doctors. This place is bloody *huge!* We need to call in to Keenan, get the other squads here fast, and *we can all then investigate together.*"

"You're beginning to sound like a yellow chicken-shit," smiled Pippa.

"I am a realist. I enjoy my internal organs, thank-you-very-much."

Pippa considered this. "Listen," she said, "haven't you wondered about the AnalysisBots? The DropBots? They come down here, do a sweep, tell us the planet is deserted of all forms of life. And then, bam! We arrive and all manner of deviated medical shit leaps out at us."

"So?"

"*So,* moron, it's a little bit suspicious, right? Why didn't the 'Bots pick up on stuff? I've seen these things in operation, they're incredibly accurate, can smell organic life from a billion paces. Why would they make such a mistake? *How* could they make such a mistake?"

"I'm sure there is a legitimate explanation," said Betezh, tightly. "Now can we *go* before that Bleasedale character comes back with a horde of legless zombie nurses?"

"I have to agree with Betezh on this one," said Miller, who had been watching the exchange with alarm, and writing in a little notebook. "It has to be said, I have been dragged beyond the call of duty, and this sort of place is no sort of place for an officer of the Royal Quad-Gal Chief Health and Safety Division of the Combined Safety and Health Institutes of Quad-Gal. It's just not right."

"We'll vote," said Pippa, eyes gleaming. "Who says we investigate? Find out what scourge is out there on those weird hospital wards?"

Pippa and Mel raised their hands.

Betezh grinned. "So who votes to head back for

the relative safety of the BaseCamp?" Pedantically, both he and Miller raised their hands. Betezh's grin widened. "That means we have a stalemate, Little Miss Twisty Exploration Knickers. And in that light, we should return to BaseCamp at once and comm Keenan for extra help…"

"No. I think you'll find *we* won the vote." Pippa hoisted the D4, checked the shell-mag, and started off down the corridor with Mel close by, claws gouging tiles.

"Wait! Hey, how do you make that out?" Betezh jogged after his squad leader, and Miller reluctantly followed.

Pippa glanced back, her bobbed brown hair swishing around her head. She gave him a dazzling smile. "Girl power," she said.

THEY'D BEEN SEARCHING for nearly two hours, and outside the sun had risen, removing the eerie green glow and making the place seem infinitely less menacing. Ward after deserted ward they searched, and although the abandoned hospital was clean, it had a desolate air, unlived in, as if long ago deserted. Beds lay empty, sheets made up and neatly tucked in a fold. Trolleys stood idle, next to monitors and strange devices none of Combat-K had ever before seen. It was Pippa who realised; Sick World had been a hospital planet not just for humans, but for aliens as well, and the weird and wonderful diseases that came about in a galactic boiling pot of sexual adventure and zero inhibition.

Betezh and Miller whined the whole way round, at first pleading and attempting to appeal to Pippa's sense of logic and self preservation, then Miller resorting to threatening court martial and the punishment of Steinhauer; finally, Betezh even tried the old *Keenan wouldn't want you out in these dregs on your own little lady* routine.

Pippa stopped, boots squealing on polished hospital tiles. "What the fuck's that supposed to mean?" she snarled, whirling about.

"I was just saying that Keenan, well, he kind of likes his women alive, yeah? And if you go and get yourself killed, then…"

"And what," growled Pippa, moving close to Betezh, "makes you think I am Keenan's woman?"

Betezh swallowed. "Well," he began. Then, wisely, thought about it. "Well," he began a second time, "well you know that thing you had going together, you know, the little romance thing, I know all about it, Franco told me about it…"

He stopped. Pippa was quivering with rage.

"Hey," said Miller. "Look. Down there. It's a cleaner."

Pippa and Betezh turned together. At the end of the corridor, distant, a figure had come into view. It seemed to be a woman, holding a large machine which hummed softly, polishing the floor.

She moved the machine backwards and forwards, buffing the tiles.

Betezh snorted a laugh. "Well that's answered that question then! There's a bloody loony cleaner on the loose, been polishing the damn floors for the last thousand years! Probably a malfunctioning AI drone, or something."

"No," said Pippa, voice soft, head tilted. "It's a woman alright."

"How do you know?"

"I can smell her perfume."

"Hey, look," said Miller. "She's naked."

"No, she's not, she's wearing... *something.*"

They stared, and Pippa led the group forward, wary, her D4 covering doorways, their boots ruining the polish. Pippa stopped, and Miller walked into the back of her.

"Shit," she said.

"Holy Mother of Monkeys," snapped Betezh, and rubbed at his eyes, as if in a dream. "You're bloody right she's wearing something, but it ain't her clothes!"

They stared at the cleaner, happily buffing away at her floor. She stopped, and glanced up at her audience. She smiled, although it was hard to tell, because most of her teeth were on the *outside.*

"What's that," said Betezh, head tilting, "that thing, there?"

They winced, scowling, staring at the wobbling item clinging to her lower back.

"That would be a kidney, I think," said Pippa, slowly. "And obviously the big red pumping thing hanging from a chain around her neck, that would be her heart." They stared at the tubes, ersatz veins, leading into and out of her flesh and connecting the external, beating heart to her lungs and arteries.

"What's that little shrivelled thing, there?" said Miller, eyes narrowed.

"That'd be her liver," said Betezh.

"Doesn't look like her liver," said Miller. "It's all black and shrivelled."

"Maybe she has a drink problem," said Betezh through clenched teeth. "The real problem *here* is *why* all her organs are on the outside."

"Ask her," said Pippa.

"What? You're kidding?"

"She's smiling," said Pippa, then shrugged, and moved forward. The cleaner was leaning on her machine, and up close Pippa could see other oddities. Her teeth were stuck to the outside of her skin, and veins roved up and down her flesh like tiny roadmaps in 3D relief. In several places, long tears were evident in her flesh, revealing stretched pink muscle within; and that heart pumped rhythmically on its chain, glistening, as if oiled.

"Hello," said Pippa, voice soft, meeting the eyes of the cleaner which, thankfully, seemed to be where God put them.

"Hello! Do you think I've done a good job?"

"Of the floor? Yes. You've done an excellent job."

"Only," the woman looked left, and right,

"I wouldn't like to be punished for shoddy workmanship. Not again."

"Have you been working here long?"

"As long as I remember."

"Can I ask you a question?"

"Sure," nodded the woman, hair bobbing. Her heart beat a little faster, making a faint *bu bum, bu bum, bu bum* sound. "Feel free. I'm just the cleaner round these parts."

"Why..." said Pippa, but could think of no diplomatic way of putting it, so just rushed the rest. "Why are all your internal organs on the outside?"

"That'd be Dr. Bleasedale," said the woman, smiling, a quite bizarre expression with so many visible teeth. "Every now and again, she has another great idea for surgery, and asks for volunteers. She's a great surgeon, you know. She's helped me acclimatise."

Pippa frowned. "You volunteered to have your heart hung from a chain around your neck?"

"Oh yes. It's portable, manoeuvrable, and I can hot-swap it when it burns out."

"Burn out a lot of hearts, do you?" snorted Betezh, in disbelief.

The cleaner threw him a sharp look, that demonstrated she was a lot less stupid than Betezh imagined. "More than you'd think, laddie," she snapped. "When you've worked these corridors for hundreds and hundreds of years, you go through a few, aye."

The cleaner squinted at Betezh, then back at Pippa. "Has he got permission to be here?"

"He's with me," said Pippa, slowly.

The cleaner nodded. "You, I know. But the others... are you sure they've got clearance? I'd hate to have to resort to some form of horrible physical violence to remove their pestilence and impurity from my clean and sterile corridors."

Betezh snorted a laugh, but Pippa gave him a stern look.

Betezh shrugged. "Well, what does she expect? I mean, look at her, all ragged and deformed, threatening to remove us! I mean, what is she, a super-deranged cleaner warrior, or something? Har har har."

"Har har har," repeated the cleaner, eyes gleaming, heart pumping faster, as she turned to face Betezh and her thumb flicked something on the handlebars of the buffer. There came a series of quick-succession mechanical clicks and the buffer reared, pistons slamming from cases and two huge circular blades spinning out from the core, each about three feet in diameter and spinning fast with razor edges. The buffer-turned-slicer slammed up around, and lunged towards Betezh with the cleaner hanging grimly onto the handlebars and Betezh threw himself backwards, stumbling, mouth a black hole of horror as the twin blades hit the floor, there came shearing screaming sounds, and huge chunks of stone and tile and wood flew up, decorating the air with debris.

"Pippa!" he screamed, and Pippa dragged free her D4 as Mel leapt back from a horizontal swipe of the huge twin blades, spinning up like an accelerated turbine with a roar of metal and stench of hot oil. The D4 *boomed* but the cleaner ducked, shells ricocheting from spinning blades with sparks and squeals as she dragged the bucking, violent, barely-controlled machine around in a heavy, pendulous arc which nearly took Pippa's head clean off. Pippa rolled, breathing deep, aware that her own weapons seemed suddenly weak and small and poor. She eyed the huge whirling blades with sour respect.

"I'm going to kill you," snarled the cleaner. "I'm going to clean you up like little stains! I'm going to polish you from the pages of history!"

She advanced, huge blades whining and jigging and barely under her aggressive control.

OLGA HAD BEEN rejected from an early age. As a child, she had been bulky, or "fat" as the many children in school liked to call her. They bullied her relentlessly, right up to the point where she learned to use her fists, and found she could move a lot faster than a fat girl should. During one Period 5 afternoon lesson, Olga, aged eleven, relentlessly hunted down her tormentors and gave them a pummelling they would never forget.

After that, Olga had respect. She had the respect of her peers and, indeed, most of the older children. Occasionally, one of the older boys or girls would make some nasty sly comment, usually about her huge bosom, sometimes about the girth of her arse. But it worked wonders what a hard sudden right hook could do, and bad news like Olga travelled fast. Soon, there wasn't a kid in the school who wasn't a] new or b] simple who dared give Olga the verbal. And these, Olga always allowed a single chance. She believed every idiot deserved one warning.

However, even with this new found power and respect, it did little to earn Olga true *friends*, and she learnt quickly that she was one of those children, and later, adults, who seemed simply destined... sadly... to be alone.

Fast forward to the present, and in Fizzy and Shazza, Olga had found a curious social equilibrium. Here, in this combat zone, she had been accepted for she was deadly enough in her own right, and the two girls seemed not to see, or at least worry about, Olga's massive size. Yes, she had enough fat to float a whale, but as long as Captain Ahab didn't rear his ugly mush, Olga was safe with her two new friends.

Until now, trapped in the aptly-named trapdoor, waiting for acid-spewing heads to dissolve her into nothing more than succulent fat strands. Below, she heard the spinning of tyres, could smell a hint of exhaust fumes, and knew.

Like her entire life of singularity, without friendship, without love, Olga knew with a deep and heartfelt sadness, knew that she was going to die as she had lived: alone. Great tears washed down her plump wobbling cheeks, and Olga took a deep breath, determined to make these little twisted genetic monsters pay dearly for eating her flesh and ruining her dreams of one day winning Franco's hand in marriage...

How could Fizzy and Shazza leave her?

Easy, she thought with a snarl.

Everybody else always had.

Suddenly, Olga felt something harsh and taut snare her legs, there came a distant roar and like an egg sucked through a hosepipe, Olga gave a massive *sclup* and was towed through the trapdoor by the power of the Buggy. She hit the ground hard, dazed, and Fizzy helped her, grunting and straining, into the vehicle.

"Hit it!" she screamed.

A ramp slammed open from the bowels of the BaseCamp, and as Heads poured into the cockpit space so recently vacated by Olga's bulk, so the Buggy slammed out into darkness and snow, wheels churning, and followed by a surge of scampering, gnashing, screeching creatures that fell quickly behind after a few short seconds of violent acceleration...

Olga, lying on her back, stared up at her Shazza and Fizzy. They were smiling. They'd rescued her!

To Olga, they looked like angels.

"Thank you," she whispered, and with a warmth and contentment in her heart, passed into a realm of honeyed unconsciousness.

THEY FOUND FRANCO'S BUGGY, deserted except for the recharging angular form of Sax. The dog snored, an odd bubbling sound like snot being sucked through a straw. His wig was curiously askew, as if he'd been through the wars.

"Where did he go?"

They peered through the storm, which seemed to increase in fury even as they stood, shivering, huddling within WarSuits and heavy jackets. The building was impressive, all glass and crystal walls, sloping zeniths and retro-wood slats.

### REC CENTRE.
### RESEARCH. EXPERIMENTATION.
### CONFINEMENT.

The three women exchanged glances. "I don't like the sound of that," said Shazza.

"What's this *experimentation* bit mean?"

"Keep your guns ready," growled Olga. She set her square chin in a square pose. "Franco needs help. I know it! We're going in."

FIZZY, SHAZZA AND Olga formed a tight squad triangle as they crept from the snowy blizzard outside, into the darkened interior of the REC. Everything was quiet, gloomy, and they moved with ease down wide corridors.

"He's got to be in here somewhere," said Fizzy, staring gloomily at her zero-reading PAD. "I still don't understand how *everything* managed to blow a fuse at the same time. It's as if the whole damn planet turned against us!"

"It'll be magnetism, or something," said Fizzy, covering her arcs of fire. "I've seen it before, often in violent storms like this. We're close to the pole as well; that sort of shit plays havoc with complex electronics."

"Still, I'd feel happier if we could reach Pippa. Or even Keenan. It's giving me the creeps, this *Franco going missing* business."

Olga said nothing, for she was still basking in the glow of her rescue by these, her two new best friends.

"Wait!" hissed Shazza, dropping to one knee. She lifted a sandal, and showed it to Olga. "Is this one of Franco's?"

Olga nodded, paling in the gloom. "That's not ze good sign."

"At least we're in the right place."

"Let's just hope he's in one piece."

"Franco is very resourceful," said Olga. "If there is ze way for him to survive, he will have taken it."

"Even at the expense of his sexual integrity?"

"Yes, especially at ze expense of ze boy's sexual

integrity," said Olga, missing the joke entirely. To Olga, Franco was a paragon of sophistication, fine morals and charisma.

"Yes. Well." Fizzy and Shazza exchanged glances, and then continued until they heard a distant fizzing sound. Somewhere, in the gloom, there came a faint glow... as of electricity.

"Olga not like that," said Olga, lifting her shotgun.

"Down here," hissed Shazza.

They cut left, down a narrow winding corridor littered with medical debris. Broken trolleys, unopened boxes half rotten with damp and showing the gleam of dulled medical instruments, rusted oxygen cylinders, piles of yellow bags of clinical waste; even body bags, which were curiously *full* and made the girls curiously *uninterested* in investigation.

Olga shuddered. "Might be zombies," she said.

"I thought Franco's wife was a zombie," said Fizzy.

"Ex-wife," said Olga, with a tight smile.

Suddenly, a scream rent the air, distant, agony-filled, desolate, frustrated, and most of all, male.

The scream died.

"Franco?"

Olga nodded, and took the lead as they pounded along the narrow winding corridor. She kicked trolleys out of the way, the shotgun small in her large and large-knuckled fists. She stopped before a door, and with a deep breath, and an apprehensive glance back at Fizzy and Shazza, who nodded their readiness, lifted her heavy boot and slammed the door off its hinges. The door hit the ground, and a sight from a nightmare met their wandering eyes. Franco hung from a hook, a butcher's slab in oil and white underpants, and surrounding him, dribbling, drooling, and in various states of dismemberment, were thirty to forty genetically modified and medical-implement-*merged* nurses, their peroxide hair permed or splayed in extravagant bouffants, their cherry-red lipstick smudged, or at the very best, applied with cement trowels.

One nurse had hold of Franco's bulge, and Franco's eyes bulged from their sockets, and Franco's bulge bulged embarrassingly from his big white underpants. "Ahh," he said, eyes falling on the stunned shocked expressions of Fizzy, Shazza and Olga. "Ahh, I know what it looks like, but – honestly – I can explain."

"Kill them all!" screamed Sabrina, waving her hypodermic syringe arms, and the nurses turned, and charged...

The following battle was not so much a battle as an explosion in a medical charnel house. Olga's D5 boomed, and the nurse with a colostomy bag for a head suddenly found out the downside of having a skull made from a plastic bag. The colostomy bag burst, and her brain and eyes ran out in a stream of diarrhoeic colostomy coolant

as her hands scrabbled for her eyeballs and brain,
fumbling them like a blind rugby player in a bath
of meatballs. Guns roared, bullets spat, and the
deviated nurse horrors slammed at the three female
Combat-K squaddies, snarling, spitting, tearing
with claws and jaws and needles and scalpels
and Franco squinted through the fine blood mist
which hung and spurted into the air as the short
violent battle raged through the room and left a
spread of mangled nurse corpses lying like so many
bludgeoned seal cubs on a Scandinavian beach.

Panting, the three Combat-K women reloaded
weapons, their bodies tense, ready for more
combat. Olga was the first to come down from the
high of sudden violence, the adrenaline of finding
herself still alive, and Franco gestured wildly with
his head. "Through there! Sabrina, the leader, she
ran away! She got away!"

Olga ran to the door, but it was bolted shut
on the other side. Olga blasted at the locks, D5
booming, but it was no good; the alloy portal was
starship hull grade, and it'd take more than shells
to loosen a hull grade rivet.

"Thank the gods!" boomed Franco. "I thought I
was a goner!"

"Looks more like a boner to me," chuckled Fizzy,
calming herself after the fight. The three women
picked their way through straggled corpses, careful
to avoid scalpel arms and hypodermic fingers.
They stood, like judges before a disgraced criminal,

peering up at Franco, Franco's underpants, and Franco's telltale bulge.

"Listen," he said, "this ain't how it looks."

"How does it look?" said Shazza.

"I know it looks like I'm oiled up and having fun, but I'm not, reet, them damn deformed nurses with their pretty faces and bobbing breasts, well, they, they," he pouted, lower lip protruding, eyes drooping, "they took advantage of poor Franco."

"Yeah, I can see that," snapped Fizzy.

"I believe you," said Olga.

"You do?"

"I know how loyal and morally righteous you are," said Olga, voice small, eyes peering up at the little fat man. "I know you would never do anything to destroy the prospect of our blossoming true love."

Franco's mouth opened and closed like a guppy fish for a moment. His teeth clacked shut. "Cut me down, there's a good lass," he said.

Minutes later, Franco was nursing reddened wrists, and he glanced about hopefully. "You find my pack? My clothes? My Kekras? They're damn fine weapons, Kekras, it'd be a shame for them to go to the mutant nurse brigade."

"We've got this." Shazza passed Franco the sandal she'd found.

Franco growled. "So, it's like that, is it? White ASDA underpants and one flip-flop." He brightened. "I've been to battle in less! They don't call me Franco 'Resourceful Bastard in ASDA Underpants' Haggis for nothing, you know! Come on squad! We must leave this place, and get back to BaseCamp! We must report this incident to QGM and seek further instructions on... on... what's that look mean?"

"It's about the BaseCamp," said Shazza, in a small voice. "It's, um, kinda been destroyed."

"Gods! I leave you three chicks in charge of the Base for a few damn and bloody hours, and what do you do? I suppose you vacuumed and polished until there was nothing left, eh? I said eh?"

"Next you'll be asking us to iron your shirts," muttered Fizzy.

"Damn right!" snapped Franco, who had surprisingly acute hearing, surprising in the fact that his job was that of *demolitions expert,* and he'd lived his whole life alongside loud bangs. "Damn good of you to offer. I'll take you up on that, just as soon as I find a shirt."

Franco took a proffered spare D5 shotgun from Olga, and strode ahead, single sandal flapping, chest puffed out, in command once again.

"What a misogynistic dick," snapped Fizzy, brows furrowed into a fearsome frown.

"Hey," chuckled Franco. "They don't call me Franco 'Gymnastic Dick' Haggis for nothing, you know?" He winked, making a strange clicking, clucking sound. "Now, which way is out? And I need to warn you about these electrocutional motherfuckers... Convulsers, they're called, give you a real sting! Better let me deal with them if we meet any. Wouldn't like you three little girls to break a nail."

He suddenly paused, and frowned, staring at something amidst the detritus on the floor. "Hmm," he said, and stooped, fingers curling around a long, thin metal cylinder. One end gleamed with a curled thread, and it was on a loop of chain, as if somebody had been afraid to lose it.

"What's that?" said Fizzy.

"It's a Leksell gamma-focus."

"Which is what, exactly?"

"Um, a device that can focus things. Like radiation. And bomb-blasts." He grinned. "If you're being naughty, of course."

"And what do you intend to do with this Leksell gamma-focus? Looks like a useless pointless piece of junk, to me."

"Hey! It may come in handy! Did I ever tell you, I'm an expert with bombs? This can be used to infuse a direct injection through an HJG grenade blast; it can be used to navigate a T5 mine-blast form-field; believe me, it can also..."

Fizzy held up a hand. She yawned. "Yeah Franco," she said. "You convinced me. Now shut up."

Grumbling, Franco hung the Leksell around his neck, and led the way through the gloom and medical detritus, the three women following, all with guns primed. Olga remained curiously silent, her eyes never leaving Franco's rump.

The darkness, the gloom, they were cloying, claustrophobic. Soon, this mixed annoyingly with an ice chill, as if the REC Centre's heating had given up the ghost and was allowing the treachery of the icy outside ice-world *in*.

At a junction, Franco stopped, sandal sliding a little on ice. He looked left. He looked right. He looked back at his squad.

"Do you know where we are?" he said, with a hopeful beam.

"No," said Shazza, slowly. "You took point. We assumed you knew the way. You mean to say you don't?"

"I've just been locked up with deranged suicidal nurse freaks from hell. How, in the name of Schwarzenegger, could I know the way?"

"Why did you take the lead, then?" said Shazza.

"Because I *always* take the lead. I am the leader. Ergo, I lead."

"Even when you don't know the way?"

"Yes," said Franco through gritted teeth. "I expect my faithful deputies to point out directions if I go wrong."

"Would that be Deputy Dawg?" said Shazza.

Fizzy giggled, moving close to her friend, a hand on her shoulder. "Hold up Shaz, come on, give him a break. He's had a rough time, I think. The last thing he needs is some rampant radical feminist lesbian on his case." She grinned at Franco.

Franco frowned, digesting this, hands on his stocky requisitioned D5, lips moving soundlessly.

"What?" he said, finally.

"What?" said Shazza.

"You said," again his lips moved wordlessly, "rampant radical feminist lesbian," said Franco.

"Yes," nodded Fizzy.

"Why?"

"Why what?"

"Why a rampant radical feminist lesbian?"

"Because I am?" suggested Shazza, revelling in Franco's growing discomfort.

Franco thought about this. "No way," he said, in a hushed and reverent tone. Around them ice crackled, like a frozen lake shifting, or some mammoth glacier retreating. The squad's collective breathing, now, was ejecting in short bursts of white mist. It was definitely getting colder. Much colder.

"Which bit?" said Shazza. "The rampant, the radical, the feminist, or the lesbian?"

"The, the damn and bloody lesbian bit!" snapped Franco, mouth open in an O. "That's just, just, just, just..."

"Just what?"

"Just damn and bloody unbelievable! I mean, look at you! Just look at you!"

"All the girls usually do," said Fizzy, moving

closer to Shazza, so that the slim flanks of their bodies touched. "It can make me real mad, but then, I'm not such a jealous girl, and we do try to have a reasonably open relationship."

Franco stared, gobsmacked, first from Shazza to Fizzy, then from Fizzy back to Shazza. "What?" he nearly screeched, so that all three women winced. *"What? You as well? You're both damn and bloody lesbians? You're both... homo and sexual? I just, just, just don't bloody believe it."*

"What's so hard to believe?" said Fizzy. "It's not like this is a new thing. Gods, it's not like we're alisexual, trikumsexual, or even DNAlesbos, sharing genetics and becoming one another, or anything." Her hand stroked Shazza's thigh, and Franco's beady eyes watched the movement with the sort of look a dog reserves for a hot meat bone.

God, he thought to himself. After what you've just been through?

Some perverts *never* learn...

"Yeah," Franco mumbled, kicking his single sandal, "it's just, I thought, maybe, one day, I might make one of you, a meal, or something."

"But you're married," said Shazza.

"Divorced."

"There's always Olga. She's a single girl. She'd do you proud, so she would."

Franco stared at Shazza with a teeth grin and narrowed eyes. Slowly, he shifted his gaze to Olga, who was staring down at him with wide eyes and a look of puppy love. She smiled, showing her missing, broken and gold-capped teeth. Her hands were clasped together meatily around her shotgun. Her breasts wobbled enticingly, like eels in a bucket.

"Now wait a minute," said Franco.

"She did bring us here to rescue you," said Fizzy.

"Without Olga, you'd be dead meat, Sausage Man."

"And she's very faithful. Like a hound."

"And look at those boobies! She'd give you some Amazing Big Loving, Franco."

"She'd give me Broken Back Loving," snapped Franco. "Just listen…"

"And you did refer to her as a 'chick'," said Shazza.

"No I didn't."

"Yes you did."

"I bloody didn't."

"You bloody did. You said, 'Gods! I leave you three chicks in charge of the Base…' You called Olga a 'chick'. This is slang for a sexy woman. Ergo, you think Olga is sexy."

Franco's mouth opened and closed again, he whirled in the ice, and strode off straight ahead, limping slightly, and muttering to himself. Behind, Shazza and Fizzy followed, chuckling, and bringing up the rear was Olga, eyes gleaming, hands slippery on her gun despite the chill. "He'll crumble," she muttered, nodding to herself. "He will give in to my feminine guile! And if that doesn't work, I'll drug ze little bastard."

Around them, with the patience of a glacier, the ice slowly invaded.

FRANCO HAD STOPPED at a window, and the three women moved close, staring out and down. Their combined breathing frosted snowflakes on glass, and collectively their mouths hung open in surprise, awe, and with a hint of fear thrown into the emotional cooking pot for spice and fire.

"That looks *bad*," said Olga, clasping her shotgun ever more tightly.

"What the *hell* are we looking at?" said Franco. He was shivering now, despite the fine protective elements of his white ASDA underpants. "It's just so... vast! How can it fit inside a hospital? Are we still inside the hospital? It's just too bloody big!"

They stared.

The cavern, for a cavern was what fell away from the iced window, was formed of rugged red rock. It fell away for hundreds of metres to a distant, smooth, polished floor of square white hospital tiles. A cool wind eased around the edges of the window, carrying the tang of iodine and antiseptic. But it was events within the cavern that blew the soldiers' minds.

Within the cavern was an *army*.

However, this was like no army Franco, or the girls, had ever seen. It was not made up of traditional soldiers, there were no infantry, no cavalry, no special forces in makeshift tents drinking brews and smoking smokes. The mad bustle of activity below in the cavern, the military squads, were all made up of...

"Are they what I think they are?" said Franco, slowly.

Fizzy rubbed at the glass with the elbow of her WarSuit, and nodded. "Yep."

"It's just, you'd think, you know, if you were an army, and you were, you know, preparing for battle, that first you'd take off your hospital gown. You know what I mean?"

"It's the backless nature of the items that disturbs me," said Shazza.

"And those machine guns look funny," said Franco, tilting his head. He watched a squad jog across the white tiles, big black boots at contrast with the puke-green backless hospital gowns. "They don't look right. I should know. I know my machine guns, I do."

"They're too long, and thin," said Shazza, slowly.

They watched for a while. The "soldiers" had quite obviously once been patients. They wore hospital gowns, boots, and many wore cam-cream smeared liberally across faces (and even arses) in some bizarre caricature of a soldier. A squad jogged past, bearing weapons, and each of the twenty-five-strong unit pulled tall alloy trolleys containing small bags of fluid. Little wheels rattled across hospital tiles happily, and Franco scratched at his ginger goatee beard.

"I mean," he said, a man stunned, "how do you go into battle dragging a fluid or blood infusion on a trolley stand? What you gonna do when you have to run across a field, or hit the deck? It hardly makes a soldier manoeuvrable. It kinda kills a squaddie's agility."

"I was wondering," said Shazza, stroking her own weapon, "who they think they're going to fight?"

The others nodded, pondering this puzzle, and watching the manic bustle of activity below. Franco counted, and worked out maybe five to six thousand patient/soldiers stationed there. Many were sat on benches, with sergeants – these seemed to wear blue patient gowns, still backless, revealing large white and black buttocks – who waved sticks and shouted a lot, as sergeants were wont to do, and prodding at map charts on moveable whiteboards.

Around the perimeter of the cavern there seemed to be a wide running track. Along this tiled tarmac oval squads pounded, many with trolleys. One song that wafted up to the peering Combat-K soldiers made Franco grin, until Fizzy punched him on the arm, bringing a large, instant purple bruise in the shape of her knuckles...

I don't know but I've been told,
A nurse on her back is as good as gold,
If you want fun in the combat zone,
Wobble those breasts and run for home,
Every nurse I've ever met,
Had the ability to make me wet,
All that flab is fun to wobble,
Every good nurse likes a tasty gobble.


Shazza cocked her weapon. She was scowling. "So then? We gonna go and earn our pay?"

"Whoa girl!" said Franco, grabbing her arm. She stared at his fingers until he let go. "Wait just a goddamn minute there, Flash. What's the hurry? What makes you think they're the enemy? And what makes you think you can take on six-thousand armed geezers, even if they are wearing backless hospital gowns?"

"No bastard sings songs like that in *my* training unit," snarled Shazza.

"This ain't your training unit, soldier," said Franco, locking her gaze. "And anyway," he continued, voice a little more gentle, "the lads must have surely sung similar ditties during training? They all do it."

"Not in my training unit," said Shazza. "I used to bust their balls."

"Have a lot of fun training, did you?"

"We weren't there to have fun!"

"Yeah, I see that."

"Something's happening," said Fizzy, peering down into the distant cavern. "Something's coming."

They watched. Into the huge space floated five huge, graceful objects. They had rigid skeletons and cloth panels, and they carried, slung below their huge, bulbous bodies, landing gantries, each nearly three hundred metres long. Their bulks, despite their mammoth size, were swallowed by the enormity of the cavern. However, the greatest surprise was their *stealth*. They moved gracefully, silently, like Dreadnought Space-Cruisers in the vacuum of space.

"What, in the name of Rancid German Sausages, are they?" spluttered Franco. Never had he seen a more ridiculous vehicle. It was all he could do not to dribble spittle down his ginger beard.

Fizzy and Shazza shrugged, eyes wide, but Olga was staring hard, her breath laboured. "You OK, Olga?" asked Fizzy.

"Ya. I know what zese things are," she said. "They are airships, sometimes called zeppelins. And yes, they are huge, and look ridiculous, but they are silent and deadly, especially at night. Just think, you could be sat in your trenches with ze warm mug of cocoa, and one of these silent bastards disgorge a thousand infantry in utmost silence. Surprise? I think it ze big nasty shock factor making you spill that cocoa!"

"Airships," mused Franco. "I think I read something like that, as well."

They watched, curious beyond belief, as the airships lowered until the huge landing platforms were within reach, and locked in place by chains just above the ground. The soldiers started to load onto gantries via ladders, hundreds of them, all carrying their strange thin machine guns. Franco squinted, noticing for the first time that not all the soldiers seemed... quite normal.

"You see it as well?" said Olga. "This place, when we enter, it called the REC Centre. Research, Experimentation, Confinement. I think these are ze key words to describe what going on down there, what we can see."

"These patients have been here for a thousand years," said Franco.

"Experimentation," said Olga, rolling the word uneasily around her mouth. The four soldiers looked at one another. "What kind of ze experimentation, I wondering?"

"And confinement," said Shazza. "What in God's name do you need to confine?"

"Whatever it is, it's armed with machine guns and getting onto large zeppelins down there," said Franco. He puffed out his chest. "Squad, this is a lot worse than I first surmised. We must escape this place, find Keenan and Pippa, and get word back to QGM. Some *weird* shit is happening down here, but I'm pretty sure it ain't anything to do with invading junk armies."

"And you'd know that, would you, sleuth?"

"Hey, they don't call me Franco 'Sherlock Holmes' Haggis for nowt, y'know, love. Come on. This way."

They moved further along the corridor, and Franco opened the door at the end. It was some kind of storeroom, with an old, rusted service elevator at the end, at least wide enough to take three stretchered bodies along with associated medical staff.

They moved warily into the gloom. Distantly, they heard the *hum* of electricity. Somewhere in the darkness, there came a fresh fizzle of blue sparks.

"Oh no," said Franco, hurrying into the storeroom. Then he stopped by a long rack of clothes. Uniforms. Nurse uniforms. They were white, with large red crosses, some blackened in places by fire and mouldy with age, and some had holes for extra arms, legs, or other appendages. But on the whole, they were a rack of fine and dandy nurse uniforms.

"Why've we stopped?" snapped Shazza. "I thought those Convulsers were nearby?"

"Disguises," said Franco, eyes gleaming.

"Oh no," said Shazza, eyeing the nurse uniforms. "You're not getting me in one of those!"

"Our lives may depend on it," said Franco, searching through the racks and pulling free a skimpy white outfit. "Here, try this for size." He threw it to Shazza, who scowled.

"What about the WarSuits?"

"Aha! There is a dial, for just this situation. It thins the fabric of the core, makes them near invisible; less protective, I'll warrant you, but ideal for our situation. You have to remove the arms and legs, but it protects your body, your vitals. Girls, if we meet more nurses or weird doctors or whatever, we will instantly be taken as deformo nurses and allowed to pass along with our business! What better way of infiltrating the REC?"

"Infiltrating? I thought we were trying to escape?"

"That's what I meant! Come on, strip off."

Franco could barely disguise his delight, then his utter anguish, as first Fizzy and Shazza dropped packs, removed WarSuit arms and legs, then thinned their core WarSuits, revealing fetching lace underwear tastefully done in combat camouflage. This was followed by Olga, who proudly showed off her Huge Silk Bridget Knickers, designed to Bulge In Your Belly™, Disintegrate Your Donut™, Squeeze In Your Sell-u-lite™, and, ultimately, Turn A Fat Woman Into A Thin Woman™ (patent pending). Franco didn't know where to put his eyes, and focused instead on getting his bra padding just right, as he clambered into his little white PVC number.

Newly disguised, they stared at one another. Fizzy and Shazza made damn fine examples of nurses, albeit without the seemingly obligatory donut rings, peroxide-blonde hair and cherry-red lipstick. Olga had manfully squeezed into the largest uniform she could find, but her bulges bulged everywhere making her look like a hippo ballerina in the world's largest tutu. "It just doesn't fit," she wailed, not unsurprisingly.

Most entertaining of all was Franco.

He was like a big fat ginger bloke, in a dress.

"Cool," said Fizzy.

"Fetching," said Shazza.

"You think so?" Franco did a twirl, and his skirt flared up showing his white ASDA underpants.

"I wouldn't do that," said Fizzy.

"The bulge kinda ruins the effect."

"Ah yes," said Franco, "but we are disguised as *deformed* nurses." He beamed, as if that answered all their problems. Picking up his shotgun, he waved the three squaddies over towards the elevator... as a background *hum* filled the air and the double doors swung open with *fizzes* and *pops* and *crackles* of discharged electricity. There were Convulsers, their hands revealing ECT pads hot-wired to battery packs. They were grinning, like a pack of wolves that's cornered a deer, their huge round hairless heads distended and each one curiously unique in its blobby shape, as if each had been hot-moulded from a piece of putty.

There were rather a lot of them.

The three women glared at Franco, then back at the Convulsers.

The *pack*, numbering perhaps fifteen, maybe twenty, it was hard to tell in the gloom with so many fizzing, popping electrical sparking appendages – it was like being trapped in an electricity generator – they squeezed and *flowed* through the doors, filling the end of the room with a bobbing, jigging frenzy.

"What now?" said Fizzy from the corner of her mouth.

Franco had gone white. His last meeting with a Convulser had *hurt*...

"I think," said Shazza, also from the corner of her mouth, "that we need to run."

"On three," said Olga.

"One," said Shazza.

"Two," said Fizzy.

The Convulsers screamed, in unity, as one, and huge arcs of electricity sprang from their ECT hands and their thin wiry bodies leapt forward, and they sprinted with awesome, unbelievable, inhuman *speed* towards the group –

Franco's D5 discharged, but shells were swallowed easily by the squirming, sparking throng...

"Run!" he screamed and, turning, found he was alone. The three women were already a good twenty feet ahead and still accelerating towards the service elevator doors.

Franco pumped his arms, as an arc of electricity sprang out, and stung him a savage and violent shock to the arse.

He leapt a foot in the air, and ran faster. It seemed the most sensible thing to do…

CAM WAS A PopBot, technically a personalised servant model. However, during earlier adventures, he had been fitted with Put Down™ War Technology, something for which Franco endlessly teased the little PopBot. However, in the real world it meant Cam could, at the expense of battery power, processor cycles, and even hardware longevity, *channel* everything into a singular process in order to achieve a distilled end result. It would leave him useless until recharged, or rebooted, but that was a price he would have to pay.

Cam ran down a series of menus, disabling function after function after function. He shut down processor cycles and channelled all power into his thrusters and, from his prone position on the sand, stretched his multi-motors to their operational limits, as Snake pulled the triggers on the D5 shotgun and the weapon discharged, so that Cam accelerated at a rate faster than a striking serpent.

Shells howled, and Cam interjected himself between Keenan's head and the hot, howling metal. Shrapnel screamed off in random directions and Keenan, sure he was dead, blinked a few times until his gaze fastened on the smoking shell of Cam, half-buried in the sand. Keenan growled, and his right straight caught Snake a savage blow to the nose, his right hook cannoned Snake's temple, and his right kick lifted the shocked man from his feet, depositing him in the sand. Keenan reached down, took the D5, and as Snake tried to formulate words with twisted lips, Keenan rammed the butt into Snake's good eye, slamming the man backwards into unconsciousness.

Keenan allowed a long breath to ease between his lips, whistling. His gaze fell on the dead body of Maximux, then he whirled on Ed, who was crawling across the sand in the opposite direction to Keenan. He strode over to Ed, and kicked him up the arse.

"Going somewhere?"

"Don't kill me, Keenan!" There was fear in his eyes, a deep understanding of what this enraged man before him could achieve.

"Why not?" Keenan's voice was low, beyond rage. He pulled free his Widow Maker tobacco, and rolled a cigarette, D5 cradled against his arm. He surveyed the desert surroundings, and welcomed – temporarily – the heat from the fast rising sun. "You were quite happy to slot a few shells between *my* ears. You, and that bag of shit carcass over there."

"No, Keenan. *Please.*"

Keenan lit his smoke, and enjoyed it for a few moments before hoisting the weapon in one hand and lowering the barrels to touch Ed's head. "You care nothing for stopping the junks, for saving millions, perhaps trillions, of people from certain death. All you think about is the cash in your damn pocket, here, and now. I can be the judge and jury on this one, no problem. I find you guilty. And I sentence you to *death*."

"No," came a tiny voice. It was Cam. In the sand. His casing was drifting smoke.

Cursing, Keenan ran over to the small machine and hoisted it in his hand. He weighed Cam thoughtfully, and there came a sprinkling of weak orange lights.

"You did a brave thing, little buddy."

"I will be useless – until recharged," said Cam.

"I'll see what I can do."

"Don't kill them, Keenan."

"Why the hell not?" Keenan's fury broke free. "They would have murdered us, both of us, Cam. And all for money." He spat in the sand. "Mercenaries. Shit-heads. Scum of the fucking earth. We put our own lives in further danger by taking them along; can't you see?"

"Not like this," said Cam. "Not in anger. Never in anger."

Keenan cursed, and gently placed Cam in his pack. Then he moved back to Ed, and stared at the cringing man for a long, long time. Finishing his cigarette, he ground the butt under his boot and threw a tiny silver filament onto the sand. Ed stared at it, then back at Keenan.

"That's a SnapWire," Ed said, slowly.

"Yep. Put it on."

"I'm not putting that on! If you try and escape, it'll cut off your hands!"

"Yeah." Keenan grinned. "I know."

"Suck my dick, Keenan."

Keenan's boot crashed Ed's face, and when Ed came around he was sat back-to-back with Snake. They both had SnapWires around their wrists, and the sun was burning their skin something horrid.

Keenan was surveying the crashed 6X6 Giga-Buggy. It was battered, tatty, the chassis a little bent. Leaning inside, he flicked several switches and the Buggy blipped and beeped. Suddenly, a TurboRam shot from the roof, flipping the car back onto its wheels where it creaked on damaged suspension, rocking from the impact. Slowly, on greased hydraulics, the TurboRam retracted back into the roof and Keenan looked to the sky, silently thanking the gods for such a vehicle.

"I didn't know it could do that," said Snake, softly.

"You should have read the manual, boy."

Keenan climbed into the cockpit, and started the engine. Fumes belched, the engine roared, and with an odd whining and rhythmic clicking the Buggy settled into some semblance of its former self. Keenan hit a switch, and armoured segments of roof folded back; the final two, near the rear wheels, stuck and started to grind in imitation pain. Keenan switched it off, pulled free Cam, and set him on the dashboard. He searched the Buggy, pulling free a recharge lead, and after a few moments of fiddling, plugged Cam in. Rainbow lights flickered across Cam's shell.

"Thank you, Keenan."

"Don't mention it. How long to recharge?"

"Not for that. For Ed and Snake's lives."

Keenan waved his hand, and climbed from the vehicle, dragging first Ed to the rear of the Buggy and sitting him down with a slap. He attached the SnapWire to the Buggy's roll-cage, and repeated the process with Snake, who was groggy from his beating. Both men glared sullenly at Keenan, who'd lit a cigarette. He blew smoke at them, and Ed coughed.

"What now?" said Cam.

"The Junkala King told me to seek the Silver River. But I've been studying the PAD maps of the planet, and it doesn't make sense. This is a normal Earth Standard planet, Y7. All the rivers are natural water, that's why it's so inhabitable, why they built the Sick World here."

"So what are you thinking?"

"North, where the desert meets the sea, there is a long arm of weird geological strata; a glacier, still retreating to the poles but able to survive the edges of the desert sun. It's the only anomaly I can find on this whole ball of rock. On the maps it's named Tekarren Ka, but translated, that means *Silglace*. That's my only lead."

"You're wrong with the translation," said Cam. "Silglace is an abbreviation of the literal. It means *Silver Glacier*, or more precisely, *The glacier which has silver at its core*. You've found something there, Keenan."

"Hmm." He rubbed at his stubble, and winced at his battered body's aches and pains. "I feel like I'm clutching at straws."

"Still no comms with Franco or Pippa?"

"No. Nothing. Not even QGM or LongWave."

"You want to explore?"

Keenan shrugged. "It's on a direct bearing towards Pippa's BaseCamp, so we might as well start there. If the Junkala King was indeed who he said he was, if this whole damn situation isn't just a prick tease, then it's the only viable option I can see."

Snake laughed, from the back of the Buggy. "Fucking heroes, out to save the world again." He growled as Keenan lowered the D5 to his face.

"I suggest you shut up."

"Or what? You'll blow my head off?"

"Exactly," said Keenan, cool eyes meeting Snake's. "You're court-martialled, son. Your days in Combat-K are over. You know it, I know it, and Cam here, property of QGM in wartime, fucking knows it. When it's upheld, you'll be Little Man. And Little Man dies as easy as any other Non-Mil."

Snake gritted his teeth, muscles on his jaws standing out, but said no more.

Keenan hit the MonkeyMan SatNav, which blipped into existence. He punched in co-ordinates from the PAD, and the Buggy's console sprang into life.

"Follow the desert north-north-east for two hundred and fifty miles," said the SatNav. "Then take a right. Ooh."

"Great," muttered Keenan, slammed the Buggy in gear, and wheel-spun through the sand.

A ROCKY MOUNTAIN range forced them north through the sand and rock fields, evidence of millennia of the terrifying Rockfalls. Keenan drove in silence, face grim, mulling over his encounter not just with Elana, but the Junkala King of a different age. Cam hummed to himself, apparently happy with the recharge juice flowing through batteries and circuits, whilst in the back, wired to the roll-cage, Snake and Ed sat in sullen silence, eyes dark rimmed, faces blank.

They pounded over harsh desert landscape, eventually circumnavigating the mountain range and turning northeasterly to compensate for navigational deviations. The landscape started to change, with more harsh, spiked plants, cacti and the occasional gnarled tree, some towering to several hundred feet in height, solitary sentinels stretching aged limbs for the sun and wearing their bark like a cancer.

No more imminent Rockfalls threatened them under the harsh, beating sun.

"I need a piss," said Snake, eventually.

"Piss in your pants," said Keenan without turning. He had one elbow on the Buggy's door, a breeze whipping his short hair, a smoke dangling between his lips.

"They say smoking kills you," said Ed, after another few miles.

"Not as quickly as a D5 in the mouth. I'll take my chances, thanks very much."

"I'm serious, Keenan, I need a piss."

And I'm serious, Snake, piss in your pants."

"You have no compassion, brother."

"I have plenty of compassion for the people I like. You don't fall into that category. And don't call me your fucking brother; if I was any relation of yours, I would have executed our mother shortly after your birth."

They continued, the Buggy hammering across rocks and through ruts and the occasional wadi. Keenan kept an eye on the console readouts, aware the engine temperature was creeping into the red.

"You're going to have to stop soon," said Cam, voice low.

"I know. I'm pushing too hard."

"And *then* can I have a piss?" said Snake.

Keenan slammed the Buggy to the right, slewing through sand and dust and shale, which spat in a wide arc like scattering rainfall. The Buggy crunched to a stop beside a towering, solitary tree, and Keenan turned in his seat, glaring at Snake.

"Are you going to whine all the way to the Silglace, Snake, or do I use the BoneStapler from the medical box to staple your fucking mouth shut."

"I'm bored."

"Nice to meet you, Bored, that's an unusual name. Some people call me Killer, for obvious reasons. Now. Keep your damn mouth shut and I won't be forced to put a bullet in your spine."

"He's cracking," said Ed.

Snake nodded, smiling. "You're a fool, Keenan."

"You reckon?" Keenan climbed from the Buggy and stretched his back, twisting in both directions to loosen tense muscles. Pain battered him dully, like punches through a pillow, reminding him of recent exploits. He could picture Elana in his mind; one minute alive, the next squashed flat. Instant death. He grimaced. She had been his key to this place... and she'd been taken away in the blink of an eye. Just like we all go, he thought. Shit!

As Keenan stretched his legs, Snake prattled on, hands suspended slightly above his head, his single dark orb following Keenan like a missile tracking a target. "There's so much about this place you do not understand."

"What, and you've got a degree in the place?"

"I've been here before," said Snake, voice quiet.

Keenan turned, stared at the one-eyed mercenary. "Yeah, right. Bull and Shit, mate."

"I swear it, Keenan. It was a long time ago, well, not by the standards of this place. But I have been here; on a mission. Far north, in the ice and snow wastelands."

Keenan moved close, and offered Snake a gun in the face. "And what pearls of wisdom did you learn whilst you were down here?"

"It's busier than you think."

"Meaning?"

"The DropBots got it wrong, Keenan. They scanned the area, but were... *misled*. There's something here of incredible power. Something of which you have no understanding; it could crush you like a leaf in a storm."

"You talk of VOLOS?"

Snake went quiet, his head dropping a little. Then he looked up, and his single eye gleamed. He sniffed, and gazed around at the desert. "He's everywhere. Can see everything. This is his planet. His world. His..." Snake laughed, "his *Sick* World."

"What else do you know?"

"Hey, wouldn't you like me to spill."

Keenan slammed the D5's butt into Snake's head, and the mercenary was punched to one side, hanging, suspended by the SnapWire which drew eager blood from his wrists. Snake coughed, and spat on the Buggy's floor. Then he looked up and grinned. "That's the spirit," he said. "Go on, beat the shit out of me. Then we'll see who QGM court-martial. You getting all this, Cam? You recording it for your *employers?*"

Cam said nothing, and Keenan glanced at the little PopBot.

"What's he talking about?"

"I am required by QGM Law to report such things."

"This just gets better and better."

"We're in a State of War," said Snake. "There are rules. I may have broken them. But so have you."

Keenan, eyes narrowed, moved close to Snake. "You listen to me, shithead, between us lovers there are no rules no more. I'll do what I have to do, to get the job done. You tried to kill me, and no doubt would have done the same to the other squads without a second thought; that makes you expendable. Now, I advise you to keep your mouth shut, or I swear by everything I hold holy, not even Cam will drag me off you."

Snake gave a nod, and stayed silent.

Keenan strode off, pissing behind the towering tree, allowing his temper to slowly dissipate. Cam buzzed alongside him. "You want some advice?"

"Fuck off."

"Don't be like that, Keenan."

"Is that true? About having to report to QGM?"

"It's hardwired into all domestic models," said Cam, his voice uneasy. "It's so the military can commandeer every AI in the event of war. We are now in the event of war. I am, technically, no longer your property."

"So you obey QGM?"

"Yes."

"And if they were to order you to kill me?"

"Technically, I'd have to kill you."

"So, you'd betray me, as well?" He looked sideways at Cam.

"Of course not, Keenan! I'm yours, and we've been through a lot of shit together. Anyway, are you forgetting the Spinal Logic Cubes so quickly? QGM don't need me in order to carry out murder; they can spike you from ten billion miles away!"

Keenan leant against the tree and lit another cigarette. He stared off at distant mountains, huge and grey and orange, shaking his head, lost in thought. "This place is so wrong," he muttered. "What's going on here, Cam? Why did the DropBots fail to spot anything?"

"It seems to be linked to this VOLOS character."

"What is he? A robot? Deranged AI? An ancient king? I don't understand. And where is his centre of operations?"

"Something's coming."

Keenan stomped out his cigarette and scanned the desert. "Where? A buggy? A hovership?"

"Something substantially... bigger."

Keenan caught the tone in Cam's voice, and shielded his eyes. Then his teeth clamped tight shut as twenty mammoth SlamShips approached with a fast drone and whizzed overhead, massive, square black undercarriages flickering with green lights against matt black alloy. Keenan watched, as momentarily they blocked out the sun, and then they were gone leaving trails of ozone and exhaust vapour.

"Did they clock us?"

"Highly probable," said Cam. "They're Mk IVs. Old, in fact, obsolete in military terms. If we had a decent Hornet it'd take out all twenty in a blink; but we don't have a Hornet so it's totally academic. Here, in this place, now, they're the most advanced hardware I've witnessed. They saw us. And they pose a significant threat."

"To whom?"

"Our mission," said Cam.

"Yeah, right, our mission is to explore. To collect samples. Our mission is a piss-steam mission. It's a lame gig, buddy."

"Unless we find something, Keenan. And you found something. You found a junk who told you of VOLOS; you found a link to the civilisation we hunt, the civilisation that threatens the very fabric of Quad Gal. Keenan, we need to get this data out to QGM. We need to establish contact."

"All comms are down," said Keenan, quietly.

"I think I can re-establish contact."

"How?"

"Those ships," said Cam. "That *warfleet*. They will have components. I can cobble something together."

"You mean DekHelix Pro-Blag LightYear Projectors?"

"Yes," said Cam. "Something like that."

"You said warfleet. I'd have to agree, it looks like that. What disturbs me, Cam, my little tennis ball buddy, is where are they going? And more importantly, who are they going to fight? Ships like that – they can carry, what? Eight, nine thousand infantry?"

"More like ten."

"This game is fast changing, Cam."

"Are we still heading for the Silglace?"

"For now. I want to track this Silver River. Can you log the trajectory of those ships? We can look them up next, put a few more pieces of the puzzle in place."

"Not only can I plot trajectories, now I've scanned mass and dimension I can track them. Theoretically. Unless VOLOS has something else up his sleeve."

"Good boy. Keep an eye on them, Cam. I can do without ten thousand enemy squaddies up my arse when I'm not expecting it."

"What about establishing contact with QGM?"

"All in good time," said Keenan. "Come. Let's get back to the Buggy. Snake and Ed are looking bored, and a little bit red. You got some sun cream? Thought not, a shame; we'll just have to let the fuckers *burn*."

\* \* \*

THEY DROVE FOR eight hours, with occasional breaks where Cam would extract water – or a thick, bitter, honeyed approximation of water – from narrow-leaved spiky plants with an interesting organic disposition: the ability to fire poisoned barbs. They filled water bottles in dribbles, and bemoaned the harsh pounding of the sun.

Keenan, head shaded by his EBH in desert camouflage colours, watched as Snake and Ed slowly broiled in the back of the Buggy, moaning and whining, their pale white skin, too long idle in brothels and disreputable bars, graduating through scarlet shades to a bright and painful lobster red. Ed's facial tattoos did funny things when combined with the scorched torture of reddened skin, making him look considerably demonic. Ed complained long and hard about this perceived abuse.

As the MonkeyMan SatNav guided them with the unerring accuracy of a digital primate, they crested a rise in rolling, undulating dunes which seemed to fill the world with apparently endless fluctuations, an ocean of sand, a desolation of desert.

Keenan caressed the brakes, and the Buggy slowed, squeaked, and stopped. He killed the engine.

Below spread the ocean.

"Wow," said Ed, eyeing the sparkling expanse of rolling blue. "Where the desert meets the sea. Romantic."

Keenan glanced up at the sun, noting its position. "I'd say we have another hour of daylight."

"So what?" said Snake, weary now, his body slumped against the pressure of his SnapWires.

"I'm thinking of that rock rainfall; and wondering if it's attached, somehow, to the night."

"You think we need shelter?"

"I think so," said Keenan. He eyed the MonkeyMan. Fifty miles, to this so-called Silglace. But would it provide any form of shelter? Improbable. They had no way of knowing. "Cam, you want to scoot ahead, see if you can find a place to hide if God begins dropping boulders on our heads?"

"Sure thing, Kee. Will you be all right with these two idiots?"

Keenan smiled. "Oh yes. They are my... friends."

Cam zipped off, and Keenan cruised down to the edges of the ocean, where blue-silver waters had smoothed the beach in a massive crescent of flat, damp, solid sand. After the bumps and bashes of the rocky desert region, this hard-packed platter was like a fine racetrack and Keenan put his foot to the floor. The Buggy growled, surging ahead, picking up speed. They slammed along the flat beach, a salt-smell of ocean in their nostrils, the sun gradually lowering over the horizon and allowing green tinges from the still-invisible moon to filter into the scene. The ocean's rolling waves turned from blue-silver to blue-green, and the desert took on an alien hue, giving the Combat-K men no doubt they were on an esoteric world. A junk world. A sick world.

"Great," snapped Ed, as they powered along.

"What's that?" Keenan did not turn.

"There's a storm coming."

Keenan turned, could see towering dark clouds in the distance. He grimaced. "Is it coming this way?"

They powered along, and Keenan glanced back after a few minutes. The blackness filling the sky was closer. They heard the deep bass rumble of thunder. Green lightning flickered. Static seemed to fill the air.

"It is getting closer," said Ed.

"Shit," muttered Keenan, boot edging lower on the accelerator. The Buggy surged ahead, engine howling, and reached its maximum speed. Keenan watched the temp gauge. It touched the red.

"It's coming in fast," said Ed, a note of panic caressing his voice, and Keenan turned. The whole sky was black now, as on the opposite horizon the sun dipped out of sight, leaving a surreal, orange glow painting the rim of the world.

"How far?" came Snake's easy drawl.

"Twenty miles."

"We'll never make it."

"You don't say?"

"You must untie us," said Snake, face locked to Keenan. "When the storm hits, the rocks will bury this car. By leaving us Snapped up, well, it's nothing short of murder. It's a War Crime, Keenan."

"No."

"That's plain evil!" snapped Ed. "We'll die out here if you don't take off the wires!"

"Then you'll die," said Keenan, settling back into his seat and watching the needle creep ever more into the red. Yeah, he thought sourly. We'll all die. We'll all die when this heap of shit decides to weld its engine into one huge lump of useless alloy.

They powered along. Thunder rumbled, deafening now. And with it came a distant *pitter patter*, a tribal drumbeat of falling rocks. Both Ed and Snake were staring out the back of the Buggy as Keenan screamed along the flat beach, the ocean crashing to his left –

And realisation dawned.

There were no craters on the beach. It was flat, unmarked, devoid of rocks. Which meant one of two things; either the Rockfall storm had never ventured this far to the coast before – unlikely, after judging its widespread ferocity the previous night; or that, just possibly, it was following them.

"Shit!"

Cam slammed out of the fading twilight like a cannon shell, and forced an equilibrium beside Keenan's head. "The Silglace is up ahead, Keenan. We're on the correct trajectory. And you were right, there's a river that runs deep into the heart of the glacier – it's silver, a river of mercury!"

"But?"

"How'd you guess? It's guarded."

"By our friends in the SlamShips?"

"No. By Cryo Medics with IceTanks."

"By…" Keenan stared hard at Cam. "You're pulling my bell, right?"

"I swear to you, Keenan. IceTanks. They distil shells from the air, from the sea spray, freeze them, and fire them. There's twenty of the behemoths, they're real old, real… odd. And fifty of the… well, I'll call them soldiers for want of a better description. They have weapons."

"Machine guns?"

"Um. Sort of."

"What's a 'sort-of-machine-gun'?"

"They fire mercury shells. They seem to be based around… thermometers."

"What?" But all conversation was lost as Ed gave an animal howl and the storm – raging behind the speeding Buggy like a solid wall of tsunami, rocks pounding the beach from a raging torrent of skies and smashing it from a flat smooth racetrack into a garbled pebble-dash of geological mush – howled with a cacophony of thunder and an incredible dazzling light-show of crackling, discharging lightning…

"Ten miles," snarled Keenan.

The Buggy's needle touched the top of the red. Steam curled from the edges of the bonnet. The Buggy's speed very gradually, began to fall…

"What are you doing?" screamed Snake over the noise of the storm. Tribal drums filled the air, deafening and terrible, like God playing with a set of world-sized tom-toms to the accompaniment of devil-run acid-house factory-hell.

Keenan pumped the accelerator, his boot stamping in rising panic. But the Buggy continued to slow.

And the Rockfall storm swept over them...

# CHAPTER EIGHT
# PARA-MEDICS

PIPPA, BETEZH, MEL and Miller backtracked fast under the screeching advancing buffer blades of the wild-eyed cleaner, who in herself looked suddenly wild, elemental, a million miles removed from any semblance of normal organic life…

"I must apologise," screamed the cleaner over the roaring of the buffer-turned-killing machine, "but you're dirtying up my corridor! You must be swept clean! Buffed to a shine! Sucked away! Scourged!" Cackling, the cleaner swung the slicer left and right, humming through the air like a bad trip, an out-of-control helicopter, and the group scattered backwards in panic.

Pippa caught Betezh's attention, and gestured; Betezh gave a tight-lipped nod.

He ran right, slamming into the wall and diving into a fast roll past humming blades as Pippa lifted, then hefted, her yukana sword, and launched it like a spear. The blade flashed through the air, and the cleaner moved fast, but not fast enough. The blade slammed through her external pumping heart, showering the floor with a splatter of blood. There came an "oof" of shock, and the deadly buffing machine slowed with a whine, left her fingers, clattered against the wall, shearing bricks and mortar in a shower of powdered debris, then gradually fell still with strangled *shrings*. The deadly blades lay motionless, battered and twisted.

The cleaner hit the floor, bleeding, grunting, and Pippa walked forward with the D4 aimed at her head. As Pippa gazed down, the cleaner fished in a leather bag at her hip, pulling free a fresh oiled and slippery heart. She fumbled for a minute, nearly dropping the organ, then unclipped the severed heart from her neck chain and went suddenly blue. With clumsy fingers, breathing suspended, she fitted the new heart in place and it stuttered, fluttering like an encased butterfly, shuddered and started to beat. The cleaner took a deep, exaggerated breath, easing herself from blue-tinged panic into calm, then turned and glared at Pippa.

"That damn well hurt!" she snapped.

Pippa lowered the D4, and poked the cleaner in the teeth. "Not as much as this will. Now listen, you freak, you're going to give me some answers because I'm fast getting sick of this place. Understand?"

"I will tell you nothing!"

"Then I'll blow off your stupid head."

"Do it!" snarled the cleaner. "You think I care? You think you can torture me more than my current existence? Well fuck you, city girl, there's nothing you can do that hasn't already been done. Torture me, rape me, cut out my organs…" her eyes gleamed. "Kill me. It matters nothing." She snarled again, like a caged animal, and spat at Pippa.

Pippa glanced up to Betezh, who gave a shrug.

"What we gonna do with her? She's mad as a brush."

Betezh winked. "Hey. Leave this one to me." He moved closer, scratching his head, then crouched beside the fury-filled cleaner who was frothing at the lips. "So then, love," he said, "we can torture and kill you? Yeah?"

"Go to hell!"

Betezh nodded, stood, stretched, turned his back on the group, and there came the sound of an unzipping fly. "Nice floor this," he said, conversationally, and started to urinate against the wall. "Must have taken you hours of work to get such a lovely shine."

"No! Wait! What are you doing?"

"It's so gleaming," said Betezh, amidst the sounds of tinkling, "so perfect, that you could almost see your own face in it. Oops! Oh damn, look here, I seem to have inadvertently pissed all over your nice clean floor." He zipped up his flies and turned, grinning.

The cleaner was incandescent with rage. "You, you, you –" she snarled.

"Me? Little old me?" Betezh rubbed at his belly, then grinned over at Pippa. "You know what Pippa, all that spam I had for supper last night has finally worked its way through my complicated bowel system. And you know what? I think I need to take a long hard dump, right here, right now."

"Noooooooo!" howled the cleaner. "Not on my floor! Not on my polished masterpiece! It took me a *thousand years* to get it looking like that! Don't defecate on my artwork, you bastard's bastard."

Betezh undid his belt, and disarmed his WarSuit rear-end flap. "So you'll talk? You'll give us answers to questions?"

"Yes!" sobbed the cleaner suddenly, "yes, yes, please don't shit on my floor. I'll tell you anything. *Anything!*"

"OK then," nodded Betezh sagely, and fastened his belt again. "Just remember, nutso. You can die, you can be dismembered, you can disintegrate... but I can always pluck up the energy to defecate."

Sobbing, the cleaner nodded and covered her eyes with her hands. Pippa sidled over to Betezh.

"Nice," she said. "Slick."

"Why, thank you."

"Only you could have dreamed up that particular angle."

"It worked, didn't it?"

"Like the best toilet flush in the world," said Pippa with a smile. "Now, Little Miss Sparkle. We want to know what's going on here, in this place, in this Sick World. You've been polishing the floor for a thousand years. You must have seen some changes."

"Oh yes," said the cleaner, climbing slowly, dejectedly, to her feet and rubbing away tears. She looked down, poking at her external heart for a moment, then focused on Pippa. "We were happy here, you know. In the beginning."

"You mean when this place was Sick World?"

"Yes. It was grand, the opening, when the Mammoth DropShips came speeding down from space. They'd built the hospitals and research centres, thousands of them, dotted all over the planet. This was going to be the premier place to recover from your illness. This was going to be another Eden, a Paradise World for the sick, the lame, the injured, the diseased. Humans and aliens came together in perfect harmony with only one objective: to get well again."

"You were here, then?" said Betezh.

"Yes," nodded the cleaner. She looked off, lost in distant memories, and she pulled out a handkerchief and blew her nose with great noise and much gusto. Her nose came away from her face in her hanky, and carefully she cleaned out the nostrils, then slotted it back into place with a *click.* "It worked. For years it worked. We were all happy. But then the... problems began."

"Like?"

"Earthquakes, first. They destroyed several of the hospitals, and a number of patients and doctors died. It was terrifying, but eminent Quad-Gal geologists couldn't discover fault-lines to explain the destruction. They said the planet, Krakken IV, did not conform to normal geological models. It was unique. An anomaly. They were stumped."

"What happened next?" asked Pippa, D4 still trained on the cleaner. She seemed submissive, subdued, but Pippa had witnessed how fast she could accelerate into a deadly mode of attack. Pippa was taking no chances, no matter how feeble the cleaner appeared.

"Then came the *pulse*," said the cleaner. She looked up, eyes bright, linking with Pippa. And in those eyes, those dark eyes, Pippa could read the freakish woman's *age*, an age which tumbled down through the centuries, long centuries of watching, of polishing, of cleaning the wards and the hospital floors... "The pulse *echoed* across the planet. That's the best way I can describe it. It destroyed *everything* electrical, across the whole world, and then people fell ill, I mean fast, within hours, and after six hours thousands were dying, vomiting blood and their own internal organs at their feet, huge sores spreading like an external cancer across their skin. Many thought it was some age-old virus, some ancient canker released to cleanse the planet. We sent out a Panic Pulse to Quad-Gal, and they sent in the ships on a one-hour drop-and-exit rescue band."

"You had one hour to reach the escape ships?"

"Yes." The cleaner nodded, deflating. "Many of us didn't make it; couldn't make it. There were sites, but millions of us were left behind."

"Doctors and nurses? Patients?"

"Yes," said the cleaner.

"Enough," said Miller.

Pippa turned, to see the Health and Safety Officer holding a Techrim 11mm pistol, aimed directly at the cleaner's head.

"Wait…" began Pippa, but Miller fired the weapon with a short bark, a bullet slapping through the air and entering the cleaner's face just above the nose, destroying an eye socket and ploughing on into the brain before exiting in a smash of mushrooming brain and skull shards. A splatter hit the wall. The cleaner stood for a moment, then one leg buckled and she hit the ground and Pippa moved and whirled fast, right hand smashing out to knock the gun from Miller's fist. It clattered down the sterile corridor, and Pippa leapt into the air, one boot catching Miller under the chin and slamming him back with a grunt and *crack* of damaged vertebrae. He landed, whimpering, and Pippa landed beside him in a crouch, the D4 shotgun pushed into his face.

Nobody else had moved.

Betezh stepped forward and squatted opposite Pippa. Slowly, he reached out and moved the barrel of the shotgun, meeting her gaze. "Don't kill him. Not yet." He transferred his gaze to Miller's scrunched and scowling face. "Now then, little man, what on earth did you go and do that for?"

"You're all going to die!" hissed Miller. "You shouldn't fucking *be here!* This is a sacred place. A holy place!"

"What are you talking about?" Pippa eased up, uncoiling from her crouch. Miller did not respond, and she stamped down, heel slamming Miller's sternum with a thud that made him gasp, doubling up, hands clutching his chest as he curled into a ball. Pippa grabbed him, hauling him whimpering to his feet. "Talk, motherfucker."

"Go to hell."

"Why are you here?"

"To make sure you die." Miller smiled then, blood on his teeth. "You couldn't do it, could you? You couldn't land the DropShip, take the rock and soil samples, then clear off. Oh no. Not Combat K, experts in shoving their noses into things that don't concern them! You had to poke about, had to try and uncover the secrets of Sick World... the secret of the *junks*..."

Suddenly, the corridor shook as pulses slammed through the building. Lights swung frantically against the ceiling and a window cracked, then splintered, glass flying out across the corridor in lethal knife shards. A sound seemed to roar from nowhere, filling the world with a cacophony of rumbling white noise as the whole world shook and the building shook and the word *earthquake* came to Pippa's dry, fear-lined mouth, and for a moment she released her grip on Miller –

Who ran for it, sprinting away down the corridor, boots pounding and head low.

Pippa's shotgun boomed, shells whistling past Miller's head, nicking his ear. Pippa dropped to one knee to steady herself against the undulating floor. She aimed again as Betezh grabbed the Techrim and pumped bullets after the fleeing figure of Miller; but he whirled madly into an adjacent corridor, and was gone.

"Shall we go after him?" shouted Betezh.

"We've got more important problems!" screamed Pippa, and turned back, glancing at Mel. "Come on! We have to get out of here!"

They ran down the corridor, the floor tilting and sending them all crashing into a wall lined with windows. Outside, they saw, or thought they saw, the reason for the quake. There were ten huge SLAM Cruisers parked, old ones, the original Mk Is, and six of them were lifting into the air, huge black bodies reminiscent of insect-shells, mammoth oil-fuelled jets pounding the concrete and landscape into a blackened choking mash of scorched fumes. Fires roared across hospital walls, smashing windows. The whole hospital was buckling to one side, and Pippa saw walls collapsing like falling dominoes.

"They've landed too close!" she screamed. "The land is unstable! Everything's going to collapse! They're *causing* the damn quake!"

"We've got to get out of the hospital," panted Betezh. A wall of fire roared towards them as a SLAM Cruiser banked and they ducked as flames slammed through skewed windows above their heads, spraying them with hot shattered glass. They crawled below the fire, then got up and ran again, sliding along more corridors and into an abandoned ward. Beds had been tossed around like confetti, and they sprinted, hurdling fallen chairs and desks, upturned beds and a slurry of twisted sheets and scattered bedpans. The hospital was twisting and rocking, and Pippa realised it couldn't be the SLAM Cruisers causing the upheaval – they just didn't have the power… this was an earthquake, a real old-fashioned nasty Miss Nature showing the world what She was capable of bastard. The SLAM Cruisers were *running away*… they were evacuating the area. They were clearing the hospital of deviants, of nurses and doctors, of patients and aliens…

Pippa grabbed Betezh, intuition flooding her. "We've got to get on one of those ships."

"Why?" snarled Betezh, face blackened and shaggy eyebrows singed from a close encounter with fire.

"What that cleaner said, about the planet destroying the hospitals, as if something ancient was trying to rid Sick World of its parasite. Maybe *we're* the new parasite... maybe the planet wants rid of us?"

"So they're running away?"

"Yeah!"

"Let's run away with them!" snarled Betezh.

They sprinted, Mel pounding along behind, claws gouging hospital tiles, pus drooling from disjointed fangs. Through more destroyed wards they careered, reckless now, filled with panic as the rumbling went on and on and on. To one side, a whole wall of the hospital disintegrated, falling away in a tumble of bricks and a mushroom cloud of dust, roaring, roaring like a vast dying animal and allowing cool air to rush in, smacking the Combat-K squaddies with *threat*.

Betezh grabbed Pippa's arm, pointing above the deafening noise. "Stairs," he mouthed. They turned, fighting the slew of the listing hospital building. Behind them, through the now-open wall, five or six storeys of height fell away.

Pippa ran, her boots starting to slide with the tilt of the building. It was like being in a jug, fighting against being tipped free to fall a hundred feet to an instant and crushing death. Grinding her teeth, sweat stinging her eyes, Pippa pushed on, reaching the head of the stairs. There came a clang, and inches beside Pippa something huge and vast and metal slammed through the wall trailing wrist-thick cables, howled across the floor in showers of sparks and disappeared from the building-sized window. Cables whipped and snapped around her head, lacerating her face, and Pippa cowered, Betezh and Mel cowering with her, until the cables had vanished with a final *twang*.

"What the hell was that?" she panted.

"Service elevator," panted Betezh, eyes wide in awe. "It nearly took your whole head off!"

"Great," spat Pippa, and they leapt into the head of the stairwell through double-swinging doors which shrieked in protest, and the vision that met them induced instant vertigo. It was all wrong, all twisted, all corrupt. Originally a stairwell in a square shaft, steps leading progressively down, spiralling against all four walls, now it was buckled and broken, with some stairs on the walls, some walls now forming a death-slippery slope, some gaping holes like maws with brick teeth waiting to mash unwelcome bones, and twisted, broken iron railings sticking like splinters and spears throughout the whole mix. Below, a heavy dust pall floated, and somewhere fire roared.

"It's the only way," panted Betezh.

Outside, more jets screamed as Mk I SLAM Cruisers ignited engines and took to the air, fleeing the savage quake... and the quake itself, rather than abating, seemed to be rising in fury, getting into its stride, pounding the earth and the hospital with elemental fists that promised no release, no surrender, no escape until everything was crushed and broken and –

Dead.

"I'll go first," shouted Pippa over the roar.

"No. Let me." Betezh pushed ahead and, sheathing his weapons, started to descend the treacherous slope, grabbing twisted iron and buckled masonry that shook and trembled and broke under questing hands.

Pippa followed, and instantly realised her error but it was too late, she was on the jagged death-slope, fingers digging into broken brick cavities, boots slipping and sliding on walls and half-severed stairs. Shit, she thought. Mel was behind her. Above her. If Mel fell, she'd take Pippa and Betezh with her.

Pippa glanced up, to see Mel's huge bulk descending, hand and feet talons gouging brickwork and sending dust and stones rattling into the abyss below.

They hit a section of steps, and ran on the rectangular twisted platforms, but the steps soon fell away into a broken wall. Still the roaring of the quake filled them with terror and Pippa realised she wanted to cry because she always understood death would come, but not like this, not trapped in a thousand-year-old decrepit abandoned hospital before she had her chance to say her goodbyes to the people she loved...

Keenan. His face flashed into her mind, surprising her.

A bad taste filled her mouth. "Shit," she said, and almost cannoned into Betezh, knocking him into the chasm over which he loomed.

"Where now?" she said.

"Down," snapped Betezh. "We sit on our packs, and we slide."

Pippa squinted through the dust. "That must be four storeys, Betezh. Sixty or seventy feet. We'll break our legs!"

"Then we'll have to break our legs." Without waiting, Betezh sat on his pack and kicked free down the insanely steep slope. Cursing, Pippa pulled her pack around, sat on it, and kicked off into the gloom and the dust. The smell of fire filled her nostrils and she realised, above them, behind them, something was burning. She glanced back, to see something large, on fire, shrieking with flames, howling down towards all three as they slid into the gloomy shaft on their makeshift pack sleds...

"Shit!"

She saw Mel glance back as the object, massive, a section of torn building, bricks and protruding rods of galvanised steel, rolled and bounced and spat sparks from the shaft walls, disintegrating steps and masonry into dust as it filled the entire shaft with bulk, filled the world with its threatening looming shrieking mass. Grimly, Pippa realised it was accelerating towards them, and there was no chance it could miss. It would crush them, smash them all into a pulp, into grease stains at the base of the hospital stairwell –

Betezh looked back, shouted something, but above the screams and the noise Pippa failed to hear him. His face was demonic, stained red by flickering fires, his facial scars twisting into a horror deformation...

Pippa ducked her head, urged her pack to go faster –

But knew, ultimately, she was doomed.

VIEWED FROM THE safety of the lift, Franco's chase was like a bad comedy sketch. He pumped through the gloom in a badly fitting and *very* tight nurse uniform, the skirt riding impossibly – and rudely – high as through the gloom fast-ambled garish little men with putty heads, batteries in mouths disgorging thick black cables, their hands flickering and charging with jumps of electricity. Every few seconds there'd be a *zzap* and an arc of blue would either discharge on some metal furniture in a shower of sparks, or strike Franco on his largest presented body part – usually his arse.

"Come on!" roared Olga, hopping from one great foot to the other, as Fizzy and Shazza hovered, fingers on the D button.

"He's not going to make it!" snapped Shazza.

"*Heeeeeelp!*" shrieked Franco, as another shock made him jump two feet in the air, legs still pumping, goatee beard standing out on end with surplus static like an electrocuted ginger porcupine.

"Over my dead body," snapped Olga, and grabbing a D5 from Fizzy she strode out, a shotgun in each huge paw, and started firing into the throng, her face gurning with concentration. Shells howled and whistled. A Convulser was punched back from its feet, and skidded back across the floor, a huge hole disintegrating the corner of its head. Another was caught in the kneecaps, devastating its legs, and it went down causing others to trip and stumble in a tangled heap of fizzing electricity and leaking battery acid. Olga aimed, quite a feat in the flickering gloom, and shot the battery in the mouth of a fallen Convulser; there was a modest *boom* and the battery exploded, taking with it the Convulser's head and three of his fellow freaks.

"Aha!" nodded Olga, settling on a system. She levelled both shotguns, blasted at kneecaps with crunches of smashing flesh and bone. Then, as the Convulsers failed and paddled uselessly on the floor, she sent more shells whistling into battery packs, exploding heads in all directions and turning the long room into an acidic charnel house…

Franco arrived, panting, and looked back, eyes wide.

"Thanks!"

"Get in the lift."

He touched Olga's arm. "No. Really, Olga. Thanks."

She gave him a smile, and backed into the lift as the remaining Convulsers, growling but wary after seeing ten freaky companions head-detonated, advanced in a slow-moving line.

Shazza hit the D button. The lift doors closed.

They descended, a rhythm of lights and floors replacing the horror of the nightmare flight. Music played, a happy little ditty by Elvis the Fifth, called *Baby, Baby Baby Suck My Balls (Ooh Yeah, Baby, That's Kinda Right!)*.

Without thinking, Franco started to tap his foot. The one without a sandal.

Olga turned, handed Fizzy her shotgun, sheathed her own on her back, and grasped Franco's cheeks between two huge hands. She planted a kiss on him, long and lingering and ignoring his frantic struggles and kicking legs. She pulled away, beaming.

"What was that for?"

"When Princess rescue Prince, she always kiss him to turn him from a frog."

"*What?*"

"My reward. For saving your life."

"Yeah. Well. Just as long as that's the *only* liberty you're going to take. They don't call me Franco 'Shy and Demure' Haggis for nothing, you know, girl. I am modest, by nature. I am a New Man. I have my high-fibre moral diet to be thinking about, capiche?"

"Ha! Rot and ze poppycock! I saw you lusting after Fizzy and Shazza before they told you they were ze carpet munchers, no-offence-meant. I know you still ze old priapic Franco I know and love." She beamed, showing missing teeth, gold teeth, and a tongue that could wrestle an octopus.

"Carpet-" snapped Shazza, eyes wide. "Hey, listen love, don't knock it till you've tried it." She glanced at Franco. "Acquainting *so many* specimens of the male of the species, makes us awesomely glad we chose the Way of the Lesbian. It's like the Way of the Samurai, only with more loving." She smiled, winked, and linked arms with Fizzy, who reached over and gave her a long, lingering, and generously erotic kiss.

Franco turned away, face like thunder, brows furrowed. "It's just not right," he muttered. "Just obscene. A waste, by gods, of far too many fine sockets!"

The service elevator descended for a long time. Through the little meshed window they saw an endless stream of deserted corridors, filled with overturned trolleys, abandoned wheelchairs, smashed waiting-room furniture, broken boxes savaged of their contents.

"I didn't realise it was so big," said Franco.

"Must go for *kilometres* under the ground," said Fizzy.

"They could have a million soldiers down here," laughed Franco, uneasily.

"Well, we're about to find out," said Fizzy. She smiled, and squeezed Franco's arm. "Don't mind

Shazza. She's a bit of a tough-nut. You're doing a great job here, you know? We're finding out stuff. Just like in our QGM mission remit. You said this was a lame gig, but somehow I had a feeling being around you could never be dull."

"Yeah," grumbled Franco, face downcast. "I attract trouble like a dog attracts fleas."

"Still, chin up," smiled Fizzy, and slapped his PVC-clad arse. "It could be worse. Those Convulsers could have taken you back to the Weird Nurse Porn Studio; next time, we might not be in time."

"Ouch," said Franco, rubbing at his scorched and wounded buttocks. "Please. I'm tenderer than a prime BBQ steak. Those Convulsers sure fried the hell out of *my* rump."

"*You're doing well; my son,*" said Father Callaghan, Franco's Temple Pill throbbing a little.

"Oh yeah? When did you decide to put *your* bloody yellow squawking feathered head above the parapet?"

"*What is, that supposed to mean, my son?*"

"You kept a damn low profile beneath your own flopping cassock when I was in the shit, didn't you lad? No advice from Callaghan, oh no!"

"*I dispute that accusation,*" said Father Callaghan. "*I believe you, did just fine on your, own. My son. Amen.*" He seemed to think about this. "*And I didn't believe you needed, any spiritual, enlightenment at that particular time. You always admitted to being a hedonist; I thought you were! relishing the experience.*"

"Yeah, right, either that or you were pissed on Communion wine. My son." Franco's sarcastic tone did not go unnoticed. "Listen Callaghan, in the future, just keep your religic borrocks to yourself, reet?"

"*I am aggrieved you feel that way* [ching]. *That is $49.99 charged to your account.*"

"What?" screeched Franco, internally.

"*You signed the contrac',*" said Callaghan. A touch smugly, Franco thought. "*That's the charge. For my advice. On; shall we say, an omnisciently agreed, rolling contrac'. $49.99 every ten minutes' religious, advice and, attempted spiritual uplifting. Cheap at half; the price. Bargin'. Cheap as; chips. Etcetera.*"

"I've been conned," said Franco.

"*Indeed, it is not the first time,*" said Callaghan, the religious AI rip-off merchant.

"Where's that scalpel," muttered Franco.

Father Callaghan shut up.

The lift chimed *bing* and came to a grinding, juddering halt. They peered out of the window, but could see only darkness. Shazza and Fizzy pulled free HighBeams and the lift door shuddered open, revealing a dark, narrow tunnel filled with six inches of water. A stench filled the lift, like a kiss from the mouth of Beelzebub.

Coughing, the group waded out, and moved along

between rough-hewn walls. The darkness crowded in, threatening some interesting nightmares. *Things* in the water bobbed against their ankles, and Franco called a quick halt. "Wait," he said, almost choking at the evil stench, "hold on. This ain't water!"

"What is it?"

Franco peered down. "That," he said, pointing, "looks like a kidney."

"And that's definitely a heart," said Fizzy, nudging it with the barrel of her gun.

"There's a foot," said Franco, his hairs standing on end. "Girls, it would seem we're in a pit of medical waste."

"Great," said Shazza. She'd covered her mouth with her little nurse hat. "Let's get the hell out of here."

They waded along to the steps, climbed them and glanced up. Above, stretching up for as far as the HighBeams would reach, pipes led out of the mammoth wall of towering brickwork. This was obviously some kind of overflow sluice. Water dribbled from a hundred different orifices. Occasionally, something larger went *plop*.

There was a door, and Franco opened it to stare suddenly into the distorted, twisted, deformed face of a man, his head almost an arch, one eye above the other on the curve of his face, his nose a tiny little flap with teeth which clacked, his mouth a foul-breathing slot in a face straight out of horror –

even after emerging from an organ sluice. Franco's own lips flapped open and closed, for he didn't quite know what to say, caught, as it were, with his ASDA underpants round his ankles. The man, dressed in a red velvet tunic, had three arms but, thankfully, only the normal quota of legs. His baggy pants were of the same red velvet, and as Franco stared at the jelly-bean shaped head, the vertically stacked eyes blinked at him and the mouth twisted in what Franco assumed was a malformed smile.

There came a rustle of guns behind him.

"At last!" said the deformed man, nose teeth clacking. "We wondered where you'd got to. They're waiting for you on the Zeppelin3. You'll need to hurry, Zegg will be hugely and mightily annoyed if you're late. You know they can't leave without the onboard medical team!"

The man ushered the four Combat-K squaddies out of the effluence organ overflow tunnel, and Franco glanced down at his badly fitting nurse's uniform. Ahh, he thought. Ahh. They think we're nurses. They think we're a medical team for the Zeppelin3. Ahh. *Ahh! Ahh? Do we really want to fly on Zeppelin3? Is that a good thing… or a bad thing?*

Soldiers arrived, a squad of twenty, all wearing green backless gowns revealing a quite atrocious grouping of deformed and hairy buttocks. Many of the soldiers had three arms bearing three guns, and quite a few had twisted features, deformed heads, some even with their heads split in two and metal plates keeping both halves separate. Some had two miniature shrunken heads, like little voodoo totems, yet others had four heads, one mounted on each shoulder like really crap designer shoulder pads, with the fourth head located in the groin area, skin stretched out to merge with thighs and stomach, so that when they spoke they really did ejaculate bollocks.

Combat K were ushered along by the red velvet jacket-wearing jelly-bean head, who introduced himself as Paddy. Paddy "to his few important friends" Pudson, failed SF comic book author, and freak-extraordinaire. Franco waddled along in his tight uniform, feeling suddenly ridiculous. He wished he hadn't picked such a tight skirt. He felt like a cheap tart. He looked like a cheap tart. He rubbed his beard, grimacing huskily, and had to admit it to himself. He was a cheap tart.

The cavern reared around the group, too massive to be real, too huge to comprehend. Above hung ten airships now, vast and eerie and silent. Seen from ground level, the world inside the cavern was a bustle of military madness. None of the soldiers were "normal" in what Franco would consider to be "normal", although to be fair, only a few limited members of the entire human species would consider Franco to be in any way "normal". Which should have made him feel right at home.

Soldiers were still running around the track,

singing their little training songs. But now Combat-K saw many had three legs, a fact lost when they had peered out from upon high at the mass. Yet other soldiers had been… blended. Some were joined sideways at the hips, and ran in curious waddling gaits, all four legs finding a curious rhythm which meant the twin-bodied soldier could ambulate with terrific and horrifying speed.

"It's REC," hissed Fizzy, jogging alongside Franco. Paddy was marching them along in a hurried deformed-arse waddle. There seemed to be some urgency.

"Wassat?" snapped Franco. He had just been distracted by a soldier who was simply four legs, joined at the hips and bent into an arch, like an upturned soup bowl, without any actual body carcass or visible heads. The four legs scampered around, like a strange white spider with human feet, all wearing different boots. Franco nearly threw up.

"REC," persisted Fizzy, face drawn and white and gaunt. "The REC Centre. Research, experimentation and confinement. These were the freaks left behind when Sick World was evacuated; these are the deviant experiments of sick sick sick medical minds. These were the bastards which needed to be *confined*. The dangerous ones. The killers."

Franco nodded, eyes on Paddy's fine red velvet. They were approaching a dangle of ropes, and

Franco's eyes were scanning fast, looking for some obvious path of escape. After all, once they were up high on an airship they were effectively prisoners.

"We have to get on," said Shazza, smiling a Big Smile through gritted teeth. "If we run now, there are thousands of the bastards to gun us down. We'll have to bide our time. Pick our moment. Wait till Paddy here is bumming his mother, who's also his sister, uncle and youngest daughter. Or something."

"If we get on, we're trapped," said Franco.

"We'll just have to play the game."

"Nobody," hissed Franco, "is going to believe we're damn and bloody nurses! Look at us! We're as convincing as fake tits."

"*But they are buying it!*" snapped Shazza.

They stopped by the tangle of ropes, and Combat-K followed them with their eyes, all the way up to a zeppelin hanging immobile and silent, like a huge war blancmange.

"Just fix these round your waists, girls," said Paddy, grinning from his lopsided head like a jelly monster from the darkest corner of gelatine hell. "Then, Zegg will have the guys haul you up."

As Paddy reached around Franco to grab a rope, he bumped his jelly-bean head into Franco's fake chest and one of the eyes looked up and closed, then opened. With heart-stopping revulsion Franco realised Paddy was actually *actually fucking winking* at him.

"Like the beard," said Paddy, nose teeth clicking. "Gives a guy something to, y'know, hang on to."

"Argh," said Franco, as the ropes went taut.

Swiftly, Combat K were hauled into the sky and the hell of medically-engineered deformity fell away. Now, they witnessed the bustle of activity in the mammoth chamber, as all around airships were being loaded in a likewise manner, some using ropes, many using ladders up which deformed nurse and doctor and patient squaddies attempted to climb. It was like some mammoth freakshow circus act. To one side, two of the zeppelins had peeled away and were making their way silently through the vastness of the cavern. The noise also dropped away and Franco glanced up to where some kind of mechanical winches were clicking at high speed, winding the ropes into slots above black iron cages.

"This is weird," said Fizzy, breathless in the cold air as they rose.

"This is hell," snapped Shazza.

"But at least that weirdo pervert Paddy isn't coming," said Franco, with a shudder which ended in the unconvincing wobble of his fake boobs.

"I think he take liking to you, fat man!" chuckled Olga, her little piggy eyes sparkling. "I think Franco a stud in this place, Franco a little pot-bellied gigolo in this place! Har har! You could settle down! Get yourself a deformo harem! Raise yourself some genetic mutations and play football with them at ze weekends. Many will have four or five legs, no? Great footballers! Yes, what is ze saying? Franco could have 2.4 freaks, har har har."

"Yeah yeah, laugh it up on your mush, Olga. How do you know there's not some huge monstrosity waiting for *you* on this airship? Eh? Eh? Maybe *you're* the one who's about to fall in love."

"Impossible," said Olga, smiling at Franco toothily. "I'm already in love."

Ropes slowed in their ascent, and Combat-K touched boots (or in Franco's case, one bare foot, one sandal) to the metal cage platform. They undid their ropes, and climbed the steps to find – row after row after row of seated soldiers, all wearing backless gowns, all bearing long slim guns, all wearing odd heads and too many limbs.

Franco glanced around, his practised eye taking in the Zeppelin3's weaponry. At the nose, there were four huge barrels attached by braided hoses to tanks which fell away beneath the airship. He nudged Shazza. "You see those?"

"What about them?"

"Military flamethrowers. Roasters. They call them Gordons."

"Gordons what?"

"Just Gordons."

"What, and they have them stashed *just below* fifty trillion tonnes of explosive gas?"

Franco considered this. "Dumb," he agreed. Then he nudged Shazza again. "And you see down there?"

She followed his pointing stubby finger, to where the airship carried long finned slots. "Go on, genius, what are they?"

"Kekra Mini-Halo Missiles."

"They're awesome," butt in Fizzy. "I've seen them in action! They were banned, weren't they?"

"Highly unstable," said Franco, nodding. "It's the T6 explosive, needs to be kept quite warm. Drop it below a certain temp and kaboom." He waggled his eyebrows.

"Kaboom?"

"Big bad badda boom," he said, straight-faced.

"So, for example, taking them out into an icy wasteland?"

"Bad move," said Franco.

Up at the head of the pew-like rows filled with deformed squaddies was a kind of open cockpit, and they could see a small, pot-bellied man standing there in an emerald green uniform, waving to the four "nurses" to join him.

The squad picked their way between the hundreds and hundreds of seated soldiers, tense and wary, feeling as if they were walking deeper into the lion's den, and subtly aware of eyes, far too many eyes, sometimes far too many eyes *on the same face*, all watching their tight-clad arses. There was a distinct atmosphere of happy misogyny.

As they approached, each Combat-K member was thinking, *this is it, the test*. Could they pass as a crack medical nurse squad? Or would they be immediately rumbled and mown down in a hail of bullets? Franco didn't have much faith.

"Hello!" roared the little man, belly pouch bouncing, holding his hand out in greeting. Above his unusually normal quota of limbs sat a tall head which was kind of curved, and bent, with a fat top-knot nipple. The arcing head was yellow, and looked just a little bit like a banana. At school, his nickname would have had to have been *banana-head*. Kids were cruel like that. "I'm Zegg, I'm the Para-Medic in charge of Zeppelin3. Welcome to my Air Ambulance! You nurses with rumpy pumpy arses are much welcome!"

"Thank you," said Franco, affecting a completely unbelievable high-pitched female squeak. "It's, um, good to be here."

Zegg eyed the four nurses, his banana-head tilting at a curious angle. It's like he's wearing a fruit-salad mask, thought Franco, and snorted, almost bursting into a panicked and hysterical laughter. He clamped his tongue between his teeth and bit until he could taste blood. Now was not the time for laughter. Now was a time to *die*.

"Who was your Mentor?" asked Zegg, slowly.

Franco flapped, his eyes growing wide, and he became solidly aware of the D5 in his hands. Blow Zegg's head off, grab the controls of the zeppelin, and send it careering for the ground. That would be their only chance at escape when rumbled...

Shazza stepped forward and smiled. "It was

Sabrina," she said, smoothly, eyeing Franco with a *calm-down-you-idiot* stare.

"Ahh," said Zegg, relaxing, "from the Porn Squad. That's great." He eyed the four unlikely nurses up and down, then gave a large, leering grin. "You should happily be up for entertaining the troops during the flight to the battleground," he said, nodding approvingly. "Some of the lads are a bit nervous. They could do with some fun sexual relief."

Slowly, Franco, Olga, Fizzy and Shazza stared back at the hundreds of deformed mutations. Franco coughed, and glanced at Zegg, who was once again staring intently at Franco's bosom like a sniffer-dog worrying a bag of dope.

"I've got to say, girls, Dr. Bleasedale did a fine job on you."

"How so?" squeaked Franco, in his unbelievable *falsetto voce*.

Zegg nodded, as if in appreciation of fine art or a priceless sculpture. "Wow. She really went to work on you four; you're the most freakish, twisted and deviated surgical mutations I've ever, ever seen!"

Turning back to the controls, the Zeppelin3 began to rise, a pebble in the vastness of the cavern, its nose turning and following the first two vacating airships. Franco glanced at Olga, and gave a weak smile.

"At least it can't get any worse," muttered the ginger-bearded nurse squaddie.

"Hello hello again!" came a voice, and down the gantries strode the red-velvet figure of Paddy, his vertical stacked eyes blinking, his nose teeth clacking. He stopped alongside Combat K. "Thought I'd hitch a lift to battle along with this crew, hope you don't mind Zegg, old chum?"

"No problem Paddy! The more the merrier! We all love to build bridges around here! Ah har ha ha!" They laughed, a comedy duo of freaks in a not-very-funny situation, linked in a deviant union by sick medical mutation. Whoever said plastic surgeons didn't have a sense of humour?

"It's just," Paddy hunched in, like a hunchback conspirator with a lopsided head sharing his deepest secrets, "it looks like the Zeppelin3, with you four sexy sex-chicks onboard, it looks likes this will be the biggest fun ride of the last, ooh, thousand years! Know what I mean?" He boomed laughter, one eye winking again, and squeezed Franco's arse.

"Gerrof!" growled Franco, forgetting to use his fake falsetto.

"Ahahaha," said Paddy. "That's what I like to see. A nurse with spirit! An utmost bubbling energy! And hands that can crack a coconut! Any more macho, sweetie, and you'll be joining the Village People! Aha ha ha ha ha. And... and and and if you don't mind me saying so, your lack of peroxide hair and cherry-red lipstick..."

"Yeah?" snarled Franco.

"Well." Paddy's eyes gleamed, and he licked his greasy lips. "Ladies. It's a real turn on."

THE ZEPPELIN3 MOVED up to the roof of the cavern, then into a wide tunnel which swallowed the vessel like a pea in an ocean. Franco and the squad took seats behind Zegg and Paddy, and as they rose through the vastness Franco experienced a strange sensation, as if he was rising from the belly of a beast, up its vast oesophagus to be vomited out into freezing ice air.

As they rose, so the temperature fell and fell and fell, until they saw a distant oval of light. Gradually, the tunnel was filled with a grey-white aura and they emerged into a perfect snowscape, cruising from a sloped shaft and up into the heavens which were gloriously clear. A white world spread out around the Zeppelin3, and Zegg manoeuvred the cumbersome vessel with skill, lifting it gradually to a high altitude where the breeze was crisp, cold and violently refreshing.

Zegg continued to prattle on, in what Franco termed a Terminally Useless Talk; he would speak, gush, froth and ejaculate, but rarely did his dialogue make any sense except to promote his own sense of self-worth and importance.

"...yes and now the Para-Medics are at the forefront of all military medical battlefield technology, and you'll find that the Para-Medics – did I mention I was a Para-Medic? – well the

Para-Medics are the most lethal in battle, the most terrible in combat, and between us we are a collective genius in the art of destruction." He beamed.

"Is that so?" said Franco.

"Oh yes," said Zegg, plodding his zeppelin through the cold skies. "Once, millennia ago, these airships were Air Ambulances, they were used for emergencies across the entirety of Sick World and the Para-Medics, even then, were held in a very high esteem but not in the same high esteem as we now demand, due to our terrible lethality in battle, did I mention we were terrible in battle? The Para-Medics are supreme in battle, and it's rare any other army can get the better of us but as I was saying, the Air Ambulances were used in emergencies and Para-Medics like me, with the Red Band, we were the top notch guys better believe it but the bureaucracy kept trying to mess with us because, hey, that's what bureaucracy does right and I soon learned that even if an emergency call came in, and say, some loon or doccie needed emergency treatment for a heart attack or vertical vein strip or something just as life-threatening, well, because of that dang bureaucracy I'd just sit there and eat my sausage and egg sandwich and to hell with all those the bastards."

Franco frowned. "So, you'd let people die?" he said. "For a muffin?"

"Oh yes," beamed Zegg. "They're all moaning whining cripples anyway, every last one of them using our dang Air Ambulances as a taxi service from one continent to another. I realised that if I made them suffer, as you do, then they'd never try it again oh no so they wouldn't."

"That's because they'd be dead," pointed out Franco.

"A valid point, yes, but, and let's be frank here, there's not *really* many people worth saving, are there?"

"What do you mean?"

"Well, I'd save another Para-Medic, of course, that's a life worth saving, but when you get old, well you kind of deserve to die, and anybody who abuses stuff, drugs and stuff, and alcohol and stuff, they deserve to die as well, and anybody of a different *species,*" he looked aghast for a moment, "I mean, you know, those non-humans, those damn stinking *aliens*. They all smell, you know. That alien smell. In the Para-Medics, we call it the ali-smell."

"So aliens deserve to die?" said Fizzy.

"Of course! Don't you think?"

"Well that solves that problem," snapped Franco. "We wondered how Sick World had folded all those centuries ago; with guys like Zegg at the helm, how could it not work?" But Franco's sarcasm was lost, for Zegg was off on another rant connected with a] the superiority of the Para-Medics, and b] the inferiority of everyone and everything else.

"When we go into battle now, we, as Para-Medics, are united! We are totally united! We have developed the much-feared Wheelchair-Bomb, Scatter Shells, Urine Clusters and Iodine Grenades! We are the most incredible air unit ever to fly a zeppelin across a planet!"

There came an odd squeaking sound, and Franco squirmed uncomfortably in his nurse outfit with just that little bit too much PVC.

"Are you OK?"

"Aye, just this g-string bit," he grunted, and tugged, "riding high."

"Ahhh, g-strings," said Zegg, his eyes glazing as his banana-head glistened. Condensation from high-altitude clouds seemed to settle on his large bulbous protrusion. "We're a big fan of g-strings in the Para-Medics. There isn't a Para-Medic who can't remove a g-string with his teeth, blindfolded. And talking of removing underwear with his teeth…" He beamed at Olga. "Hey, you, chunky, I can stick this baby on AutoP. We could nip back to the Bedchambers, I can show you what a Para-Medic is *truly* capable of!" He winked, just so she got the idea.

"Not now," said Olga. "I have ze headache."

"That's a dang shame," said Zegg, rubbing at his engorged crotch. "Back when I worked the Air Ambulance service, there wasn't an ill, stunned, depraved or unconscious patient who wouldn't lie back and think of the Greater Glory. Ahhh, those were the days. What about you?" He pointed at Fizzy, but she shook her head, face a stony glare. "And you?"

"Sorry," said Shazza.

"This is very, very unusual," said Zegg, frowning, his hands on the controls of the zeppelin. "I've not been turned down for a bit of rear-end sexual coupling for hundreds of years now! And Sabrina's porn squad are usually the hottest little hottie nurse chicks on the block. You dig?"

Finally, his gaze came to rest on Franco, who was squirming uncomfortably amidst a series of squeaking sounds, his face contorted in a parody of pain. "So then," said Zegg, forcing a smile which looked wrong on his face. "What about you, sexy bearded nurse type?"

"You can kiss my big hairy arse, dildo-head!" snarled Franco, as behind him Shazza and Fizzy slowly placed their heads in their hands and closed their eyes in horror. Oh no, they thought. In these circumstances Franco can not and will not *shut up*...

"What is this insolence?" snapped Zegg. "What is this insubordination? Nurse hotties *do not talk like this!*"

Franco was still squirming, his tight uniform still squeaking, and the seemingly sentient bit of tight white cloth chose that moment to pop a button. The button, from beneath his crotch, went *ping*, and flew across the cockpit catching Paddy a stinging sting to his lopsided jelly-bean forehead.

From Franco's groin area erupted his disjointed, squashed and severely abused Mr Roger. His ASDA underpants were all scrunched up to one side, and Franco panted at this sudden welcome release from tight-crotch agony.

"Ahhhhh…" said Franco.

"Wow, baby," beamed Olga.

"Hey!" snapped Zegg. "You got a dick! Nurses don't got dicks! What you doing, having a dick? You shouldn't have no dick in your pants. I was going to *explore* your pants! The horror of the dick!"

Franco pumped his shotgun. He assumed the Game Was Up, and gave a big beaming grin. "Shit," he said. "You've sussed me there, bozo. The cop's a fair one. You have me bang-to-rights, guv'nor."

"Get the imposters!" screamed Zegg.

Franco fired the D5's quad-barrels, and Zegg's head was neatly removed and deposited in a thousand pieces around the cockpit interior. Franco whirled on the remaining soldiers – numbering perhaps a thousand. They stood up, in perfect unity, as a single well-honed military battalion, and with a synchronisation that would make aerial display teams weep.

They brought about weapons, and aimed them, as one, at Franco.

"Help?" suggested Franco, and in panic fired his D5 with a savage quad smash…

*  *  *

As the Buggy, still growling, still decelerating, was consumed by the Rockfall and the terrible darkness of the storm swamped them, so thousands of huge boulders fell around Keenan and his prisoners, pounding the beach into instant oblivion. Face grim, as if in a trance, blocking out Ed and Snake's screams and howls as they pulled frantically against their bindings, Keenan guided the Buggy left, then right, following some unseen sine curve which weaved an almost mystical path between the quick succession of falling, thumping boulders. Nothing touched the Buggy, no rock large or small; all fell wide, or were left in the wake of Keenan's psychic cruise...

"What are you doing?" growled Cam.

"I've... no idea."

"What's guiding you?"

Keenan threw Cam a wild grin. "Must be my alien blood."

"Well, something wants to keep you alive!"

"You... don't... fucking say."

"I can fix the engine."

"Do it."

"But it'll reduce operational life expectancy."

"You'll burn it out?"

"Aye. But we'll clear the Rockfall."

"Do it!"

Cam, spinning fast, leapt forward and, with tiny extruded grippers, wrenched free the Buggy's bonnet revealing a huge pulsing behemoth of an engine within. Buckled, the bonnet flew off over the Buggy and was instantly crushed in the violent Rockfall. Cam dropped into the engine compartment, integrated with a *grind* into the vehicle's injection system, and knowing this would disintegrate the physical engine in just a few short minutes, slammed the engine full of fuel, nitrous, and PK5. The Buggy lurched forward with incredible acceleration, howling, body panels vibrating. Keenan clung on for dear life, teeth grinding, following his path of magic through the Rockfall and within a few seconds they burst free, leaving the darkness, and the hammering boulders, behind...

The Buggy continued accelerating, suspension pounding, six huge wheels eating ruts and slamming across the flat beach in a blur of speed and noise and fire. Sparks erupted from exhausts alongside spiralling slivers of shaved pistons.

Grimly, Cam continued to pump his heady cocktail mix into the injection system... until he saw the Silglace ahead.

The tail of the glacier towered four thousand feet in the air, a huge wall of white and glinting silver, veined, embedded with ice-trapped rocks, and completely at odds, at a violent contrast, with the desert. The glacier snaked off as far as the eye could see, and rather than being swallowed by the ocean, it was the Silglace which was doing the swallowing, an ice fist so vast it created its own weather and gravity and magnetic pull. Keenan watched, mouth open in awe. Never had he seen a wall of ice so huge. It was like approaching a sheer vertical mountain, a cliff so vast it filled his vision from left to right, dipping into the sea a little and meandering off like its own discrete continent.

"Hell," said Keenan, softly.

"You saved us!" screamed Ed, laughing manically.

"Not so fast," snapped Keenan, and nodded ahead.

Where the beach, sea and glacier converged in an unholy triumvirate of churning water, burning sand and stoic ice, so a huge chamber became visible, like a mouth scar at the foot of the Silglace. It was an opening, a cave a whole kilometre wide, a dark and cool and threateningly unwelcome maw. The beach turned to frozen sand within a few short feet, and on that ice-rimed desert sat the IceTanks and a scattering of soldiers.

"They shelter in the Silglace," realised Keenan, chewing his lips. His hands vibrated on the Buggy's wheel. More fire belched from exhausts, and the engine, like some dying shrieking animal, started pissing oil in a long sick slick from a fast-melted sump...

"Cam, are they friendly?"

Before the PopBot could answer, bullets started popping and pinging around them, several glancing from the Buggy's cracked and battered windshield but failing to penetrate. Keenan ducked involuntarily, and there came a sudden *krump* from one of the IceTanks and Keenan dragged on the steering, the Buggy slewing on sand, tyres churning. A crater appeared in an explosion of frozen sand and ice needles which rattled across the Buggy. More *krumps* filled the air, but they were moving too fast, leaving a long oil slick in their wake as the Buggy screamed at the IceTanks and the soldiers, who Keenan could see wearing large black oily suits and gas masks with thick rubber tubes leading from mouth to chest packs. The soldiers scattered as the Buggy roared at them, leaping a sand dune and sailing over the arc of tanks with ratchet-clicking guns trying vainly to track their leap. The Buggy landed, grinding out on suspension, clanging and banging and sliding sideways, wheels churning, hot oil spray arcing out as Keenan fought vicious controls to send them howling into the dark of the crescent-mouth cave.

Cam appeared in the black. "She's gonna blow!" he screeched, and zipped at Snake, and Ed, cutting their bonds with a flicker of laser.

They swept into the cool interior of the Silglace, twilight killed by a switch. "Jump!" bellowed Keenan. They leapt from the Buggy in a tangle of mad confusion and noise and heat and spraying oil, hitting the frozen ground hard with thumps and rolling, stunned, as the Buggy slammed a solid wall of ice and *detonated*. Fire roared, billowing out over the three cowering men. Hot twisted panels of metal scythed through the air, and rattled from distant walls of ice. Heat gusted through the cavern. Fire swept along the trail of oil and out from the cave towards the charging masked soldiers, what Cam had dubbed Cryo Medics. More fire roared outside, and soldiers were consumed by fire as a huge wall of flames seared through their ranks and the Rockfall, catching up on the fleeing Buggy, pounded the IceTanks and men and set about nibbling at the edges of the vast glacier, the monolithic mountain of ice that defied nature and gave a middle finger salute to the sun.

Keenan groaned, and rolled onto his back, coughing on acrid fumes inhaled from the fire. Everything hurt. Pain slammed up and down him like an elephant dancing on his bones. There came a *click*, and Keenan opened his eyes to see Snake's face, worryingly close, his eye-patch torn showing an angry red socket within, face scratched and streaked with oil and smoke and grime, his battered, trembling hands holding a D5 up close, the barrel under Keenan's chin.

"Funny how things turn out," he spat, and rocked back on his heels. "Tell that bastard Cam no funny business." He kept the weapon tight under Keenan's chin and moved behind the Combat-K squad leader, holding him close, eyes scanning the smoke and gloom, his features flickering red in firelight.

"Those soldiers will be on us in a few minutes," said Keenan, voice calm. He couldn't see Cam, but noted Ed had gathered the rest of the weapons and held them, crouched, looking nervously about.

"I wasn't planning on going back outside," said Snake, with a hiss. Ed was searching around the burning debris of the Buggy. The flames had died down now, but thick smoke still filled the air, acrid and evil.

"Here's Cam," said Ed, to a twitching, nervous, hairline-trigger Snake. Ed tapped the blackened, singed, smoke-damaged PopBot with the toe of his boot. "Little bastard's dead. Well, we can hope, right?" He gave a bitter laugh, looking to Snake for some kind of peer-group approval.

Keenan looked on with dark, shadowed eyes.

"There!" hissed a voice from the smoke, and bullets roared around the three men who ducked in reflex, rounds crashing around them – only, they weren't *really* rounds.

"What the hell are they shooting?" shouted Ed, as rattles ricocheted from the ice wall behind him.

"Who cares!" growled Snake, and opened fire into the smoke, quad-barrels screaming harsh screams of smoke and promised death. There were grunts from the smoke, and the thud of a body hitting rock. "This way," snapped Snake, taking charge, and prodding Keenan before him.

Keenan moved off into the dark, lit dimly by silver veins in the glowing ice, and a light that seemed to appear from a million miles away. With Snake and Ed behind him, growling, twitchy, heavily-armed, Keenan allowed himself to be cajoled along... after all, he thought with a smile, it was the direction he wanted to travel.

The cave narrowed, roof dropping, until it was a glowing tunnel of ice unnaturally carved. With Ed taking a rearward defensive position, his guns booming every thirty seconds or so, they moved into and *below* this glacier, the Silglace, following the narrow tunnel until it emerged on the banks of an underground river.

A river of mercury. A river of silver. Just like the Junkala King had promised.

There was no sound from the underground tributary, just a lazy wide flow of liquid metal. And bizarrely, it flowed *away* from the sea. Towards the heart of the glacier. A place Keenan, with his alien intuition, knew he had to now explore. Would it surrender VOLOS to him? He smiled. He doubted it.

"What you grinning about, monkey?" snapped Ed.

Keenan shrugged. "Careful where you wave that thing, Ed. You might take off your own damn head."

"If you don't shut your mouth, I promise I'll remove yours."

"Ed, shut it," snapped Snake. He was looking left and right along the narrow, winding banks of the river, unsure of which path to take.

"If you go left, you'll emerge into the ocean," said Keenan softly.

"And how the hell would you know?"

"Cam told me."

"What about the other way?"

"The Silglace, the Heart of the Glacier."

Snake peered at him suspiciously, his uncovered eyeless socket reddened and irritable. He rubbed at the socket, making it weep, then scratched his stubble. "If it's a trap, dickhead, I'll blow your head off."

"Really? You don't say."

"I haven't forgotten how you killed Maximux." His voice was soft, eye gleaming. "Go on. Follow the river."

They moved through ethereal gloom, along the low bank of the gently shifting mercury river. Only a few inches away, Keenan could reach out and touch the silver surface; but some primeval instinct, or maybe the traces of his alien blood, or the alien *joining* in his system, warned him against such foolishness. It's not mercury, said a voice in his mind. It's something else. Something alien. Something *dangerous*.

As they walked, following the narrow ice trail which was, in itself, treacherous and slippery, promising a swift descent into the silver river, Keenan thought back to his... how could he quantify it? His alien *integration*.

*I can see Eternity*, Emerald had said. *I can see beyond Time. I can see the pulse of The Galaxy Soul.*

And Keenan *understood*. It had seemed like a simple kiss. A joining of lips, an alien kiss, so simple, so innocent. And yet, like molten hydrogen, thoughts had flowed into Keenan's brain with the simplicity of binary. Lights illuminated. In place of human thought came machine truth. A digital epiphany. The *truth* and the *shift* and the *Dark Flame burning* came from Emerald, the Kahirrim, an ancient *alien* from an ancient, once-extinct race.

She had kissed Keenan. Flowed with him, merged with his blood and fluids. She had recognised the seed in him, the seed of the Dark Flame, the seed so desperately sought by Seed Hunters across the Quad-Galaxy...

And for a short moment, they had been *one*.

*Kiss me,* Emerald had said, *and I will know you, understand you, I will delve your deepest desires and fears and needs, I will flow with your saliva and blood and semen, I will be a part of you and you of me, fluid, joined, together for an eternity...* When Emerald possessed him, flowed with him, joined with him, *merged* with him, so she had left something behind, some residue of her alien self, some substance clinging to the inner walls of his organic shell that had subtly *changed* him.

Emerald had taken away Keenan's humanity.

Now, only God knew what he was. He smiled, a long grim smile. Because he certainly didn't.

Everything was eerie, silent, filled with the silver glow of weird life under ice. It was surprisingly warm, and Keenan felt himself sweating as he moved onwards, his mind worrying about Cam, about Franco and Pippa, about the mission, the junks, everything was a swirl and he wondered, not for the first time in his life, how he managed to end up so perennially in the shit.

"Wait," said Ed, stopping.

"What is it?"

"I saw something. In the silver."

"What?"

Ed looked up, eyes gleaming. "Treasure," he said, his tattooed face filled with a rising greed, a lust for wealth.

"Fucking mercenaries," snarled Keenan, eyes narrowed. "You're a fucking pestilence on the world. Look at you, on your hands and knees, grubbing about in the shit looking for any scrap of gold. Where's your honour, Ed? You were Combat K, once. Not any longer. You sold out in the name of hard cash."

"You shut up!" screamed Ed, pointing, his eyes haunted. Keenan could read ghosts flowing behind false shutters of self-denial. "You don't understand what it's like, you could never understand..."

"Show me what you saw," said Snake, distracted for a moment, creeping towards Ed who had knelt, was reaching out towards the slow, sluggish silver.

"Down there," said Ed, pointing, reaching forward...

Keenan glanced up. Far down the trail, he saw the first of the Cryo Medics creeping along the path. His dark PVC-type gas-mask gleamed in the gloom, reflecting the silver of the river. He clutched a long thin machine gun, and Keenan fancied he could hear the rasping of an alien respirator...

Ed leaned closer. There, just below the surface of the silver, they saw a glimmer of coins, a tumbling fall which rose and spun, dancing like a quick-moving eel of golden scales. Suddenly, Ed lunged forward, up to his elbows, and screamed a scream so high pitched and nauseating Keenan slapped fists over his ears as Ed pulled back his arms, where the flesh was eaten away to the bones, arms now nothing more than pitted crooked skeletal limbs. Even as he pulled free, his flesh was falling like molten wax, tumbling from his bones. Ed screamed, and screamed and screamed, staring in disbelief at this horror, this unrecognisable mutation being visited forcefully on his flesh...

Snake stared, open-mouthed, stunned.

Keenan slammed his fist into the back of Snake's head, a savage hard blow that dropped Snake immediately. Keenan took the D5 shotgun, and stared at Ed with pity, no longer feeling rage at this pitiful enemy, no longer suffering hatred. Keenan stared at a simple sick animal in need of quick death.

"No," wept Ed. "I don't want to die like this!" He flapped the useless bones of his arms. Even now, the tibia and fibula were starting to deform, to soften like runny putty, and melt into drooping unrecognisable blobs of molten bone-matter –

"I'm sorry," said Keenan, voice little more than a whisper. Four shells smashed Ed's chest, powering the small man back into the silver river. Eyes closed, Ed sank, flesh dissolving instantly from his frame so that Keenan's last glimpse was of a skeleton, splayed back, reclining, bones fast – dissolving in the powerful acid...

Snake's head smashed up. "Keenan. The Medics are coming. Give me a gun..."

"What, and have you shoot me in the back of the head? Get to fuck."

"*Keenan!*" Snake's face was pleading, and he glanced to where Ed had disappeared. "I don't want to die, Keenan. The two of us have more chance escaping this shit if we work together."

Keenan stared hard at Snake, then tossed him his Techrim 11mm. Snake weighed the gun thoughtfully, and ducked as bullets whined over the two men, chipping shards from the ice. Keenan and Snake returned fire, guns booming in the hollowed out glacier with incredible ferocity. Bullets howled through the grey gloom, smashing the Cryo Medic from his feet to topple into the silver river. More came, creeping along the path, and Keenan saw they had circuit boards welded to their arms and chests, and several of the soldiers – further back – carried tall back-pack tanks.

Great, he thought. Flamethrowers. Just what I need to end a bad day.

"Let's go."

With heads down, they sprinted along the ice-slippery path, which wound to the left blocking out their pursuers. More machine gun bullets whined after them, and one deflected from the tunnel wall and skittered to a halt on the path before Keenan. He stopped, knelt, and picked up the... bullet. He grimaced, showing it to Snake.

"They're firing hypodermic syringes," he said, head tilted to one side, analysing the short, stubby syringe. It was about the size of a 7.62mm round, so a hypodermic in miniature, with a hardened tungsten tip and an injection payload. "They have machine guns which fire syringes! How... bizarre."

"Yeah, well they can still kill. Let's go."

Keenan pocketed the projectile and ran, with Snake close behind. After a few minutes the path suddenly widened, and opened into a large oval ice cavern. The path rose onto a bridge, or series of many narrow ice bridges, below which the silver river opened up, disappearing into at least fifty different tunnel openings. At bridge level, each strand of silver river was followed by a new tunnel, so as Snake and Keenan breasted the ice-rise they saw fifty gawping tunnel entrances ready to accept them, to swallow them whole.

"Which way?" snapped Snake.

Keenan opened his mouth to reply, then felt a

*pulse* in his chest, in his veins. Something beat in synchronisation with his heart, and for a moment, a fleeting glimpse of time, showed him a sliver of pain greater than anything his human shell had ever endured. Before his mouth could open to scream, the pain had gone, but Keenan dropped to his knees as if punched, all breath knocked out of him, squinting and wheezing under the eerie ice light.

Snake whirled. "Have you been hit?"

"No." Keenan wheezed. He pointed. "That tunnel."

"You sure?"

"Yes."

Snake moved forward, stopped, turned and hurried back. He hoisted Keenan to his feet, his face close, and hissed, "Come on, soldier. Those bastards are not far behind..."

Even as he spoke, they poured onto the strands of ice bridge and opened fire. Compact syringe bullets whined over the two Combat-K men, and they broke into a run, returning fire, bullets kicking out powdered ice slurry and punching Cryo Medics from their feet in sprays of startling crimson. "At least they bleed!" shouted Snake, laughing suddenly, leading the way. Keenan hobbled after him, feeling as if his heart had imploded, feeling an alien *blood* raping through his veins.

Two of the Cryo Medics had reached the summit of interlocking bridges, and turned long slick nozzles towards the two fleeing men.

"Fire!" screamed Snake suddenly, loosing off more panicked rounds. But he was wrong. The Medics pulled triggers, and ice burst from the weapons, a massive outpouring of ice smoke, ice shards, snow and sleet slamming out on a horizontal plane and filling the chamber, flooding towards the two Combat-K men like a mushroom of poisonous gas –

They sprinted, into the tunnel, and were slammed in the back by the wall of ice-smoke. It felt like being hit by a brick wall, and instantly Keenan and Snake were smacked down, unable to breathe, ice in their lungs and in their eyes, blinded, incapacitated, fingers frozen solid to guns, bodies shaking with the shock of sudden impact.

Keenan tried to speak. He could not.

He felt the passing of the smoke and ice, and heard boots, many sets of boots, sprinting into the corridor. He heard the rasp of respirators, and felt hands on him, rolling him on to his back. The pain in his eyes dissipated enough to allow him to make out blurs, simple grey shapes, and he saw sketched the image of the gas-mask wearing Cryo Medic standing over him, rasping, hypodermic machine gun in his gloved hands. The Medic pulled free his mask, and Keenan blinked rapidly, staring up into a face that was a circuit board, or more precisely, had had many circuit boards welded to the flesh so that only the eyes showed through tiny diodes and transistors, coils of copper and flickering digital LEDs.

The Cryo Medic seemed to grin behind his electronic mask, and his words were metallic, like that of a robot.

"You should not have come here, Keenan, Combat K man. But we have been waiting for you, nonetheless. Waiting for *centuries*. Welcome to our Lair. Welcome to The Electronic Medical Institute For Integrating Human and Machine!"

A wave of nausea and darkness slammed him.

And Keenan remembered no more.

# CHAPTER NINE

# MADWORLD

PIPPA COWERED BEHIND her arms, waiting for the house-sized slab of masonry to engulf her... but it did not come. She slid, sparks erupting from her pack, swords and gun, as they connected with debris in the stairwell shaft... massive crunches rent the air, and glancing up, she saw the masonry had caught on an out-jutting of stone, snagging it. Then it broke free, tumbling, falling towards Mel again. Below, she heard Betezh shout and suddenly flip away, disappearing from the shaft. Pippa reached out, catching the lip of ledge and hurling her body through the opening. She hit Betezh, who had just gained his feet, in the back and they both went down like skittles amongst fires and crumbling bricks. A second later, Mel hurtled through the opening, and behind her there came a *crunch* and dust billowed into the chamber engulfing them, making them cough and choke and clogging nostrils with filth.

"Come on!" snarled Betezh, and they ran under an overhang of crumbling hospital wall, out into a buckled, heaving courtyard. Even as they watched, cracks snaked along the ground and cobbles tumbled away like stone dice into a deep stench-filled crevasse.

"There!" screamed Pippa. "The SLAM Cruiser! We've got to get onboard, it's our only hope!"

Even as they watched, through the fire, dust, billowing smoke and mushroom clouds of exhaust fumes, the SLAM revved engines high and hard and shifted, floating, its loading ramp moving away from the gantry in a shower of sparks and crumbling stone. They ran, sprinting across the courtyard, cobbles falling from beneath their boots into deep pits of molten stone. Betezh, surprisingly, took the lead, moving damned fast for a fat man, in fact, faster than Pippa had ever seen him move.

Betezh leapt, boots thudding the ramp. The Mk I SLAM Cruiser reared above him, like a towering black hotel, tiny yellow windows twinkling through poisonous exhaust. Pippa came next, leaping, fingers gripping the edge of the ramp and scrabbling madly for a moment, legs kicking as the wind was knocked from her. Betezh reached out, powerful hand curling around her wrist and lifting her bodily onto the ramp. He grinned at her. "Got you," he said.

They turned.

Mel was struggling. She'd slipped on a downfall of tumbling cobbles, her claws scratching out at rock, scoring marks on stone. Pippa watched with her heart in her throat as Mel clambered over the edge of the sudden quake-induced precipice, and sprinted like a dog, on all fours, claws gouging the earth. She pounded up the gantry, long spools of saliva drooling from twisted zombie jaws, and leapt –

Pippa reached out towards her, both arms outstretched...

But the SLAM Cruiser chose that moment to ignite afterburners, and leapt into the sky with a roar that shook the remains of the quake-battered hospital into a collapsing, tumbling, mushroom-engulfed oblivion. Huge walls toppled, towers screamed and rocked and fell, huge clouds of dust billowed amidst rockslides of brick and stone and steel support columns. Sheets of fire painted the underside of the clouds.

Pippa looked into Mel's eyes, as they pulled away fast, and Mel disappeared without a sound under the tumult of cascading bricks and stone. Dust occluded her. In a roar of deafening, final collapse, Mel was gone.

Pippa slumped back on the ramp, exhausted. Tears eased down her cheeks, scoring wide lines through settled dust.

"Get up," said Betezh.

"But... Mel! She's dead."

"And if they catch us here, *we'll* be dead," snapped Betezh. "On your feet, soldier. Chin up. All that guff. Come on bitch, I don't want to die!"

Pippa stood. She shouldered her pack, and withdrew her precious yukana sword. The black blade gleamed, a single molecule, frictionless, deadly. "I'm in the mood for death, now," she said. "I'm in the mood for some killing." Her cold grey eyes gleamed, like a machine.

Betezh blanched. "Hey, don't take it out on me! Blame whoever sent the quake."

Pippa gave a single nod, and without another word, took the lead. They moved forward, and behind them, upon some digital instruction, the ramp started to slowly lift, closing them in the belly of the SLAM.

"Trapped," said Betezh.

"Good," said Pippa. "Let's find the cunt who's running this show."

"They'll kill us. Or. Even worse." Betezh shuddered. "They might operate on us!"

"Just let them try," snarled Pippa.


"I AM DR. Farook," said the tall man, with curly black hair and two extra arms welded into his neck. All four arms waved yukana swords, an absolute fortune in rare, antiquated blades, and Pippa crouched, watching the four blades, calculating their financial worth and seemingly ignoring her approaching, imminent doom –

"*Pippa!*" hissed Betezh.

Farook hurtled at Pippa, and she leapt with awesome speed, a blur, seeming to dance between all four blades and her yukana made a single horizontal cut, and then she was through the whirling wall of metal death and landed lightly. She turned, resting her own blade on her shoulder, smiling at Betezh through the still whirling wall of silver yukana steel.

"But…" said Betezh.

Doctor Farook slowed in his dervish of death, each blade faltering. One knee went down, he stumbled, and his head suddenly detached from his body. The corpse slumped to the iron deck of the SLAM Cruiser, and blood gushed out, noisily.

Betezh gave a single nod. "You are indeed skilful."

"No," snapped Pippa. "They are indeed inept. Why are there so many bloody doctors about? It's like A&E on a Saturday afternoon. Oh no, silly me, my mistake. All the docs would be off playing golf, then." She smiled, sardonically.

Betezh fell into step beside her. "This is a hospital ship?"

"Perhaps. But what I really want to know, is what the hell went on with Miller?"

"This is one screwed up mission."

"Yeah." Pippa gave a horizontal smile. "Tell me about it. It looks to me like there's so much weird mutated shit going on down here, no way in the Quad-Gal could DropBots be so deaf, dumb and blind. Which kind of hints at a few possibilities. Either the DropBots and AnalysisBots were reprogrammed or deceived in some way; improbable, as they are extremely advanced AI designed with a singular purpose. And looking at the mess of the, um, medical staff we've met, I just can't believe they'd miss this apparently global shit. Another alternative is that QGM wanted Combat-K dead, so they sent us on what we thought was a piss-easy gig, and blam, we're suddenly in the shit without the right equipment or weapons."

"No," said Betezh, voice low. He was casting about, eyes nervous, across the myriad criss-crossings of the SLAM Cruiser's black alloy decks. Admittedly, they'd met four pockets of resistance, and admittedly, Pippa had slain all four pockets single-handedly in the blink of an eye, taking on odds that had made Betezh pale; but he was still waiting for a burst of sudden gunfire bringing a burst of sudden death. It wasn't a nice feeling. "You're wrong. I used to work internal affairs."

"Oh yeah. I'd forgot." Pippa gave a nasty smile.

"If Steinhauer or QGM wanted you dead, there are easier ways of killing you off. After all, you've got spinal logic cubes; he can pull the plug at any moment. I've got a more viable proposition."

"Which is?"

"Steinhauer suspected foul play down here. If he'd really thought it was that simple, he wouldn't have sent you, Franco and Keenan in command of your own squads. How many elite soldiers do you need to gather rock samples? So, he's got a nagging suspicion of junk foul-play down here, sends us down, knows we'll kick up the shit and start hunting down the problem... especially *without* the permission of superiors. When Miller was assigned, Steinhauer was shitting bricks. And it's looking to me like Miller was a plant; I've no idea who he was working for, but he wanted to stop this mission good."

"Hmm. I don't know. How could Steinhauer be sure something would happen down here?"

"Well, look at Keenan and Franco! Hell, even yourself! You attract trouble like a hamburger attracts ketchup. If Steinhauer had even the slightest sniff of illegal intel, then it was going to happen, Pippa, like night follows day, like... like Franco follows hookers."

"Why send us so under-equipped?"

"You call Military Grade DropShips which convert into BaseCamps under-equipped? We have enough weapons and bombs to start our own little war. Giga-Buggys, QGM comms, no, this was no simple infiltration. Steinhauer had an idea something bad was going on down here; he might not have realised the extent, but he has your files. If something was going to be uncovered, then you're the guys to do it."

"We've uncovered *shit*," snarled Pippa. "What have we found out? That there's a deviated medical population? That there are desolate hospitals, earthquakes, and lots of fucking twisted doctors who want to experiment with our flesh?"

"At least you know it ain't no picnic. And the minute you start giving Combat-K questions…"

"Yeah." She laughed. "We'll go looking for answers."

"In the words of Van Gok, ding dong!"

"I'm still confused."

"You're supposed to be. That's the nature of the beast. But we're on the right path, Pippa, I promise you. I can smell it."

"This your Internal Affairs sniffer-dog nose at work?"

"Yes. They don't call me Harry 'Bloodhound Snout' Betezh for nothing, you know."

Pippa snorted a laugh, and slapped Betezh on the back. He beamed from behind his Frankenstein-stitching facial scars. "You're a dickhead, mate. But at least you can make me laugh."

"I'll be laughing a lot more when we vacate this heap of shit ship."

"One step at a time," said Pippa, voice low. "I want to know where it's going, and what it's doing. For now, we need either the pilot, or the captain."

"So we need the SLAM's Bridge?"

"Yeah. It's this way," said Pippa, her good humour evaporating.

USING CUNNING AND stealth, Pippa and Betezh had avoided any extra excessive conflict on their journey to the control centre of the rumbling SLAM Cruiser. As doctors and surgeons surged up and down corridors, many deformed, many bearing extra limbs or bizarre examples of human-alien cross-surgery so that all manner of physicians had tentacles and horns and tufts and suckers, much to the wide-eyed open-mouthed horror of Pippa, and the cynical deep breathing of Betezh (been there, done that, bury me in a Y-shaped coffin baby), so the two Combat-K operatives leapt into deserted side-chambers, or hid in narrow gaps between steaming pipes and smoking engine units. The urgency on the SLAM Cruiser seemed to have increased; they could only surmise somebody had found the bodies.

They spent a while, crouched by a small portal staring out from the SLAM Cruiser's flanks. Below, forests and lakes rolled by and they felt the Cruiser bank, the ground shifting beneath them. "Look," said Betezh, finally.

"What am I looking at?"

"Snow," said Betezh.

And he was right. Ahead, the forests were tinged with ice, and the edges of lakes gave way to crackling sheets.

"It's getting colder," said Betezh.

"We must be approaching another continent," nodded Pippa.

Forced from their sanctuary, they'd made their way deeper into the ship, towards the Bridge, the control centre, and the helm of operations. They pounded galvanised walkways, slipped through narrow apertures blasting hot oil smoke in their faces, and slithered on their bellies under oil-dripping tanks. They were smeared, blackened, ingrained with filth. Pippa caught sight of herself in a mirror, her hair lank and oil-drenched, and she gritted her teeth, scowling. This was *not* the way it was supposed to work out.

"I look like shit," said Pippa.

"Don't worry. Doctors will fuck anything."

"That's not a very funny joke."

"Who said I was joking? Har har."

They continued through the mechanical hell of the SLAM Cruiser's rough internals. Now, only minutes from the Bridge, their lives had gone from bad to worse to hell. "I told you not to kill so many doctors," whined Betezh, as they hung by their fingertips under an oil-smeared bridge, whilst above their heads boots thundered, followed by the sucking slug-squelches of some unfortunate human-slug hybrid wearing a surgeon's mask and carrying twin scalpels in slug-sucker appendages. "All you did was raise our profile. Now the entire bloody ship's looking for us!"

"Listen, dumb arse," growled Pippa, "what was I supposed to do when confronted by a sword-wielding maniac? Roll on my back and let him tickle my belly?"

"All I'm saying," persisted Betezh, wriggling, his fingers slipping and sliding on the slick galvanised rail as his legs kicked above an awesome drop to certain death, "is that by killing so many surgeon bastards, you made things a lot worse."

"How can I possibly have made it worse? If I hadn't killed them, we'd be dead!"

"But you're missing the point," said Betezh.

"Dickhead," snapped Pippa. "Now I understand why Franco carved chicken nuggets out of your face. You're the most irritating son-of-a-bitch I've ever had to suffer a mission with."

"That's a little harsh," said Betezh, pouting.

"Why? You look like Granny took her knitting needles to your face. I've seen better looking models in a morgue."

"Some wear our scars on our face," said Betezh, voice solemn, "and some wear them in our hearts. Look inside yourself, Pippa, my pretty little pretty face. When it comes to God's good-person roll call, I know where I'll be standing. What about you?"

Pippa ground her teeth, but as she was about to reply, a beam of light shone on them. Both looked up, and saw a small nurse-soldier type creature, crouched, torch aimed from the barrel of an MPK held in seven fingers. He grinned, with five sets of teeth. "What have we got here, my little, bloody, sterile swab-creatures? Hiding under here, are we? Trying to escape from us, are we?"

All around the gantry, faces started appearing. Or rather, what approximated to faces appeared. Small stubby arms held guns, and eyes peered from slick damaged faces which Pippa and Betezh couldn't quite place in the gloom. One thing was for sure; there was something wrong with these soldier-types; something horrible.

A myriad of cackles emerged.

"Good hiding place," muttered Pippa.

"Hey, it worked for a while, didn't it?"

"Just not long enough," said Pippa.

"Get the Net," said one of the stubby little soldiers.

There was a *fizz*, and a *pop*, and something elastic and gelatinous and encompassing splodged and swirled around the duo. It spread, like a fast-growing opaque shroud, covering the Combat-K squaddies and nipping at their fingers until they let go. With yells, they fell, and hung suspended, swinging gently beneath the gantry.

"A JellyNet," said Pippa. "Great. I'll never get this shit out of my fucking hair."

"Stop moaning," said Betezh, pulling at his glooping fingers which were sticking to the all-encompassing, stretching, quivering mass, "it could be worse, we could be dead."

"If you don't stop pacifying me, you soon will

be," muttered Pippa, and shuddered as the still-expanding JellyNet spread over her face and into her eyes, ears, nose, throat, anus and vagina, creeping swiftly down the lining of her Permatex WarSuit and hugging her like a second skin of jelly strands. The JellyNet, biological AI entrapment device that it was, invaded her every orifice, locking her rigid with a sudden tightening pull, and Pippa felt sick deep down to her core. JellyNets were reputed to be made from the coagulated souls of sexual deviants. A JellyNet enjoyed its job. In every hole.

She shuddered again, and felt them hoisted up from their dangling and dragged along the floor. Little legs stomped in stumpy boots, but that was the only sound Pippa could distinguish as she bumped along the ground, the JellyNet inside her, massaging her, hugging her, caressing her in a sickly fashion.

SLOWLY, THE JELLYNET retreated. And as Pippa coughed and choked, rolling on her back like a beached turtle, she scooped jelly goo from her eyes and focused on –

Dr. Bleasedale.

"That bitch," she growled, and lunged forward. There came a *barrage* of clicking, locking machine guns in a circle around her form, and Pippa glanced down, where the JellyNet still locked her wrists and ankles together. She was still trapped:

a prisoner. She looked up, grinning at Bleasedale, and with slightly manic wide eyes. "It's your lucky day."

"Indeed it is, my dear! Ya, haha, daarling!" Bleasedale grinned from behind her purple facial burn scar. She removed her small peaked white cap, ran a hand through short curly hair, then replaced the cap. She still wore a starched white doctor's uniform and high leather boots. She still carried her short black stick, which she *whacked* across Betezh's head with a crack.

"Ow!" he said, rubbing his head with jelly-manacled hands.

"I should have you instantly minced!"

"Oh yeah?" snarled Betezh. "How the hell you gonna do that?"

Bleasedale pointed with the stick. "I have an industrial Becker & Harris Limb Mincer in the corner. There. You see? The big stainless steel box."

"You mean a lamb mincer," said Betezh.

"No no, a *limb* mincer." She smiled. "Used after *amputations* to dispose of the waste. I am reliably informed it takes a whole human carcass. Whether it be dead, or," she savoured the word, "living."

"That's sick," said Betezh. "You mean you'd mince someone alive?"

"Oh yes," smiled Bleasedale. "And we have done so, on... what would you say the Mince Count is so far? About seventy-six Stringers? Is that right, Glob?"

"Yeah yeah yeah," growled Glob in a husky voice, hopping from one military-shined boot to the other, and for the first time Pippa and Betezh focused on one of their diminutive captors without the disability of jelly-gunge in their eyes.

"Holy shit," said Betezh.

"He's like a fucking Oompa-Loompa!" snapped Pippa.

"Hey!" growled Glob, "less of the insults. I'm part of a refined and cultured culture, I am. So cut it out with the crap. No, I haven't seen Snow White. I haven't worked in a chocolate factory. And I'm *not* the bearded bloody brother of Gimli. Right? I'm a Porter."

"A Porter?" Pippa frowned. "Like, in a hotel?"

"No, you slack-fanny mop-bucket, like in a *hospital*. We, you know, take patients to and from the wards, down to theatre, help out, jip about, have a fag, mince and moan, that sort of thing." He stared hard at Pippa, and she couldn't help but notice his face was a flurry of open sores. She shuddered. Glob winked.

"How about it, chicken?" he said.

"Um, I don't really *fancy* any chicken right now, thank you, on account of being bound and incarcerated by a raving lunatic with a Nazi-uniform fetish."

The Porter moved close, his eyes widening amidst his horrific facial sores. Pippa caught a whiff of putrefaction, and noted some of the Porter's wounds were heavily infected, tinged with green and black. She half-imagined she saw the curl of a maggot's tail in one wound. She shuddered.

"I was calling *you* a chicken," breathed Glob, heavily. It was the laboured breathing of the rapist.

"You mean, what, no way mate, you mean that was a fucking *line?*"

"Hey, us Porters are renowned for being sex on a stick. Bulging in the bean-pack. Ferrets in the sack."

"I don't want a ferret in the sack. I want a man whose face isn't entirely made up of necrotic tissue."

Glob leant close, almost conspiratorially. He nudged Pippa in the ribs. "Look around you love, babe, chick. I'm the prettiest one here! A pretty boy, for sure." He beamed, showing black teeth. "It's been clinically proven a hospital porter is *the* most sexually active creature ever created. A true sexual athlete, for sure. It's also been proven we can *pull anything*. Oh yes. You'll be coming to me soon enough. And coming on me, if I'm not mistaken. I can tell. You're begging for it, right now, here and now. Gagging for it. Let me put something huge and wholesome in your mouth babe-chick."

"Over my dead body!" snapped Pippa, looking sideways at the freak.

"If that's the way you want it," smiled Glob. "Living, comatose or dead, I'll pork anything that

moves. Or doesn't. Takes more than a stiff to scare
away my, err, stiff."

Glob wandered off, presumably on an important
mission, and Pippa did indeed stare at the other
porters, and did indeed note that Glob was, indeed,
the prettiest pretty boy of the bunch. In their manic
Brownian-motion trajectories, it was hard to spot
their disease-laden faces at first; but then Pippa's
eyes focused, and locked, and she noted how the
Porters carried facial sores like a badge of rank,
or something to be proud of. Many had faces that
were, simply put, one huge open necrotic wound,
with eyes peering out from peeling reddened pus-
green flesh like dinner-plates floating on a murky
shit-swamp. Many Porters sported lumps and
bumps on heads, necks and arms, but it was faces
that drew Pippa's horrified vision back time and
time again. Sores, incisions, boils, warts, scattered
and layered, sores on warts, boils on sores, pus
leaking from burst spots and all filling happy
little sexually-leering faces like a chameleon cloak
of putrefaction. Pippa shuddered, watching the
Porters' many pointless activities. They seemed,
like many an office worker, to have perfected the
art of doing absolutely fuck-all.

Seemingly ignored for a moment, Betezh and
Pippa gazed around the Bridge. They were on
the SLAM Cruiser's main control deck, a wide,
flat, open room stacked around the edges with
complex computing containing clocks and dials

and pumps and gauges, some dribbling steam, and many used for controlling the vintage spacecraft. One huge curved wall was flex-window, showing the ever-increasing snowy wilderness outside. Even as Combat-K watched, the trees dropped down a long flowing slope to the sea, and they powered out over a choppy, violent ocean.

"Where are we going?" asked Betezh.

"To battle, daarling!" Dr. Bleasedale turned, tapping her stick into the palm of her free hand. She seemed heavily preoccupied, and ignored the scampering capering little Porters who seemed to be running around on a million pointless missions, criss-crossing and jumping over one another, some pushing rattling trolleys with a dicky wheel, some empty wheelchairs, many just lounging and smoking and leering.

"What kind of battle?" asked Betezh suspiciously.

Bleasedale leant close, her breath bad like used alcohol cotton swabs. "A battle between continents! We are at war, you hopeless ignorant fool. Sick World is a battleground! And we will be victorious! We will quell our enemies!"

"What enemies?" scowled Betezh.

"*Our* enemies!" screeched Bleasedale, gesturing wildly with an arm in the vague direction of the ocean. "We have been at war for hundreds of years, ya? The three continents, Yax, Kludek and Second Djio. Sometimes, we conduct raids, either by ocean or air. Sometimes we organise pitched battles to settle the score – once and for all."

"And that's what this is?" said Pippa.

"Yes! We will win! We will crush the enemy! Storm their trenches! Take down their machine gun nests! Conquer and slay and maim and kill!" She stared hard at Pippa. "Why the hell do you think we're short of organs, daarling?"

Pippa shook her head.

"It's our Bullet-Wound Guarantee Replacement, Standard Policy v4.7. If you get more than two rounds in an organ we replace it, ya? After you pay your voluntary excess, of course. And providing you have some No Claim Discount."

"Your soldiers have their organs insured?"

"Standard Kludek Guts Policy. After all, we *are* specialists in Medical and Surgical Care, and Rehabilitation Treatments for our lucky, lucky patients. Aren't we?"

Pippa caught Betezh's eye, and gave a little shake of her head as thoughts rioted through her skull. Battles? A war? What the hell was going on across Sick World? A war of dominance and power between deformed and deviated doctors and nurses? What kind of sick world was this? She spotted the global joke. She couldn't bring herself to laugh.

Huge engines throbbed in the bowels of the SLAM Cruiser, and Pippa and Betezh found themselves increasingly to the rear of activity as hundreds of Porters flooded the Bridge and went about spinning dials and valves, turning wheels, pressing buttons, tapping on keyboards and pushing the odd wounded doctor across the platform in a wheelchair, usually with a comedy leg stuck horizontal and banging into things with comedy yelps. *WHACK!* "Sorry!" the Porter would say, his sore-ridden face all screwed up and panting pus. *WHACK!* "Sorry! *Sorreeeee!*" *WHACK WHACK CLANG!*

"We've got to get out of here," whispered Pippa, shuffling closer to Betezh.

"Yep. And kill Dr. Bleasedale."

"Why is that a priority?"

"Because it is," said Betezh, scowling. "Some life-forms just don't deserve to exist."

"They'll be distracted when they go into battle," said Pippa. "Wait for my signal, then we'll kick-off royally. You think you can reach the yukana sheathed on my back?"

"Only if you get down on your knees."

"Yeah. Right. Just don't get any ideas."

"Wouldn't dream of it, Pippa. After all, I ain't a pretty boy, like these around us."

The SLAM Cruiser groaned, engines droning and thrashing deep in the craft's bowels. They banked again, and a land mass hove into view, a jagged, fractured landscape of broken ice and snowy peaks. The SLAM lifted, clearing the mountains, then dropped towards a vast, endless ice-field and as they drew close, like a mammoth lens coming into focus, so the world and the battle preparations and the *armies* came sharply into view –

"Wow," said Pippa.

"Hell," said Betezh, and he was right; it was a vision of hell.

Two vast armies faced one another across the icy plateau. Each faction, separated by perhaps a kilometre of No Man's Land, numbered perhaps twenty or thirty thousand... *troops*. Only these weren't soldiers in the traditional sense, for these were legless nurses, straightjacketed mental patients, doctors with external organs, Porters with wheelchairs mounted with guns, and a whole host of deviants merged with alien and metal and implements and equipment. It was like a gathering of lunatics. It *was* a gathering of lunatics. They carried swords and spears and machine guns, which they brandished regularly like amateur fanatics, waving them above their heads and firing off rounds in a clatter. Edging closer, Pippa saw that vast trenches had been dug and carved out of the ice, facing one another ready for battle, and each army stood behind their trench in what could only have been described as the most pointless gathering of proposed trench warfare ever devised.

"What's the point of the trenches?" said Betezh, "if the whole damn army stands behind it, waiting to get shot?"

"It's idiotic," said Pippa.

Betezh nudged Pippa, and gestured towards Dr. Bleasedale. "Did you expect anything else?"

Outside, the SLAM Cruisers, which had picked up troops from the hospital prior to its earthquake bruising and subsequent collapse, were already disgorging their payloads at the back of the gathered army. Bleasedale's SLAM Cruiser slowed ever more so that it was practically hovering, and jagging left and right for stability, waiting for its turn to put down on the icy wilderness and unload its medically-themed battalions.

"Right!" Dr. Bleasedale turned, and placed her stick against her narrow lips. Her eyes gleamed. "You humiliated me back at the hospital. You practically refused my kind offer of replacement organs, and then you... then... you killed *Gerry.*"

"Gerry?" said Pippa.

"The decapus," whispered Betezh.

"Now." She smiled again. It looked wrong on her face. Just wrong. Like a dog with three dicks. "It's time to feed the army."

"Meaning?" snapped Pippa.

"They like sausages," said Dr. Bleasedale, moving closer. In her peripheral vision, Pippa noted a group of Porters had suddenly detached from their aimless melee and circled the two Combat-K captors, guns primed, sore-ridden faces gleeful. Nearly twenty guns were trained on Pippa and Betezh... nobody could outrun that many bullets.

Pippa stepped close to Bleasedale. "So what?"

"We need more sausage meat."

The Porters surged, grabbing Pippa and Betezh. Pippa's head slammed forward, breaking a sore-ridden nose in a splat of pus, and her legs shot out, snapping kneecaps with terrible crunches. Betezh used his elbows, whacking left and right with thuds and yelps and the dry-twig snapping of bones. There was a surge of activity, of sudden acceleration into violence and Dr. Bleasedale minced backwards, on tiptoes, fingers wiggling as if fearful of getting involved in this sudden drunken pub brawl.

It was Glob who brought Pippa down with a tackle and smack to the head. Pippa grunted, and through her dazed vision saw the Porter held a small lump-hammer. A swarm of Porters bore Betezh to the ground and started kicking him, viciously. He was lost under a flurry of scrunched-up, boiled-up leprosy faces.

Glob, aided and abetted by a few other stumpy Porters, half-dragged and half-carried a dazed Pippa to the base of the huge, stainless steel mincer, the Becker & Harris. Behind, there stood a robust set of steel steps leading to a kind of plank. It was the same set up pirates had used for a million years.

Pippa was manhandled, groaning and drooling blood and saliva, up the steps. Glob took the lead, dragging her along the narrow and treacherous steel plank above the Becker & Harris inlet, which was basically a huge cone filled with gears and half-moon knives and corkscrews of gleaming steel. As Pippa slumped down on the plank, Glob leering over her, the machine gave a *jolt* and gears meshed and the cone started to spin beneath the plank with a high-pitched whining, like a gauntlet across a chalkboard.

Pippa struggled to her knees, and looked up at Glob. She saw the gleam of triumph in his eyes, saw the erect bulge in his pants, and realised, one way or another, she was about to be properly fucked.

"You should have listened to me *before*, chicken," snarled Glob, waving his machine gun. "If you'd come out back for a bit of fun, and you were good, I could have *saved* your ass. Now, your ass is going to get minced."

"You know something?" slurred Pippa, still groggy from the beating, feeling incredibly sick, a huge egg-sized lump on the back of her head slamming her with nausea, bile, and a need to lie down in a cool dark room with an ice-pack. "I'd rather go through the fucking mincer than spend a single second near your little waggling sore-minced maggot, maggot." She smiled. It was not a nice smile.

"That's OK," said Glob. "Because that can be arranged." He lunged at her, fist powering in a hook that would have sent her neatly to her death, had she not leapt forward herself at the same time, head crunching into Glob's erect and bulging groin and making him howl in dick-fire agony. Glob staggered, and Pippa rocked backwards and swept her boots out, slamming left, taking Glob's stumpy little legs from beneath him. He fell, caught his face on the steel plank with a crunch and splatter of open wounds, bounced up a few inches, then slapped down into the cone of the grinding Becker & Harris Limb Mincer. His legs went in first. The mincer slowed, given some proper work to do, and Glob looked up screaming, his hands reaching out towards Pippa who slowly climbed to her feet and stood on the plank, gazing down at the spinning mesh of sharpened steel. Glob was dragged round and round, like scum sucked down through a plughole, and gears meshed beneath the machine as it stepped up the party and ejected a stream of sausage meat onto a long table already filled with waiting sausage skins...

Below, Betezh surged to his feet – and Pippa ran, and flipped off the Becker & Harris, landing suddenly amongst dazed Porters. Betezh grabbed a yukana as, in the same movement, Pippa ducked and twisted, allowing the blade to be drawn from her pack, and Betezh slashed down, severing the JellyNet which still bound her hands. The JellyNet strands screamed, quivering and vibrating as Pippa took the yukana by the blade, flipped it over to catch the hilt, then stared hard at the stunned, open-mouthed Porters.

"Boo," she said, and in a vicious slamming horizontal stroke took four heads from bodies with a *schlup schlup schlup schlup* of vibrating weapon. Machine guns howled with hypodermic rounds, but Pippa was ducking, whirling, moving, and several Porters pottered forward, abdomens open, bowels jiggling free into cupped hands. Pippa stood, back straight, and drew her second sword in a fluid arc. One yukana slashed down, freeing Betezh's screaming JellyNet hands, and he grabbed a syringe machine gun and stared at the weapon, then shrugged. "When in Rome."

They faced a sudden, frozen horde of Porters and Dr. Bleasedale, who stood, shaking and purple with rage, vibrating on the spot, so filled with fury they thought she might possibly explode.

"Get them!" she howled.

The Porters charged, but were used to dealing with elderly patients in wheelchairs, not two highly trained and extremely pissed Combat-K special forces killers. Pippa and Betezh leapt forward and carved an easy path through the Porters to Bleasedale, leaving behind a scatter of body parts and the odd rolling head. The rest of the Porters carried on their charge right out of the Bridge's doors, to leave the place suddenly, silently, deserted. The two swing doors swung backwards and forwards, like the portal of a wild west saloon, until, with a squeak, they were still.

"You can't kill me!" belched Bleasedale. "I am the doctor! I make things well! I repair that which is broken! I fix that which is ill! I am a doctor! I am *the* doctor! You do not *fuck* with the doctor! The doctor is always right! Wrong is something that happens to *other* people! I am a *professional*," she spat the word on a shower of spit, "and I am *not used to these intrusions and you are messing with my concentration and there is a battle to be fought and sausages to be cooked and you cannot stop me now when I am about to become the Leader of Kludek under VOLOS!*"

Pippa strode forward. As the little black stick came up, Pippa cut the fingers from Bleasedale's hand with a swift stroke of her yukana. Dr. Bleasedale stared down at the severed stumps, and howled suddenly, like a toddler who's just had a lollypop removed.

"Tell me about VOLOS," said Pippa, voice low.

"No! I cannot! He'll kill me!"

"I'll kill you."

"His death will be a thousand times more painful!"

"Wanna bet?"

Bleasedale smiled, then, and nodded. "Oh, ya, daarling." Suddenly, she turned and launched herself at the SLAM Cruiser's controls. Screams ran around the walls in the form of wailing alarms and the SLAM lurched, made several deep vomiting sounds, then dipped its nose towards the ground and accelerated violently.

Pippa and Betezh were wrenched from their feet and slammed across space, whacking against the curved cockpit vista. Below, they saw dopy nurse-soldiers begin a slow-motion scatter as the huge Mk I SLAM Cruiser howled towards its own stationed army...

"We will all die together!" screamed Dr. Bleasedale. "Ya! Together in a meat slurry!'

# CHAPTER TEN

# LEAD ZEPPELIN

THE ARMIES OF Kludek were busy little bees. Squaddies were happily climbing into trenches ready for the first round of battle, and indeed, whistles were being blown in readiness for the grand kick-off. Across the expanse of No Man's Land it was a swirling, icy waste where wind whipped up eddies of churning, powdered snow. The opposing army of Yax was also climbing into its trenches and blowing whistles and readying heavy-mounted G52 machine guns. The two vast armies were preparing for battle, generals issuing orders, captains filtering orders, sergeants screaming harshly at troops with badly polished boots, and above it all banners snapped in the wind and flags wavered and pride slammed through these readying armies of two of the greatest continents on the planet...

Above the Yax armies, huge airships were delivering the last of the nurse soldiers, along with a battalion of chained Convulsers, electricity sparking and crackling and filling the air with ozone. Behind the Kludek lines, the last of the SLAM Cruisers were hovering, waiting to disgorge military payloads of infantry into this new arena of war, onto this battlefield of insanity, into this... game. Everything was going smoothly. Sergeant Caligula, of the Fifth Battalion Porn Troops, checked his wrist-clockwork. It ticked and tocked and told him they were nearly ready for the Great Off, the Big Push, the Enema Rush. He blew his whistle. More whistles echoed back down the trenches, telling him his trench troops were ready, and that all machine guns were primed in case the filthy dirty enemy tried a surprise attack charge over No Man's Land...

However.

Something seemed to be happening across the icy kilometre stretch of No Man's Land. The Kludek army seemed to be in some disarray and at first Sergeant Caligula rubbed his hands together, realising that any disruption in the Kludek ranks would give them a clear head start in the slaughter stakes.

In the sky, one of the huge hanging SLAM Cruisers suddenly dipped, and accelerated towards the ground. It connected with a deafening roar that physically shook the entire ice-shelf on which the great armies stood, and ploughed along through its own army scattering thousands of troops, who were picked up on a broad flat nose-cone and spat into the air like wailing ragdolls. With engines roaring, the SLAM Cruiser powered on, carving a furrow through its own military trenches, squashing a thousand bestethoscoped doctors armed with paracetamol machine guns, orange tans and a Big Ego, and continued, on into the sacred holy-ground of No Man's Land and –

Towards the Yax battlelines.

"It's a trap, a trick, a con!" screamed Caligula. "The dirty stinking cheating bastards are trying to get one up on us! Advance advance advance! Charge charge charge!" He blew his whistle, and nurse-soldiers streamed over the trench walls trailing peroxide curls, and charged – waddling – into No Man's Land.

Heavy machine guns started to roar, firing prosthetic limbs.

The sky filled with arms and legs. It was quite a sight...

Seeing the attack begin before the allotted time, the Kludek army screamed and blew whistles and charged, also accompanied by the music of machine guns, this time firing vials of piss, and in the midst of the two charging armies the SLAM Cruiser ploughed on with the tenacity of an advancing glacier, pushing up thousands of tons of churned ice and snow as, deep in its belly, fire blossomed and barrelled and ignited *gas* and *boomed* and worked its way towards the billion-gallon fuel tanks...

Armies clashed like knives. Bullets howled, made from needles and scalpels and surgical saws. Flesh *whumped* in chunks from shuddering bodies. Voices roared in appreciation. Screams shrilled. Engines churned. Swords decapitated. Syringes punctured. Blood flowed into the mud and squatted in glistening puddles... as the doctors, nurses and patients of Sick World went to war.

Franco's eyes gleamed. He could see his ginger goatee beard, his tight nurse uniform, his heavily-muscled biceps all reflected in the polished gleam of a thousand targeted machine guns. He clutched at the Leksell gamma-focus flapping loose around his neck, but knew in this situation the bomb-focus would be no use; although he wished, and wished hard. He staggered back under a force of snarling, almost physical, hatred which rolled out to meet him, and his generous arse cheeks met the Zeppelin's control panel –

There came a clatter of ratchet levers. Franco whirled – but too late! "Franco!" screamed Fizzy. "That's the..." Engines roared, and the stationary Zeppelin dipped its nose and powered towards the ground.

Guns roared, as a thousand deviant doctors

opened fire. Hypodermics whistled around Franco, who threw himelf behind the console and winced and gurned and hung on for grim life with a grim face and dark grim thoughts.

Olga slammed down next to him, her great hands clamping the console so tightly the alloy buckled. Franco, straggled goatee streaming, forced his head around and saw several deviant doctors with way too many wavering legs and suckers plucked from their seats and slammed back in the slipstream, vanishing.

An idea crawled into Franco's mind like a slug under a cabbage.

"Aha!"

With great force of will and muscle he hoisted himself up, and saw they were about to plough into the ground and no doubt suffer a certain, messy death. He reached out, teeth gritted, and grabbed the controls. There came a noise like crashing battleships, the Zeppelin lifted its nose and climbed for the sky. Behind, several doctors flopped from their bench seats, bounced off the flanks of the helium-filled vessel, and sailed spread-eagled towards the warring factions below…

Franco grappled his way into the pilot's seat.

"What the hell are you doing?" screamed Shazza.

"Saving the day," rumbled Franco heroically, puffing out his hairy chest from behind his skimpy nurse uniform. "And there is still no charge for awesomeness!" With all his puffing, his fake boobs nearly flopped out. Somehow, the effect of sexy coquettish nurse was quite lost on Shazza. "Hang on tight," he said. "Real tight." And then he winked. It was quite awesome.

Franco, despite appearances, despite sexual perversion, despite the beard, was a quite amazing and adept mechanic. Where machines were concerned, he could pretty much fix anything, and they didn't call him Franco "Grease Monkey Mick" Haggis for nothing. Genuinely. As a result, a hurried glance across the console told him everything he needed to know about controlling the Zeppelin3 airship. He grabbed a lever, and spun a dial. The Zeppelin3, despite its bulky appearance, was an advanced evolution of a primitive concept. Engines growled, and the machine shot up further into the sky until the icy battlefield was nothing more than a chequered gameboard; and then, idly, the cumbersome vehicle suddenly spun, flipped, and hung upside down...

Screams, squawks and grunts echoed from the pews in the Zeppelin3, as a whole battalion of deviants detached from their particular greasy perches and, some with machine guns still spitting hypodermic bullets, performed spread-eagled freefalls without the aid of a parachute.

Franco, hanging onto a gear lever, glanced across at Olga. She was scowling at him, as her immensely powerful hands slowly compressed a layer of alloy and steel. Her fat legs kicked rhythmically. Her tattoos gleamed under a layer of sweat.

Fizzy and Shazza, long hair streaming, hung on with grim looks as the Zeppelin3 sat, suspended, upside down with engines thrumming. Franco threw a glance back at the deformed soldiers. There were only three left. Three, and Paddy Pudson, who had clasped hold of a steel stanchion with his nasal teeth.

"Dop it! Dop it!" he wailed. "Pud us da wide way ud!"

Franco gestured with his head, but his own colleagues were far from impressed; probably as they were about to fall to their own deaths.

"Turn us over!" instructed Olga with the voice of an avalanche. Unstoppable. There came a squeal of steal, and one hand broke free clasping an oyster shell of metal. She dangled, huge bosom bobbing like footballs in a bin bag. Franco stared with wide eyes.

Wow, he thought. I have been a blind man!

Just... look at those!

Think of the... incredible fun!

Think of the *fumbling!* Think of the *wobbling!* Think of the *nipples!*

After all. He smiled, lost in his reverie. In an infinite universe, nothing's nice as tits.

Olga saw the stare, and frowned in confusion. She had been pursuing Franco – and Franco's arse – for many a month now, and hanging upside down from a Zeppelin3 seemed an unlikely place for his libido to come alive.

Franco slammed controls, and the Zeppelin flipped around like a whale changing direction, engines growling. Everybody hit the deck, but Franco was sprinting before anybody could move, his single sandal slapping forlornly across the deck. A right smash broke a doctor's jaw, a right side-kick with a stumpy leg left another deformed GP rolling in the aisles clutching testicles compressed to lemon pips. The third three-legged doctor squaddie, sporting an external kidney and five grafted ears, backed away, hands held up. Franco grinned, a gleam of teeth, showing a dark gap where one had been knocked free in a pub brawl.

Franco stomped forward.

"No!"

There came a ripping sound, and Franco stared at the kidney pulsating and wobbling in his hand. The three-legged doctor reared back on his back leg, and tried to kick Franco – who danced back, turned, and hurled the kidney over the side of the aircraft.

"I *neeeeeeeeed* that, youse bastards!" The doc ran, and dived over the side after his precious, spinning kidney.

And that just left –

Paddy, who sat, slumped in the aisle, nose-teeth clacking quietly in agitation. He looked up, vertical eyes blinking. "Don't kill me," he whimpered. "I'm a coward, really, honestly, I don't want to fight, I never wanted to fight, I shout and abuse and offer my opinion, but I don't want to fight no matter what insults I give... I'm just in charge. I have ideas, you see, clever ideas, and I think I'm really clever, and everyone thinks I'm really clever and funny and bright, but we all know here that I'm not very clever." He pulled out his lower lip. Franco stared, without emotion, wiping his kidney-smeared hands on his skimpy PVC uniform. "You see," continued Pudson, lips wobbling, fifteen fingers kneading his velvet clothing, "I'm a very creative person, honest, I mean look at my clothes! I made them! And my arms! I grafted them! And my nasal teeth! A product of my cheap science fiction! But I've got a bit carried away with myself, haven't I? Please don't kill me. Please please please."

"Pudson?"

"Yes?" Pleading.

"Shut the fuck up. And you damn well stay fucking shut up, if you know what's good for you. Capiche?"

"Yes sir! Thank you sir! I'll do anything sir! Thank you sir!"

"PUDSON!"

"Yessir?"

Franco gestured to Fizzy, who was panting, sweat-streaked, but had the ghost of a smile on her lips. "Fizzy, if this misogynistic misplaced bastard son-of-a-bitch moves..." he smiled. "Blow his fucking head clean off."

Fizzy grinned. "My pleasure, Franco." She grabbed a long, sleek weapon and cocked it, analysing the hypodermic gun's flanks with a military interest. "Although it might take a while."

"Take your time, babe."

Franco moved back to the control panel and glanced down through glass-floor panels. Below, the battle raged. Even at this high altitude they could hear the clash of the medically deformed armies engaging in battle.

"What now?" Olga moved close, and placed her hand experimentally on Franco's arse. He did not complain, so she did not move her fingers.

Franco frowned, brows knitted, and fished out his PAD. It was still dead. As dead as a dodo burger. He shook it vainly, in the hope that some miracle of motion would spark the tiny device back into life. It did not.

"Pippa's down there," he said, softly.

Olga shook her head. "No, she was placed ze thousand kilometres away on a different continent. Remember?"

"Hmm. No. She's down there. I can feel it in my blood. In my bones." He stared hard at Olga. "She's Combat K. I can *sense* her."

Olga nodded. "If you say so, Big Boy. We should go and have ze look?"

"Yes. Hold on, everyone! We're going down."

Franco dropped the Zeppelin3 through layers of cloud towards the rampaging armies beneath.

Huge swathes of nurses battled doctors, dragging their legless and machine-melded torsos through the blood-churned snow, hacking at one another with sharpened stethoscopes and throwing quad-scalpel shurikens with unerring accuracy. Many of the deformed combatants resembled porcupines, with all manner of medical implements protruding from faces and heads and torsos. It made for extremely grim viewing.

"It is horrible," said Olga.

"Savage," agreed Shazza. "Like the BBC Quad-Gal News. What can we do?"

"Very little, I think," said Franco. "These battles have been raging for a thousand years. We are temporary interlopers. Only God knows what these poor bastards are searching for. An end to war, I would suspect?"

"Or an end to medical experimentation," said Fizzy, moving closer to watch the rampaging thousands. An explosion roared, throwing up chunks of ice and bodies. A lower torso with four waggling penises arced past the windshield, and the nurse-clad squaddies exchanged worried glances as the Zeppelin3 rocked on concussions of energy.

"We're too low," said Shazza. "We could detonate."

"I'm looking for Pippa," said Franco, quietly.

"You're insane! What do you hope to see in *that?*" She pointed with her own weapon, towards the smash and thrash of battle insanity. Nothing was clear. Smoke rolled across the ice. Bullets whizzed and whined. Explosions spat icefall in arcs. Everything was a madness. The world had turned a deep arterial red.

"Take us up higher," said Fizzy, shuddering as a missile fashioned from three oxygen cylinders tied together with straightjackets went wild, howling and spinning through the air, to explode only feet away. Fire roared, heat washing over Zeppelin3's lower flanks.

"No." Franco set his jaw. He turned, suddenly, bent and removed his remaining sandal, and launched it at the crawling, whimpering Paddy who was making a break for the edge of the airship. The sandal cracked the back of Pudson's weirdly-shaped head, and he slapped the floor, unconscious. "Fucking cardboard tough-guy. What a creep! What a creepy sexist bastard!" Franco brushed down his nurse uniform, face in a frown. "It makes one feel quite abused." He turned back to the battle, and banked the Zeppelin to the right. They drifted through smoke.

"There!" he screeched, as he spied Pippa crouching behind an overturned truck. Fire licked along the chassis. Beside her was… Franco groaned. Betezh. But still, it was another set of hands to hold a machine gun!

"Pippa!" he yelled. "Pippa!" But she couldn't hear him over the roar of battle, and the whine and slap of bullets. He turned to Fizzy and Shazza and

Olga. "We're going in!" The three women nodded. They could recognise an obsessive lunatic when they saw one; but understood his motivations. Franco was going in... to rescue his friends.

He dropped the airship, and saw Pippa glance up, lifting her weapon. He waved frantically, and saw her face, smeared with dirt and gun-oil, suddenly soften. Shazza tossed a ladder over the side, which unravelled to the ground, and Franco, with Olga holding his ankles, hung over the side with a Sick World machine gun in each fist, covering Pippa and Betezh as they ran for the ladder and clambered up like monkeys on mescaline.

Panting, they dropped to the deck and there came a brief succession of embraces. Another explosion rocked the Zeppelin3, and Fizzy grabbed the controls, lifting them into the air with the roars of a powerful engine.

"Wait!" snapped Franco. "What about Mel? And Miller?"

Pippa glanced at Betezh, then back to Franco. Something in her face made him go cold. "Miller betrayed us," said Pippa, slowly, placing a hand on Franco's arm. "He did one, when we were in a bad situation. We tried to take him down, but he was too quick. He escaped."

"And Mel?"

Pippa's cold grey eyes, usually full of an emotionless calculation, were full of tears and she realised, realised for the first time how incredibly fond of Melanie she had become – zombie or no. Her hand squeezed Franco's flesh, hard. "I'm sorry, Franco," she heard herself say, detached, a million miles away. "Melanie is dead."

Franco closed his eyes. He swooned.

He hit the deck, and remembered no more.

FRANCO SWAM IN a murky wilderness inside his own head. He stepped from dream to dream, always an observer, unable to interact with his own self as he watched through another person's eyes. He watched himself, the bad decisions of his life, the violent choices he made, the sexual perversions he endured. He watched himself tortured at the Mount Pleasant Hilltop Institution, then watched him eke out a pitiful revenge on Betezh. And finally, he saw himself married to the monster known as Melanie, and their wedding night (he watched, detached, in stunned disbelief; he even appeared to enjoy some of it). And finally, ultimately, came their divorce. Franco sat stiff in a nylon suit, as the lawyers outlined his list of misdemeanours and Mel stood in the witness dock, drooling drool that melted 1,300-year-old hardwood timber, and staring at him with frustration and annoyance. And yes, Franco had to admit, he was not the easiest dude to live with… but when you were divorced by an eight-foot mutation with body-odour problems that would make a skunk weep, you had to start taking a good hard long look at yourself. However, despite the animosity Franco had always nurtured a dream, a small pebble of hope clutched in the sweaty fist of improbability. That one day, Mel would regenerate into her beautiful original self, and come running, falling into his arms, giggling, her fresh hair like flowers in his face, her tongue like honey in his mouth.

Franco grunted. Shit. Life wasn't like that. Bad things happened to good people. The evil weren't always punished. And it was fucking rare there was a happy-ever-after ending. Not in this world, not in this life. Well. Not in Franco's world, anyway.

Franco opened his eyes from beyond his pounding head, and found he was lying on his back, staring at thick hairy legs sporting huge tufts of black spider-hair like coagulated rugs. Franco looked up, weakly. Olga sat beside him, holding his hand.

"Hi," he said. *Bum budda bum budda bum budda bum* went his headache. But hey. It was better than a sermon from Callaghan.

"There there," Olga said.

"What happened?"

"You found out about ze Melanie." Olga patted his head, as if he was nine years old, which was exactly what he didn't need when the drummer from drumming band *Bang Da Drum* seemed to be playing a solo in his skull. Franco struggled up onto his elbows, and realised they were moving, or rather, the Zeppelin3 was moving, at speed. He stood, shaking his hand free of Olga's bear-like grip, and padded over to the control section. On a bench to one side was Pudson, head hung low, wearing defeat like a cloak. Franco kicked him on the shin, and he squawked with his nose teeth.

"Hey Pippa? Where we going?"

Pippa turned. Gave a brief smile. "We've had a signal. Must be from Keenan."

"What kind of signal? I thought all comms were down? Are the PADs working, then?"

"Use your head," smiled Pippa.

*Bum budda bum budda bum badda bam bam bam* went Franco's pounding skull. "What d'ya mean?" he frowned, and looked around, searching for his single sandal which had been used as a weapon against Pudson's deformed head.

"Can't you hear it? Keenan is one crafty motherfucker."

"You mean my headache?" said Franco, eyes wide, realisation dawning.

"Yep," said Pippa. "We three have spinal logic-cubes that detonate if we betray one another. Right?"

"*Yee*-arse?"

"So? How do they communicate?"

"I see where you're going," said Franco. "Somehow Keenan's tapped into the frequency and is giving us a banging headache with a message. Why, that crafty crafty bastard. I suppose he must be in trouble, then?"

"According to the maps, he's beneath a vast glacier."

"How'd he get there then? I thought he was in the desert?"

Pippa shrugged. "We've all been on the move, Franco. Sick World is far from a normal place. Soil samples? Hah. I hope to God I'm the first one to get my hands on Steinhauer if we ever get off this diseased hardcore rock alive!"

Franco deflated, and moved to the low edges of the Zeppelin3's platform. Below, the landscape sped by icy mountains and frozen lakes. A cold wind whipped Franco's beard, and a hand touched his arm.

"Not now, Olga."

"It's me again," said Pippa, and Franco breathed her scent. He gazed into her cold grey eyes and realised he was in love with Pippa, had always been in love with Pippa, and would love her until the day he died. He knew, however, his love was unreciprocated and a dream to which he must aspire, and ultimately, never achieve. He shrugged. It didn't matter. One day, he might catch her off guard – when she was drunk.

"This game's getting serious," said Franco, morosely.

"Yes," said Pippa. "People are dying."

Franco nodded, and stared out over the snow.

Pippa wrestled with herself. She wasn't used to being nice to people. "I... I'm sorry about Mel, Franco. I know she still meant a lot to you."

"Yeah."

"What do you want to do now?"

Franco shrugged. "Pick up Keenan, I suppose. I feel weird, like a directionless familiar. Like a puppet, with some bastard controlling the strings and making me dance a stupid jig. But hey, I usually feel like that, so some fucking things will never change."

"We need to get off this planet." Pippa leant on the rail, staring the same way as Franco. The cold chill ruffled her bobbed, black hair. "Find Keenan, and get the hell off. They weren't joking when they called it Sick World. A fitting name, on so many different levels."

"It's not that easy," said Franco.

"What do you mean?"

"Well," he took a deep breath, "all those people, all those doctors and nurses, mutated patients, the lot of 'em, they were abandoned here, right? Quad-Gal left them to rot a thousand years ago. Something's happened down here. Something bad. Something which just ain't right. And I want to find out *what*. To hell with the junks, to hell with QGM. This matters, here and now, to these damn and bloody mutants."

"You want to save the world? Again?"

Franco puffed out his chest. "Well, somebody has to do it."

"This is too big, Franco. Way too big! We should pull out. These deviants, these mutations, they mean nothing to us. Why the fuck should we care?"

"I care," said Franco, staring hard into Pippa's eyes. "And if I can find out who's responsible for Mel's death along the way… well, I'll have me a handy slice of Revenge Pie whilst I'm at it." He grinned, showing his missing tooth. Then sighed. "I was hoping you and Keenan would tag along for the ride."

Pippa grasped his hand, wrist to wrist, in a warrior's grip.

"I thought you'd never ask," she said.

CAM LAY BREATHLESS (although he had no lungs) and in pain (although he had no pain receptors). He was stunned (although, technically, he could not be stunned) and he was supremely pissed off. This, he could endure, because Cam was a GradeA+1 Security Mechanism with advanced SynthAI and a Machine Intelligence Rating (MIR) of 3450. He had integral weapon inserts, a quad-core military database, and Put Down™ War Technology. He was, to all intents and purposes, registered as core life. He could feel a close approximation of human emotion, albeit through a deviation of accelerated binary. After the addition of a backstreet bootleg Profanity Chip, Cam could also swear like a trooper and think *bad* thoughts unbecoming of a GradeA+1 Security Mechanism.

Now, as Cam lay smouldering, blackened, his shell crispier than a crispy fried duck, his circuits shorting and energy draining away towards a digital equivalent of death, *anger* pumped through him, electronic adrenalin surged his circuits... and Cam got good and proper mad.

He scanned. All around, Cryo Medics were messing about, analysing things, their guns loose, their attitudes relaxed. The threat had passed, moved on, and a little frizzled PopBot obviously offered little or no threat. He wasn't even worth sweeping up!

The *bastards*, thought Cam. *I'll show them, think they can abuse and torture a helpless little PopBot and then not have the decency to finish the damn job properly? Think they can just leave me here bleeding what bit of power I've got from my circuits like a dying fish flapping on the top of a pond? Eh? Well I'll bloody show them!*

Cam reached out. He needed power. Lots of power. A nuclear blast of power! Yes, that'd sort out his processor. His chips. Cheap as chips! Ha ha. It'd be funny, if it wasn't so painful. A digital death, so to speak.

However. There were no advanced mechanisms lying around in the foyer of the Silglace. There was nothing of advanced military spec Cam could hijack. No vast power reserves he could tap into. No underground wealth of stored energy from which he could take a humongous Lucozade sip.

"Damn and bloody blast!" said Cam.

Then paused, in embarrassment.

He realised he was beginning to sound like Franco. And that would never do.

Smouldering and fuming, Cam reached outwards to the only power source available to him, and locked. It was simply the fires surrounding him, burning merrily, ignored by the poking Cryo Medics.

Very, very slowly, Cam started to recharge.

He watched the 0.0000000001% edge ever-so-slowly up towards the 0.0000000002% marker. He gave a very big sigh. At this rate, he was going to be stuck for a thousand years... but there was one thing he could do.

Cam focused. He sent a tribal beat of pulses on a back-line cube-whip to Pippa, and Franco.

Combat K, he decided, needed one another.

Keenan, groggy, aware of little more than muffled sounds and hazy vision, felt his arms locked to his sides. Gradually, awareness started to return, but as it did so heavy *clanks* and metallic *thuds* filled his senses, introducing panic and fear. Where am I? What's happening? What the fuck hit me in the back of the head?

Then, he remembered. Cryo Medics. With faces like circuit boards. What had he called it? The Electronic Medical Institute for Integrating Human and Machine? Shit. Shit! He had to get out of there... and fast!

His eyes flickered open, and his breath hissed with sharp intake. An inch before his face was what appeared to be a platter of ice. He could see his own breath dusting the surface with steam. He struggled, and found he was locked tight, arms by sides, ankles together, and he felt panic welling inside him because he was essentially mummified, buried, entombed, and a fist plunged into his heart and held it beating in an iron grip and he choked, could not breathe, and the lack of air, lack of oxygen, lack of *life* spread out from his heart, first spread out from his inner self and encompassed him, *consumed* him with the evil of utter and total and universal claustrophobia...

Keenan wanted to scream, but could not take in air.

Suddenly, he felt motion. A jerk, then whatever he lay within began to move. Slowly at first, and he heard a rhythmical thumping sound, a *du dum du dum* as if he was in a carriage on rails. Then his feet dipped, dropping away, and he tried to scream as he fell vertically, feet to the floor and head spinning and –

*Breathe. With me. Be calm.*

Keenan felt honey spread through his mind like a gentle narcotic. A warm yellow light infused him. Reality became a distant second-hand experience. As if through drug smoke, Keenan said, *Who are you?*

*I am within you. I am part of you.*

*Who are you?*

*I am that element of you which linked to the Dark Flame.*

*Who are you?*

*I am Emerald.*

*The Kahirrim? I thought you died…*

*We never die. We simply shift phase. Be calm now. Be still now. Relax, and open your eyes, and you will live through this, I swear.*

Keenan's eyes flickered open, and still the drug-smoke lethargy infused him. The carriage, or whatever had entombed him, was shifting at colossal speed. Down, then twisting and turning, banking, rolling, and then… it eased to a halt. There came hisses, of releasing pressure, and above Keenan the world shifted. A face loomed over him, little eyes amidst a barrage of electronic boards. Only, now, and this close, Keenan saw they weren't quite right; it was an electronics technology with a difference, each board consisting of tiny, tiny loops and wires, scalpels and needles… as if it was an electronics technology invented by somebody with an utter obsession for medical implements.

There came a *snap*, and Keenan was freed. A gun poked over the rim of the pod, or capsule, or whatever the hell it was, and Keenan sat up, slowly, rubbing at bruised wrists. Reality came slamming back and he was poked and prodded out of his… he looked back. It looked like a sarcophagus fashioned from crystal. On wheels. Attached, roller-coaster fashion, to a track. Keenan saw Snake being similarly disgorged from a second mummy-coaster and pushed, complaining, towards Keenan.

"You all right, mate?" said Snake, with a scratching rub of his whiskers.

"Been better," said Keenan, looking around.

They were inside a dome, under the ice. The place was a bustling hive of activity, with perhaps a thousand Cryo Medics rushing about their business. They worked at machines set at chest height, their circuit-board faces flashing occasionally with sparks of electricity. Around one section of the dome's wall squatted huge metal canisters, hinged and ribbed, and fashioned from what looked like an ancient black iron. There were many pipes and tubes emerging from cast valves. In the distance, by one of the chambers, two Cryo Medics were working. One held a yellow bag of medical waste, whilst another shovelled something from inside the chamber, depositing *lumps* into the yellow plastic. Keenan shivered.

"You, follow us," snapped one Cryo Medic, prodding his gun in Snake's chest. Snake grabbed the barrel with a snarl, and around them twenty guns *clacked* into action. Snake held up both his hands, and rubbed at his torn eye-patch. Beneath, flesh was weeping.

"OK, OK, be cool, dudes. But keep the damn gun out of my face. It's been a long day, and I might just ram it up your... up your diode chute."

"This way. Cryo Locum wants to speak with you!"

The circle of Medics gestured with weapons,

and Keenan and Snake moved forward across the dome's floor.

"Where do you think we're going?" mumbled Snake from the corner of his mouth.

"Not sure," murmured Keenan. "But whatever happens, don't let the bastards put you in one of those chambers."

"Why's that?"

"I think this is where they make... themselves. Earlier, the Medic who captured us – he said something about integrating human and machine. Only I've got a feeling things don't always go well; hence the sick bag and shovel. See?"

Snake peered at the shovelling. Steam was still rising from the cubes of meat. "Understood, Keenan. Very deeply understood."

Their boots padded across the dome's floor, and Keenan stared up at the arches in wonder. They were white, but covering the entire interior surface of the Institute was a very fine golden thread in an incredibly complex pattern. It was so fine it was almost invisible against the white of the cavern, and as they walked Keenan found himself tracing patterns with his eyes; some of the wires glowed momentarily before fading back into gold, so that the entire surface looked like a vast network of optic fibre decorations.

"What a tacky load of shit," snarled Snake, following Keenan's gaze.

"No," he said. "It's beautiful."

Snake cackled. "Is this the Great Man Keenan going all soft at some tacky festive bauble? It looks like what it is, Keenan, a huge quivering tripe pie covered is a plethora of gold shit. Get real, man, this entire place is a retro-electronic graveyard."

"You don't understand," said Keenan, voice soft. "It's a map. A huge map."

"What?" scoffed Snake. "A map of what? My arse cheeks?"

"No," said Keenan, forcing his gaze to break from the glowing vision of the dome interior. He found it hard, almost impossible. He had been drowning in the vision; addicted worse than any Spuke-Crack addict. "It's a map of the entire planet. Sick World. Only... it's inside out."

Snake stared for a long time as they marched. It was cold, and their breath formed smoke streamers.

"Bollocks," said Snake, at last. "You're winding me up."

Keenan shrugged, but continued to stare. It was like spaghetti pooling across the front of his brain, twisting and turning and shifting. And then it went *click,* and moved into focus. And Keenan could understand the map. He could decode the information shifting between several dimensions before his very eyes, and he realised, knew, understood it was his alien blood, his contamination, his *taint* that made this possible. Keenan was something more than human. Or maybe something less.

He followed the map. He could see their path, in real-time, glowing and fading and glowing and updating and fading, even as he watched. He read the Silglace, and the trip here to this dome. With a frown, Keenan realised he could read his future path... and this shift of phase was his, and for him alone, and he was looking at the ArcPass, a mythical map a billion years old, something he'd read about in QGM broadsheets and kubes and ggg broadcasts. Keenan was staring at myth. At the impossible. At a legend. A bad dream.

"I can see our future," said Keenan, voice a drift of ghost-smoke.

"Are there lots of naked women in it?"

"Sort of."

"Great!"

"I... don't think you'll be happy when you meet these babes, mate."

"Where are we heading, then?"

"We're heading down," said Keenan. "We're going to find VOLOS. We're going to stop him. And there's only one route that can take us to the bastard."

"Which way's that?"

"Through the Asylum," said Keenan, his voice grim.

THEY STOPPED, AND were manhandled so they stood side-by-side. Before them on a throne of crystal sat the Cryo Locum. He was larger than the Medics, verging on eight feet in height. As a human specimen he would have been magnificent, a towering powerhouse of muscle and sinew, his fists the size of dinner-plates, his biceps thicker than Keenan's thigh. His entire face and naked upper torso were riddled with a hundred circuit boards, soft-welded into flesh, joined to slightly leaking veins and arteries, to the Cryo Locum's own natural electrical circuitry, and to his spinal and lymphatic systems. To his very brain.

He stood, as Keenan and Snake were prodded forward, and gazed down with tiny black eyes hidden under folds of green and red circuit boards. Charges of electricity flickered along channels. The circuit boards moved, shifted, and Keenan realised he was staring at a smile on the face of an electronic human lunatic.

"Nice to meet you," growled Keenan. "What's your next party trick? You switch on a light bulb poked up your arse?"

A boom of crackling laughter rolled out, and Keenan gave a nod. It was nice to see that brain-fried, circuit-board faced, eight-foot cryogenic lunatics had a sense of humour. Although, Keenan realised, it was probably going to go *bad*.

"Keenan. You think we don't know who you are? Or why you are here? VOLOS knows everything!"

"Can he see us? Hear us? Now?"

"Of course!" boomed the Locum.

"Hey VOLOS!" shouted Keenan. "Your days

are numbered, fuckhead. We're gonna root you out and fuck with your game. You understand?"

Locum boomed his laughter again, shoulder shuddering, electricity crackling along circuits and diodes. Then he stepped down from the dais on which his throne rested, and Keenan and Snake did everything they could not to take a step back. The electronic man was awesome.

Snake leant towards Keenan. "Do you ever get a really, really bad feeling we're going to have to fight this fat-arsed motherfucker?"

"Happens to me all the time," muttered Keenan.

"This is the way it works," boomed Cryo Locum, leaning forward a little, as a Towering King would address his little subjects. "We are going to change you, Keenan, and little Snake Man, you are going to join the ranks of my Cryo Medics! You will become Integrated Electronics! You are going to Combine with the Circuits! You are going to Electrify, little men, Electrify!"

A cheer rent the air, and all the surrounding Cryo Medics – which now seemed to be the entire thousand-strong workforce in the domed arena – had formed a huge circle, and many fired off ice-guns into the air in plumes of freezing, shattering, tinkling ice bullets.

"But?" said Keenan, head to one side and taking a step back. Reading his intent, Snake moved back also, rolling shoulders and stretching his ligaments. Both men could sense it was going to kick off worse than any Nottingham nightclub at closing time. They began loosening themselves ready for battle. None of the Cryo Medics intervened. They were obviously looking forward to the entertainment...

Cryo Locum placed his huge, white, almost albino-skinned hands on his hips. When he spoke, ice-smoke ejected from between the circuit boards of his face. "We need to put you into the machines." He gestured, to the dark, foreboding chambers, witnessed previously full of human cubes – or chunks, as Cam liked to call them. "But you are currently too volatile. Too violent. We cannot repair these machines if broken, so they are indeed precious to us. Instead, first, *you* must be broken."

"And you're gonna do it?" snapped Keenan, taking another step back. The Cryo Medics had formed a circular ring of flesh. He didn't have much further to retreat. There was nowhere to hide; nowhere to run.

"Breaking little men, well," they could almost feel Locum blush, "it is a great vice of mine. A great, shall we say, sexual pleasure." As if on cue, a bulge appeared in his component-inlaid pants.

Keenan shivered.

Snake screamed and charged, both boots launching at the huge figure's grotesque groin. Snake connected, and arcs of electricity shot up and down his body in sparkles of red, green and blue. Snake hit the ground with a grunt, steam rising from his clothing, and Locum kicked him in the ribs, a slow, easy, pendulous gesture that picked Snake up and accelerated him across the chamber. The ring of Medics parted, and Snake rolled over and over, slapping the ice, to lie still, panting, staring down at the floor in shock. He glanced over at Keenan, grinned, and spat out a mouthful of blood. "Your turn, Big Guy," he croaked.

Keenan moved forward, gritting his teeth... and cursed the day he'd been born.

CAM CHECKED HIS sensors. 0.000006% and rising. It was slow. Far too slow, especially with him sending the pulse comm signals. Frustration screamed through his circuits. Anger battered his CPU with a disintegrating ALU. Binary chased hex chased base 10. He needed more power, or he'd spend an eternity bleaching scabs of energy from pointless pitiful power sources like moss on a rock sucks distant sunlight.

Damn! Damn and hot bloody blast!

And there, he'd done it again. A Francoism! Damn that little ginger midget!

Idly, Cam watched the Cryo Medics messing about, searching through the remains of the Giga-Buggy. And then... it struck Cam like a sock full of marbles. Of course! He'd been so stupid! Dim-witted! No brighter than a Philosophical Hoover (a *PhilHoov*), no more intelligent than a Psycho-Analytical Toaster (a *PsychoAT*). Doh!

The Buggy's battery.

Garnering his energy, Cam used what few micro-amps of surge remained to roll his battered shell across the rocky ground towards the disintegrated Buggy. And there! He sensed the trickle of gradually leaking energy. Cam jigged himself along, then clattered to a stop beside the black cube, spinning a little. With the last remnants of dying power, he extruded a monofilament and drilled into the battery cells…

It was being born.

Like the blind, given sight.

Like the lame, discovering the ability to walk.

Cam yodelled in machine code, quite a feat, even Cam had to admit, and sucked in juice like a junkie guzzles Lemon Crack. Power flooded his circuits, and despite the blackened frizzles to his shell Cam ran a quick machine-gun succession of diagnostics and found he was –

Alive.

"Right, motherfuckers," he grumbled, and lifted unsteadily into the air, wobbling. The few remaining Cryo Medics turned towards the blinking red lights which scattered like angry hornets across Cam's casings.

Guns turned on him, bullets whined, and Cam shot out in a wide arc, cracking skulls in quick succession, and like a bowling ball scattering skittles he decked the twelve remaining Cryo Medics in less than a second.

Cam yowled in glee. Gurgled in gluttony. Bopped a jig of joy with a funky dance of death!

He checked his power.

1%.

"You've got to be kidding!" he moaned, and realised in horror that the Giga-Buggy's battery, whilst powerful for a vehicle, was minute when aligned to the requirements of an advanced AI PopBot. In essence, he needed more juice... or, he checked his run-time, in another sixteen minutes, he'd be on the deck again.

Cam did a quick circuit of the chamber, then sped out into the corridor down which Keenan, Snake and Ed had fled. And there it gleamed like a silver snake, the river itself, a winding twisting platter of silver.

Cam scanned for power – and could sense nothing. And yet... and yet he suddenly *knew* there was a power source in there, somewhere, a source of energy which would revitalise him, make him whole again.

Cam moved, dropping to a single millimetre above the surface. He fancied he could hear voices. Ghosts. And that was impossible. Cam didn't believe in ghosts. In his digital world, they could not exist.

Cam hovered, uncertain. He tried to scan component elements of the silver river, but it came back blank. Which meant this river was fashioned from a substance found nowhere else in Quad-Gal, and thus not supported in Cam's chemical database. Either that, or it was sentient and shielding itself. Which meant it was living, or AI. Which meant it had power cells, organic or otherwise.

Cam readied himself to plunge in –

What if it's dangerous? asked a tiny voice at the back of his mind.

Ha, scoffed Cam to himself. It's only a silver river. How dangerous can it be?

KEENAN CIRCLED THE Locum warily, fists raised, and the huge monster watched Keenan without motion. Keenan moved in, and the Locum raised his fists, and Keenan stepped back. The sound of Snake vomiting blood did nothing to calm his raging mind.

Be calm, he thought.

Be still.

He relaxed, body and mind and soul, and distilled everything to this moment. For long seconds nothing existed outside this arena, outside this simple match of one on one, and there was no bigger mission, no bigger picture, no chamber or Cryo Medics or map-infused inner dome... just Keenan, and the enemy.

He charged, a blur, and the Locum leapt towards him, a huge fist swiping out. Keenan ducked the blow, which whistled past his temple, twisted, rolling into the Locum's legs with a thud designed to knock the Locum from his feet – instead,

Keenan was winded, and he saw a huge boot lift into the air and he moved fast as it slammed down, cracking the ice. Keenan kicked out, both boots slamming the Locum's knee, and the Medic took a step back. Keenan slid forward, delivering another blow to the same joint, and a third. There came the faintest of splintering sounds, and Keenan rolled as a fist slammed at him, thudding into the ice. Keenan drew a knife from his boot, and rammed the blade into the back of the Locum's circuit-board covered hands. Sparks raged and leapt like fireworks. The Locum let out a high-pitched shrill scream, long and warbling, and Keenan pushed himself back as the Locum stood up straight and stared down at his fist, pinned into a club by the long blade. He reached forward, started working at the dagger, then let go and screamed again, an almost electronic sound like a fast transfer of data, and Keenan ran, both boots connecting with the Locum's face, making the huge lumbering figure dance backwards, off-balance, and buoyed by his success Keenan leapt again – into a right blow that moved so fast he hardly saw it coming. The fist slammed Keenan's chest and he was knocked, twisted from his trajectory and sent spinning across the ice. He slid to a halt, and sat, coughing, pain raging through him, fire burning him and, wondering if the bastard had broke his sternum... the Locum charged with heavy ponderous steps and, stooping, picked Keenan up in one huge hand, with Keenan beating and slamming his elbow into the giant's limb. The Locum hurled Keenan, who curled into a ball, slamming from the ribbed and finned exterior of one of the huge *blending* machines. Metal struts cut Keenan like whips of steel, and he folded around the curves of the machine's flank, then rolled limply to the floor. Pain and blood-red images of impact danced through his mind. He heard footsteps, saw the ponderous approach of the Locum, and he spat out a tooth. Bastard. *Bastard!* Keenan pushed himself up, then staggered to his feet. The Locum swung its damaged fist, Keenan swayed back and struck out, slamming the embedded knife with the palm of his hand to a grating soundtrack, the snapping of several severed tendons, a grunt of shock… Keenan dropped, slammed three blows to the Locum's groin, then rolled free as a boot tried to stamp his head. Now, the Locum had turned, had his back to the machines, with their age-old iron alloy and promise of flesh and metal and electronics merging to form a wholesome whole.

"Enough!" roared the Locum, and his voice was edged with raw agony.

"Hurt, does it?" sneered Keenan through a mask of sweat, and dirt, and blood.

"You will die now," said the injured Locum. "No integration for you. Medics! Get the other!" Cryo Medics converged on Snake, and grappled the man to the ground but even as this happened

Keenan attacked, thundering blows in the Cryo Locum's transistored face. His fists beat wires and complex electronics, sparks showered, and Keenan felt a PCB board crack under one heavy blow. The Locum took a step back. Keenan ducked a whistling sweep, and leapt, boot cracking the Locum's face. Blood dripped from beneath the boards, and one twisted and dangled from his face revealing the pale white flesh beneath, skin mottled, flaked, like a wound left to fester under sick bandages for years. A terrible stench of putrefaction rolled out, making Keenan gag, but still he attacked, raining blow after blow into the now staggering Locum's huge figure – until he stumbled back, and slumped down heavily on a bench just inside the machine. Keenan reached out, and slammed shut the corrugated alloy door. Locks hissed. Suddenly, the Locum surged to his feet as understanding flooded him and Keenan whirled on the console, the entire panel in an alien lexicon, but he felt a pulse of dark blood within his veins and he felt Emerald with him in brain and blood and soul... he reached out, fingers caressing the console, and stroked a series of keys, first in one pattern, then a second, and finally a third –

"No!" screamed the Cryo Locum, voice muffled, beating against the inside of the machine. His damaged circuit-board face appeared at a little window. "Let me out!" he pleaded. "Please! I won't have you killed! I'll let you both go free! Honest!"

The machine gave a low hum, a jolt of massive power, and inside there came a whirlwind of gold and snowflakes and the machine started to dance, rattling backwards and forwards on heavy iron legs and inside the Cryo Locum was screaming and wailing like a man about to die... which he was.

Keenan took several steps back, and glanced over his shoulder. The hundreds of Cryo Medics were staring, transfixed, at their leader trapped in the machine. They stared, dumbly, and then, kicking into lazy gear, three rushed forward and grabbed at the control panel –

But too late.

Power, huge and raw and unrestrained, crackled at the summit of the machine and flooded down through the gold dust and swirling organic snowflakes and *Cryo Locum* himself, and he screamed and screamed, pounding at the interior until there came a sudden, vast, explosive *squelch*.

Keenan turned. The Cryo Medics were staring at him. They were close, now.

He smiled, and leapt, and slammed a right hook, ducked a return blow, dived at a second Medic, both fists pounding its mask, then he took its machine gun and sent a stream of ice bullets mowing into the ranks of enemy before him –

Flesh splattered, bullets whining and drilling holes in torsos, legs and heads. "Snake!" screamed Keenan, and he saw, perhaps fifty feet away, Snake struggling viciously with five Medics, punching and kicking until he, too, held a gun. Weapons roared, and Cryo Medics were shot out and up, bodies riddled with ice bullets as Snake and Keenan worked grimly towards one another, guns yammering, barrels glowing blue cold with ice round chill until they stood, back to back, and for a moment the hundreds of Cryo Medics backed away, forming a circle around the two men –

They ceased firing, Snake with only one mag left, Keenan already on the Dead Man's Click.

"We're fucked," said Snake from the corner of his mouth.

"Don't be so pessimistic." Keenan eyed the Cryo Medics warily, wearily, and saw the door to the machine behind them open. Several Medics started laboriously shovelling out the chunked remains of their recent leader. "I'm out of rounds," he said.

"I've thirty."

"Then we are fucked," agreed Keenan.

A low growl echoed around the domed chamber, and Keenan and Snake stared hard at the hundreds, perhaps thousands, of twisted mutated Sick World enemies before them. The combined growl grew in volume, ferocity, and then pace, rising almost like a war chant and Keenan's eyes searched vainly for any weapon within reach –

As the mass of Cryo Medics seemed to *bunch* with energy, fury, and intent.

As one, they charged.

# CHAPTER ELEVEN

# NIGHT NURSE

FRANCO STOOD, LEANING against the rail, watching the snowy world speed beneath him. Pippa approached.

"We're nearly there. Another ten minutes."

Franco nodded, and glanced back towards a frozen forest zipping beneath the huge, near-silent Zeppelin3. "It's beautiful here, Pippa. Have you taken the time to look around? To admire the scenery?"

"Yeah, but something went badly wrong. That's why it's called Sick World."

"It stinks of Man, not God," said Franco, mood turning sour.

"We'll see."

Pippa went back to the airship's controls, and Betezh was the next to approach Franco. He slapped the small pugilist on the back, and guffawed down his ear. "How's it going Franco old buddy old boy what do you think of the gig so far, eh? Quite a turn up for the books this place being populated by medical deviants an' all, eh lad?"

Franco glanced at Betezh, at the Frankenstein's Monster stitching that ran up one side of his head. Franco sighed, weighted under Betezh's enthusiasm. Betezh was a hard man to put down, a seemingly eternal optimist and, some would say, just as mad as Franco... only on a slightly different plane.

"Yeah. It's a bit crazy," smiled Franco.

Betezh changed tactics, and leant alongside Franco, staring out across the snow. "I'm sorry about Melanie," he said, after a while.

Franco nodded.

"It was quick," said Betezh.

Franco nodded again.

"Her death, I mean."

Franco frowned. "That's kind of what I assumed you meant."

Betezh sighed. "Yeah. Having a whole fucking hospital come crashing down on your head, BAM! straight in the back of the skull, boy, that had to hurt like a bastard, all those bricks tumbling over you, bouncing on you, crushing you, and if you were real unlucky then the mushroom clouds of dust would choke you, invading your lungs like a cancer and slowly suffocating you to death, cutting off your oxygen supply until you choked and choked and choked and hell, yes, maybe that didn't happen but instead she was squashed, trapped under the rubble and slowly starving to death and what chance would there be for a rescue party, eh? I ask you, eh?"

Betezh stared at Franco, whose face was far from friendly.

Betezh coughed. "Yes. Well. What I mean to say, is, well, it must have been quick."

"Betezh, fuck off and leave me alone with my thoughts."

"Yes buddy, no problem, whatever you say." Whistling loudly, and with hands thrust in pockets, Betezh wandered away and Franco spat over the side of the Zeppelin3, but no matter how much he hawked and snorted and regurgitated, he could not rid himself of the sour taste of failure.

"THERE!" POINTED PIPPA.

"Where?"

"There!"

"There's nothing bloody *there,*" snapped Franco, staring at the trees, the ice, the snow, more ice, a bit more snow, and a snowy wall of a glacier which blended in nicely with the rest of the snow and ice.

"Inside the glacier," said Pippa.

They stood for a while, the Zeppelin3 bobbing on gentle eddies of cold air. After a while longer, Franco said, "Oh," and they stared some more.

"You mean, like, *inside* that there huge trillion billion million tonne glacier?"

"It would appear so," said Pippa.

"You see any tunnels?"

"Nothing so convenient, mate."

"I have an idea." Franco brightened, and he turned. "Right," he shouted, gaining the attention of Fizzy, Shazza and Betezh. Pudson stayed with his odd head in his warped hands, his desolation and despair a tangible thing. "I want everybody to move to the *back* of the airship."

Everyone stared at him.

"Go on then!" he shouted. "They don't call me bloody Franco 'Bright Idea' Haggis for nothing, you know."

"Franco, what's the plan?" Pippa gripped his arm.

"It's a surprise."

"What kind of fucking surprise?" she snapped.

"Hey, trust me." He winked. Pippa groaned, and released her hold. "Just don't mess this up. We're a long way from home, and Keenan needs our help."

"Hey, they don't call me Franco 'Lucky Bastard' Haggis for..."

"I know, I know."

Franco moved to the controls, and familiarised himself with the myriad of dials, sliders, wheels, levers and buttons. Then he stared ahead, grinned, released a deep breath, and muttered, "Keenan, baby, we're coming to get you."

*  *  *

IN THE SUBTERRANEAN gloom there came a *boom* like the colliding of worlds, and several plato-penguins standing by the side of the underground lake waddled across ice and plunged into the almost freezing pool. They bobbed for a moment, looking up through surreal under-ice light, and watched as a huge crack jigged and jagged across the ceiling. There came another *boom,* and the ceiling caved in with a million tonnes of ice crashing down in a teeming shower. Gradually, the icefall slowed, and from the eerie glowing tunnel emerged the huge, ominous shape of the Zeppelin3, cruising silent, the bulky airship filling the confines of the tunnel like a well-engineered piston.

"There's a huge cavern!" yelled Franco, back to his terror-stricken colleagues. Only a madman would bring an airship beneath the ice.

"Cavern cavern *cavern,*" echoed the cavern. "CAVERN CAVERN AVERN, ERN ERN ERN ERN." Franco blushed, for here was a man who did not readily like the sound of his own voice. Quieter, this time, he said, "Pippa, are those Gordon's Military Flamethrowers charged?"

"Yes," came her sombre response. She appeared, superficially at least, to be in a less than fine mood.

"Rasta billy!"

Pippa strode forward, glancing up at the dangerous and teetering roof of the internal cavern. "Franco!" she hissed. "When you said you had a plan, I didn't realise it meant nuking the fuck out of the glacier, following a series of dodgy ready-to-collapse internal tunnels, then flaming your way through the rest of the fucking place!"

"Oh? Didn't you?" he placed a hand against Pippa's chest, the flat of his palm outwards, as a warning. "Stand back now girl, this is a dangerous place and certainly no place for a little lass like yourself."

"I might be a lass, Franco, but you're an *ass*. This is *dangerous!*"

"You think I don't know that?" She stared into his eyes, and beyond the swirl of madness saw concern, and sincerity, and hope. He gave a deep sigh. "I used to work the mines for CB," he said, eyes misting, "a long time ago. I know about tunnels and caves, fractures and faults. We're OK." He glanced at the ceiling. "For now."

"OK," breathed Pippa. "As long as you know what you're doing."

"I've already lost Mel," said Franco, quietly. "I'm not about to let Keenan, or you, go the same way."

Pippa nodded, and retreated down the ice-slippery deck of the Zeppelin3. Engines gave a drone of power, and they floated forward, and *down*, into the cavern. Franco had been correct in his predictions. It was big. No. *BIG*. So big the Zeppelin3 was like an ant in a football stadium.

They sank towards the vast, ice-chunk filled

lake, stagnant, still, and drifted across an icy, blue-tinged darkness. The silence was awesome. Smoke billowed from the Zeppelin3's exhaust. Occasionally, there came a distant cracking or creaking sound, which snapped like sudden machine-gun blasts through the eerie gloom. But then, gradually, stillness and silence, would return to this vast endless subterranean space.

"It's wonderful," breathed, Franco, almost to himself. Hs eyes were pinned wide in childhood awe. His lips wet from eager anticipation. "Wow," he said, staring at natural ice formations not witnessed for a million years.

"Just a shame you had to blast your way in," snorted Betezh from the back of the airship. "Nothing quite like destroying a million years of sculptured ice. Nothing like deforming Nature to give a man a good appetite for breakfast."

"Ach, shut your face," snapped Franco, and focused on the co-ordinate compass. Not far now. Just a single kilometre... east, and *down*." He moved to Pippa's side, his breath steaming, his deviant nurse uniform crackling with frost. He shivered. It was cold. Damned cold. He touched his beard, which was frozen stiff, each bristle a tiny icicle.

"I hope Keenan's OK," said Pippa, and Franco read the pain in her eyes. She still felt for him. Hell, she still loved him; but Franco knew this was a sore topic, an insanity yo-yo bouncing between love and hate, madness and calm, death and life. And all it took was a swift tug to send it careering in another direction again; possibly with very bad results.

Franco sighed. "Yeah. Me too. I miss me old buddy. We've been through some shit together, me and Keenan." He glanced at Pippa. "The three of us, in fact. Hey, you remember that alien AI wire, the Tangled? Down in that bunker? Just before we were…"

"I remember," said Pippa, her voice a little too tart, her tone hinting at disapproval. She relaxed a little, hands on the controls, guiding the Zeppelin3 down. A tiny blip on an analogue monitor showed their progress.

Franco pointed. "That uses magnetic bands," he said.

"What do you mean?"

Franco shrugged. "The monitor. It's not electronic, like we're used to. It's using Sick World's magnetic field for navigation. It's variable, to an infinite degree. Unique. I've never seen anything like it."

"So this planet's weird? Despite the obvious, of course."

"Yes, it's damn and bloody odd," said Franco. "I've seen several thousand different designs for navigation; but never anything like this." On a whim, he pulled out his PAD and tried to boot the little machine. It gave a flat zap, and refused to light up.

"You think it might be the strange magnetic field?"

"Yes. There's way too much interference. The PADs were designed to operate in any environment... but they can't handle it here. The environment isn't natural."

"So it's a created thing?"

Franco gave a deaths-head grin. "We're about to find out, lover." He patted her arse.

Pippa stared straight ahead. "Franco?"

"Yeah, sweetie?"

"Touch my arse again, and I'll surgically remove your fingers."

"OK, sweetie."

They dropped into the silence, and the ice.

"IT'S A DEAD end," snapped Pippa, hands hovering over a control dial. The Zeppelin3 shifted uneasily, up and down, in strong rising under-ice air currents. It was a struggle to keep it steady.

They floated in a high but tight tunnel, where the Zeppelin3's flanks brushed against potentially sharp ice. There came several squeaking sounds, and she exchanged glances with Franco and Betezh, who'd moved forward, a look of acute nervousness on his horrifically scarred face.

"Problem?" he growled.

"It's through there," said Pippa.

"Stand back," said Franco. "We'll blast our way

through!" He beamed the sort of lunatic beam which had got him locked up.

Pippa snorted. "You might bring the damn roof down."

Franco glanced up, but saw only the underside of the Zeppelin's huge bulk. "That might happen anyway," he said, painfully aware that billions of tonnes of glacial ice squatted just above the intruders, a trap for the unwary treasure hunter, a Rockfall for the reckless.

Franco primed the Kekra Mini-Halo Missiles.

"No," said Betezh, placing his hand on Franco's arm. "I've got a bad feeling about this, buddy. A real bad feeling."

"Trust me," said Franco, voice impossibly soft. Ice creaked and cracked above, below, all around. They all *felt* the glacier shift, move, and settle, like a huge dinosaur resting slowly back to die. He flicked several switches. Motors whirred. From somewhere deep below them, there came a subtle *whine*.

"We might die," whispered Pippa.

Franco stared at her. "This is for Keenan," he said.

She gave a nod, and Franco fired twin missiles into the heart-ice of the glacier...

KEENAN AND SNAKE stood, back to back, weapons primed in grim, steady hands, breath smoking in the cold of the domed chamber. Gold flickered across the mammoth arched ceiling as minute changes in the *map* integrated and meshed; a digital update.

The Cryo Medics were screaming, charging... but their mammoth noise was suddenly superseded by a high scream which blasted through the chamber. Weapons rattled as they were realigned and eyes fixed on Keenan and Snake, cold eyes behind frosted gas-masks, and the eyes were brittle with ice, not an ice of frozen water, but of frozen compassion, chilled empathy, solidified humanity. There was no give there; the Cryo Medics would kill anything without remorse.

Suddenly, fire blossomed across the underside of the dome with a crackle of detonation, and ice rained down in chunks and cubes, splinters and knives. A hundred Cryo Medics were crushed by a hotel-sized cube of compressed ice that *whumped* into the floor and left smears of strawberry topping. Yet more Cryo Medics were slammed by spears of ice, several pierced through their open, screaming mouths and impaled, quivering and twitching, releasing their bowels onto the gore-slippery floor. From the rage of billowing fire emerged the Zeppelin3, slamming into the cavern with heavy 7.77mm guns yammering, dropping through ice and smoke and fire and raining debris, skidding around in a tight air-arc and levelling guns at the suddenly panicked and cowardly Cryo Medics...

Guns roared.

Keenan and Snake backed away, their own guns slamming into the Cryo Medics, who were suddenly pincered between two opposing forces. A hundred went down in a heavy swathe of spent ammunition, and the rest buckled like foil, panic slamming through ranks like a bush fire. They ran, sprinting for the many exits from the dome chamber, weapons forgotten, an urgency for survival overtaking brains. The Zeppelin3 expertly tracked them, guns pounding, barrels glowing hot like the embers in a fire. Cryo Medics were smashed in the back, hearts and lungs punched through chests, bodies splintered and torn, dancing like ragged marionettes on the way to the frozen floor. Blood spurted, fountained, ran in streams, described webs of splayed crimson, tattooed Rorschach patterns against the ice, curiously symmetrical in a simple artistic splendour.

The remaining Medics fled the chamber. The guns silenced, smoke rising from glowing barrels.

The Zeppelin3 lowered, gently, as if on silent wires, and this Deus Ex Machine turned to focus on Keenan and Snake, still tense, guns aimed at this huge silent vehicle, eyes narrowed and waiting for yet another explosion of enemy guns –

"Keenan!" boomed Franco, and Keenan felt a huge weight lift from his chest, from his mind, from his heart. He uncoiled from his defensive crouch, pushed shoulders back and, for the first time in what felt an eternity, smiled.

A ladder clattered over the side of the platform, and Franco leapt out before it touched the ice, swinging and swaying as he descended, one sandal flapping on greased rungs. He dropped to the ice, and held out his arms. "Keenan, babe!"

Keenan grinned, stepping forward, and hugging Franco. "You mad little fucker. How the hell did you get *that*," he eyed the huge Zeppelin3, "so far down *here*?"

"Bombs," beamed Franco. "Lots of bombs. An orgy of bombs! You're looking well! A bit pounded, a bit bedraggled, but well, my man."

"And you look… like a porn-star nurse."

Franco stared down at his tight-fitting nurse attire, then grinned even wider as Keenan rolled his neck and shoulders, pulled out his small silver case, and rolled a cigarette with Widow Maker tobacco.

"Hot damn, I forgot how sexy and chic I appear to your average common mortal man." He coughed. In a whisper, he added, "I don't normally dress like this, y'know?"

"Hey." Keenan held up a hand, watching as Pippa, Fizzy, Shazza, Betezh and Olga all trooped down the ladder, one by one, the whole frame shaking madly under Olga's immense weight. "Each to his own, buddy. Different cultures, different customs, yeah?"

"It's still damn good to see you." Franco punched Keenan's shoulder, and Keenan groaned, touching the place tenderly.

"Just lay off the violence. I feel like Olga stomped my head." He eyed the group of ragtag nurses and bedraggled squaddies. Snake stood to one side, uneasy now, realising the odds had switched, and were somewhat against him.

Pippa stepped close to Keenan. "We came for you."

Keenan nodded, lighting his smoke. "Thank you." He glanced around. "Thanks, all of you. I can see by your appearance you've all been through the wars; but we'll have time for swapping adventures soon enough." His eyes narrowed. "Where's Mel?"

"She died," said Franco, voice a little strangled.

Keenan placed his hand on Franco's shoulder. "I'm sorry about that, buddy. Real sorry. She'd been through a lot of shit with us; she was a part of our team. One of us. Combat K."

"Yes," said Franco, voice unnaturally quiet. He had lost his usual bubbling bounciness. "She was my true love."

Keenan took a deep breath, pushing it from his mind. He had other priorities; like their impending slaughter, and the desecration of the planet during the last thousand years. "Now," he glanced up, "we have to follow the map. We have a direction. We have a goal. A purpose."

"We do?" said Pippa, moving close, voice barely more than a whisper. She was close enough to lean forward, to kiss him. Keenan stared deep into her cold grey eyes, saw the insane tangle of hatred and love, or gentleness and violence, and he smiled. He drew on his cigarette, and Pippa gave a little cough that made his smile widen. It was always the little things that touched him.

"We're gonna find the bastard who did this to the planet; to Sick World. He's called VOLOS." Keenan crouched, touching the ice floor. "He lives deep down, beneath the planet crust, deep within the rock. He helped create the junks, or rather, deviated an existing species into what the junks became. They were once a proud, fine race, a species of humility and love and culture. He knows *everything* about the junks. He knows their weakness. And, well, VOLOS twisted this place. Twisted the Junkala. He made Sick World, and the sick deviants who inhabit it. VOLOS changed the doctors, the nurses, the patients – turned them into the sorrowful horrors we have all faced."

"So we're going down?" said Franco.

"No jokes," said Pippa, glancing back at him.

Franco's face was straight. "Would I?"

She laughed. "Yeah, deviant, you would."

"Hey, that's a gross misrepri... misrapre... a *wrongful* presentation of my intentions, that is. So it is."

Snake moved forward, still uneasy, his gun *almost* facing the ground as if worried he might suddenly be pounced upon. He glanced at Keenan, and at the array of hardware bristling before him. The odds had well and truly shifted.

"What about me?"

Keenan stared at him. Something hard and cold in his heart pushed to the surface, but he forced it away. His senses screamed at him to put a bullet in Snake's brain. But he could not. Would not.

"You've got a reprieve, fucker. For now."

"Do you want my gun?"

"Not yet. Just make sure you don't wave it near me, or I might get the wrong idea and blow your motherfucking head off. Yeah?"

"Yeah, Keenan."

Keenan stared at the ceiling. Then around, at the reunited squaddies. "Well, guys. It's time to go to work."

KEENAN SAT CROSS-LEGGED on the floor in the exact centre of the chamber. Surrounding him stood the remnants of Combat K, battered, bruised, but defiant and hard and unyielding.

Keenan closed his eyes, felt himself drifting, felt the pulse of alien blood in his veins. And when he opened his eyes he was alone and this place was a million years distant. Cold ice-smoke drifted across the floor, and everything seemed... new, gleaming, bright. He stared up, tracing golden line through the ice, and it shifted subtly and rotated and he felt something in his mind go *click* and then was back in the present, and he could see both images superimposed and he knew. Knew the way. The way down to VOLOS...

"Follow me," he said, standing.

"Where are we going?"

Keenan took a deep breath, eyeing each soldier one by one by one. "Below this chamber lies the Asylum. A thousand years ago it was the secret project of Sick World, the deformed child locked in the cellar, the embarrassment brushed under the rug. When things started going wrong, going *bad,* they tried to put it right. But because of *money,*" he spat the word, "and *sponsors,* they kept on going, kept on trying to make Sick World the premier service for getting people and aliens well; and taking their hard earned dollars in the process."

"But some went mad," said Pippa, eyebrows raised.

"I'm not sure. But I'm warning you now, whatever's down there, down in the Asylum, what they called Ward 1 – well, it's going to be a thousand times worse than anything else we've experienced. They sealed it off, in the end. Before Sick World was evacuated. They sealed it off and left everyone in it to die… deep beneath the world, beneath the layers of strata… and you only do that for one reason. When there's no other way. Now. I understand if anyone, and I mean *anyone*, chooses to stay up here, near the surface. You can return to the last SLAM ship, protect it against deviant nurses, whatever. Nobody should have to witness what we're going to suffer beneath Sick World's supposed *normality.*"

Keenan didn't look at Franco, but could feel the ginger squaddie's eyes boring into his skull. He turned, finally, when Franco made a little strangled sound, like a cat in a bag tossed into a canal.

"You mean we're going down *into* an age-old mental hospital? A big underground one? One full of loonies?"

"Yeah, a very secretive and a very *bad* one."

"And you got all that from the sparkly roof map?"

"Let's just say I was inspired," whispered Keenan.

Franco paused. It was a painful pause; like a fart in a lift, or bared bollocks at a wedding ceremony. Finally, he said, "But I'm only a little fella," his voice the squeakiest of mewling mewls.

"That's what I mean," said Keenan, not unkindly. "There's no shame in staying behind to protect our single exit path from the planet; after all, it could become a bigger warzone up there than... the deviated place down here, beneath. Under our boots. And in the darkest recesses of our minds."

Franco considered this, and met the gaze of Fizzy, Shazza, then Olga; he connected with Snake, and Betezh, and finally with Pippa, who gave him a little smile, an honest smile, which was a rarity to see on her cruel, snarling face. Franco puffed out his chest, and took a deep breath. He noted with some pleasure that Betezh looked deeply uncomfortable, squirming beneath his scarred skin, for it was Betezh who had been instrumental in breaking Franco's spirit at the Mount Pleasant home for the "mentally challenged". Betezh had done a lot of bad things. He carried shame like a badge.

"I'm coming with you," said Franco.

"It'll be dangerous, and mad," growled Keenan.

"Hey, they don't call me Franco 'Kick Danger in the Balls' Haggis for nothing, you know, mate. I'm with you; all of you. Right to the fucking end, and beyond. Just show me where to sign." He bared his teeth; more in horror than smile.

"Good man!" Keenan slapped him on the back. "Pippa?"

"Yeah, Kee?"

"Get that airship primed. We're going in. We're gonna need lots of missiles, lots of guns…" he smiled wryly, "and a big fucking sense of humour."

"I'm on it, boss."

Keenan watched the ragtag squad climbing the ladder, until he stood alone on the ice amidst chilled corpses of massacred Cryo Medics. He stared again at the shifting map, and saw again the imprint of VOLOS's face melded into the contact points, the contour lines, the geographical features of mountain and lake and valley. Instinctively, he realised VOLOS was a part of this place, a part of this world; as old as the rocks, the trees, the ice, the deserts, the mountains.

· VOLOS was, perhaps, the greatest foe they had ever faced.

"I'm coming for you, fucker," said Keenan, stamping out his cigarette. In grim silence, he climbed the swinging ladder.

PART III

# THIS IS HARDCORE

# CHAPTER TWELVE

# PSYCHOIATRY

THROUGH ANCIENT ICE tunnels they cruised, silent, reverent, passing through halls of ice lit by distant eerie light, sparkling blue and white, filtered through towering cliffs of ice, through walls of snow, through chilled stalactites and waterfalls locked in stasis for a thousand years. Keenan, Franco and Pippa leant on the Zeppelin3's rails, breath smoking, eyes shifting uneasily as occasional cracks echoed through the vast tunnels, the gargantuan halls, the blue tinged caverns of a perpetually shifting, easing, crawling glacier.

"It's so big," said Pippa, whispering, because somehow to speak loudly seemed very wrong.

"We are intruders," nodded Franco.

"You two have a vivid imagination," snapped

Keenan, and glanced back, where Olga sat with a shotgun pressed nonchalantly against Snake's side; not in a direct threat, but more as an act of suggestion. A suggestion of murder if he put a greasy weasel fox-foot wrong.

They cruised for a day, through endless tunnels and halls, but one constant remained, a trait which every vast space, every narrow corridor, shared. They travelled downwards; sometimes it was nothing more than a gentle decent, sometimes vast vertical cylinders seemingly scooped from the ice by precision machinery. As they descended one such vertical tube, Keenan pointed to rails set in the ice. Old rails, glinting like brass in the beams of their gun lights.

"Nobody would be that crazy," said Franco, uneasily, watching the rails *thrum* past. "What idiot would want to build a base down here?"

"Not a base," said Keenan. "A hospital. The original hospital, the first hospital and the last hospital. Ward 1. The original Sick World; where all this madness began. It's down here somewhere. Towards the core."

"The walls are too neat," said Pippa. She held her PAD, which was fluctuating wildly between differing states of operational status. A thin blue laser shot from the PAD and bounced from ice walls, then spun in a circle of piercing sharpness. Then died. Pippa read the results. "It's a perfect cylinder," she said. "It's impossible this was formed naturally; this tunnel was excavated. By machines."

"Were they mining, do you think?" said Keenan.

"For what?" frowned Franco, shivering a little. Then he perked up a bit. "Maybe it was for *gold*."

"Maybe it was for *death*," said Keenan, and lit a cigarette. Smoke trailed up above them, into a deep velvet, blue infinity.

"You're a proper miserable bugger, going and ruining my fantasy like that," mumbled Franco. Still in his nurse uniform, his skin was going gradually blue, but he stubbornly refused extra clothing, exclaiming that a real man, a proper man, a *macho man* could put up with any excess of chill.

"Yes," pointed out Pippa. "Right up to the point when you're *dead*."

Keenan shrugged, and smoked, and watched the descent.

They dropped a long, long way.

THE ZEPPELIN3 BOBBED to a halt. They were lost in yet another vast cavern system, a star sparkling in the centre of the galaxy; but this time it was different. This time, on the ice floor far below, something gleamed.

"Take us in slowly," said Keenan.

Nodding, Pippa scrolled dials and the airship lowered, engines a rhythmical thrumming. Super-cool air streamed past. What looked like tiny toys on the ground eventually enlarged, and it was with stunned awe Combat-K realised just how *big* the machines actually were. They weren't just *big*; they were *vast*.

The Zeppelin3 bobbed above them, and even Paddy made an effort to stand up and hobble to the side of the airship, bound tight in SnapWire, nose teeth peering over the edge, chattering.

"What is zey?" rumbled Olga, eventually, the first one to break the silence.

They gazed over the sea of machines, perhaps five thousand in all, glinting silver, and black, some with swirls of red; many of the huge cubes and rectangular alloy blocks contained odd blade attachments – each blade the length of an eighty-storey skyscraper – and each one looked positively lethal, on a world-building scale.

"I think we just found the excavation equipment," said Keenan, rubbing his hands together despite his WarSuit. The cold was really getting to him. He was a tropical kind of guy.

"I wonder if they still work?" said Franco, oddly.

Pippa looked sideways at him, aware of Franco's obsession with machines, and engineering in general. Motorbikes, cars, rocket ships, guns; Franco got a regular hard-on for anything that went click. "Why would you ask that?" she said.

"Just wondering," he smiled.

"Don't even be getting the stupid idea," snapped Pippa, frowning.

"I'm sure I don't know what you mean," said Franco, who'd crashed more QGM Warships,

Cruisers, Shuttles and SLAMs than the entire QGM Crash Test Fleet put together. Whilst Franco loved machines, it would appear machines did not always love Franco.

"Yes, I'm sure you do," said Pippa, "you've got that bloody glint in your eye, like the time you ran that ten million tonne oil tanker up the Jajunga Beach on Kimo, knocking over three hotels and ruining a *lot* of beach holidays. Including the QG Mayor's."

"Hey," said Franco, "that was the controls, that was. An illogical layout."

"No Franco, it was your *lack* of control at the controls, dickhead. So, and you listen good my little ginger friend, the *last* bloody thing we need is you taking control of a fucking machine capable of ploughing down to the core of the planet. You hear what I'm saying? Sick World is unstable enough as it is without a mad burrowing ginger maggot cutting holes through entire tectonic plates."

"I am sure," said Franco, primly, "that I don't know what you're talking about. However," he turned and stared at Pudson, leaning over the rail, vertical eyes blinking in the cold ice air, "I'm a-wondering if he does."

Franco scampered over to Pudson, and shoved a Kekra quad-barrel machine pistol in his face. Pudson gawped, stupidly, like somebody with a machine gun in his mouth.

"Talk, muppet."

"What would you like me to say?" It was more whine than speech, and subtly impeded by inches of ice-rimed steel. However, Paddy made a good effort at answering the question.

"What are those machines?"

"For digging. Can't you see?"

"How long have they been here?"

"Longer than us humans."

Franco stared at the deformed freak before him. He clicked his tongue in annoyance. He wanted to say, "Human? You're a bloody long way from being human, mate," but instead focused on his questioning. "Do they still work?"

"I don't know that," said Pudson. "I've never seen them before. I've only heard rumours. Legends, if you like. There was supposed to be a place deep under the ice where the World Builders stored equipment." Pudson went suddenly red, and snapped his mouth shut.

Franco prodded him. "Tell me more."

"No."

"I'll toss you over the side."

"If you do, I'll... I'll... I'll kill you!"

"How? You'll have been tossed over the side! Idiot!"

Paddy Pudson looked suddenly crafty, quite a feat on such a deformed facial construct. "I wasn't going to do it *now*," he whined, like a kid deprived of a jelly baby. "I know what I'm doing, I am. Oh yes. I'm playing the long waiting game, you see. I'm patient. I will have my fame and fortune and gory glory gold one day! I'll be great! You'll see! It's called the long waiting game. It's always worked for me. Waiting works, you see? You see, don't you?" He grinned like a maniac, which surely he was.

Franco withdrew, returned to Keenan, and scowled at the hunched form of Paddy Pudson, crusted with ice, eyes gleaming malevolently as he stared down at the *trillion*-tonne machinery below, presumably used to excavate these vast caverns through which Combat-K now travelled like a worm through a rotten apple.

"What a fool," said Franco. "Fame and fortune? The only fame and fortune he's going to achieve is on the end of my fucking boot. What do you think, Keenan?"

"I think we're nearly there."

"Nearly where?"

"Look."

The Zeppelin3 had been drifting as Franco had his little chat with Pudson, and a wall like a cliff face reared above them, shearing off in a gentle curve into the distance of this ersatz interior sky. At the base, where the vast machines ended, they were replaced by *fields* of trucks, freight containers and tanks, all ancient, all coated in thousands of years of frost and ice. And here, Combat K could see an arch so vast they could pass fifty Zeppelin3s beneath its wonderful stone curve.

On the zenith of the arch, in kilometre high letters, was an ancient carving.

It read: WARD 1.

"We're here," said Keenan. "Get your shit together. We're going in."


"IT'S CREEPY," SAID Franco, as they floated near-silent beneath the arch. "It's spooky. It's freaky. It's giving me the heebie jeebies."

"Shut up," said Pippa between clenched teeth, her gun trained on... a wall. Of black ice. Slowly, they descended and touched down on rock. Behind, a cold wind howled through the Ward 1 archway, and before them, in the mountain-sized mass of humped cubic black ice, was a normal, white, hospital ward set of swing-doors. They were tiny, a sparkling contrast, like a diamond lost against the backdrop of a galaxy.

"Looks fishy," said Franco.

"As well as creepy, spooky and freaky?" snapped Pippa. "Gods, Franco, can't you learn to keep your big flapping mouth shut?"

"No," said Franco, in all seriousness. "I was Captain of our School Debating Team. It trained me to keep my mouth open at every possible opportunity, especially when being addressed by a particularly foxy young squad killer." He leered at Pippa, and gave her a wink... as something large and shovel-like, pressed against his arse.

Pippa turned from the hospital doors, which

seemed to glow, almost surreally, with a hint of whiter-than-white.

Olga loomed over Franco, beaming. "Hello sweetie," she said.

Franco coughed. "Um. Hello love," he said, and reaching up, pecked her on the cheek.

Pippa blinked a lazy, tomcat blink, and bared her teeth in a sudden wide and understanding grin. "So then," she drawled, as with deft hands she settled the Zeppelin3's engines and killed the power. The huge vehicle gave a *sigh*. "You two, you know, a bit of an item now, are you?"

Franco's smile was tighter-than-tight. "Yes."

"So, you fancy a slice of Olga pie, do you Franco?"

"Shut up."

"Fancy getting your face between those two massive ripe peaches of bosom, do you?"

"Shut up."

"Fancy giving her a bit of the slick Franco loving?"

"Shut up."

"After all, they don't call you Franco 'Horny Stud Muffin Who Can Fuck All Night' Haggis for nothing now, do they, eh Franco?"

"Shut up."

Pippa turned, and Keenan was pulling on his pack. Fizzy and Shazza had sorted out their kit, and removed the tight-fitting nurse uniforms which Franco seemed strangely reticent to remove. Snake was ready, with Olga his appointed guardian (for Health and Safety reasons, i.e. Snake's Health and Combat K's Safety). Betezh was packing guns, raided from the Zeppelin3's armoury, and only Franco seemed to be messing about, with Olga's hand apparently permanently spot-welded to his arse.

"We ready?" she said.

"Most of us," said Keenan, eyeing Franco warily. "You up for this gig, Franco? Or are you going to stay here and play with your fat girlfriend?" He switched to Olga. "No offence meant."

Olga grinned with teeth that could bite through live electric cabling. "None taken, stick man whom I could break like a brittle twig with one great blow of my great fists!" She leered close and winked. "Understand that, little jelly-man?"

Keenan laughed, and Pippa smiled. It was the first time she'd heard Keenan laugh in a long, long time; offset slightly by the fact he held onto his damaged ribs, and finished the laugh with a bout of painful coughing.

"Come on. Let's roll. The ice is beginning to close in on my brain. I'm starting to feel like I need one of those Rainbow Pills. Franco lad?"

"Yeah boss," said Franco, miserably, as he wrestled two-fisted with Olga's great, spade-like hand.

"Put some boots on, there's a good lad. The tight tits I can live with, but we can't have you hobbling around the place like a leper on ecstasy, can we?"

"Sure thing boss."

"What shall we do with him?" Pippa pointed at Paddy Pudson, who cringed back, cowering, face contorted in raw fear unlike any show of cowardice Combat-K had witnessed in a *very* long time.

"Slot him," said Franco, pulling on some thick-soled army boots. "Put a gun up his chuff and give him ten rounds."

"I implore thee," whined Paddy.

"For fuck's sake," muttered Keenan. "Tie him to the rail with some acid-rope. Good and tight. I doubt there's much he can get up to out here on his lonesome. We good to go, people?"

Everyone gave Keenan a nod, and Pippa unrolled the airship's ladder, which clacked to the rocky cavern floor. With only the whine of the wind moaning through the giant archway, they descended and walked across rock, guns primed, to stand behind Keenan at the doors to Ward 1. A ragtag band of miscreants and cutthroats, they looked more like a hardy crew of mutinied pirates than a professional group of elite special force soldiers.

Keenan placed his hand against the double doors, and pushed.

Bright white light greeted them.

Like lambs to the slaughter, they trooped inside the Asylum.

*  *  *

"WOW," SAID FRANCO.

They all stared about. The corridor was long, and wide, and brightly lit. The floor tiles, an alternating chequered pattern of green and white, gleamed. Everything was quiet. Still. Motionless. No breeze, no noise; a hiatus in time.

"It's so... clean," said Pippa.

"It's too clean," growled Keenan, MPK muzzle pressed against his cheek. "I don't like it. Get ready for something bad to happen... I can smell it on the breeze."

Franco gave a deep sigh, and Keenan looked sideways at him.

"What?" said Franco. "*What?* It's just this place mate, it's so, so, so reassuringly *clinical*. Not like those other bad places we visited with all the demented nurses and stuff. This is better. This is what a hospital *should* be like. I have spent a long time in hospitals and I know these things!"

"Stop talking."

"Yeah boss."

They eased forward, boots squeaking on immaculate tiles. They passed trolleys which gleamed, chrome shining like a waxed automobile. They passed wheelchairs, motionless, PVC buffed to a shine, tyre-rubbers a perfect gleaming grey, axles smeared with a dab of grease. They passed a wheeled stretcher, and Keenan reached out slowly, as if afraid the apparition might vanish. He touched crisp white cotton. He leant forward, and sniffed it.

"Well?" said Franco.

"It has a hint of lemon," said Keenan, frowning.

."This is a cool joint," said Franco, beaming a smile.

"How can it be a cool joint, dickweed?" said Pippa. "It's a damn hospital corridor!"

"You don't understand." Franco looked almost dreamy. "I had some reet good times at the Mount Pleasant."

"I thought they electrocuted your testicles?"

"Hey," Franco nudged Pippa, grinning, and looking quite delirious in his tight nurse uniform. "You could always give it a try, if you like."

Olga muscled forward, and didn't quite push between Franco and Pippa. She smiled, a broad smile that reminded Franco of an alligator yawning.

"Olga uneasy," said Olga, and cracked her tattooed knuckles. She hoisted her D5 and stared around. "This place, it smell like... like a lunatic place."

"How would you know that?" said Franco.

Olga shrugged her huge shoulders. "She just does! Stop asking ze questions. You get Olga all confused."

The woolly silence was broken by the sound of distant footsteps, and a bristle of weapons crackled through the corridor, too many muzzles pointing at the distant set of double swing doors.

Keenan eased the team forward, their movements fluid now with the promise of further combat, their faces streaked with dirt, and sweat, and blood, and droplets of pus. They looked worse than any deranged combat squad had a right to look; and against the pristine and immaculate surroundings of this virginal hospital corridor, there seemed to be a curious visual reversal.

The footsteps grew louder, ponderous in their measured pendulum. They stopped just beyond the double doors, and Keenan moved forward, gun before him, eyes hardened and face a mask. His weapon lowered, jaw muscles tightening, and Pippa read his intention... to put rounds through the wood.

"No," she said, her words drifting down the sterile avenue.

The double doors swung open and, stooping to fit his bulk through the wide expanse, a huge, *huge* man pushed himself through the portal, like a turtle's head emerging from its shell. He was big. No. He was *big*. He didn't walk into the stretch of corridor, he rolled into it, his layers of fat falling over themselves in an eagerness to obey gravity. The man's head was like a potato, with a thick shaggy mane of brown hair, huge laughter lines, and deep brown eyes, each as big as a man's fist. He had a huge shaggy beard which reached almost down to his waist, and was not so much a singular entity as a continuation of the mane of hair he wore on his head, giving him the look of a huge potato-lion.

In terms of fashion, there was no sign of the recurrent medical theme here. He wore what could only be described as a baggy smock, rainbow-striped, thick-knitted, loose and, one presumed, easy to move in. It was a dress. It was a tent. However, it could not disguise the battle of the flab, currently lost. His arms and legs were thick, powerful, and naked. He wore boots that had seen better days, and laced with bright colourful tassels. Overall, he gave the impression of a fat hippy grizzly bear.

"Holy bat shit!" said Franco, his tongue lolling out.

Keenan simply cocked his weapon with a single, echoing, determined *click*.

The bear-man beamed down at them, as if they were his newly-found best friends. He roared with laughter, suddenly, a blast of hot mirth that made Keenan cringe, and the giant rolled forward a few steps and placed his hands on his hips, head touching the ceiling.

"Welcome!" he boomed. "I am Lunatrick, and you have entered my domain!" He laughed again, a great bubbling geyser outpouring of sound that welled from his considerable belly and emerged like a flow of comedy lava.

Franco eased forward. He coughed. "Um, Lunatic?" he said.

"No no!" The huge bear waggled a finger, and Franco found himself momentarily hypnotised by that gesticulating digit. "I am Lunatrick! I am the king! This is my Ward! My Asylum! The Mad Morgue! The Looney Bin! The Chamber of Comedy Conniption!"

"Um," began Franco, who could be a pedant.

"And yes," roared the giant, Lunatrick, "you are *very welcome!* We don't get visitors often and I'm not sure why! Yes you are, we had those visitors the other decade and you crushed them in the Randy Rollers! No, I don't remember that, what are you talking about? Actually, you're both wrong because there *were* visitors but they had guns and tried to shoot us, me, him, all of us, and we ended up putting them in the Boiling Pot of Horrors where they, um, boiled to death, remember? I remember no I don't!"

Lunatrick beamed at the stunned gathering. Weapons bristled uneasily. Franco toyed with the pin on a BABE grenade. It would be so easy... one pluck, one twist, roll it under the fat man's practically immobile body and *boom!* Lunatrick, specialist organic wallpaper.

"Actually," said Pippa, forcing a smile, "what you said, just then, didn't actually really make any sense."

"Yes it did no it didn't it's because they don't know but should we tell them because if we tell 'em they might get scared and think we're... mad."

Lunatrick beamed again, and something scuttled through the shaggy mane of hair, surfaced, tiny little beady eyes staring, and then disappeared like an otter in a pond. "Sorry. It's complicated."

Keenan pulled out his silver cigarette case, shouldered his weapon, and rolled himself a smoke. Lunatrick watched Keenan, a huge smile on his broad chops. Keenan lit the weed, took a deep puff, and blew smoke in Lunatrick's face.

Lunatrick gave a little cough.

"Why don't you explain it," said Keenan, with a tight smile.

"YES!" boomed Lunatrick. "I might but it could get complicated so listen very careful! Especially those at the back!" Lunatrick beamed at Fizzy, Shazza and Snake. They scowled at him as one, guns not quite pointing away from him and his big beard.

Lunatrick settled himself on the ground, his colourful rasta-robes spreading out around him, like a chicken settling on a batch of eggs. "You are in my Kingdom, my World," he began. "I am the Asylum King, and Ward 1 was the original ward of Sick World, of Krakken IV. I have been here from the beginning. Yes. That is so."

"But..." said Franco.

"Yes?"

"That'd make you over a thousand years old!" blurted the little ginger squaddie.

"Yes. It has been a long hard struggle, often backwards. Here, we are a thousand *looonies*.

We are the maniacs, the greebos, the vagabonds, the freaks, the gypsies, the deviated, the frankies, and we number more than five thousand now, an incredible feat, for coming by extra body parts is a real bitch."

He smiled again.

"You said looonies," said Franco, again, the pedant.

"Yes. Looonies."

"Don't you mean loonies?"

"No. We have extra oomph. You'll see. When you meet them shall we show them? Yes, that would be wise. But only after we've told them. That makes sense. Not to me it doesn't. Don't be such an idjit. Now then, back to business, telling you about my army. The Army of the Mad. That's me, Lunatrick, and my droogs, the Army of the Mad."

He paused.

"You are *insane*," hissed Pippa.

"Exactly," said Lunatrick.

"But he's blocking the way," whispered Keenan, "and it'd take more than an elephant gun to shift the bastard. So let's hear him out; maybe the looony can help us."

"I was the Ward Manager," said Lunatrick. "In the beginning. I was human. Once. Sort of." He giggled, and rocked back and forth. Long pools of saliva drooled, pooling in his lap, but he seemed not to notice. "But things changed, the luna went ding-dong, and topworld cut us off, cut the chain, pulled the plug, cast us out and down and twisted into downside, madworld, luna, but they called it luna meaning *lunatic*, not the moon, the green moon. Why don't you tell them about the Upsamid? Yes. That would make sense, for we've been waiting for the Keenan for a thousand years. Ever since boy-o told us about him. Yes. He did, didn't he? Yes. He sure did glad we got that all sorted out and straightened away."

"What the hell's wrong with you, lad?" snapped Franco. "Can't you speak proper like what I does?"

"I am tri-polar," said Lunatrick smugly, playing with his strings of drool.

"You mean bi-polar," said Franco, a self-appointed expert on all things mental. "I knows about that, so I do."

"Tri-polar," said Lunatrick. "I am home to three personalities. Unfortunately, we never get on we fucking well do, no we don't you two muppets are always arguing and I'm the only sane one anyway looonies why are you two arguing when we should be discussing the Upsamid? Yes, the Upsamid, tell Keenan about what the Junkala King said about showing him to the Upsamid."

"The Junkala King said I would come?" Keenan's eyes were shining.

"He saw you. In a fast-forward dream. A twisted prophecy, no less. I we us have to take you to the Upsamid, show you how to reach the Elysium Casket and that will point you in the direction of VOLOS will it? Yes it shure nuff will and that's what these dudes want a way of finding VOLOS to sort out this godforsaken cursed ball of mango." Lunatrick's look suddenly shifted, in a way very reminiscent of Franco; Pippa and Keenan exchanged knowing glances.

"What's that mean?" scowled Franco.

"It's the crafty witch-look of the mad," said Pippa.

"Conniption," said Keenan, tapping his nose conspiratorially.

"Yeah, conniption," smiled Pippa.

Keenan took several steps closer, and the huge bloated Lunatrick looked up at the soldier. "You want something, don't you?" said Keenan. It wasn't really intuition, because Lunatrick observed a kind of genetically-modified Arthur-Daley-ducking-diving-fucking-skiving aura that befitted every used car, buggy and shuttle salesman Quad-Gal wide. "What is it? What do you want?"

"I want a new world," said Lunatrick, eyes gleaming.

"Meaning?"

"Exactly what it says on the tin. I was here, Keenan, from the start. I was here at the beginning of Sick World. I watched the Sick Crates being lowered, helped smash off the sides and watched the wounded, the lame, the diseased, watched the krooped, the muffled, and the kijangered, watched them all limp, walk, hop, and slither from their

Sick Crates. But we never cured them, did we? We never helped them... we just made matters worse."

Keenan realised with a start that Lunatrick was crying, huge tears from his huge brown eyes. Despite his obvious lack of secure screws, it was still a touching sight. Lunatrick cared about the deviants of Sick World. Because he remembered them when they were not so; remembered the abuse of medical trust.

"OK," said Keenan, throwing Pippa a scowl. She shook her head, and rubbed at weary eyes. "I'll make a deal. Lead us to VOLOS and QGM will find you a planet. Uninhabited. And we'll do an airlift for all who want to leave. How does that sound? A fresh start. The chance to begin again."

"There's something else," said Lunatrick, rubbing at his eyes and sucking up huge drools of snot that hung from his over-large nostrils. He chewed for a few moments, thinking, then swallowed.

"What do you want next, our fucking eyeballs?" muttered Pippa.

"Shut up," snapped Keenan. Then, "Go on, what is it?"

"You must reverse the mutations," said Lunatrick. "Everything you see here, on this planet, it is as a result of VOLOS. We are his personal playthings. The wars they fight up above," he gestured with a hand the size of Franco's head, "they are engineered by VOLOS. But more importantly, we are a test bed for the junks, guinea pigs, experimentations,

VOLOS serves a Higher Purpose. Or so he thinks. I we us are tired of seeing the abuse and endless suffering. We want it to end."

"We can end it with napalm," muttered Pippa.

"I will do what I can," said Keenan, "because I understand, understand VOLOS, I can see glimpses of his mind like water droplets in ice. And, bizarrely, VOLOS is intrigued by our little escapade. I don't think he'll hinder us, too much."

"Why not?" snarled Pippa. "He's done a damn good job so far."

"Because," said Keenan, eyes narrowed, "he wants something."

"What's that? Our testicles?" said Franco.

"No," said Keenan, staring hard at Lunatrick, who had started gibbering and playing with his fingers. "When the *Kahirrim*, Emerald, entered each of our minds, she left a residue, a substance which has altered us from human. Made us…"

"Hot damn superhuman!" exclaimed Franco. "I always knew I was special!" he beamed.

"Yeah, special fucking needs," said Pippa caustically.

"I'll give you some special needs," Franco said, and licked his lips.

"Only when I'm unconscious," said Pippa.

"That can be arranged."

"You're a bloody pervert!"

"I try," said Franco, with a grin.

"He wants us. To experiment with." Keenan's

smile was glass-cold. "He wants to add us to the Sick World gene pool, see what new and interesting breeds he can develop. This place has become stale for VOLOS; there's no new blood, no new meat. There's been no new genetics for a thousand years; the place is a DNA ghost-ship."

"Except for us," said Pippa, voice cold. "Shit. Keenan, we've come stumbling in blind. They've not been trying to kill us, not all of them; they've been *playing* with us. We're the icing for the cake. The cherry on the Bakewell."

"Using Emerald's special powers," said Keenan, quietly. He could see it, now, the colossal cold spaces of VOLOS's brain; or at least, whatever the thing was that formed VOLOS's brain, "I can *feel* him."

"He's not human, is he?" said Pippa.

"No. He's trapped here. He's stuck. Locked in place. All fresh meat has to come to him; he has to use a carrot, a lure, bait to entice you into his trap. I bet he threw a party when they set up Sick World; I bet he was like a naive kid in a brand new sweet factory."

"I'm losing this," said Franco. "Who's the kid in the sweet factory?"

"Just check your bombs," said Keenan, voice cool. "We're gonna need lots."

LUNATRICK LED THE way, down spotless corridors, past immaculate wheelchairs and trolleys and wheeled stretchers. They crossed wards full of sparkling equipment, polished floors, beds made up with fresh linen just waiting to receive patients – patients who would never arrive.

"I don't get it," said Franco, as they followed Lunatrick down a long ward containing perhaps fifty beds, all neatly made, all with immaculate bedside cabinets containing jugs of fresh water, sprays of colourful flowers, handmade "Get Well Soon" cards and cardboard piss-pots. There were TVs on extendable arms. It was most civilised. "Why keep it so neat? So tidy? What happened to entropy? What happened to the damn and bloody kipple, eh, I ask you?"

"Because," said Lunatrick, whirling and causing everyone to back-peddle. He smiled. "I have pride in my work." He turned, and continued his ponderous march on heavy boots, flab bouncing.

Franco composed his ruffled feathers. "Hot damn, he nearly got a D5 shotgun blast up his nostrils." He shouted, "Hey mate, don't do that again, reet? I nearly shot your big fat head clean off!"

Lunatrick stopped before large white swing doors. Beyond, there was a roaring sound, a little bit like a waterfall. He focused on Franco, and said, "You wouldn't be the first, my friend, no he wouldn't would he tell him about Big Bill Bates and the Mighty Morphine Shotgun Sellers oh we can't what do you mean we can't why can't you two simply be quiet when I'm trying to have a damn conversation all that bloody happens is you confuse the situation and everyone gets mentally mashed up and we don't know who the hell is talking to who. Right? Right. Right." He smiled, nodding in understanding; an understanding only he understood.

Franco was about to utter a retort when Lunatrick pushed open the swing doors and Franco's jaw clacked shut. For beyond was a hospital ward bigger than anything Franco, or the others, had ever seen. It was like a football pitch. No. It was like *ten* football pitches. The roof was high and airy, the whole place suffused with a strange white light, not quite daylight, but near enough. There were beds. Thousands and thousands of beds, all laid out in neat rows. Amidst this apparent order scampered and cavorted Lunatrick's Army of the Mad. Five thousand mental inmates, more loony than loony, locked away inter-breeding for a thousand years to create –

"Wow," said Keenan, honestly stunned; and not in a good way.

"It's like an inter-galactic gene-pool gone wrong," said Pippa.

"It's cool!" beamed Franco watching a *flock* of about a hundred patients, wearing straightjackets, go swarming across one area of the massive ward in very much the manner of a shoal of fish.

"What are they all doing?" said Keenan, in awe.

"They are keeping the place clean," said Lunatrick, voice soft as he led the group to a balcony which overlooked the vast ward. "Awaiting the day the great god from the sky rescues them and takes them to a New World."

Franco moved close, and patted Keenan on the shoulder. "That'd be you, then, mate," he said, relishing the irony.

"Shut up," said Keenan from between clenched teeth.

"God to Five Thousand Looonies!"

"Shut up."

"Father to an Army of the Mad!" Franco persisted, never one to let go of a good bone.

"I'll give you an army of my *fist* in the middle of your *face*," said Keenan.

"Now now," said Franco, holding up a hand, "no need to be like that! Getting all violent, like. I was just making an observation."

"*'Getting all violent?'*" snarled Keenan. "We're bloody soldiers!" He calmed himself, and focused. He saw Shazza and Fizzy grinning at him, and gave a short laugh, rubbing his eyes. "Gods, this isn't what I expected when we touched down... well, what seems over a month ago now!"

Olga moved forward, eyes watching the thousands of cavorting lunatics down below. "You are doing well, Keenan. Let's go an find ze VOLOS, no? Let's kick his big Sick World ass to the moon and back, no?" She rumbled with laughter, and cracked her knuckles.

"This way," said Lunatrick. "We need to get on the LooonieTrain. It will take us through the Layers to the Upsamid." They moved down wide metal steps – all scrubbed spotlessly clean – and beneath the staircase stood a small, white train, which gleamed with chrome parts and polished steel. It had a single carriage, filled with luxury.

"This is one damn strange place," muttered Franco.

"Get in," hissed Pippa. "And don't say a word."

"Why, what's the problem?"

"Nothing."

"It's made of bone," said Olga, leaning close to Franco, so close he could see the small blue dots tattooed on her cheeks. "Ze whole thing, carved from one huge piece of bone! It is most disturbing to see, if you take ze step back!"

"Holy hot damn and bloody crotch bollocks!" snapped Franco, staring, eyes wide at what he realised was a very *clever* piece of... sculpture. A modern art masterpiece, no less. He moved close, eyed the polished tracks of the narrow-gauge lines, then ran his hand down the train's gleaming flank. It was smooth, and polished, like aged ivory.

Lunatrick gestured, and the group piled into the carriage. Lunatrick moved to the engine block, which even now was hissing softly and emitting thin jets of steam. Suddenly, a horde of lunatics came sprinting over the beds and down the ward aisles, gibbering and chundering, drooling and monkeying, some in straightjackets, some with their arms on backwards, many with only one leg, hopping enthusiastically, eyes a-gleaming. Franco leant back, boot raised to ascend the carriage with a squeak of rubbery PVC nurse uniform and revealing one huge and hairy buttock, but the lunatics swarmed past Franco, unseeing, and crowded around Lunatrick, hoisting the fat King's bulk up and heaving, squashing him into the engine cockpit like a rat squeezed into a matchbox. Lunatrick made many grunting, moaning sounds. Franco stared, eyes wide.

Shazza prodded him with her gun. "Get *in*, idiot."

Franco gawped, but climbed into the carriage and sat on the polished bone seat. The squad piled in, bristling with guns, and stared around at the smooth, polished environment. Despite its cleanliness, it was the cleanliness of a carcass picked clean by buzzards. Despite a lack of stench, it was the non-stench of a quarantined leper colony. Despite its bloodlessness, it was the bloodlessness of a vampire-scourged city. Drank clean.

Franco shivered. "It's like a morgue," he said.

"Don't be so melodramatic," snapped Pippa. "It's a damn train carriage. Act your age."

"No, I agree," said Keenan, and lit a cigarette. Harsh Widow Maker tobacco filled the small compartment. Snake started coughing, and Olga's gun wavered towards the eye-patch wearing mercenary who had remained strangely silent since rejoining the group. Keenan hoped it was a form of contrition; but he doubted it. "This is so plain and simple, yet so creepy. Inside a hollowed out bone. The question that leaps to my mind is, what sort of creature made the bone?"

"It was a big one," said Pippa.

"A big bone," said Franco, slowly.

"Don't," said Pippa, wincing.

"Oh. My. God." Franco's face went wide. "We're inside a cock!" he snapped, face white with shock, straggle-haired beard bristling. "I can't bloody believe it! I've been inside an arse, I've been inside a giant dildo, and now a steam-powered cock! Does the god of Franco Humiliation *know* no bounds? Does the many-spined omniscient monstrosity of Mocked Francos *have* no remorse? Of course not! Because Francis is here to be ridiculed by the Many Gods of Humour Central, to be joked about, to be mocked and slapped and ribbed and poked! If Nature is a natural entity, She is having a laugh, She is pointing Her finger, and She is rolling on Her back spewing comedy situations for our heroic hero, that's me, that is, Franco! to fall and stumble and tumble into unexpectedly like a flickering fly into a Venus Fly Trap, only probably! yes probably! with a giant vagina at the bottom, or maybe a giant vagina bottom, at the bottom! Ha!"

"Here," said Keenan, and handed Franco a small blue pill.

"Cheers mate."

Franco chewed in silence, as everyone stared at him, many with horror. Thankfully, Lunatrick chose that moment to fire up the bone engine and, with a jolt, they eased away from the huge steel staircase and set off between thousands of rows of neatly-made hospital beds.

"What a place," said Keenan, smoking, and watching the lunatics scroll past. Many waved, those without arms encumbered by straightjackets. Keenan waved back.

"It's horrorshow," agreed Pippa, and watched Fizzy and Shazza talking quietly, heads leant close together, eyes shining. They seemed upset. Fizzy reached out, and stroked a strand of hair from Shazza's eyes and *something* went click, inside Pippa, inside her breast, inside her heart. Suddenly, she realised she missed contact. Real, honest, naked physical contact. She was so caught up in the process of violence and death, destruction and detonation, that she had forgotten, or pushed aside, the simple needs of the woman inside, the girl inside. To be held, to be touched, to be kissed. Simple, real, human contact.

Pippa sighed, and looked at Keenan. He returned her gaze, and smiled. He was ragged and battered, torn and bloodied. He had two broken fingers strapped tightly together; luckily, one wasn't his trigger finger.

Outside, the simple bone train picked up speed. It chugged. Steam formed a billow around the funnel as it sped between hundreds and hundreds of rows of hospital beds, all manned, cleaned, perfected by the Army of the Mad.

Pippa gave a little shake of her head, caught Keenan watching her, and she returned his smile. Then with a sudden start, she wondered how she looked and stood, locating a polished plate of chrome by the door. She stared into the face of a stranger, a battered, bruised, bloodied, tattered hooligan, a street-tramp with crap in her matted hair, grease and dirt-streaks on her swollen face. "Shit," she muttered, equating that to the way she perceived herself now. Something touched her hand, and looking down she realised it was Keenan's questing fingers. She took his hand, and he squeezed her fingers, and in that simple single moment, in that spark of connection, of brushed skin, of honest intimacy, she suddenly realised everything was all right between them. Well, not *all right*, but the kill had gone. Keenan no longer wanted her dead. And that, in itself, was a massive leap forward; a milestone achievement of incredible understanding. Possibly even forgiveness.

*I didn't do it*, she said to herself.

And she almost believed it.

*I didn't kill his family.*

It was a set-up. I was framed.

But how? Why? And by whom?

And a word leapt to her mind, and somehow, deep within the pulse of her blood, she felt a tickling sensation that swept through her veins and this connection with Keenan, this reawakening of trust, sent sparks running up and down her spine and seemed to *ignite* the alien essence left in her by the *Kahirrim*, Emerald. Ganger, came the word. Search the ganger. And Pippa knew; knew it was her *employer*, Quad-Gal Military, who had turned her into what she had become; but more than that, they had betrayed her, made Keenan hate her. In a flash of understanding she realised QGM had murdered Keenan's family. But why? Why would they do such a thing? And how had they used *her* as the puppet?

Did she *really* use scissors?

With a start, Pippa realised she was crying, and Keenan stood, his body close to hers and rocking gently with the lull of the charging train. The rock pushed them together, and for a brief instant the lengths of their bodies touched. Then they shifted away, like a tease, and Pippa looked up into his eyes.

"It wasn't me," she said.

"Shh," said Keenan, and touched her lips.

"I wouldn't do that to you."

Keenan grinned, like a skull on speed. He wanted to say, *of course you wouldn't, I believe you, I love you, I know you would never do anything to harm my family*. But he didn't believe it. He knew; knew Pippa was a killer, a psycho assassin of the lowest order. He knew it. She knew it. And she knew he understood her soul. The dark corners. The dark places only she, alone, could explore in the lost hours of the night.

Instead, she rested her head against his chest. And was happy with that.

Further down the carriage, where Franco had gone to calm himself after the twisted realisation he rode inside a giant phallus, and thus needed medication to straighten his warped brain, Franco suddenly became aware of a proximity. By the time she was there, it was far, far too late.

"Hi sweetie," rumbled Olga, and sat down, taking up two seats which flexed, creaking in protest.

Franco stared into that wide brutal face, with its tiny dark eyes, and he sought as hard as he could to find something to complement her on. "Um," he said, grinning wildly, the narcotics in his system playing sudden havoc with his reality; with his major malfunction. "Your ponytail is looking very neat today," he said.

"I oiled it," said Olga, and leant in close. She stank of sweat and gun-oil and cordite. Her huge bosom pressed against Franco urgently and he laughed nervously, wondering what it was about him that attracted lunatic women who didn't understand a simple "fuck off".

Franco went to shift, but she was there, nuzzling his neck, his throat clamped in one powerful hand. Her tongue wormed trails of saliva across Franco's neck and cheek and forehead.

"Ahh," he said. "You see, the thing is... ahh..."

"You like, no?" said Olga, and nibbled his nose.

Her free hand, the one not clamped around his throat in a strangler's iron hold, stroked along his inner thigh.

"Um, I was just a-thinkin', we, should, possibly, wait, a, like, a minute," said Franco uselessly. He was like a turtle on its back. A newborn chick. A fly caught useless in a web... stuck and struggling.

"Om," said Olga, as her mouth clamped over his, and she French-kissed him with a strength, power and ferocity he'd totally expected. She was like a drowning woman coming up for air. She was like an industrial bolt-sucker. She was a turbine in reverse, only she didn't just suck him of fluids, she sucked him of life, and when she finally released him from her predatory grasp, gasping and flailing like a gassed and headless chicken, blue in the face from oxygen starvation, swooning from a manic head-rush, the small blue pill finally kicked in, surging Franco's system with a *flood* of narcotic craziness that sent his mind spinning and his brain pulsing. New colours were invented in nanoseconds. New tastes skimmed Franco's palette. He tasted red and smelt chords and saw the essence of peaches and cream.

"Wow," he said. "Do it again!"

And so, as the train chugged through Ward 1 with Franco kicking and flailing like a murder victim, he had the snog of his life.

THE TRAIN JOURNEY went on for longer than anybody expected. Occasionally, Lunatrick would shout back through the open window of the carriage from his perch in the engine's cockpit. Things like, "Over there we installed five hundred new beds, just waiting for the next delivery of needful mental patients no we didn't actually excuse me I think we did gods I wish you two dickheads would stop your jabbering," and, "That's where we had the great Diazepam Wars of the Fifteen Decades but we all agreed on different sides and it's hard trying to direct a battle when somebody else in your own head knows your plans and sells them to the opposing force for extra dollars for sugary donuts in the canteen." The occupants of the bone carriage nodded, sagely, and wondered just how big a *ward* could actually be. They also wondered just *when the hell* Lunatrick would realise that he and the other patients were in a closed circuit, a loop, and no matter how well he maintained his Asylum – well, they weren't ever getting any new patients. Period.

The train started to increase its speed, accelerating over the horizon of beds. They thrummed past, and Keenan glanced at Pippa. "How many do you reckon there are? A million? Two?"

"At least," said Pippa. "It's a gross misappropriation of hospital funds. The management should be fucking ashamed of themselves. Ha ha."

Keenan gave a smile halfway between nasty and sardonic. "Well," he said, grimacing, "why change the habits of the last fucking millennia? It's always the hospital management that fuck it up, with deviated funding, backhand bonuses and under-staffing. They should be fucking skewered."

Snake eased forward down the carriage, and sat beside Keenan. "It's going all weird," he said.

Keenan stared at Snake as a lion stares at a human; in base hatred, distaste, but with the wariness of meeting a despised cunning and lethal fellow predator.

"What is?"

Snake nodded to the window. "Look."

Outside, the speeding passage of beds seemed to *bend*. The whole vision of the outside world was curving, and the mental patients had fallen behind, now leaving nothing but vast acres of spotless, neatly-folded hospital beds. Millions of them. Waiting for patients that would never come.

Even as Keenan watched, the curve became more pronounced and he stumbled to his feet, glancing over at the other members of the squad, all of whom were agitated. All except Franco. He was staring out of the window, whistling.

"What do you see?" snarled Keenan.

"Nothing," said Franco, giving Keenan a strange look. "You OK? You look like that time you had seventeen pints of Wife Beater and that dodgy ostrich kebab. You were sick all over that homosexual lap-dancing senile delinquent. Those were the days!"

"It's curving!" said Keenan. "The whole world outside is curving!"

Franco glanced outside, then back to Keenan. "You're drunk, mate," he snorted. "It's fine, reet?"

But the world wasn't fine. They were moving faster and faster and faster, and the curve became a ball into which they sank, or sliced, down and down through layers of hospital beds, through stacks of arched bedside tables, and Keenan ran to the front of the carriage and bellowed, "Lunatrick! What the hell's going on?"

"Don't worry," boomed Lunatrick, his fat jowls wobbling under his huge beard. "We have to accelerate to enter the Globular Plain, we need to dissect the Layers to get to the Upsamid. It's a protection mechanism, to keep out unwanted thingies, just sit back and relax, and let old Uncle Lunatrick guide you."

Keenan slumped back, and felt the curvature pinning him to one side of the carriage. They were all holding on now, grasping brass door handles and black leather seat-straps as the pull of G-force edged them across the carriage towards the right-hand side... all except Franco, who sat perfectly still, unmoving, staring at the other members of Combat-K in shock and horror, with maybe a sprinkling of confetti confusion and a big dollop of craziness.

"What the damn and bloody unicorn-radish hell are you all playing at?" he snapped. "Are you all *crazee*, or something?"

And that was it, Keenan realised. They weren't insane, but were entering a place of insanity – a distillation of madness. And in that place, only the truly insane could happily exist. Keenan ground his teeth under the agony of forced pressure, eyes fixed in jealousy on Franco's relaxed body, his wrinkled brow, his flexing fingers ready to come to the aid of his dodgy and quite obviously *ill* friends in need...

"You mad bastard," muttered Keenan, and to the rattling shrieking clanking of the engine and carriage, he was forced away from reality, and passed out, and rattled on into a seemingly endless oblivion.

CAM SAT ON the bottom of the Silglace river and was trapped, pinned down, made a prisoner. He felt the savage acids attacking his case, organic and intelligent in their simple methanol-based intelligence, but he was smug in the knowledge that they could do nothing to penetrate his advanced shell and bodywork. He was not simple flesh and bone, but a PopBot! Yes! A War Machine! He had survived Biohell! He was, it had to be said, a GradeA+1 Security Mechanism with advanced SynthAI and a Machine Intelligence Rating (MIR) of 3450. I have integral weapon inserts, a quad-core military database, and some severe Put Down™ War Technology. He grinned. He knew it.

However.

The Silglace, vegetable-sentient, knew it was having little effect on the *invader*; thick tendrils of silver mucus encased Cam, and held him there, pinned to the bottom as he frantically sought a power source from which to scour a recharge.

After a billion possibilities, Cam realised with a start, and a seeping feeling of dread, that there was *no* central power source, no wholesome seat of energy to which he could attach, vampiric, and drain the host of valuable resources.

No.

And without power, Cam would never be able to prime his motors to break free of the Silglace's pull. They were entwined, locked together, and if the Silglace so chose, it would last for an eternity... or until his shell eventually rotted and crumbled to powder.

"Bugger," he said. "I buggered this one up." It seemed the most succinct response.

He sat for a while, angry with himself, fuming

with himself, and wondering what the hell he could do.

All comms were down. Except the spinal-logic pulse idea. But that, hell, that only worked on humans, right?

Cam gave himself a smile. He had an idea.

He sent a *pulse* using the Silglace as a carrier.

And thousands of kilometres away, something snoring woke up.

Keenan awoke slowly, as if from a Sunday morning slumber. The world was fuzzy, a distillation of disorientation. His mouth felt like feathers. His eyeballs were stuck to their sockets. He groaned, and sat up with wooden teeth and tartan thoughts, to see the rest of the squad similarly coming around as if from a toxic anaesthetic. He glanced back, but the train was nowhere to be seen – only Lunatrick, big and fat and grinning, with his rainbow robes billowing, his eyes sparkling. He scratched enthusiastically at his beard.

"Come on, come on! Up up up! We have a long way to go!"

Keenan glanced to where Lunatrick pointed, across an undulating white landscape to the distant *bulk* of the Upsamid. He squinted, but could make out no details through an early morning haze. *Impossible, right? We're inside the planet, inside Sick World, how can there be a bloody atmosphere?*

Franco bounded up, and punched Keenan on

the arm. Keenan winced, because Franco had a powerful right straight, as befitted a pugilist.

"Ey up!" he said. "Look here! *And* to our benefit, we're no longer inside that cock."

"It was a train, Franco."

Franco pouted. "Looked like a big ol' cock to me! And the only cock *I* want to get inside is, an, an, an, um…"

"Yes?" said Pippa, sweetly, moving beside Franco. "So you do fancy a slice of Man Pie every now and again?"

"I didn't say that!"

"You suggested that there *was* a type of cock you'd like to get inside. Now, whilst I'm not quite sure how one would accomplish such a feat, I'm sure you'd give it your best shot, Franco, little buddy. Ain't that so?"

"No!" he went red. "I'm being misrepresented!"

"You misrepresent yourself," snapped Keenan. "Fizzy, Shazza, Snake, I want you up front with Lunatrick. I've got a nasty feeling about this place, and I like to trust my intuition. Betezh?"

"Yeah?" Betezh had been quiet for a while, and seemed to be nursing a hangover.

Keenan stared at him. "Have you been drinking?"

"No! Well, yes. Just a little."

"What did you drink?" said Keenan through gritted teeth.

"Just a bit of voddie. To warm myself, you know, against the cold."

"And where the *fuck*," said Keenan, "did you manage to get vodka in this desolate shit-hole?"

Betezh glanced at Franco. Keenan turned. Franco was whistling a little tune.

"Well?"

"Look Keenan, it was just a nip, alreet? Found it in a locker. T'was *medicinal* vodka, so that's all right, isn't it, because we were just using a medicine, not the alcohol, reet?" He beamed, as Keenan pushed past him roughly, and followed the ambling mass of Lunatrick across the – now he thought about it – *soft* white landscape.

"If you two idiots drink again on my mission, you'll be going home with your balls in your rucksack. You understand?"

"Yes Keenan."

"Yes Keenan."

Franco leant in close to Betezh, and whispered, "He's a damn spoil-sport, the old grump."

THE WORLD WAS filled with a diffused glow, and Pippa found herself staring hard at the sky. It was curved, gently curved, and she felt as if she stood inside a snow globe, peering out. The more she looked, the more her eyes decoded what she saw; the whole sky was a tapestry of tiny ward beds, millions of them, forming a hazy bright pattern.

"You see the sky?" she said.

"I'm worried more about the ground," said Keenan. He paused, knelt, and touched the white.

Then, he pulled off his glove and squeezed the substance. "It's a hospital sheet," he said, glancing up at Pippa with a frown. "Rolling, like desert sand dunes. But the whole thing is white cotton, soft to the touch."

"Strange."

"Odd."

They moved off, following Lunatrick. They seemed to walk for a very long time across the squishy, padded, cotton floor. Above, from different angles, as if witnessed through a sky-size diamond, different facets of Ward 1 could be witnessed on angular planes. It was disconcerting, as if the world had gone mad; as if the sky had deformed and forgotten its insanity pill. They approached a dark forest, which spread on their left up the flanks of a hill. It was only as the squad grew close they realised that what they saw were not, in fact, trees.

"What is that?" said Pippa, squinting.

Franco stared. He had the best eyesight in the group, as befitted the official sniper. "They're hypodermic needles," he said, eventually.

"How do you mean?"

"The trees," replied Franco with a tight smile. "The trunks are made up of thick hypodermic needles, and each branch is a twisted needle. Each needle drips fluid from its tip, and the leaves are... are..." He scowled.

"Yeah?"

"Sanitary pads," he said, face straight, eyes just a touch glazed.

"So the landscape is medicinal," said Keenan. "It's taken on the characteristics of the hospital. The land itself has changed into an organic version of the medical. This is complete warped madness."

"Or logical," said Franco.

"What do you mean?"

"The entire technology, machine guns, weapons, all of it is based on hospital technology. It seems like the whole planet, the whole of *Sick World* has absorbed what data it can and modelled itself. Look!" Franco pointed, and they all stopped, lining the banks of the narrow river. To one side, distant, was a bridge spanning the thick flowing grey water. The bridge was made from a giant leg-straightening brace, complete with leather straps and rods controlled by screws. It shone like new chrome.

Pippa knelt by the river edge, dipped her finger in the water.

"Wait," said Franco. "Don't taste it. It ain't water."

"What is it?"

"Morphine," Franco grinned amiably. "I recognise the smell. It's one of my smells of choice. And they don't call me Franco 'Bloodhound' Haggis for nothing, you know. I can smell a poppy from a thousand mile mountain top. I can smell the cheese from a goat's teat. Baby, I can smell *sex*."

He leered for a moment, but Lunatrick lumbered over to them. He appeared nervous, which looked just plain wrong on his huge bearded face.

"What is it?" said Keenan.

"We must hurry. We have company."

"What kind of company?"

"Bad company," snapped Lunatrick, frowning. Even as he spoke, the last syllable was drowned by a massive, distant concussive *crack*. Instinctively, everybody looked up and through the millions of facets of the sky, saw a surge of activity, flashes of colour, and more bright violent explosions.

Lunatrick, wobbling now at a fast run, and surprising everybody by his sheer turn of speed, ran for the bridge. They crossed the chrome expanse with its flapping leather brace straps, and then headed closer to the hypodermic trees and on towards the Upsamid.

Lunatrick was panting hard, now, and a muffled sound followed them. It was the sound of machine guns, the roar of detonation, the crack of HighJ explosives. There was a battle being fought in the underground realm of Ward 1.

"They're invading," panted Lunatrick, face serious and dour. "The bastards! I never thought they would invade."

"Who's invading?" said Franco.

"The deviated doctors and nurses, from above. VOLOS's armies! They know you are down here. They want to stop you, halt you from finding the

path to VOLOS. But they are too late!" His eyes
shone with triumph.

More booms echoed, and ahead of the group the
Upsamid grew quickly huge. It was black, slick,
frosted with ice. It was a pyramid, but completely
inverted and standing on its tip. From ground level,
the tip of the upside-down pyramid's slick smooth
walls travelled outwards towards its massive base
high in the sky, probably a kilometre in width. Like
an impossibility of engineering, the Upsamid hung
stable and solid. It drew their eyes, and twisted
their minds, like a geometric puzzle made real.
Strangely, being upside down, the Upsamid seemed
more solid, more frighteningly... *real*.

"I'm not going in *that*," snapped Franco.

"Why not? You've been up a few weird and
wonderful pipes in your time," smiled Pippa.

"Shut up."

Cracks of detonation rattled across the faceted
sky. Suddenly, on fast-ropes, crack doctors
rappelled down from a very great height, tiny white
and pink dots that grew at a phenomenal speed
chasing hissing, uncoiling ropes. Guns bristled.
Bullets slapped across the padded landscape with
*thumps* as Combat-K dropped to their knees, guns
training on these fast-falling deviated doctors
and nurses, all wearing backless war-gowns and
showing plump and pimpled arses in fast descent –

Guns roared. Keenan's MPK howled, Franco's
quad-barrel Kekras smashed in his brutal fists,

and Pippa stood, D5 shotgun resting on her hip as her cold grey eyes surveyed the attackers, and discharged shells into their midst. It started raining bodies, that thudded softly on the ground.

"The sky's been breached!" screeched Lunatrick. Weaponless, he stood, jaws agape, watching as Betezh, Snake, Fizzy, Shazza and Olga rotated like a well-oiled machine, guns roaring to pluck attackers from the sky. Bullets snapped and whined. Cordite formed clouds. Several crack abseiling doctors hit the ground and charged, hypodermic machine-guns pumping. Olga was hit in the shoulder, and pitched back with a roar as her own shotgun blew the doctor's head clean off. Another grew back, and Olga steadied herself, blood pouring from her wound, and she shot the second head off. This time, the double-headed GP hit the ground and was still, grey blood leaking from a steaming neck wound.

Snake was cool in the midst of the fire-fight, firing controlled three-round bursts and picking attackers neatly from their uncoiling fast-ropes. Bullets and needles whined around him, but he did not flinch, did not hide. His single eye was devastating at picking out targets.

As the last of the attackers rappelled, ropes hissing, Combat K's guns thundered through the sky and so one fat nurse landed, feet sinking up to her ankles in the cotton landscape. She was huge, with a bush of peroxide-blonde curls like an overgrown bush, and bright cherry-red lipstick that had gone nuclear. With screams and wobbling jowls she charged the group, and she carried short fat guns which discharged cubes of steel. Combat K's guns turned on this charging, suicidal, peroxide bouncing nurse, and bullets cannoned into her mass but for long moments she seemed to *absorb* everything thrown at her, and with body smoking from many puncture holes, and with her tight white PVC nurse uniform squeaking in punctured agony, she fell towards the floor face down as the last of her guns discharged –

Cubic bullets *whumped* across the clearing, and several hit Shazza in the face. In an instant her head was disintegrated by the small steel cubes, pounded in a flurry of metal to nothing, and Shazza stood for a shocked moment of incomprehension, her own gun pointing at the floor. Then her knees bent and she folded slowly to the ground.

"No!" screamed Fizzy, running to her lover's side and dropping, weeping, throwing her arms across Shazza's perfectly unmarked body. Only the head was missing, no face, just a ring of battered, bludgeoned bone. "*No!*"

Pippa ran to Fizzy and knelt by the woman. She glanced back at Keenan, who gave a nod then returned to scanning the skies with the hot barrel of his machine gun.

"We've got to get moving," said Pippa, placing a gentle hand on Fizzy's shoulder. "More could come."

"I'm not going anywhere," snarled Fizzy through tears and snot. "She's dead, Pippa, she's dead!"

Pippa said nothing for a moment. Keenan made a quick military hand gesture, and the group started moving away towards the Upsamid and a tiny entrance near its base.

"Come with us," said Pippa.

"No," wept Fizzy, digging her hands into her lover's clothing. "I'm staying. Staying here with Shazza."

"She wouldn't want this."

"I don't *care!*" Fizzy's eyes were wild. "You go. I'll protect the entrance. Buy you some time." She showed her teeth, which were stained with her own blood. She had bit her tongue, savaged herself in agony at her loss. "I'm going to kill some fucking nurses!"

Pippa nodded and looked to the skies even as more invaders started to fall. Fresh guns rattled and Pippa turned, sprinted towards the Upsamid's entrance where Franco was moaning about having to climb into tight little slippery holes.

"If you don't get in fast," snarled Keenan, "I'll shoot a tight little slippery hole in your bastard skull."

"All I'm saying, is..." muttered Franco, as he disappeared into the black square.

"Come on!" shouted Keenan, and Pippa ran past him, diving through the entrance. Keenan, left alone in this weird place, gave a long last glance at Fizzy, standing over the body of her dead lover. He watched, as she lifted her gun and with expert, single shots began to murder the fast-dropping attackers... bodies began to fall, and Keenan's expert eye picked out a perfection of headshots. Suddenly, fire roared out from some kind of flamethrower and engulfed Fizzy, and the body of Shazza. From within the flames, still Fizzy calmly picked off doctors and nurses, and the odd twisted, screaming, deviant patient...

Keenan leapt through the hole, and landed on a sandy floor. Lunatrick did something to the wall, and huge crescent-shaped plates of stone slid into place. Outside, bullets pinged like the music of chiming crystal.

"We are safe. For a few moments."

Keenan nodded, and released a long breath. The sudden deaths of Shazza and Fizzy had shocked him, and he could feel the mood of the group change. A sense of mortality fell like a wide black shroud, covering their heads and shoulders in death fallout, entering their mouths and noses and eyes and filling them with an icy-cold sense of despondency.

"They're both dead," he said, quietly.

"Let's move out," said Snake, starting across the sand.

"Have you *no* fucking compassion?" snarled Pippa, her gun training on Snake. He stopped at this threat, his single eye focused on the weapon without emotion. He gave a shake of his head, and a narrow smile.

"Better them than me," he said.

"You bastard." Pippa's hand was shaking.

"Do it," said Snake. "You think I give a fuck? Don't you understand? We're moving further and further into Sick World, going deeper into the core. There's no escape from this place, Pippa. Shazza and Fizzy, they were lucky I think, they bought it first. I just hope my time comes as... quick." He smiled then, and his eyes moved to Keenan, who reached out and lowered Pippa's gun.

She looked at him questioningly, and suddenly read in his eyes the truth. There was no escape from this place. They were indeed going down to confront VOLOS, to save the millions of twisted deviated medical staff and patients of Sick World... but, in Keenan's mind, this was a one way journey; a suicide mission. There was no return.

"Hell," she breathed.

"We're already there," said Keenan, quietly.

"You think we're not coming back?"

"I don't believe in miracles," he said.

"So you think we're all going to die? And you stand there, smug and arrogant, and play with our fucking lives and drag us deeper and deeper into this mess, this insanity, and expect us not to fight our way out?"

"Look around," said Keenan. "How the hell did you think we were going to escape?"

"Roll over and fucking die, then," snarled Pippa. "But I won't!" She glared at him. "I thought you had more fight in you than that!"

She stormed off, to where Lunatrick waited by a sandy-floored tunnel that led so steeply up they would have to traverse it on hands and knees. "We must hurry," he said, stroking his thick beard. "They will soon blow a hole in the Upsamid's wall. It is an ancient relic, not a fortress."

"And where are we going now?" snapped Pippa, eyes wild, finger tight on gun trigger.

"Through the core of the Upsamid," said Lunatrick. "Down. Down and down, to the Star Lakes, and down through those, and on towards the Hardcore: Vela. VOLOS's *hospital.*"

Around them, the Upsamid started to vibrate. Sand and pebbles skittered across the floor, and the whole edifice was suddenly shaking as if seized in the fist of a savage earthquake.

"What is it?" shouted Pippa. Franco was slapping at his PAD, but down here, it was effectively non-functional.

"Quickly!" shouted Lunatrick. "Follow me!" His face was contorted in horror. "They have sent the Eartheaters! Oh gods, I cannot believe VOLOS would unleash them on his world, in this place..."

"Eartheaters?" snapped Pippa.

The rumbling increased, and suddenly a hole appeared in one wall in an explosion of rock and dust and snapping teeth. The Eartheater was there, its huge head seemingly made of meshing steel wheels and teeth and eyes, all of them spinning and intertwining like a kaleidoscope from a metal nightmare. It's body was long, the thickness of a man, a putrid stinking brown corrugated sausage-skin, and suddenly five guns trained on the creature and bullets screamed and roared and the whole world became a madness of violence and snapping teeth, Combat K members scrabbling and trying to get back and away from the savage vicious spinning mouth, teeth, gears, saws, wheels, grinders, and eyes. More and more bullets roared and howled, slamming and smashing the Eartheater into a battered bloody limp pulp. There came a *slup* as the long worm body fell from the fast-excavated tunnel... But still the Upsamid shook.

"That wasn't so bad," said Franco, grinning suddenly, and kicking the long, dead worm with his boot. He surveyed the mash of head which served not only as head, but as an excavation tool capable of burrowing through rock and stone.

"That's the first," whispered Lunatrick. "There will be more! Hundreds more! Quickly, follow me!'

## CHAPTER THIRTEEN

# VELA

THE REMAINING MEMBERS of Combat-K scrambled up the steep slope, using fingers and knees to help their ascent. Dust rained down, choking them, filling their eyes with grit, and they struggled against the violent earthquake of Eartheaters. Behind them, in the chamber vacated, they heard five or six creatures thud to the ground and begin a curious screeching, rotating, gnashing of teeth and gears and facial grinding appendages.

"They're coming," boomed Betezh, who had somehow managed to get himself to the back of the group. He kept looking behind in what would have been a comical manner, if the consequences hadn't been having legs chewed off. In a panic, he fired off ten bullets down the steep tunnel – and at the noise, the Eartheater's heads snapped up and they wriggled towards the opening.

"Dickhead," snapped Pippa.

At the top of the incline they ran until they reached a huge cone, the point of which slotted neatly into the tip of the Upsamid. The interior of the cone swirled black on black on black, in what should have appeared a solid blackness. However, here there were a million different shades of black, all coalescing like black cream in black coffee, and the group stared down into this spinning display, and looked to Lunatrick for guidance.

"We must jump," he said. "It will accelerate us down to the Star Lakes. The Upsamid is a transport device, a focus, if you will. It will *concentrate* you down towards Vela. And, ultimately, VOLOS."

Franco gave a big sigh. At the bottom of the tunnel, the Eartheaters, now numbering twenty or more, made a spirited attempt at climbing the tunnel ascent with face blades gnashing.

"Show me," said Keenan.

Without a word, Lunatrick stepped off the rim and into the swirling black. He vanished, instantly.

Franco nudged Keenan with his elbow. "Hey, how do we know he wasn't just vaporised?"

"We don't."

"So, what do we do now?"

"We jump."

"After you," grinned Franco manically.

"As you wish."

Keenan stepped off the ledge, into the spinning cone, and was gone. No sound, no drama, no fuss. Pippa followed, and Betezh, and Snake and Olga, until only Franco was left alone on the rim, jiggling from one foot to the other, looking nervously into the spinning black and then back at the Eartheaters making their way up the steep tunnel...

"But how do I know you haven't *all* been vaporised?" he moaned to nobody at all. He glared at the Eartheaters, who gnashed their way towards him. "And you lot can stop fucking grinning as well!" he screeched, turned and, as fangs and circular razors and grinders lurched for him, he leapt. And, even then still moaning, was gone in a flash.

FRANCO SWAM THROUGH oily blackness, and slowly emerged through the sky as if floating through airborne treacle, to stand on a platform looking across an infinite lake of glittering gold and silver, and a rainbow of colours which merged and meshed and constantly interchanged.

"Far out, dudes," he said. "Why can't the worms follow us?"

"They are machines," explained Lunatrick. "Mechanical constructs. Made from leftover medical equipment. VOLOS is inventive like that. And so, the accelerator cone only works on organic. Even now, they'll be jumping in and getting mashed all up into cogs and gears and bits and shit."

"Neat," said Franco. "I like it." He stroked his beard and stared out over the Star Lakes. He glanced at Pippa. "Hey, fancy a swim?" He laughed, but his laugh petered out into nothing as he saw their faces.

"It would appear you're right. A swim. Yes. In crushed proto-matter; the birthing agent of *Stars.*"

Franco stared at the colourful, swirling matter beneath him. So, he thought, this is the stuff which creates a sun? Wowsers! And I have to swim through it all? Damn and bloody bollocks! That's amazing, that is! Reminds me a bit of those fabulous Rainbow Pills I used to get from Mount Pleasant!

"So we keep going down," said Keenan, eventually, voice weary. "What will we find beneath the Star Lake?"

"This is the final barrier," said Lunatrick as he stroked his beard, voice lugubrious. "And one through which I cannot pass. VOLOS knows me, he knows my genetic code, my DNA keys. I am locked out of Vela, as are all of those Highside. Only you, with your new genetics, will be allowed into the genepool."

"Hey, what kind of genepool?" said Franco. "There ain't nobody stealing *my* genes. I'm damn fond of every last bloody one, despite some rips in the knees." He was attempting a joke, but nobody took him on.

"It means having been genetically excluded, right?" said Pippa. "This Star Lake, it's like a giant biocomputer. It knows the codes for every lifeform on the planet; and subsequently, can force them out. Keep them away from VOLOS, yeah? Only us, with our new and original codes, out twisted mutations, only we can progress."

"So we just jump in?" said Franco, who was actually quite keen to begin swimming in star-matter. He could sometimes be a little perverse, he was the first to admit; bizarrely, this kind of *did it* for him. Before he realised what was happening, Olga was beside him, close beside him, *very* close beside him, rubbing at him and crooning, and she had taken his hand in her great scarred tattooed paw. She squeezed him, and Franco yelped, sure she'd broken a couple of fingers, so prodigious was her strength.

"We go swimming together in the birth of the universe, ya?" she said, and Franco could smell her musky scent.

"Don't get any ideas, Big Girl."

"We swim naked, if you like. It like being born in a star! I heard it quite ze invigorating experience!"

"The thing is," said Franco, "I'm kind of pining. For Mel, you understand? Now, I know she was an eight-foot mutation. And I know she drooled pus from every conceivable orifice. *And* I realise she divorced me. But, well, Olga, the thing is, I miss her puckered up little brown-mottled face, you know?

I miss her growls, grunts and farts. I miss her slimy kisses and the thrill of her sharpened claws around my erection. I suppose what I'm trying to say is that although I've warmed to you, lass, in the last few days during these mad and mental bloody adventures, although you hold a big fat place close to my heart, although I must admit I quite fancy a hairy-lipped snog every now and again and the chance for you to show me those wrestle-fuck moves you keep going on about, the thing is, I'd feel like I was betraying her memory. And I can't be having that, lass."

There was a long pause, and Olga nodded, bent down, and kissed Franco on the cheek. "That was ze beautiful, Franco. Olga will wait for you. Olga will be there for you, when you are ready, no matter how long that take." She ambled off, and gave Betezh a friendly punch on the arm; a blow that disabled him for the next thirty minutes.

Keenan leaned close. "Eloquent," he said.

"Cheers, ears."

"I was being sarcastic."

"You were? Hot damn, you disguise it well, Keenan."

"I'm not looking forward to this. It's a gang-rape of the lowest order."

Franco nodded, and Pippa moved close. "Keenan?"

"Yeah, babe?"

"I'm sorry. About my little outburst. Before."

Keenan grinned, and took Pippa's chin in his hand in a rare moment of affection. His thumb stroked her cheek and, leaning forward, he kissed her, a lingering slow kiss, then turned and faced the Star Lake.

"What was that for?" Her voice was low.

"Ach, fuck it, it wasn't for anything. I kissed you because I could. Because I wanted to. Because I'm sick of this evil between us and the minute we head down there, down to Vela to face this *thing*, this *alien* called VOLOS, then there's a high probability we're going to end up dead. This place is too advanced for us, too *weird* for us. The way we got here, through the Levels in Ward 1, through that Upsamid cone accelerator... that isn't normal, girl. We're dealing with a... with a *technology* we barely comprehend. This isn't a simple assassination; we can't just wander in there and kill VOLOS. If we don't like what he has to say, if he wants to take us apart gene by gene then, in all reality, there's probably little we can do about it."

"You could contact Cam," she said, in a small voice. "Get him to come fizzing on out to our aid." She laughed. She didn't sound convinced.

"I keep trying, babe. I keep trying; but the little fucker isn't answering."

Pippa moved to the edge of the platform, and gazed out over the Star Lake. Below, colours whirled and twisted through strands of gold and silver. The whole was a beautiful thing, but as

Pippa had learned in life, during many a painful experience, beautiful things could often be deadly. Including herself.

She took a deep breath, took hold of Keenan, and kissed him back. He let her hold him, and only pulled away when he saw Franco, in his peripheral vision, hopping towards them in a curious sideways crab-like movement which he sometimes employed. Franco was grinning from ear to ear, as if his head had been opened up by a machete.

"What do *you* want?"

"Sorry to split up you two lovebirds, eh? Eh?" Franco nudged Pippa viciously in the ribs, and gave her a ribald wink. "Eh love? Eh? I saw all that, tongue action and everything, it was a pleasure to watch, a pleasure to observe if I may say so myself." He licked his lips. And coughed. "Anyway, Lunatrick says we have to go now. Vela awaits. All that kind of crap. So, guys, we going or what?"

"Let's do it," said Keenan, and kissed Pippa again.

They moved to Lunatrick, and Keenan shook the huge man's hand. "Wish us luck, Big Guy."

"Keenan, be careful down there. Trust nothing, nobody, trust not your senses, nor your instincts. VOLOS is old, older than you could ever believe possible; older than worlds, older than Leviathan."

"There's that name again," muttered Franco.

"Not now," said Keenan. "That's a battle for a different time; a different age."

"Are you returning to the Asylum?"

"Yes." Lunatrick nodded. "The inmates will have formed barricades, battle walls, defence lines; long have we waited for such an attack. I just never realised your arrival would be the trigger to initiate hostilities. Still, we will hold, Keenan, my lads are a brave lot. We will hold, waiting for you to return. To fulfil your promise."

Keenan looked into Lunatrick's eyes, and saw that the great man believed it. He nodded, and understanding was there. Lunatrick had to believe in Keenan, for without that belief he would have to give up hope of ever saving his people; of ever freeing them from the slavery imposed by VOLOS.

"VOLOS is greater than a god," said Lunatrick. "Be careful."

"Ach, I'll look after him!" boomed Franco, and slapped Lunatrick on the back, a move which made Lunatrick turn slowly to survey the little ginger squaddie with a baleful scowl.

"Hmm," said Lunatrick.

"So, we just jump in then?" said Franco.

"Yes." Lunatrick gave a sombre nod. "Jump in, and swim *down*. Swim down as if your lives depend on it. Because they surely do."

Franco turned, just as Keenan placed a home-rolled cigarette between his lips. He lifted his lighter, and Franco leapt forward, grabbing the small Zippo and closing his fist.

Keenan stared at him. "Yeah?" he said.

Franco grinned weakly. "That Star Lake, Keenan. I don't know what exactly is in it, but it's volatile. *Dangerous*. I knows my bombs, reet? Best not to be lighting fags around this gooey colourful shit. After all, we've got the Asylum directly above us. You could have blown it to Kingdom Come!"

Keenan removed the Widow Maker, and looked forlornly at the bedraggled weed. "I was so looking forward to that. It might have been my last cigarette... ever."

"Yeah. Well. Time for a swim, I'm thinking. But think on this. If we need an instant mega-bomb..." he rolled his eyes madly, and gestured with his shaved head, "here's the stuff, baby, a trillion fucking gallons of it, you get what I'm saying? Y'know? For that last minute *Deus Ex Machina* type shit going down that you see at the end of films and stuff? The Big Bang? Indeed, the *fucking* Big Bang. To, y'know, maybe blow up VOLOS, and stuff?"

"Yes." Keenan coughed. "Whatever. After you." Keenan forced a smile.

"Hey, no problem! They don't call me Franco 'Swimming Through Shit Champion' Haggis for nothing, you know." With that, he stepped from the platform, tipped into a dive, and zipped neatly below the surface of the Star Lake.

The others followed, one by one, until only Keenan, Pippa and Lunatrick stood. Pippa dived in an elegant arc, and disappeared. Again, Lunatrick took Keenan's hand.

"Free my people," he said. "Free Sick World."

"I'll do my best," said Keenan, and dived into the Star Lake...

To be consumed by the birthing agent of stars.

FRANCO PUMMELLED HIS way downwards as if fighting his bedclothes in his sleep, and was soon overtaken by Pippa with her long, graceful, elegant strokes. Down they swam, as if through honey, through a billion billion twisting threads of gold and silver and rainbow hues, all flickering and twirling, down down down through strands and although there was no oxygen to breathe and none of the squad attempted to breathe, they were sustained. Franco fought his way ever downwards, and found his mind drifting, the world drifting, and everything was so beautiful, so totally serene and two elements flooded his mind like an overdose of brilliant happy narcotic – realisation and fulfilment. Here, Franco was perfect, this place was perfect, and there was no fear, no hate, no war, no death, and Franco knew he could live out an eternity of perfection and he need never worry again, never feel fear or anger or frustration again. All he had to do was cease his swimming, cease his struggle, and just... hang, baby.

*It's a trap*, squeaked a little voice in the back of his mind.

*Like a fly in a spider's web.*

*A flapping fish in a shark's radar.*

*An organic crumb in a SPAW's radiation field...*

Franco fought the urge to give up and, twisting, he saw Pippa falling behind him and he slowed his descent, realising it had her; but Keenan swam down behind, grabbed her, shook her and she nodded, gave him a thumbs up, and then they were swimming again and Franco fought his way down.

Down.

Down through colours, down through threads, down through a living matter of sub-organic protons...

And Franco saw gems, diamonds and rubies and emeralds, floating beside him close enough to reach. He passed a diamond the size of a Buggy 6X6, and a sapphire the size of a house. Eyes wide, Franco slowed and turned, and saw Snake homing in on him. Franco gestured, and Snake nodded, single eye mercenary-wide, understanding passing between the two greedy money-orientated gold-grabbing bastards... here was wealth, the greatest wealth they had ever set eyes upon! Only three eyes, but enough eyes to see they could be rich! And it could all be theirs! All they had to do was find a Freighter, rig it with kilometre long slings, and *bam!* they could be so much Richer than a Very Rich Rich Man.

Keenan's hand slapped Franco's face, a slow-motion blow which nevertheless stung like a bitch and brought Franco kicking back to reality. He blinked, and the images of wealth faded and he saw Keenan give a little shake of his head, and shame burned Franco, burned his cheeks with the burning red brand of Greed. Am I that bad? he asked himself. Am I really that greedy, that base, that uncouth and petty and driven purely by money? Well, money and sex? Am I so bloody *impure?*

He considered this.

*Yes*, he thought. *I am.*

He swam down.

But hell, it *was* a fucking BIG sapphire.

Down he swam, following Keenan now with Snake close behind, and the swim, the experience as a whole seemed to go on and on, for hours, for days, for weeks and time no longer had any meaning and Franco remembered thinking that this journey might never end but then, that was a good thing, because the world within the Star Lake was perfect.

A perfect place to live.

And a perfect place to *die.*

Franco blinked, and heard a splash, and then he was falling through a complete and total darkness. He fell rather a long way, and hit the ground very hard. Consciousness left him, and he had a short vicious dream about big worms with lots of vicious bastard teeth.

When he awoke, he could smell chloroform.

* * *

KEENAN SAT UP in total darkness. He coughed, and seemed to vomit a long, long stream of viscous fluid which burned him on rapid exit. Crawling onto his hands and knees, all pleasant memories of being inside the Star Lake vanished, to be replaced by a reality of pain, and burning, and a feeling that his body, his every atom, had been raped by some alien force he did not comprehend.

"Kee?"

"Pippa."

A light came on, fixed to the barrel of Pippa's D5. Slowly, the others came round, all vomiting thick brown streams to the damp black stone floor. As the group pulled itself together, Pippa's light played around the place and they found themselves in a wide, ancient corridor. Old pipes, rusted and green, ran at ceiling height, although there was no ceiling, just a vast and cool openness. Somewhere, up there, was the Star Lake. They had passed through with their lives, but only just; each and every member recognised the danger of what they had just survived. It had been a reawakening of their insecurities; their private lusts. And it scared them all to the core.

"It was a mind trick," said Franco, at last, spitting on the ground and hawking up another ball of phlegm. "Designed to keep us from reaching... here. Wherever the hell *here* is."

"This is Vela," said Keenan, eyes dark.

"Yes," said a voice, although it wasn't a voice

that transcribed through air, it was an essence, a being, it was something created inside each person's head and imprinted like hot brands of fire on the front of their brains.

"And you are VOLOS." Keenan's voice was halfway between snarl and spit.

"Perceptive, Mr. Keenan." They got the impression of a smile. Of humour. And humour denoted life, or at least, life as far as Combat-K could understand it.

VOLOS seemed to sigh. The world seemed to hold its breath.

"Welcome to Vela," said VOLOS. "Welcome to my Underworld.'

There was a long pause, an eternity, so it seemed. Long enough for stars to be born, and for stars to die.

"What happens next?" whispered Franco.

"He watches us," said Keenan, gently. "He's been watching us all the time, haven't you VOLOS, you fucker?"

There was no answer.

Light swept into the corridor, as if painted sideways by a brush. The slow-motion action imbued disconcertion.

Combat K gazed around and Snake stepped forward, rubbing wearily at his eye-patch as if satisfying an itch beneath. "Well," he said, "this sure is a *shit*-hole. I kind of expected the lair of the great VOLOS to be something better, something far more magnificent."

Keenan looked across at Snake then, and frowned. "You sound like you expect a certain… standard." An intuition took Keenan in its fist and squeezed his guts. "You're here, aren't you? Here for VOLOS?"

"Yes."

"And I thought you were a cheap mercenary."

"Just tagging a ride, Keenan. Just using you and Combat-K as a donkey; you have no idea what you've stumbled into, my friend. You have no idea how big the Game is, no concept of the complexity of the Puzzle."

"It can't be bigger than your ego," said Keenan, gently.

He turned then, to the left, and watched a figure approaching down the decrepit corridor. His eyes tracked left and right, surveying debris, the entropy, the rusted pipes hissing steam, the dangling cables sparking with discharges of electricity. Everything had a damp, ancient feel, like a long abandoned warehouse. Yeah, he thought with a grim internal smile; a million year abandonment.

The figure was small, slim, and clothed in a simple grey robe. It was impossible to determine sex, but his, or her, skin was a pale and flawless white, milky to the stage of translucency. However, what made Keenan breathe deep and brought a rattle of weapons from the rest of the group was the face, for the hairless head and face were featureless, a blank oval, like a pale and milky peeled egg.

The figure stopped.

"Let me take it," whispered Franco, quad-barrel Kekra by his cheek.

Keenan waved Franco away and moved forward; only after a few footsteps did he realise Snake was right behind him, at his heel, like a faithful hound. Keenan masked his irritation and stopped, staring at the flat blank platter of skin.

"You are VOLOS?"

"Yes." The blank face seemed to swim, as if formed from viscous liquid, and a mouth opened at the centre of the face to utter the single word; then rolled back into position, languidly, like a ripple of molten wax.

"He's lying," hissed Snake in Keenan's ear.

Keenan turned a little. "Will you *fuck off.*"

The figure lifted a hand, and Keenan felt a *blast* of pressure slam past his cheek. Snake was picked up and tossed a hundred feet down the corridor, wailing, arms flapping in a vicious acceleration that slammed and battered him from pipes and abandoned furniture like a toy ragdoll; he hit the ground, rolling over and over and over. He lay still.

"Did he really think he could come here and fool me?" said the blank-faced creature. Then the mouth formed a smile. "He is a Spinner. He can take a room and spin it through time. Quad-Gal Military's greatest weapon, I fear." The figure laughed, a soft melodious sound. "He is here to kill me, or so he believes, and yet he does not truly understand VOLOS." There came a deep sigh. "VOLOS is open and honest. Snake is... a snake. He believes what he believes. VOLOS is misrepresented in all of this game. This charade. This battle. This war."

Keenan turned, and stared at Pippa and Franco. "A Spinner?" he mouthed, and they both shrugged. Keenan could not help but notice fingers tight on triggers. Snake's acceleration had nearly taken their heads clean off.

Keenan turned back, and his eyes narrowed. "I don't think you're being quite straight with me," he said. He watched the face, but could discern no reaction, no emotion, for there were no features to read. "I don't think you are VOLOS. I think you are a servant. A messenger, of sorts."

"Very astute." The face seemed to flicker a smile. "I am the avatar of VOLOS, but I contain his mind, contain his blood, what you would know of his soul. I am an extension, if you like; in a way you would extend your hand, and your fingers are still your own flesh, your own organic matter. Thus, I am a limb of VOLOS."

"OK." Keenan nodded, watching the avatar. "Why haven't you killed us?"

"You must travel through the Hospital. VOLOS wishes to commune with you directly."

"Why?"

"Only VOLOS can tell you this."

"And there's a catch?"

"As I said. Astute. Yes, Mr. Keenan. The Hospital is a dangerous place. More dangerous than you could ever believe. It is a place of birth, of life, and ultimately, of death."

"And yet you've just walked through unharmed?"

"There was an element of matter projection."

Keenan nodded. He glanced back. "What would you have us do with Snake?"

"Leave him. I will take care of him."

"You'll kill him?"

"No. He will be held until you accomplish your mission. Or die in the process."

"I didn't realise we were on a mission," said Keenan, with a wry smile. "Not for you, for VOLOS, at any rate."

"All life is a mission, a striving towards goals," said the avatar. It turned, and pointed with a long, elegant arm and thin tapered fingers. "That way, Keenan. That is where you must go. You must work your way down through the three levels of the Hospital. It is up to you whether your colleagues accompany you; only you can decide whether they will aid, or hinder, your progress."

The avatar turned, and began to walk away, swaying hips gently in a hypnotic movement reminiscent of the feminine.

"Wait," said Keenan.

The avatar stopped, turned, and the blank face surveyed Keenan in a way that made him shiver. "Yes, Mr. Keenan?"

"I don't understand," he said.

"You will," said the avatar. "Believe me, you will."

THEY WATCHED THE avatar of VOLOS depart. Pushing through double doors, the figure seemed to gradually dissolve and disseminate amidst the entropy of the wide, abandoned corridor.

Keenan gestured to Pippa. "Check Snake."

"Yeah boss."

Keenan dropped his pack, and started rummaging through, discarding certain items and affixing others, mainly weaponry, to his belt.

"Franco. Check out your PAD. See if there's any sign, anything *at all* from Cam, QGM, Fortune, or any of our dodgy off-world contacts. We need information on what we're going to face down here."

Franco toyed with the PAD, but shook his head. "Keenan, it's limper than a junkie's todger. Sorry mate, we're still on our own."

"Then, I'm going in alone," said Keenan.

"Oh no," said Franco, staring hard at his friend. "We're brothers in this, bruv, you're not going anywhere without your faithful companions in sleaze. We could be some serious help to you when the shit hits the fanny fan!" He glanced around, at Betezh's scars, at Olga's rolls of flab, at Pippa's cold grey eyes narrowed in his direction. "Well," he said, "I could be, anyway." He grinned the grin of a maniac.

Pippa returned. "He's out cold. In some kind of coma, but he's alive. What the hell is a Spinner?"

"Never heard of it."

"That sounds like a Ganger Agency thing. I'm sure I heard that somewhere."

"Maybe. We've got bigger problems at the moment; I don't like the sound of this Hospital place, but I'm damned if I can work out how it'd be more dangerous than the collective shit we've just been through."

"Lunatrick warned us about down here," said Pippa, voice soft. "That's why we're all coming with you."

"I work better alone."

"No. We work better as a team."

"I don't want to get you all killed!" snapped Keenan.

"What, you don't think we're big enough boys and girls to make our own decisions? We're part of a *squad*, Keenan, part of a *team*. We work together, play together, and we damn well die together. So stop your whining and let's get tooled up and on the move. I, for one, am curious as to why VOLOS hasn't just blasted us from afar."

"I think," said Franco, voice cool, eyes strangely intelligent from behind their mask of insanity, "he's lost control."

"What?" snapped Pippa.

"This VOLOS. The Big Guy. The Bloke in Charge. I think he was a Big Dude round here once over, and helped create, or formulate, all these medical deviations. But I think something happened, maybe he lost his powers or something, but he's trapped down here now, just like the rest of the freaks. He needs us for something, guys, he wants our help. That's why we have to fight our way through his defences... he no longer controls them."

Keenan looked sideways at Franco, as he reordered his pack, down on one knee. "You know Franco, for a madman you sometimes have an alarming sense of clarity."

"Hey!" he grinned, "they don't call me Franco 'Global Brainbox of the Globe' Haggis for nothing, you know. I'm a damn genie, a geena... a mastermind, so I am."

Pippa snorted, but conversation died as they readied themselves. Weapons were checked, primed, locked and loaded. Betezh and Olga had serious looks on serious faces, and the five remaining members of the Combat-K infiltration team stood in formation and faced the swing-doors leading deeper into VOLOS' Hospital.

They moved forward, and Keenan placed a gloved hand against the double doors.

"Geronimo," said Franco.

"What?" snapped Pippa.

"It's a saying. Y'know? When you're about to dive in. I usually reserve it for acts of candlelit cunnilingus, but hell, this situation felt just damn right, somehow."

"You're a sexual deviant, Franco Haggis."

"Amen to that, my sweet little pudding."

Keenan pushed open the doors, and cool air wafted over them. They stepped forward, and the light seemed to dissolve and rearrange as the corridor shifted from entropy to clinical perfection.

The doors swung shut, clicked, and locked behind them.

Finally.

The core members of Combat-K were in the Hospital.

COMBAT K STOOD in the cool sterility of the Hospital. A short corridor led to a long ward, so long it went on further than the eye could see. Beds were neatly made. Lights were low, dimmed. The smell of disinfectant wafted in the air like a sweet disease, like leprosy.

"I don't like this," said Franco, easing forward.

"You don't like anything, Big Man."

"This is too nice. I preferred the last corridor, with all the shit."

"Let's move out," said Keenan, and they walked forward, slowly, in battle formation, eyes constantly scanning and guns weaving, covering arcs of fire.

Distant, they heard the sound, a sound so alien to the environment that for a long moment they all frowned. Then Pippa's face softened, but Keenan gave a savage shake of his head, scowling at her.

"But it's a baby," said Pippa. "A baby, crying."

The sound died; dissipated.

"Do you really think, in a place like this, there'll be a baby?"

"Even deviants are born," said Pippa, and Keenan could see by Pippa's enlarged eyes that she was being maternal. He sighed, and glanced over at Olga for support. However, the huge psychopathic tattoo-knuckled fat squaddie also had a dreamy look about her small, pig-like eyes.

"Must be a woman thing," muttered Keenan. "Come on."

Again they moved, between the perfect beds, until they came to a central office area. They stopped, and Keenan and Franco cleared the room. It had neat desks with stacks of papers, several IN and OUT trays, and a kettle and a toaster. Hardly the threatening items of deepest dark nightmares. Outside, there came a *buzz* and the lights flickered.

"Keenan," said Pippa. He emerged, and she pointed to a sign on the office's external wall. It was small, and neatly engraved. It read: **MATERNITY WARD**.

"So this is where the freaks, the deviants, the greebos and mutations come to give birth?" snorted Keenan. Then he looked at Franco, Pippa, and Betezh, and scowled. "Shit," he said. "Let's get moving; let's get out of this place, it's giving me the creeps."

As they progressed through the Maternity Ward environment, so the lights gradually dimmed, and dimmed, fingers of grey creeping over the world. The hospital ward had windows, but they were hung with heavy drapes. Keenan crossed between two beds and pulled back the dangling drapes; the glass was grey and blank, like the lifeless eyes of a long-dead corpse.

"Great."

At that moment, distantly, a babe started crying. Keenan held out a hand, stopping Pippa from rushing forward, and he took the lead again, moving slowly down the ward. Here, the beds were interspersed with baby cribs and incubation chambers. Everywhere lay evidence of babies: blankets embroidered with teddy bears, tables strewn with rattles and baby baths, baby creams and shampoos, even cards in pink and blue denoting messages of congratulation.

"It's giving me the bloody heebie jeebies," said Franco.

"I don't know why," said Pippa from the corner of her mouth. "You've fathered enough kids in your time."

"What's that supposed to mean?"

"Exactly what it says on the tin."

"So you mean to tell me," he considered, "you think I'm a dad?"

"You've had sex, haven't you?"

"Lots of times! I am," he puffed out his chest, "a sexual athlete."

"So, the law of averages state you must have fathered *some kids.*"

Franco considered this. "Oh," he said, finally, and seemed unable to grasp the concept. Eventually, he shook his head. "Nah, not me, I'm Franco 'Lucky Sperm' Haggis! I'm Franco 'Zero Ovulation' Haggis! Babies are little tykes that happen to other people. I take precautions, I do."

"Yeah, right," smiled Pippa. She pushed forward to Keenan. "Come on, I want to see this squawking child."

Keenan shrugged, MPK tracking towards the baby wailing as they gradually approached. The annoying guttural sound seemed to become even more abrasive as they neared, and Pippa and Olga pushed past Keenan to reach the edges of the incubator in which lay the tiny pink thing, wrapped in blankets, wailing.

"Aww," said Pippa, leaning close.

"Cutchy cutchy coo," cooed Olga, leaning close from the other side.

"Wahhh wahhh wahhh," squawked the baby.

"It's so small and helpless," said Pippa.

"Just look at that little fella's hair!" beamed Olga.

Both women leant over the incubation crib, pulling aside soft white blankets, cooing and aahing and oohing with brains as runny as their eyes.

"Be careful," growled Keenan, looking up and down the ward. This could be a come-on, a prick-tease, a *decoy*. He'd seen it before, a thousand times; just never using a newborn. But it'd work. It'd work damn well.

"Wahh!" said the baby, and opened a beady black eye. It stared at the two women, caught in rubber-faced poses of soothing ululation. The baby's crying stopped. Immediately.

"See?" said Olga, turning and winking at Franco. "I have ze mother's touch!" She turned back just as the baby leapt into the air, both tiny pink feet slamming Olga's face with the force of a sledgehammer. Olga staggered back, blood pouring from her nose as the tiny pink babe bounced, once, and head-butted Pippa on the chin, sending her sprawling backwards across a bed, D5 shotgun blasting an ND into the ceiling. The baby sailed through the air, Keenan's MPK tracking it but... he could not pull the trigger.

The baby slammed through ceiling tiles in a crumble of plaster.

Everything was silent.

"Wah wah bloody wahhh!" said Franco, scowling as Pippa and Olga rubbed their damaged faces. "Some damn and squawking bloody baby that was! It was a human hammer! A toxic newborn!"

"Shut up," growled Pippa, dignity ruffled, eyes scanning the ceiling.

There came a crash, further down the ward, and the baby emerged from a hole and hung by its toes, surveying the group. Its tiny wrinkled face was indeed human in appearance, as was every other part of its wrinkled body, right down to the newly-clamped umbilical.

The baby gurgled, with the sort of lovely wobbly baby sound only a baby can make.

And attacked...

It bounced like a mad little Yoda amongst the group, kicking and punching, head-butting and biting. Like a thing possessed, the tiny naked pink baby growled and spat and bounced and tore at flesh with tiny clawed fingers. Franco's gun fired, a slam of quick succession bullets that tracked the baby as it spun fast past Betezh. There came a *whum whum whump*, the final bullet embedding in Betezh's shoulder and smashing him back onto his rump. The babe landed on Betezh's head, and both hands slapped him on the forehead with stunning force, making him reach up and grab it. It squealed, wriggling and clawing at his powerful fingers.

"Shoot it! Shoot it!" screamed Betezh, half in triumph, half in horror. Baby fingers tore at his flesh, drawing blood, snapping his fingers, as both Franco and Keenan aimed uneasily, guns weaving, aware that an incorrectly placed bullet could blow Betezh's head clean off.

"Hold it still!" bellowed Franco.

"It's fucking *biting* me!" yelled Betezh, "how can I hold it fucking still?"

Keenan's gun *cracked* and the bullet slammed the baby's chest. However, instead of separating the baby into baby bits, its body accepted the spinning bullet with a *plop* that seemed to *stretch* flesh and skin and shake the baby as if it was a pink flesh rattle.

The newborn kicked backwards from Betezh's grip, and landed lightly on disjointed legs. It scowled at Keenan, eyes dark and narrowed, then gurgled something unintelligible in baby-speak which might have been, "Urgle wurgle bubble cubble", then bounced off down the corridor in a curious mixture of running, jumping, bouncing and leaping, using floor, beds and walls to aid its mad dash.

Franco tracked with his Kekras, but couldn't bring himself to shoot a fleeing newborn in the back. "Damn," he said, then glanced at Keenan. "Man, you're a savage shot."

"What's that supposed to mean?"

"You shot a fucking *baby* in the chest!"

"It wasn't a baby."

"It looked like a baby!"

"Guys, guys, I'm bleeding over here," said Betezh weakly, and Pippa and Olga knelt by him, rummaging in packs for bullet pads as Betezh did his own impersonation of a baby wailing.

Keenan and Franco stood guard, scowling as Betezh moaned about Franco being a bad shot, and how it was bad enough with the damn and bloody enemy firing at you without your own damn and bloody team putting a bullet in your muscle.

"Shut up," said Franco, through gritted teeth.

With Betezh patched and nursing an injured arm, they moved off down the Maternity Ward again, only this time far more alert, and not about ready to be overcome by the con-cries of an apparently innocent babe...

THERE CAME A final, terrible *buzz* and the lights died. Combat K cursed, to a man, and flicked on the barrel lights on their weapons. The Maternity Ward seemed suddenly a *much more* eerie place; a place of long shadows and strange shapes, all imbued with the stink of iodine.

They moved slowly, with care, guns tracing every shadow, every flicker of movement. All were hairline triggers waiting to be tripped; all except Franco. He seemed quite laid back about the entire proceedings.

"I gotta admit," said Franco, "I just don't like babies."

"Well, one did just try to kill you," said Keenan.

"No, not because of that. I mean, in general, sort of thing. On a day-to-day basis. I just don't like the little buggers."

"What a stupid thing to say," snapped Pippa.

"How can you not like babies? What's not to like?"

"We-*eell*," said Franco. "They're ugly, ain't they?"

"Ugly? What is ze craziness of this man?" boomed Olga.

"They are, admit it, every damn baby ever born is damn and bloody ugly. They're all wrinkled up and squashed up, with the funny little putty faces and big mouths with no teeth going 'Wah!' and 'Wurh' then covering you in baby sick. It's quite a revolting thing, really. Humans are quite revolting."

"Are you *mad?*" snapped Pippa. "I've never heard such drivel in all my life! Babies are cute!"

"Cute like my arse," said Franco.

"You're a heathen idiot," said Pippa.

"Maybe," said Franco, smugly, "but it doesn't remove the fact that all babies are ugly. To a man. Woman. Boy and girl, I mean." He beamed. "And they smell. That kind of weirdy milky puke chocolate smell all babies carry like a bad, um, smell. You getting the drift of my argument?"

Olga's fist whacked Franco on the top of his head, and he grunted, head shunted down into his neck like a turtle retreating into its shell. He scowled at her, and hissed, "Violence isn't the answer to everything, Olga."

"It's ze answer to your drivel!"

"If you can't argue your bloody corner, then retreat with dignity!"

"Grrwl," said Olga, clenching her fist again.

"OK, OK!" Franco held up his hands. "Come on, let's stop bickering, we have a mission to attend!" He trotted forward to where Keenan walked point. "Tsch," he said, gesturing backwards with his thumb, "women, hey?"

"You'll feel different," said Keenan.

"Eh?"

"When you have your own kids. They're an awesome experience, mate. Like nothing on earth. It's just... there's nothing worse than other people's children. All the good things become evil." He smiled at Franco's confusion and melancholy.

They moved through the darkness.

Occasionally, they heard scrabbling sounds, as of something small and quick scuttling into a recess. Sometimes, a solitary baby wail echoed distantly, as if sent to taunt them; to mock them with its high-pitched music.

"What's that?" said Franco, shielding his eyes. "Over there? *Right* over there? It's stairs!"

"The end of the Maternity Ward," said Keenan, relief in his voice.

"Well!" beamed Franco, turning to beam at Pippa, Olga and a pale-faced Betezh. "This wasn't so bad, was it? A single pinky and wriggly baby sent to stop us! No problems battling something like that, eh, people?"

There came a roar, only this wasn't the roar of men charging into battle, or the roar of a caged or cornered lion; this was a roar of a thousand tiny baby voices squeaking in hatred, each strand of sound entwining to form a terrible high-pitched vibrating, ululating whole. The noise rushed over Combat K, and from the darkness they came like a wriggling pink tide, sprinting and bouncing, climbing and running along the walls; babies, lots of babies, hundreds of babies, all shapes and sizes and colours, pink ones and white ones, yellow ones and brown ones, thin ones and scrawny ones, wobbling ones and fat ones, some so obese they dragged themselves across the ground like huge pink wriggling slugs. They came with a roar, and Combat-K stood, stunned, rooted to the spot with something other than fear, something far greater than fear. This transcended fear right off the bloody scale past horror and on its way to an indescribable insanity-inducing disbelief.

"Run!" screamed Franco, at last, voice like a girl.

This broke the spell, and Combat-K pounded down the Maternity Ward, pursued by the fast-moving tide of babies, gums snapping at heels, finger clipping boots and WarSuit legs as they ran and crawled and spat and hissed...

A baby leapt onto Franco's back, tiny pink-brown arms encircling his throat. "Gerroff!" he screamed, "Gerroff!" He turned, and the baby puked sick into his eyes, stinging him, blinding him and he stumbled backwards as claws raked his bearded face and there came a *boom*. Pippa's D5 shell plucked the baby from Franco's back and spat it upwards and out into the throng.

Still running, Franco whirled, and scooped baby sick from his eyes. "Thanks, chipmunk," he panted, and realised in horror one of his Kekras had gone. "Damn and bloody blast bloody babies!"

Overcoming their uneasiness in the face of claw-like fingers and sharp baby gums, Combat K opened fire as they ran, bullets and shells whining and blasting into the pursuing ranks of deviant hunting babies. Babies were shot from walls and ceilings, blasted in flails of tiny limbs, gums gawping, dummies truly spat out as they whirled under a hot metal onslaught only to fall, roll, and be trampled by the hordes of their scampering fast-crawling bouncing comrades...

"I've never seen so many babies," panted Pippa, sprinting alongside Keenan. "Duck!" Keenan ducked and Pippa's D5 blast picked the spread-eagled, leaping baby from the air and smashed it away into the darkness, separating it into five separate baby pieces with an almost comical "Waaahhh*hhhh!*"

"I can see the stairs!" screamed Franco, and Combat K, gun-barrels glowing, pounded on. Betezh, ahead of Franco now (after all, Franco was only a little fella) had a fat baby land on his back, and Franco grabbed the little tyke and for long seconds found himself staring into wide baby-blue eyes. "Wah!" went the baby, and "Wah!" went Franco before he tossed the kid backwards over his head, to be trampled by the stampede of hungering baby flesh...

Combat K stumbled onto the landing, bouncing from the wall and sprinting onto the stairs.

Suddenly, all noise ceased... and Combat-K faltered to a halt, panting, slick with sweat. They glanced back, and found themselves staring at a sea of tiny, wrinkled faces, eyes blinking, some sucking on dummies, many wearing nappies and bibs, but all suddenly, strangely motionless as if they'd met some invisible barrier they could not cross.

"Hell," hissed Franco.

The babies blinked at him, sucking on soothers.

"Looks like it from here," said Keenan, panting, and wiping blood from his forehead where a baby's savage talons had slashed a long line through his flesh. "Come on. I think we're safe from them."

Franco pointed at the mass of babies, numbering in the hundreds, and he shouted, "See here, you little bastards! If I happen to come back through here, reet, then you lot are in for a kicking so you are!"

Pippa leant close. "You tell those damn babies," she said.

"Well!" snorted Franco, indignantly. "They messed with the wrong squaddie, didn't they?"

"Yeah, Franco. You saw them off just fine."

"You think so?"

"No, *idiot*."

Combat K scrambled down the stairs, which seemed suddenly infused with a thick, grey fog, oily and spun around corded grey tendrils. The fog filled the stairwell, almost blinding the group as they moved fluidly down steps... and in the process, managed to become totally and hopelessly separated.

PIPPA STOPPED ON the stairs, deeply disorientated. "Franco?" she hissed. "Stop being a dick, Franco, where are you?" No answer. "Keenan?" No answer. Now she started to get edgy, and with arms stretched out before her in the oily smoke, and coughing a little on its thick, intrusive fist, she descended further, down and down, her boots making faint slapping noises on the concrete.

The steps ended, and Pippa stumbled. Smoke cleared, and she saw herself in a huge, huge warehouse-type space. Far above, the ceiling was a corrugated slope. She moved forward, could discern distant walls, distant boundaries; parts of the interior space were filled with huge stacks of cargo containers, as used on Stack Truks and Grey Ships. Their huge rectangular bodies, in a myriad of subtle colours, were strangely eerie, so huge, so silent, in this massive cold place.

Pippa moved forward, then turned back to see if her colleagues emerged from the stairwell. She could not see the stairs, only a perfectly flat wall of smoke, rolling and coiling behind an invisible barrier.

I've been moved, she thought. Shunted. Like a rat through a maze. Shit.

Her gun felt hopelessly inadequate in her gloved hands, and Pippa moved warily across the vast expanse of matt black floor. She began to weave between stacks of containers, eyes narrowed, gun tracking, searching out possible new targets.

She smelt it, before she saw it.

Fire.

Or, more precisely, *burns*. Charred flesh. Scorched skin. The aroma of frying, human fat. The sizzling stench of a cooked person.

Pippa shivered, in horrible anticipation. And recognised the reality of her waking nightmare.


NOTHING SCARED PIPPA. Nothing. Not guns, not knives, fists, boots or bombs. She'd endured broken ribs, broken legs, even a broken neck once in a skiing accident. She'd been shot on no less than sixteen occasions; once in the head, the scar now happily concealed by her thick, bobbed hair. She'd been stabbed in the belly, and in the right kidney, and had two fingers amputated in a sword fight with a GG AI (now, thankfully, grafted back on). None of those things brought so much as a tremor of fear to Pippa's steel-like countenance...

But fire. Fire was a different story...

She'd been six years old. She remembered, vividly, her mother putting her to bed and reading a story about a magical tortoise with a shell like Doctor Who's *TARDIS*, in which he lived a life of tortoise luxury with three female tortoises and a stack of mouse burgers. After the story, as Pippa dozed, so her mother kissed her brow and put out the light, remembering of course to leave the landing light on, and the door ajar, providing just enough ambient glow, just enough idea of sanctuary.

Pippa drifted into happy dreamland, in which she was a tortoise living in an over-large shell. But noises infected her dream, shouts and screams and they were screams of panic, of fear, of pain and she opened her eyes and was coughing even before she was awake on thick acrid smoke...

She sat up, a sudden movement, rigid with fear. She could hear a *roar*. "Mummy!" she yelled, but by shouting she sucked in great lungfuls of smoke which sent her slamming into a choking fit. She climbed out of bed, rushed to the door which was hot to the touch, but she was too young to realise the dangers... she threw open the door and fire rushed in, a living dancing demon, hammering her like a wall of glass, shattering over her, taking her in a fist of flame and crushing her, mercilessly.

Glass smashed.

Something smothered her, a fire blanket, and she felt great strong hands patting out her flaming *She Girl* pyjamas. Something pressed over her mouth and she was flooded with a precious sweet oxygen which she gulped at, like a dying fish. She blinked up at this huge strong man, with his crooked nose and yellow helmet and awkward but reassuring smile, and for moments thought it was her daddy come to rescue her but realisation dawned. It was a fireman, and he lifted her in powerful arms, cooing as if she was an injured fawn, and he carried her to the window and she remembered seeing the brutal fire-axe leant against the wall with its battered, scarred head. He climbed out, amidst smoke and searing flames, and she heard the gasp from below, then the cheer and the turntable ladder rotated and lowered, hydraulics hissing, ratchets clanking, until the smiling dirt-smeared fireman delivered her into the arms of her weeping mother...

"Where's daddy?" she asked, wondering why her daddy hadn't rescued her.

"He's been burned. In the fire."

Then the paramedics were there, checking her over and rushing her into the ambulance and away, to the burns unit of the local hospital. Most of her hair was scorched away, and the back of her neck and entire back seared by flame to a black, charcoal cinder. When the firewall had leapt at her, she turned to run...

Pippa blinked, now, remembering the following months of pain, the skin-grafts, the agony. Tears developed at the corners of her eyes, for here and now the smell of frying flesh reminded her of her own, all those years ago, when she'd been nothing but an innocent little girl. She discovered, much later, her father had fallen asleep, in bed, with a cigarette. The happy glowing little cig had burned down to its filter, a long and delicately balanced cylinder of ash, a mocking middle finger of grey which gradually crumbled, and ignited the duvet. In seconds her father's legs had been consumed, and he had run from the house screaming, setting fire to the stairs and landing in his fast, self-preservation exit – thus condemning Pippa to a fire-ensnared tomb. If it hadn't been for the bravery of the firemen, she'd be dead...

"Bastard."

The word ejected from a snarl of lips, and even now Pippa felt the old scars on her back itching, and she thought of her father, and she hated her father. She remembered the thick yellow cream, remembered vividly the many skin-graft operations continuing for a further six years, simply to return her to a semblance of normality. She remembered school, and her torture at school: kids were evil little bastards at the best of times, she knew, and even now she shivered, remembering the other kids chasing her with matches and lighters, making dolls of her and burning them in the classroom and playground. She'd wept, oh how she had wept and begged to be left alone. But the bullying continued, merciless, endless. Her parents couldn't stop it, her teachers couldn't stop it, because bullies were clever, cunning, they knew when to strike in those tiny moments when nobody else was around, nobody else there to witness the pain. The worst – Emelda, a big butch lass with legs like girders and a spotted face like a burst melon, with facial lumps and frizzy hair like bad candyfloss – Emelda, yeah, Emelda had taken particular delight in torturing Pippa, chasing her on long winter mornings across frosted fields, throwing lit matches at her in class, singing "Burn the witch, burn the witch, *burn the witch!*" This went on for years. For long, agonizing *years*. Years of subtle fear, of checking the coast was clear before leaving school and before joining the dinner queue; always the last to enter the classroom, just after the teacher, much to the amusement and general hilarity of Emelda and her group of mocking cronies. Pippa the Prick, they called her. Pippa *takes* Prick. Pippa the Witch. Pippa the Bitch, Pippa the Walking Corpse, *fucking burnt bitch, you should have died in that fire with your mum and dad, you should be a blackened stick-corpse stinking like fried pigmeat, lying in a mass grave for the burned, all curled up together like burnt bacon and your fingers like black twisted twigs.*

They caught her by the local shops. Ironically, her dad had sent her to buy cigarettes and matches, and she stood, arms limp, matches in one hand, as the girls formed a semicircle cutting off her escape and Emelda, with her frizzy mass of back-combed curly hair, snarled words filled with poison and hatred and Pippa did not understand, did not understand this *hate*. What had she done? She said it, finally plucked up the courage to say the words which burned in her breast.

"Why, Emelda? What did I do to you? Why do you hate me?"

"You fucking burnt witch, we want you to die, we hate you, hate your stupid little bitch face and stupid little burnt-stick arms and legs."

There was no reason. Something *clicked* inside Pippa.

She smiled, even as Emelda slapped her a stinging blow across the face, making skin smart with an imprint of fat, red, crooked fingers, making blood trickle from a split lip and Pippa's eyes turned triumphant in a cold, analysing, grey glow.

"Burn      the      witch?"      she      whispered, understanding flooding her, and she struck the match and threw it into Emelda's frizzy hair in one swift movement. Emelda's hair was a monstrosity of curled hair filled with *hairspray*. Flammable. Her head went up like an inferno, curls crisping and Emelda screaming like... like a live *pig* on a spit.

Pippa smiled as Emelda rolled around on the floor, screaming, trying desperately to put out her blazing hair. None of her friends helped. They backed away, like the cowards they were, and faded into the shadows for eternity.

Pippa stood, watching Emelda squirm, head tilted to one side, eyes bright, screams now gone as her lips melted, her skin melted, but the eyes were there, would always be there, watching her, haunting her...

Now, Pippa blinked.

Now, her own eyes were bright. She rubbed at them savagely, and rolled her shoulders, feeling the scar tissue stretch. She'd stopped moving, was frozen to the spot, nostrils twitching at the scent of burnt flesh. She heard sobbing, distant, muffled, and padded forward between huge stacks of industrial containers... unsure of what she might find. Emerging from between teetering stacks she found the containers arranged in a large square, and within the square was set up an emergency field hospital with perhaps fifty benches. Each bench contained a burn victim; men, women, even children; most had entire bodies scorched, skin blackened, arms stretching out with crooked fingers, faces contorted in hot fire agony and painted by patches of colour, raw pink, angry red, charcoal black. Pippa gasped. Amongst these many victims ran three nurses, tall, slender, with peroxide-blonde hair and cherry-red lips. They did not complain, they simply hurried about, administering jabs and offering support with soothing voices and calming smiles.

Pippa moved forward, and one of the nurses turned. "You! Help, over here! *Please!*"

Pippa slung her D5 across her back and hurried towards the nurse. With a fire-dry throat, eyes wide as she took in the flame-carnage, she croaked, "What do you want me to do?"

"Here, inject them with this."

"Painkillers?"

"Yes."

Pippa moved amongst the wounded, the scarred, the burnt, the desecrated. Bacon lips pleaded for help, whimpered in agony, screamed and croaked with fear, but it was the eyes, the eyes were the worst, the pleading in deep, watery depths. Pippa came upon a young girl, six years old, her back savagely burnt, her limbs moving in exaggerated slowness as if she swam through the air, as if trying to crawl away from the pain, the *burning*, which had ravaged her. *It's me,* thought Pippa, tears streaming down her own face. *It's me!*

"Help me," said the little girl, and Pippa gave her an injection but could see that it did little to relieve the pain. "Please, please help me." She was weeping, the burnt husk of her body shaking as sobs wracked her skeletal, pork-crisp frame.

Pippa gave her a second injection, and the girl slumped forward. Pippa felt a nurse's hand on her shoulder. Cherry-red lips tickled her ear. "You'll have to kill that one, pretty. She's beyond our help." *No,* Pippa wanted to scream, she's not beyond help, I can help her, I can save her and she was back there, in the fire with the flames ravaging over her and she was back there, watching Emelda squirming on the floor trying vainly, and with slow weakening struggles, to put out the fire in her own hair as the skin on her face melted like hot wax and the whole merged and blended until Pippa screamed, long and harsh, and jabbed the hypodermic, delivering a sweet injection of euthanasia.

"Well done," said the nurse. She pointed. "Now the next."

Pippa moved on, killing the burnt husks, the damaged beings, one by one until she reached the end of the row. Then she turned, and came down the next row, delivering her injections of mercy and crisped body after burnt husk slumped to the benches, sighing, expiring, and Pippa was crying, sobbing, weeping openly as she murdered and murdered but this was right, wasn't it? This was the right thing to do, because these people were dying, dying slow horrible deaths under slaughter of the flame and she had the power of *life and death* in her hands, she had the power of...

God.

Pippa finished at the last row, and the final body slumped, dead, to the cool flat bench. Weeping, Pippa looked up, and felt suddenly that something was wrong. The three peroxide nurses were stood together, on the other side of the space, huddled together, watching her with suspicious eyes.

"We should call you the Goddess of Mercy," said one, voice deeply sardonic.

"You are a Killer, that's for sure," said the second.

"A Bringer of Death," said the third.

"I was helping them!" shouted Pippa, "I was putting them out of their misery!"

"Are you happy to be alive, fucker?" snarled the first nurse, peroxide curls bobbing.

"Maybe somebody should have put *you* out of your misery."

"If that fireman hadn't arrived, you would have been toast."

"Roast pork Pippa."

"Cooked toddler-girl."

"Fried female eunuch."

"Burn the witch," said the first nurse. They started to move, walking slowly through the aisles, spreading out, and Pippa became aware of movement, from around the space, as between the containers emerged more nurses, hundreds of nurses with their smart, tight, white uniforms, their bulges of generous belly and bosom, their peroxide-blonde hair and cherry-red lips only now, *now* they didn't look so pretty with their curled claws and blackened teeth stumps and glittering, feral eyes which set them apart, a million miles apart, from the human...

"Burn the witch," they chanted, crooked croaks rising in volume as they swarmed towards her like a plague, "burn the witch, burn the witch, *burn the witch!*"

Pippa screamed, covering her ears, then dragged her D5 shotgun from her back and blasted a nurse from her feet. She accelerated backwards, a flailing rag doll, a hole through her midriff showing burnt and blackened intestines. The nurses opened mouths, and flames curled from pink eel tongues, flames burned in their eyes and every single nurse was on fire, on fire *within* and Pippa tried to back away between the benches but there was no escape, no retreat, nowhere to run that the burning nurses could not follow. They had her cornered, a rat in a corner, a fish in a net, a six-year-old girl in a burning room with no help, no rescue, no love, simply waiting to die.

"I don't want to die," sobbed the six-year-old Pippa.

As she waited for the flames to come.

CHAPTER FOURTEEN

# CRASH & BURN

"Wait!" hissed Pippa. "No. I won't let it end like this. I won't die like this. I won't fucking *kill* like this!" Tears streamed down her ashen face, and she threw her weapon to the ground. "I will not fight you," she said, voice a hoarse whisper.

The nurses surged up to her, their breath fire, flames curling from lips, and their hands touched Pippa, caressed her, stroked her hair and body and she gave herself to them, no longer caring, and she knew, deep in her soul, she should never have burned Emelda, it was wrong, it was evil, and now she stayed her hand, did not toss the match into Emelda's hair, instead taking the beating and crawling home, weeping, for revenge could never be the right way.

Pippa breathed, deeply. She opened her eyes. Stared into the burning, glowing orbs of the nurses.

"*I will not fight you,*" she growled. "*Do your worst.*"

She closed her eyes, and waited for death, but opened them again as she felt the nurses retreating. The benches were gone, leaving a large cool space, and in the middle of the area something glittered on the matt floor. Pippa walked forward, and knelt, and picked up the single match.

She smiled.

And felt a great weight lift from her heart.


EVERYTHING WAS NOISE and chaos. An eternal tumbling of worlds, planets clashing, smashing, colliding, a roaring and twisting and bashing of steel, stone, concrete, all rushing and clashing together in a madness. She threw up her hands as the insanity took her, and was pulverised by the chaos, battered and bashed, torn, pulled down in a rabid violence which left her totally stunned.

Gradually, the roaring subsided. It was an avalanche in reverse, starting fast and gradually decelerating through smashes and cracks, until only occasional concussive *booms* detonated the silence. Then there were more cracks, and bangs, and the trickling of dust which seemed to go on for a long, long time, so long she wondered if her breathing space might fill with dust and fine debris; suffocate her with a liquid solid.

And then... silence.

A period of time passed, but she was concussed, battered from a very great height. She had no idea how long had passed, only that time *had* passed. She felt as if she meandered in and out of consciousness, although she could not be sure. She could taste blood, which ran down her throat, lubricating her dryness; and for this she was thankful, yet at the same time worried. It was not good to drink blood. If the bleeding continued, she would obviously... die.

To die.

For months, she had never considered the concept. Even during her extensive Biohell adventures, she had never once stopped to think about the risks of her actions, the possibilities of death in the violent environment in which she operated. But now, when she thought about it, thought about death, she wondered what would be in store for her.

After all, was there a God for eight-foot transmogrified mutant zombies?

Was there some kind of flesh-hanging, pus-ridden, brain-eating deity?

Did zombies have a heaven? A place where the flesh was always rotten, the brains always ripe and chilled, and people didn't run screaming the first second they laid eyes upon you?

I'm delirious, thought Mel. It must be the battering. And the loss of blood. And the loss of... Franco.

Dear, sweet Franco. Didn't he see? Didn't he realise? She had divorced him *for his own sake!* She had killed their marriage because, despite loving him to bits, she knew in her heart of hearts that a fine strapping squaddie like Franco couldn't possibly spend the rest of his life married to an eight-foot monstrosity, with breath like a fetid corpse and who got slick every time he took off his hat and exposed the pulsing beat at his temple.

Brains, y'see? thought a dazed Mel. It all came down to the brains.

Man brains, woman brains, kiddie brains; hell, even fish brains. It was all the same bucket of mush to her. They were sweet, they smelled sweet and by God they tasted finer than any vintage Champagne. Mel would swim an ocean for a platter of raw brains, she would climb a volcano, crawl across a continent of broken glass, abseil the world!

And sex? Zombies alive! Don't get Mel started on sex!

As a woman, Mel had contained a healthy sexual appetite. But as a zombie? Mel didn't understand the exact biological workings of a zombie, but by everything that was holy, her libido had increased to the extent she was milking Franco like an over-milked goat. The poor, bleating, deflated little bugger.

And now. Here. Trapped.

Trapped under a collapsed hospital. Waiting to die.

Tears formed in Mel's tiny black zombie eyes and, gathering her strength – which was considerable – she heaved at the bricks and steel around her. Muscles squirmed up and down her arms and shoulders, but nothing shifted and Mel released a pent-up breath of anger and frustration. Dust trickled over her face, and made her cough.

Entombed, she thought sombrely.

Buried alive.

How long would it take a super-strength super-zombie to die from starvation? Then a horrible thought bit her. *What if* she couldn't die from starvation? What if, being a zombie, that sort of long-drawn out agonising death was denied her? What *if* she was tougher than tough, tougher than *death*. And she would have to spend years, decades, trapped down there beneath the rubble?

"Grwll grwll mrwl brdwll," she growled, and heaved and heaved, muscles bulging, eyes bulging, heaving and straining and straining and heaving, but the steel stanchions would not shift, the rubble barely creaked, and Mel, after perhaps twenty minutes fighting her entombment, slumped back into her tiny cubby hole, shaped in a random scatter of chaos to cruelly preserve her life.

Bugger, she thought.

And wished Franco was there...

Distantly, something made a grinding sound. The ground beneath, and indeed *around*, Mel shook. Stones started to vibrate, dust trickled and blinded her. As she blinked it free the grinding accelerated into a *clanking,* a deeply-throbbing mechanical sound like some great and titanic form of earth-moving equipment.

A pounding began, and scatters of sound which thudded through the earth and hurt Mel's ears. There were scrapes and bangs, metallic squeals and Mel, with a feeling of elation, suddenly realised somebody was *digging.*

Rescue! Franco had come to rescue her!

Franco, Pippa, Betezh, Olga, they had seen her buried in the rubble of the collapsing hospital and dug out some earth-moving equipment and they were attempting to free her from imprisonment. The joy! The elation! Oh how she'd give Franco the fucking of his life for this! She'd ride him till he bled, in a simple appreciation at his loyalty, at his unstinting belief in her failure to be squashed.

The pounding and grinding continued, and through vibrations she felt the digger getting closer and closer. Then a horrible thought occurred. What if the digger *dug* through her? After all, those huge bucket teeth were savage and made no distinction between flesh and brick!

Mel's teeth started to gnash and gnaw in frustration. It would be a savage and unfair death! Rescued, but murdered in the process! Oh how the God of Zombie Comedy liked his little japes! The bastard.

Suddenly, bricks and steel shifted above her, the whole world seemed to tilt and wobble and move, and a grim dull daylight flooded in. Mel realised it was evening, turning to darkness. Green tinged the bricks, and the huge shape of the digger with its seven mechanical arms, caterpillar tracks, and four huge hydraulic legs which were currently lifted above it, giving the whole giant machine the appearance of some kind of deformed robotic spider-octopus hybrid.

Quad engines droned and roared, exhaust fumes plumed, and the digger dropped again, grasping a H-section of steel weighing perhaps eight-hundred tonnes and tossing it aside easily. Mel shrugged free of her imprisoning bricks and started to wave her arms. Spotlights strobed across the scene.

"Grwll grwl!" she shouted, as the digger turned and whirled, caterpillars crushing bricks into dust. It spun again, many arms flipping and flopping, great steel limbs which suddenly dropped towards her. She ducked, to avoid decapitation, and the machine dug out another scoop of bricks.

Mel scrambled quickly up the mound of debris, waving her brown mottled arms and screeching a high-pitched zombie screech she knew might attract the driver's attention over the roar of engines. "Dwn herww!" she shouted. "Dwn herww!"

The digger whirled over her head, trailing bricks.

One bounced off Mel's domed skull, and spun off into the pit from which she'd emerged. Mel scowled, and her lower jaw moved out with *cracks* of annoyance and twisted tendon.

Suddenly, the digger quietened and spotlights swivelled on ball-joints to focus on Mel, standing atop the pile of bricks. She shielded her eyes from bright light, piercing in the fast-falling gloom of late evening, and breathed deep on engine fumes as the digger, motionless now, filled her with a sudden, quiet, dread.

"Hello?" shouted a voice.

Who was it? Betezh? Franco? Keenan?

"Grwll, grwl grwl grwwwll!" bellowed Mel.

She sensed, more than heard, the driver's uneasiness. "Oh, I'm terribly sorry, there's been a terrible misunderstanding. I saw you buried, but now I realise… I thought you were somebody else."

*Thought you were somebody else?* Mel was an eight-foot super-soldier, a man-made zombie creation with mottled pus-oozing skin and a head like a football on a long, corrugated neck that wouldn't have been out of place as roofing material. Who the hell had he mistaken her for? How many zombies roamed *Sick World*?

"Grwll?" she said, and little linguistic clues clicked to form a whole. She recognised the voice. She recognised the shape in the digger's cab. Oh damn, she thought. Oh hell. It was Miller. Miller the Health and Safety Officer. Miller, the turncoat.

"Just climb back down in the 'ole, there's a good girl," Miller was shouting from the high cab. "I'll pile in a few hundred tonnes of bricks and we won't say anything else about this matter, aha haha."

Mel growled, and took a threatening step forward…

"Or maybe not," said Miller, and the digger sprang into action. Arms with teeth and buckets whirled over Mel's head, and she leapt, narrowly missing being cut in half. Despite the digger's sheer size and weight, it could move fast, and was surprisingly nimble for something weighing in at eight thousand tonnes. Caterpillar tracks crushed bricks, quad engines throbbed and Mel landed on a slope, rolling down in a tangle of bruised limbs.

The digger pursued, rumbling, and Miller shouted, "I really am sorry about this, Melanie old girl. But it seems you contravene Health and Safety regulations. You stink, a bit, you see. And you're a bit of an abomination against humanity. Ha ha!"

A spike slammed towards her, and Mel skipped sideways, arms stretching out and encircling the huge steel point. She was hoisted high into the air, the digger's arm crackling and surging, Mel's legs dangling at crazy angles as she was hurled through the green-tinged evening. She screamed, as much as a zombie could scream, and heard Miller cackling within the safety of his cockpit pod. She glimpsed his face, a demonic mask through spider-webs of cracked glass, and it was the *glee* in his face that rankled Mel more than anything and sent her surging into a bizarre zombie berserker rage.

Laugh at me, will you?

Laugh at my pus and deformities?

I'll show *you!*

She climbed up the vibrating, swinging mechanical arm like Spider-man, and leapt with a feat of great agility onto the rolling cab of the digger. Miller heard the thud, and glanced up, scowling. One of the bucket arms swung towards the cab, and Mel ducked as it hissed overhead, bent, then slammed her claws through steel and peeled back the lid like the lid from a baked-bean tin.

"Argh!" squawked Miller in disbelief, and lost control of the awesome machine for just a few moments. Mel reached in, gripped him by the throat with one set of claws, and hoisted him out, dangling like a rubber rag-doll.

"Frwlcker," she growled, and shook him.

Miller did a hangman jiggle, hands clawing at Mel's muscles as he turned slowly blue. Eventually, she released him, and dropped him back into the cab where he spluttered and choked. She squeezed in beside him, and draped one arm over his shoulders in a moment of intimacy.

"Wherww werww thrww shrpwss grwing?"

"Eh?"

Mel gave him a backhand slap, the kind of lazy backhand slap which could remove a head from shoulders. Miller's spit and blood decorated the inside of the cab, and he held his hands up before his face, squeaking.

"No no no! Not the face! I wouldn't like to get, um, deformed." He stared hard at Mel's disfigured image. "No offence meant." He watched the glint in her eye, and caught on fast. "OK, OK, you want to know where your friends have gone? That's easy! Easy peasy! Look, I have this tracker." He pulled out a small black bauble, with a flashing blue light. "We can track them with this! It's linked to their spinal-implanted... logic... cubes."

He faltered to a halt, aware he'd made a huge mistake. "Um," he said. His voice dropped, low, so it could only just be heard above the rumble of quad engines. "It was given to me. By Quad-Gal Military. So I could, y'know, keep an eye on you lot. Make sure you didn't... find... anything."

Mel took the tracker, scowled, and put the digger in gear. Pulling on levers, she retracted the many arms and spikes and buckets, and then roared over a mound of bricks scattering debris and steel and the remains of the collapsed, quake-ravaged hospital...

"'Ranco," she said, eyes moist. "I'rm crumming frw youww!"

THE DIGGER RUMBLED over hill and down dale. The landscape, Mel soon realised, even under the light of the green moon, was doing strange things. Things a landscape shouldn't be doing.

It was moving, for a start.

"Well look at that!" said Miller, leaning forward to peer through the cracked windshield. "That forest over there is running like water!" And it was; the trees flowed across the landscape, branches and leaves wavering, as if washed away in a mudslide – only the ground was solid, liquid solid, and shifting uneasily like a cunning sort of quicksand.

"Don't be driving in that!" said Miller, urgent now. "We'll bloody sink!" He thought for a moment. "This landscape contravenes Health and Safety guidelines, Section 15B of the *Guidelines for a Safe Landscape* pamphlet, you know. Any landscape should be a stable landscape, and trees should not move around in case they hurt people, or affect their health, or their safety." He seemed quite happy about this. He felt like he was doing his duty. Like a good and efficient Health and Safety Officer should.

"Grwl," said Mel. As an abomination, she had a pretty poor view of Health and Safety Officers, and Health and Safety in general. After all, her very *existence* went against everything Health, and everything Safety. She killed people and ate their brains, for a start.

"What's that?" shrieked Miller.

"Grwl?"

"It's the river! It's solid! But it was sunny today! How can it be solid?"

And Miller was right. The river, despite moving like a river, was sluggish, a kind of liquid solid, and quite disconcerting to watch. Mel rumbled to a stop beside the embankment and one of the digger's arms reached forward and prodded the river. It glooped in a dangerous sort of manner.

"That," began Miller, and Mel smacked him. "OK," he said. "Be like that. I was only going to point out…" She smacked him again. One of his teeth rattled against the cockpit windshield, and he grabbed at his face with injured hands and injured pride.

Miller stared hard at Mel. "You're a bad girl!" he yelled, blood spittle foaming around his lips as one hand probed inside his mouth. "You shouldn't do that to me! It… contravenes…"

She glowered at him. "Shrt fuwrk up!"

"OK! OK!"

Mel eased the digger into the river, or rather, *onto* the river. The digger, despite being many thousands of tonnes in weight, failed to penetrate the surface. Instead, it was like a fat man walking on a saggy trampoline, and they bounced their way across the river in uneasy silence, like a hushed audience waiting for a drunk tightrope walker to fall.

They made the opposite bank, and the digger churned up the mud wall and sat on a ridge of rock, silhouetted by the green light of the moon. It clanked, groaned, and sighed, settling on its haunches.

Mel examined the small tracker in her claws. She gazed off across the landscape, which seemed to squirm before her eyes, as if she were drunk, as if she were high. It was unreal. Surreal. A vision of madness, as if the very land itself possessed life, possessed a sentient will.

With a clank, the digger lifted from its caterpillar haunches, and lurched off after Franco.

FRANCO STUMBLED DOWN the stairs, through oily smoke, and stopped as the smoke cleared and he realised he was alone.

"Huh? Keenan? Pippa? Olga?"

Silence reverberated down the cold corridor. In fact, it wasn't just cold, it was *freezing* and Franco's man-breast nipples stood out through his PVC nurse's uniform in a quite garish and horrifying display of faux excitement.

"Hot damn and bloody bollocks! I'm alone! Where did everybody go? What kind of depraved and arse-like magic is this?" He gazed around myopically, his Kekra little comfort after the sudden disappearance of the other Combat-K members.

Franco stepped forward, squirming uncomfortably in his requisitioned second-hand boots. He hated boots. Sandals were his thing, even if he ran the risk of blowing off his own toes with grenade shrapnel. Franco didn't care. He'd risk toe amputation, or *toeputation* as he called it, just to let a bit of air circulate. After all, Franco suffered something chronic from athlete's foot. It had been said, in drunken military circles, that Franco had the worst feet in the Quad-Gal. The smelliest. The stinkiest. Like a chicken-farm gone bad. Like sour cheese and rotting fish. They were bad. Hell no. They were *baaad*.

"Ho hum. Why's this always happen to me? I thought I was doing too well, and people should stop calling me Franco 'Lucky Dick' Haggis because they're using up my luck and it's starting to run out! Hot damn."

Franco stopped, breath streaming. The corridor, with its many glass windows, was long and straight and rimed with ice. Franco reached out, touched the glass, and yelped, withdrawing his finger and leaving a strip of skin against the pane.

"Bugger! That's cold, that is."

Franco was talking to himself, a trait he often developed when he was feeling alone, or stressed, or alone and stressed. He frowned. This wasn't looking good. "It's not looking good," he murmured, and pressed his Kekra against his cheek. He yelped again, as the gun – so cold, it was white with frost, and dripped frozen icicles of oil – stuck to his skin. With a tearing sound, he ripped it free with a high-pitched feminine squeal reminiscent of a woman having her fanny waxed.

Franco stared at the gun. Some of his beard, replete with skin, was stuck to the rectangular barrel.

"Damn and bloody bollocks! Where is everybody? KEENAN?" he boomed, not caring who heard anymore. "PIPPA? BETEZH? WHERE ARE YOUSE FUCKERS?"

A head appeared, further down the corridor. It was a stern-looking woman, broad and stocky, wearing a tight blue uniform and with her hair fastened back in a tight bun. She had a round face, pointed nose, and arms as thick as Olga's; and that was thick. They could bend steel bars. Crack open coconuts. Crush a man's head. All with a simple blip of the throttle.

"You!" she shouted, and her voice dripped with so much authority Franco almost snapped to attention. Almost. Decades of slovenly ways had taken their toll. "Stop your shouting! We have patients here! Have some compassion!"

"Yes, ma'am," mumbled Franco, lowering his face submissively and shuffling forward. "Very sorry, ma'am."

The nurse stepped out, stern face appraising Franco as if observing a diseased-riddled chicken dancing before her. "Yes. Well. As long as we understand one another. And no need to stand on formality, young man. No need to call me ma'am. My name is Nurse Armbreaker. And *you* may call me Nurse Armbreaker."

"Yes, Nurse Armbreaker. I'm Franco, Nurse Armbreaker. Listen, can I ask you something, Nurse Armbreaker?"

"Of course, young man."

"Where *am* I?"

Nurse Armbreaker scowled. "This is The Clinic of Anonymity."

"The... what's that supposed to mean?"

"It is where," said Nurse Armbreaker stiffly, "men and women come when they have certain, shall we say, problems."

"Problems?"

"Down there."

"Down where?"

"Down there."

"You mean in your arse?" snorted Franco.

"Sometimes," said Nurse Armbreaker stiffly, "the anal region is afflicted, but of course in these sort of cases, any part of the genitalia can suffer all manner of problems." She smiled, a cold stiff smile, breath steaming from her nostrils.

Franco, face locked in rigid spasm, was animated suddenly and he rubbed his chin. "You mean this is a *VD* clinic?"

Nurse Armbreaker rolled her eyes. "I suppose some would describe it as such, although here we just refer to it as The Clinic."

"Har har har," said Franco.

"Excuse me?"

"I mean," snorted Franco, chuckling and rubbing his beard, "this is where you get willy and fanny problems, reet? Where todgers turn green and fall off, where grapes grow on pouting pussies, where slack and loose individuals get their comeuppance for *not being careful!* Har har har."

Nurse Armbreaker stared hard at Franco. "There is no comedy," she said, "in Venereal Disease."

"Oh there is, I tell you, there is, there was this one guy in the squad by the name of Big Bucket Bollocks, or that's what we used to call him on account of his testicles being shaped like comedy buckets, and this also linked to the joke about his sperm being grittier than sand, oh how we all did laugh over that one, then there was Sally Slack, who it was said shagged a whole platoon and in the process she gave them all *Weeviles,* a most terrible parasitic infestation whereby they takes your todge, right, and then burrows millions of tiny holes in your bulging helmet making it look like the bloody surface of a bloody moon, or something, and Slack spreads this all around the blokes with her easy ways and we're all standing on the parade ground, and those who was scratching, we'd nudge each other and say, 'Heh, he's added a bit to Sally's Slack', and how we did roar with laughter at that one, then there was this other geezer called Freddy Full Load, suffering from a bout of rabid Cumitis, and he used to have that much spunk in him he could pretty much fill a pint bottle every hour, and that's what he used to do and we'd leave it out for Gunnery Sergeant McKinnon to put in his tea. Oh Gods, how we did laugh at that one."

Franco rambled to a stop, lost in distant reminisces. He noticed Nurse Armbreaker's face, and his grin fell quicker than a whore's panties at the flash of a gold crown.

"I see," said Nurse Armbreaker.

"That was a long time ago," said Franco, shuffling his feet. "By the way, why is it so cold in here?"

"To help the patients. It slows down the acceleration of the many rare and wonderful venereal diseases which appeared after humans and aliens started..." she scowled just a little bit too hard, "having *intimacies.*"

"You mean sex?" beamed Franco.

"I mean *intimacies*. We don't use the S word in the Clinic. It just isn't right."

"What about blow jobs?" asked Franco.

"*Excuse me?*" snapped Nurse Armbreaker.

"What I mean is," he coughed, "you know, other sexual terminology? Like cunnilingus? Anal entry? Sloppy pussy? That sort of thing?"

Nurse Armbreaker had gone whiter than white; quite a feat in the freezing environment of The Clinic's corridor. Then her eyes narrowed, and a smile crept across narrow lips.

"Can I *help* you, Franco Haggis?"

"Eh? Yeah, sure, I'm looking for my friends, we seem to have become separated, there's this big dude called Keenan, thinks he's the boss but we all know little ol' Franco is the one really in charge, then there's Pippa, a right feisty one her but I have it on good authority she bangs quicker than a madman on a drum-kit, and is as slippery in the vagina department as a bucket of soapy eels." He grinned, face leering as he imagined Pippa naked. He'd seen her a lot, in his imagination; and he had her well-installed in a variety of sexual simulators using modified DNA to recreate a digital doppelganger. Better than life? Damn fucking right!

"Not like that," said Nurse Armbreaker, voice husky, and strangely quiet.

"Like what then?"

Nurse Armbreaker stared at Franco's groin. He laughed, but the laugh was wooden and tinged with just a little bit of fear. "No no no," he said, "you've got it all wrong, there's absolutely nothing deviated about Franco's tackle, mate, nothing wrong at all. All plumbing is working very well, thank-you-very-much."

"Really. Didn't you just scratch?"

"No, I don't think I did."

"Seize him!"

"Eh?"

Two beefy, stocky, butch nurses grabbed Franco from behind, and Nurse Armbreaker stepped forward, close, intimate, and removed his gun. She stared at him, from a face lacking in any sense of humour. Franco strained, and one arm broke free, but quick as a flash Nurse Armbreaker showed why she had that particular name. She grabbed Franco in a head-lock, and lifted him easily from the floor. The other nurses stepped away, thick black sensible shoes squealing on the chilled floor tiles, and Nurse Armbreaker single-handedly carried Franco in a kind of twisted embrace, his head and neck under one arm, trapping him.

Franco squawked, kicked his legs, then tried to head-butt Nurse Armbreaker. In response, she tightened her grip and Franco choked, red in the face, turning to blue as she literally *crushed* the life from him.

With a final twitch, Franco passed from consciousness.

The last thing he heard was his Kekra hitting the floor.

NEVER LET YOUR guard down. Trust nobody. Be ready for surprises. Be alert. These were Franco's mantras, his internal diatribes which formed his personal philosophy when on a mission. However, as he groaned, his whole body feeling as though it had been through a car-crusher, he realised he had broken Rule 1. Yeah, and Rule 2. And possibly Rule 3 and Rule 4 as well.

"Shit and bugger," he groaned, although the words were unintelligible to those surrounding him, and Franco's eyes fluttered open and he stared up at bright white lights. The lights of an operating theatre. He groaned. "Not *again*. What *is it* with these medical muppets?"

He tried to sit up, and found he was restrained. Leather straps fastened his wrists, upper arms, waist and ankles. He had been stripped naked. If he tried, he could lift his upper body about six inches from the – he suddenly realised – wheeled trolley, and this enabled him to see he was not, in fact, in an operating theatre. Oh no. This was much, much worse.

"Where am I?" he squeaked, voice far less than the usual Franco drawl.

Nurse Armbreaker stepped into view. She wore a smile, but her eyes were cold. Indeed, colder than the liquid nitrogen used to freeze off public pubic warts. "Franco Haggis. Welcome back to the world of the living. Thank you so much for volunteering to take part in our medical experimentation into alien-human hybrid venereal disease."

"Wha'?" said Franco, still groggy from his crushing, although the bright lights and tangible *fear* were bringing him around fast. "What's going on? Eh?" He strained against his straps, and jiggled the whole trolley which reminded him *so much* of life back at Mount Pleasant when he'd been incarcerated as insane. "What you doing to me, woman? I demand to be released this instant!"

"No," said Nurse Armbreaker, "I have your medical consent form here." She flashed a document beneath his nose. He caught the words... *sexual, disease, help us, experiment, grotesque, and severe*, plus his own genuine signature, before it was whisked away again. Franco paled. *Grotesque*, it had said. Franco didn't like the word grotesque. It reminded him of grotesque things.

"Now listen here," he said, and Nurse Armbreaker, who had been sneaking forward, attacked him with a syringe which jabbed his arm and injected amber fluid, straight to his bloodstream.

Euphoria flooded Franco, and he felt his lips and tongue turn to rubber, his muscles turn to jelly, and his penis enlarge and engorge at quite an alarming rate. Wow, he thought, as he watched himself stand proud, as stiff and robust as it could ever be. What happened there, then?

"A penile stimulant," said Nurse Armbreaker, face stoic. "It has the unfortunate side effects of making your brain quite ridiculously simple, but we can't have everything, can we, and for the purposes of this medical experimentation, intelligence is unnecessary."

"You viagra'd me!" slurred Franco.

"No." Nurse Armbreaker smiled, a glitter of teeth. "This is something much more potent."

"Help!" wailed the conversely enlarged and enfeebled Franco.

"There is nobody to help you," said Nurse Armbreaker sternly. "Take your medicine like a man! Be upstanding! Uplifting! After all, your dreams are about to come true. Bring in Candy!"

"Candy?" thought Franco. He perked up a bit. Maybe things were looking up? He heard sniggering, and twisted to see several of the beefy nurses from before, all wearing blue uniforms, all carrying clipboards and tiny pencils. Occasionally, one scribbled something. They were observing him! Him! Franco Haggis!

He turned back, and caught sight of the screen. It was illuminated from behind, and he saw the shadowy outline of the perfect woman. She was tall, with an hourglass shape, wide hips, huge globes for breasts. Her hair was long and flowing, and her silhouette was one of the most perfect things Franco had ever seen. He watched the silhouette undressing, and his mouth began to drool. I wouldn't have needed none of that penile stimulant, I tell ye! he thought. What's going on? What damn and bloody game are they playing here?

"Come out, Candy," cooed Nurse Armbreaker, and Franco's eyes went wide in anticipation as from behind the screen stepped... a green jelly-monster from his worst nightmares. It was as if a huge and wobbling mound of jelly had been formed into the shape of the perfect woman. Candy was semi-transparent, and apparently made *from* some kind of wobbling sentient vegetable matter.

"Candy?" moaned Franco, struggling weakly against his bonds. The amber liquid had made him as weak as a new kitten. And his mewls were about as manly.

"This is Candy," said Nurse Armbreaker, voice stern, face a puckered focus. "She is a Viss, from the

Gregfarory System, Cluster XXII. She is a perfect alien-human hybrid, and unfortunately, riddled with a variety of, shall we say, diseases. It would be an interesting experiment, for Clinic purposes of course, to see what effect these deviated bacterium have on a singular entity human body. Proceed!"

"Whoa!" shouted Franco, "just wait a goddamn minute!"

The Viss, Candy, proceeded. She walked coquettishly across the clinic experimentation room, past beds and trolleys, past cabinets of drugs and sterile stainless steel pans containing sterilised medical implements, most of which looked like deformed birthing tongs, or over-large scalpels.

"Wait!" roared Franco, but Candy was in full flow, body wobbling in an exaggerated manner, breasts wobbling more than any breasts had a right to, and she reached the edge of the trolley and placed a hand on Franco's chest. It felt like being handled by a wet fish.

"Hello," said Candy, and started climbing aboard him.

"Geroff!" shouted Franco, struggling, but Candy engulfed him with her green jelly and placed her mouth over his, and her vagina over his hardness. He sank into her in all directions, and screamed, muffled, as she began to hump him.

IT WAS LATER. Much later. Franco opened a beady eye as if coming round from a particularly bad drinking session. He groaned, the after effects of the drugs kicking his system like a kid with a ball. "Shit," he said. "Bollocks." Then just for good measure he added, "Arse" to his triumvirate of waking expletives.

*I cannot believe that*, he thought.

I can't believe what she did to me!

It, he corrected himself. I can't believe what *it* did to me.

I feel quite abused.

Argh.

As full consciousness invaded his system and he realised he was *still* in his waking nightmare, he spied Nurse Armbreaker and gave her his worst scowl, the one with thunderous eyebrows and squinty eyes and a pouting mouth full of broken teeth. It had little effect; she was talking animatedly to several skinny little limp doctors with officious looking clipboards.

So, thought Franco. It's gonna be like that, is it?

He pulled at his straps. They were tight. They were strong. Stronger than Franco, anyway.

Then he spied the... alien. The Viss, Nurse Armbreaker had called it. It was cowering against a wall, wobbling and green, and seemed somehow smaller now and Franco felt a sting of pity. The creature seemed somehow demure, submissive, and he realised the Viss was as much a victim, as much a prisoner, as he.

OK. Plan of action? Don't get stabbed with a hypodermic again! That seemed like a good one. Nurse Armbreaker started towards him, trailed by a gaggle of beefy nurses and feeble doctors. They were all subtly deformed, with spots and lesions around their mouths. Franco frowned. Several of them scratched at their genitals.

"And here," said Nurse Armbreaker, "we have Specimen 12,568. Franco Haggis. Human, or as near to human as we've been able to acquire. In poor health, judging from his complexion, his beer belly, and his manically exaggerated libido which hints at childhood repression and problems mating with others of his species for long periods of time."

"Less of the species," muttered Franco.

"Ahh. The specimen is awake." Nurse Armbreaker pulled free a long scalpel, which gleamed in the glow of The Clinic's lights. "As we can see, the Viss has successfully infected our human specimen with a variety of diseases, and it will be educational and extremely valuable to medical science to see how they deform, coagulate, spread and mutate.

Franco strained to see his own penis, but couldn't *quite* get the elevation required. *Deform, coagulate, spread and mutate?* Franco went a little bit cold, and a little bit dead inside. Franco had *never* been infected in his life! Or nothing he could readily remember, anyway. Or at least, nothing that hadn't been cured by a fifty-day course of

QG nuclear antibiotics. This sounded serious. This sounded like... alien VD.

"Oh Gods," he muttered, and did a quick self-diagnostic. How did he feel? Not in his head, nor even his body, but down there in his little willy?

Actually, when he thought about it, and focused all his attention on his groin area, he felt quite odd. His Roger felt a little bit inflamed. In fact, it felt like a different size. Hell, it even felt like a different damn shape!

"Let me see it!" he blurted out, a sudden fear and hypertension taking hold of him and squeezing, hard. "I want to see it! Curse you, I want to see what you've done to me! *Damn* that alien VD!"

Nurse Armbreaker gave him a stern look, and lifted the scalpel, speaking backwards to her gaggle of supporting staff. "Here, we will *pop it* and see what emerges..."

However, as the scalpel lifted from prone to attack, Franco took the only opportunity he could. The scalpel passed his hand, and he grasped it in a sudden jerk, reversed the blade and cut neatly through the leather strap. His right arm snapped up, clutching the scalpel. It gleamed with a nasty silver light.

"Hey!" came the gravel gasp of Nurse Armbreaker. "Specimen! You can't do that!"

"Can't do what?" Franco slammed the scalpel down with a stabbing motion, cutting a long bloody streak in Nurse Armbreaker's thigh. She screamed, a long canine shriek, and grabbed the blood-gushing limb. "Get him! Murder him! Kill him!"

Shit, thought Franco. Bugger! This game's up!

The scalpel whizzed through the air, parting the leather of the second strap. Now he had both arms free. A doctor rushed at him armed with a long needle dripping amber nectar. Franco's upper torso twisted, as the thick needle flashed past his eyes, and he poked the scalpel into the doctor's masticating, frothing mouth, straight into the back of his throat. The doctor stumbled back, vomiting blood. Franco leant forward, missing the swing of a fire-axe (*fire-axe?* howled his mind, *where the hell did a fire-axe come from?*) which embedded in the trolley with a *thud*. Franco deftly slit the straps on his ankles, elbowed a nurse in the face, bursting her cherry-red lips and forcing her to drop the scalpel she carried in fat fumbling fingers, then leapt from the trolley, which squeaked a little, shifting on its little chrome wheels. A doctor snarled in that curious way only a doctor can snarl, and Franco hurled the scalpel. It embedded in the doc's eye, and he hit the ground on his back, twitching.

"I'm a bloody damn specimen, am I?" roared Franco. He was good and mad now. "Infecting my todge with diseases and alien VD! I'm just not bloody having it, reet?"

He whirled, grabbed the axe from its temporary embedding in the trolley, and wrenched it free. He stood, naked, quivering, dangling, holding the axe and scowling with hatred. Then he looked down, and almost dropped the axe at the sight of his little fella. It was swollen, engorged, and most definitely blue. It dribbled a toxic looking blue substance. It was, to all intents and purposes, an infected alien todge.

"Nooooo!" howled Franco.

"Now you listen here," snapped Nurse Armbreaker, stalking forward, limping on her slashed leg and wagging her finger at him as if reprimanding a naughty child. Her bun quivered. She looked most seriously exasperated... As if the naked man with the axe before her was someone to be chastised, and not avoided like a heady dose of bubonic plague. "This has gone far enough! You are Specimen 12,568. You have been delivered here for our medical purposes, and *you will do exactly what you are told you naughty little man, put that axe down on the floor this instant and step away from the trolley!*"

Nurse Armbreaker was used to getting exactly what she wanted, when she wanted. She was used to being obeyed – instantly. Which was why Franco's actions quietly surprised her.

Franco swung the fire-axe, and lopped off her head.

Nurse Armbreaker's decapitated noggin rolled sideways and gave a *slap* as it hit the floor. A half-hearted fountain of blood came from her carcass, which folded to one side. Nurse Armbreaker's eyes stared up at Franco, and her surprised mouth was formed into a surprised O of utmost surprise.

Franco glanced up at the remaining doctors and nurses, perhaps ten in total, who had armed themselves with a variety of twisted medical implements, a curled needle here, a corrugated scalpel there, and for the first time Franco realised everything in The Clinic was slightly twisted, slightly bent from the norm.

The doctors and nurses, also, wore an O of surprise on shocked faces.

Franco grinned.

"Come on, let's dance, fuckers," he said, and with bare feet slapping the tiles and his blue todge swinging in rhythm, he charged at them, hefting the axe.

WHEN IT WAS over and Franco stood in pools of blood, staring around himself as his fury bled away, he looked down at himself again, at the streaks and smears covering him as if he was some savage at the end of an esoteric religious ritual. Which, maybe, he was.

"Damn and stinking chipmunks!" he snarled. "Now, where's me clothes?" He turned, bloodied axe still tight in his grip, but could see no clothes, and more importantly, could see none of his weapons. "Damn and raggedy whores! Will nothing ever go right for me? It's like the whole Quad-Galaxy is constantly against me!"

His eyes fell on the jelly alien. She quivered, yet smaller now, her great wobbling breasts deflated, her rotund arse a mere shadow of those great ripe peaches which had been pounding on Franco's thighs only a few short hours ago.

Franco stalked forward, feeling the heat of hatred rise once more within him. The Viss cowered, covering her head with her arms to create a quite bizarre vibrating image of semi-transparent woman vegetable.

All work and no play make Franco a dull boy, he thought. He lifted the axe. Blood dripped in long gloops from the gore-streaked head. Tiny slivers of sharpened steel could be seen through the gore, and the terror of the Viss reflected in this polished steel mirror.

She infected you, snarled Franco's hate.

She poisoned you with her toxic fucking.

She has diseased you for an eternity...

Franco weighed the axe thoughtfully. Kill her. Kill it. It deserves to die! It is an alien, a heathen, a simple jelly vegetable woman, an abomination against all life...

Franco scowled, and threw the axe to the ground. "Hey lass," he said, "there's no need to be frightened. I'll not do you any harm. I know now, I understand you're a prisoner here just like me, they infected you, just as you infected me. We're both victims, yeah?"

The jelly woman stood, and turned, and seemed to be looking at him with jelly eyes, although he could not be a hundred percent sure because everything was green, her eyeballs, her eye sockets, her head, and all merged in a gentle wobbling manner.

Franco took a deep breath. He held out his hand. "Are you OK?"

"Yes," came the softest, most gentle and, ironically, most *feminine* voice Franco had ever heard. It was the voice of an angel, the voice of a queen, the voice of a goddess. "I am Greya."

"Nice to meet you," came Franco's gruff response. He looked around. "Now then, how the hell do we get out of this damned hell-hole?"

Greya turned, and pointed at a solid brick wall, painted in the sterile puke-green colour which could only appear on a hospital's deranged palette. "That way."

"But it's a wall."

Greya stepped forward, and her arm seemed to enlarge suddenly, swelling and punching out with savage unstoppable force. Bricks exploded, steel shrieked, dust billowed, and within a single second there was a rough and crumbling doorway.

"Now it's a door." Franco gulped, as Greya's arm returned to normal size, then he glanced at the axe, and gulped again. He was pretty sure it would take more than a simple melee weapon to destroy *this* particular creature.

"This way," she soothed, taking him by the hand.

"OK," squeaked Franco, scooping up the axe, and stepping through the portal.

\* \* \*

KEENAN STEPPED FROM the oil-smoke stairs and found himself at the edge of a playground. Keenan had seen this sort of thing before, in huge hospitals built around central hubs or courtyards; an outdoor space, usually a square, surrounded by towering hospital buildings and used by unfortunate children staying in hospital for whatever reason. Keenan had always suffered uneasiness around such medical playgrounds, for whilst their intentions were obviously noble, they simply reminded him of disease and death... and not just disease and death in general, but the affliction of the young.

He glanced around uneasily, his guns feeling wrong in his hands. What is this place? What am I doing here?

He realised immediately that they'd been forcibly separated, and intuition told him it was VOLOS. So then, a test of some kind. A test before they progressed to meet the maker of Sick World? Keenan gave a sick smile. *How fitting*, he thought.

He moved forward, slowly, carefully, gun tracking and waiting for the next enemy. Around him the windows were like eyes, small, square, black, and lacking any emotion, any sympathy. They were a testament to sterility; the sterility of medicine. The hopelessness of the dying. The bitterness of the dead.

And something smelled.

Something smelled *bad*.

Keenan stopped, fake grass crunching underfoot. Before him were a row of four swings, a climbing frame set with two slides, a rubber tyre suspended by chains, and a sand pit. A cold wind blew, and autumn leaves drifted crackling across this sterile playground. Keenan shivered. He looked up at the stars, but there were no stars in this place, just a terrible velvet blackness which coated the sky like tar. And then he remembered: he was far under the world. In a fake place. An ersatz hospital world. A *sick* world.

Keenan turned, the cold wind ruffling his brown hair. His eyes narrowed, and he saw movement at a window. It was pushed open by thin white arms, and Keenan saw a young girl there, no more than ten years old. She leant out slightly, looking down at him, and something chilled Keenan to the core of his soul. She was pretty, with long black hair, but her eyes were black, lacking emotion, devoid of empathy. They stared at him as if he were a bug in a killing jar.

Keenan fought the urge to wave, and he watched her watching him. Her lips moved a little but no words came out.

"Hello," said Keenan, voice quite low. He didn't want to advertise his presence. But then, if this *was* a test by VOLOS, anything of danger already knew he was there. "Shit." He raised his voice. "Hello, girl; can you show me the way out?"

"There is no way out," she said.

"Where am I?"

"The playground of death," she said, and turned, as if talking to somebody within. Keenan saw the back of her head, then. It was caved in, crushed, showing yellow shards of bone emerging from a pulped skull. He could see blood, and he could see the terrible blue-grey of the girl's brain. Even from this distance he could distinguish maggots crawling in her flesh, in her living tissue, in her brain-matter, and Keenan felt the urge to vomit well swiftly inside him –

His hand slapped over his mouth, as along the hospital wall more windows opened, high and low, right across the expanse of the hospital face. Behind, he heard clasps being undone and hinges squeaking, and Keenan turned and watched as a thousand windows were opened by a thousand children, all eerily quiet, all staring with the same black eyes, the same lack of emotion, the same essence of the damned.

"What is this place?" he whispered, spider-legs creeping up and down his spine. Keenan shivered again, his hackles rising, his blood chilling, his heart stopping, his soul dying, as he turned and turned and turned, and watched the hundreds of children, each with a very special wound or illness or disease, each and every one different, unique, and *special*.

One girl had no eyes, just bloody eye sockets. A little boy had a slit throat, blood pumping down his chest. Another boy held hands out with only stumps for fingers clasping the sill. A girl had a screwdriver in her head, the shaft protruding around bubbling brain-matter and blood. Yet another had facial burns, a little girl had a disease of the mouth and nose which left huge, gaping holes in her face through which her working soundless jaws could be seen. More and more and more, each affliction unique, each devastation destroying a child's happiness, future and, ultimately, hope.

"Stop!" he cried, pain flooding him.

"Welcome, Mr. Keenan," said the first girl who'd appeared. Keenan stopped his cycle of turns, and stared at her. His mouth was dry, head pounding, and by God he could have savoured a long cool draught of Jataxa spirit. The whole fucking bottle, in fact. It was on days like this Keenan wished he was dead; dead and eking out an existence in damnation, with his murdered little girls.

Once an alcoholic, always an alcoholic, he thought sourly. There was no such thing as a cure, he knew. Remission was just a temporary shelter until the day he began again. Keenan licked his lips.

"Who are you people?" he said, eventually, voice a lullaby. "Why are you all here, like this? Why are you all so…"

"Injured? Wounded?" The little girl smiled, although her black eyes held no emotion, no humour, no understanding. Her eyes were piss-holes in the snow. Portals to another, darker, dimension. "This is the Children's Ward, Mr. Keenan." She savoured the words, her little pink tongue like a quick, darting fish. "This is where we come to suffer, to be tortured, to feel agony, and to die."

"No," said Keenan.

"Yes," said the little girl. "I am Amra. I am here to show you that dreams are worse than reality, I am here to show you that life can be worse than the horror of imagination; I am here to make you suffer, Mr. Keenan. I am here to make you pay."

Suddenly, all the wounded children started screaming, the boys and girls howled high-pitched and loud, ululating cries ringing out and out and filling the cubic playground with pain and terror.

"STOP!" bellowed Keenan, but his voice was drowned as by a waterfall of sound. The screams continued, all merging into a whole of high-pitched squealing noise which seemed to pierce Keenan's ears and drill right through to his brain stem. He covered his ears, and felt something hot there, and when he looked at his fingers he realised it was... blood.

The screaming continued, an endless river of sound, and Keenan turned around, useless gun clasped in useless hands as he realised, for the first time in his life, despite his personal armoury of guns and bullets, knives and bombs, his elite training and decadent, single-minded purpose, he was effectively unarmed, helpless, weak, more childlike than the screaming children who tortured him. He tracked with his weapon, but dropped it. How could he shoot injured children? And what was their crime? To scream? To show their pain and endless torture?

Across the playground, a gate suddenly opened. It was a wooden gate, painted in bright, gay colours. It squeaked, a penetrating noise through the cacophony of deranged children, and Keenan's gaze snapped to see –

His mouth fell open, for there were his two young girls, Rachel and Ally, and they ran to him across the playground, eyes bright and excited, faces flushed with joy. They wore long dresses and sandals, and hair flowed behind them as they ran. They stampeded across the playground, seemingly ignoring the hundreds of screams, and they fell into their daddy's arms and he was on his knees, holding them, smelling the fresh scent of their hair and feeling the soft warmth of their skin.

Keenan fell into his little girls, fell into their smell, into their essence, into their very being. As they hugged, so the screaming backdrop began to subside, began to drop in pitch, declining like a turbine winding down. Eventually, the screams were gone, and only Keenan's peripheral vision showing hundreds of faces, mouths twisted in silent Os, like automatic kids with the volume on mute, disturbing his equilibrium...

"We missed you, Daddy," said Rachel.

"We love you, Daddy," said Ally.

And Keenan was sobbing, great tears of mercury falling down chilled cheeks. A cold, ice-filled wind blew, ruffling his hair, cutting between their embrace like a nitrogen knife. Keenan pulled back a little, looked into their eyes and they smiled sweet beautiful child smiles and something *cracked* inside Keenan's heart, like a delicate rare bird's egg breaking to spill out precious yolk. There was something wrong. Something twisted. Something *deviant*.

They are not real, whispered a part of his soul.

They are... *dangerous*.

But he was overcome, with joy, with grief, with regret, with frustration, and he chose to ignore the warnings because the love he felt, the great surging uplift of joy and thankfulness, quelled any and all negative energy and Keenan decided, there and then, that if he had to, he would die with them, die for them. No regrets. No bullshit. He would be with his girls, forever.

"Will you take us on the slide, Daddy?" asked Rachel giggling.

"And the swings oh please the swings first!" cried Ally.

And it was there, the strangeness; the looks on their faces were wrong, as if they were wearing human masks, and Keenan pulled back a little, frowning, and this action saved his life. The knife blade whistled a millimetre from his throat, so close it almost kissed his flesh, and he blinked, hard, staring at Rachel whose face had changed in an instant from love to hate, from create to destroy.

"Motherfucker," she snarled, and stabbed forward with the blade, young face twisted into a vision that should never sit on a child's face. Keenan swayed, fast, an instinctive movement, and his right arm smashed up and right, knocking the blade away. He rocked back on his heels, took several steps back, and surveyed the two girls.

"What are you?" he whispered.

"I'm going to kill you, Daddy," snarled Rachel, advancing, the long knife held out. Keenan saw ice glittering on the blade. More cold wind blew, sending leaves skittering across the playground. It smelled like fresh snow.

"I'm going to cut out your liver, *Daddy*," said Ally, and she was more calm than Rachel, less filled with dark emotion. "I'm going to eat your organs. *Then* we'll see how much you fucking love us." She giggled, the sound jangling, out of place, echoing and hollow like dice in a tomb.

Rachel charged, and she was fast, a blur of movement, too fast to be human and Keenan twisted as she leapt, the blade flashing past his face, but Ally was there, also leaping and Keenan ducked, whirling around and back, backing away, reclaimed gun limp in his hands and he could shoot, should shoot, should mow them down because they weren't his girls, weren't his dead children, they weren't human, no human could move like that, twisting and bending, spider-like in their flexible leaps, but they *looked* like his children and his finger slid from the trigger. How could he kill his little girls? How could he kill them, again?

Crying, Keenan was backing away. Rachel and Ally spread out, grins elastic on pale faces.

"Gonna cut you up."

"Gonna fuck you up."

They charged, moving fast, twisting and bending and Keenan backed to the see-saw and tripped, fell hard. All wind was knocked from him and Rachel and Ally appeared above, demonic faces gazing down, sneering at him, mocking him.

"Not so tough now, soldier boy."

"You're going to taste death, you pointless cunt."

Keenan blinked, in lazy-time slow-motion. The world descended into a hazy, snow-filled globe and everything was moving slowly, disjointed, unreal. Keenan lifted his hand and stared at his fingers, and they were pale white, fish-white, and he moved them, in slow-motion, as the girls continued to speak but their voices were slowed, lethargic, deep and masculine and making no sense. They lifted their knives, a unity in destruction, and the blades plunged down fast, hard, intent on death and Keenan moved so fast he felt his muscles straining and tendons tearing and self-preservation kicked him up into the sky from a deep well of despair and he slammed sideways into the girls' legs, toppling them like skittles and rolling fluidly to a crouch, eyes narrowed and lips compressed and gun, now real, no longer a dormant thing, in his hands.

"You want to kill me?" he growled.

The girls climbed to their feet, legs heavily bruised, and snarled at him with strings of saliva and snot pooling from clacking jaws. They shook their heads from side to side, as a dog shakes a bone. Their eyes were black now, and feral.

"You're going to have to work for it."

They leapt, and Keenan dropped his gun and lunged, right fist slamming out and snapping Ally's head back. A spray of blood burst from her nose, and Keenan ducked Rachel's blade and smashed his right elbow into her face. She hit the ground, still, breathing ragged. Keenan turned to Ally, but she was stunned, lying on her back, the knife lost beneath the swings.

Keenan uncoiled, releasing a slow breath. He retrieved his gun, and stared in abject curiosity at the matt stock. Then he looked up, suddenly, into a sea of faces.

As the fight had unfurled, so the children had filed out from the Children's Ward. They were no longer screaming, but instead filled the playground with their diseases, their abnormalities, their injuries, their cancers and their amputations. The girl with dark hair and dark eyes stepped forward, and spoke to Keenan.

"Kill them," she said.

"Why?"

"They tried to slaughter you. They deserve to die. They are evil things, they should not be in this place. This is our hospital. This is our ward. This is *our* playground!" Her voice had risen, and spittle flecked her dark lips, her neat teeth, and her eyes were filled with tears of passion.

"No," said Keenan.

"Kill them!" she shrieked, lurching forward, then stopping.

"No," said Keenan, and he lifted his eyes, met the gaze of the dark child. "I cannot. And I will not."

"Then we will murder *you!*" she hissed, and pulled free a long, glinting scalpel. The rest of the children produced weapons, and their eyes were fixed on Keenan, and they smiled dark smiles and their knowledge was infinite, their malevolence a deep dark ancient thing. "We will cut your heart out. And feed."

Keenan threw down his gun, his face bleak, his eyes tired. "So be it," he said, as the MPK clattered.

He closed his eyes, as hundreds surged over him...

# CHAPTER FIFTEEN
# HARDCORE

CAM LIMPED INTO the huge domed cavern after a myriad of miniature yet death-defying nighmare encounters he would rather not talk about, withhis twisted scanners only registering at 13%. He tried, again and again, to grab fixes on Keenan, Franco, Pippa, or any of the other members of the squads. And, infuriatingly, the only one he could determine was Sax, the robot dog with the bad wig, asleep and snoring as he recharged back at the Giga-Buggy at the REC Centre, amidst a fresh fall of deep snow.

Cam spun slowly, blue lights flickering. It was very quiet, and very cold.

Above him, the massive dome was smashed through, and the floor below littered with debris. Something had forced its way down here. Something big. And something with devastating firepower. It stunk of Combat K.

Did they leave? Exit by the tunnel?

And, with little other option, Cam had only one set of co-ordinates in his damaged and fizzling memory.

Sax. He would locate Sax.

But then... what was that? Cam detected a huge field of crushed proto-matter; the birthing agent of *Stars*. Hmm, he thought. If Combat-K are in danger, I could add ignition to that huge source of proto-matter... what a source of detonation! I can damn near destroy half the planet. Inside, Cam's Put Down™ War Technology twinkled. It would be like an entire World War! Started by him. He coughed. To save his friends, of course.

Cam rotated.

Which way?

Out of the tunnel, towards Sax and the Giga-Buggy? Or down.

Towards the bomb.

Cam whistled a little tune, and made his decision...


KEENAN SPAN IN the vastness of space, the vastness between worlds, between dreams, the place where nightmares were spun and made real. Slowly, he drifted for a billion years and the pulse of alien blood in his veins beat harder, and faster, and it burned him for he was merely human, his shell not designed to take such substances.

*You are the Dark Flame,* said a voice in his mind. *You are special. So very special. This world depends on you.*

Keenan opened his eyes, slowly. His eyelids were rigid, almost solid, soiled with a sticky glue. He forced them up and stared at white dust, like flour, which filled his vision. Keenan groaned, and a *puff* inflamed before him, a mini holocaust. Keenan realised he was lying on his belly, and he rolled over to his back, slowly, the dust soft beneath him and covering his WarSuit, his hands, his hair with its fine powder. He coughed, and chemical needs fought for precedence in his system. Cigarettes, or Jataxa? He realised he wanted a smoke more than anything, and crawled onto his knees, the dust sinking beneath him, soft, pliant, almost dragging him under with its instability.

Keenan glanced left, saw Franco emerging from dark dreams. Franco sat up, powdered in the dust, and glared at Keenan. "Nobody said it would be like that! I had a bastard of a time, I did. It was all... urgh!" He shivered, and checked his penis manically, eventually calming down and giving a big sodden sigh. He looked at Keenan. "How about you, Big Man?"

Keenan shrugged, and climbed unsteadily to his feet. "It was a test. We were on our own, facing our own little nightmares, I think. What happened to you?"

"Mad VD clinic," said Franco, face grim. He scratched his groin. "You?"

"Hundreds of diseased and dying children trying to kill me." He refrained from mentioning his own girls; the memory was too painful, like a glowing hot splinter through the centre of his brain, placed there by the tender caress of a sledgehammer.

"Hey, guys!"

It was Pippa, trawling towards them as if wading through fine sand. She was coated in the substance, and appeared from the gloom almost as a ghost. She stopped, and started laughing at their appearances.

"You two look grim," she said.

"It was a grim time," said Franco, scratching again. "Damn that VD clinic. Damn that dodgy alien sexual disease!"

"What happened to you?" said Keenan. He had found his small tin, and rolled a cigarette. He glanced at Franco. "Is this shit explosive? Because if it is, we're all going up in a ball of flame."

Franco wet his finger and tasted it. Shook his head. "No, nothing detonation worthy here. Feel free to cancer yourself out."

Keenan lit, and Pippa shrugged. "It was a... burns unit." Keenan nodded, understanding evident. He knew Pippa's history, knew exactly why she was such a fine example of damaged goods.

"Sounds like a walk in the park compared to *my* experiences," Franco muttered, and pushed his hand down his pants, pulling a funny face as he once again fumbled and fought with his own tackle.

"What the hell are you doing?" said Pippa.

"Rearranging the old meat and two veg," scowled Franco. "Leave me alone, reet? It's a very delicate process."

"We obviously passed the tests," said Keenan, staring around himself at the bleak, endless white desert. It rose on dunes, rolled away like a sea of powder, an addict's wet dream. "But where is Betezh? And Olga?"

Pippa searched, eyes wide. "Are they dead?"

"There's only one way to find out. We need to meet VOLOS. But where do we go?"

"That way," said Franco, confidently, pointing in one direction.

"Why?" said Pippa. "What distinguishing feature of the featureless landscape attracts you?"

"I'm just telling you, it's that way."

"Why?"

"Because it is."

"Yeah, dickweed, but *why?*"

"Because my seventh sense tells me so! They don't call me Franco 'Lucky Compass' Haggis for nothing, you know!"

"There is no direction," came the voice of the avatar. It stood, ankle-deep in white powder, watching them with a featureless, translucent face.

Keenan frowned. "You cheated us. You never said we would be split up; we operate as a unit. A squad. We are Combat K." He gave a grim smile. "Until the day we die."

"It was no trick," said the avatar of VOLOS.

"Where's Betezh? And Olga?"

"They did not pass the test," said the avatar, grimly.

"So they are dead?" bleated Franco, fists clenching.

"No. I did not say that. They are merely... somewhere else. In a holding cage. With the one you call Snake. They will not be harmed, but they may not enter this domain. You see, VOLOS has to make sure you are worthy before you enter the inner sanctum. Once inside, he is defenceless against you despite his might, his age, and his vast intelligence. VOLOS needs to know you are not too... twisted, as examples of your species. He needs to make sure your genetics are of the right calibre, shall we say. VOLOS may be old, but he is wary. He doesn't open the door to those he does not trust."

"I like words like *defenceless*," muttered Franco, and Keenan could see it, could read it in his comrade's eyes. *Get in close and blow the motherfucker away. VOLOS was a scourge, an ancient evil, he had created the junks and now they spread through the Quad-Gal like a pestilence, a horde of insects, destroying everything in their path, toxifying every living planet and species with their vile poison...*

Something shimmered in Keenan's mind. He began to comprehend. He began to grasp the strands, and weave them together into a rope of understanding. What made VOLOS evil? Perception. And yet, what did he want with Keenan? With Franco and Pippa? VOLOS was mighty. He could have taken them apart at any point, plucked them from the surface of his planet, his *Sick World*, and done what he liked with their corpses. Why go through this elaborate charade?

"You are beginning to realise," said the avatar, blank face turning towards Keenan. "That is good."

"We are?" said Franco, and puffed out his chest. "Superb!"

"Keenan is," said Pippa, understanding the situation implicitly.

"Is VOLOS coming here?" said Keenan.

"No. This is the Furnace. VOLOS would not venture this far out."

Franco, who was tasting the powder again, scowled. "It's a bit sour, this stuff, so it is, and it ain't going to win you any culinary awards mate," he said. He laughed at his own joke. "Why do you call it the Furnace? A bit damn and bollocks over-dramatic for what is, if I am not mistaken, a huge sugary bowl of white dusty shit!" He grinned, showing his missing tuff.

"You *are* mistaken," said the avatar, no element of emotion in its asexual voice. "You walk upon the powdered remains of a billion dead souls. They are cremated in the Furnace. This place is also known, to some on Sick World, as the Mausoleum."

Franco choked, and started scraping coagulated white paste from his tongue. "You mean to tell me you stood there watching me taste powdered dead people?" Scrape. "Their remains?" Scrape scrape. "Their bloody damn and bloody ashes? You sick sick son-of-a-bitch!" Scrape scrape *scrape*.

"Curiosity killed the cat," said Pippa, smugly.

"Shut up, fine words coming from someone who's bloody frigid."

"Frigid! Why, you…"

Pippa's voice tailed off. Keenan gestured, and Franco, too, halted his erratic oral scrapings.

"There is one more test," said the avatar, and seemed to look up at the sky, agitated now by demeanour, if not expression.

"Do we have a choice?" Keenan's voice was little more than a whisper.

"Not this time. You have come too far. You made your choices, many of them, over previous hours, previous days. Now you are here. Now VOLOS *needs* your counsel. But first, you must prove yourselves worthy to enter the inner sanctum. I will take you there, when you are ready."

"What's the next test?" blurted Franco.

"So far," said the avatar, "you have been through the world of the child, the babe, the infant. The world of birth. Then you endured individual experiences – moments from your lives which are there like vivid scars deep within brain tissue; not so much earned, as inherited. And now... now you will face..."

"Death," whispered Franco, eyes wide.

"Yes," nodded the avatar. "You must cross the Morgue. Only then can you enter the core of VOLOS's domain."

"What do we have to do?" said Keenan, grasping his gun tight.

"Absolutely nothing," smiled the avatar, "although so far you have been tested on your intellect, and your mercy." The avatar licked alabaster lips, an opening in the blank, a pink stain, a crimson scar. "Now you will be tested on your savagery." Like a flow of quicksand the world dissolved and Combat-K were falling, spinning down through the powdered remains of a billion doctors and nurses, patients and madmen, through the sterile purified dust of the twisted, the deformed, the injured, the lame, the diseased, the toxic, and ultimately, the dead...

down,

down,

to the Morgue.


THE CORRIDOR WAS old. Ancient. Pipes hissed and steamed at ceiling level, a high gothic ceiling filled with stone arches and rusted brackets, swinging chains and rust. Rust dominated, an entropy of corroded, eaten metal.

"I don't like this," muttered Franco.

"You don't like *anything*," said Pippa.

"Yeah, well, it gives me the heebie jeebies."

"At least we're together."

"Shh." Keenan held up a gloved hand, his attention focused. He gestured above them, where a wide metal sign, pitted with rust and battered flakes of old paint, read: **THE MORGUE**.

Keenan led the way through a wide archway, then through a gradually reducing tunnel of increasing rust and accelerating decrepitude. They came to a square door, made from black iron and boasting huge rivets. It was solid, in the same way a castle portcullis is solid, and Keenan grasped a thick bracket and tugged, half expecting the door to resist his efforts. Instead, it swung easily open on well-oiled hinges revealing a huge space, football stadium huge, and completely tiled with small, square, white ceramic tiles. The isolated pools of light were weak, green orb islands between seas of black.

Combat K stepped through the iron door, and only Franco turned when it eased shut behind them, grinding shut and giving a tiny, metallic *click*.

"We're locked in!" bellowed Franco, and his voice slammed down the giant tiled space, acoustics taking his diarrheic words and bouncing them from wall to wall to wall. "IN IN IN," boomed the echo, and gradually, eventually, faded to silence.

"It's a solid door, indeed," mused Pippa. "I thought it was to make sure we didn't get in, but it opened easily enough."

Keenan gave a nod, eyes fixed ahead, body tense, alert, ready for combat. "A thought occurs – that the door, possibly, is not so much to keep us from getting in... but rather, to keep *something* from getting out."

Pippa swallowed. "That's a bad thought, Zak."

"I have bad thoughts all the time," said Keenan, glancing towards her and giving a wry grin. "Come on. We need to clear this space. We need to get to VOLOS."

They moved forward, easing through the black and green globes of light. There came a sudden clatter, as Franco kicked an object which rolled out from blackness and rocked to a halt in a pool of light. "Damn and chicken bollocks!" he snapped, and his echo was picked up and smashed around the interior. "OLLOCKS, OLLOCKS, LOCKS, LOCKS, OCKS."

Keenan glared at him. "Idiot!" he hissed.

Franco gave a shrug, and trigger fingers tightened on twin Kekras as his eyes fell on the object to stub his toe. It was a skull, gaping, with the lower jaw missing. Franco stooped and scooped, and stared into the eye sockets of the skull.

"Nice place."

"What's that over there?" Pippa shifted her D5 shotgun, and the barrel light lit up a dim line of cylinders. Franco eased over to them, treading warily through the gloom. They were old. Older than old. Decrepit, with faded markings and long-ago peeled paint. The brass nozzles looked... broken.

Franco reached out...

"No!" snapped Keenan, but it was too late.

Franco twisted, and there came a hiss. Franco sniffed, then squeaked shut the valve. He held up a hand. "Hey, it's OK, it's cool. They're oxygen cylinders, alreet? Don't be all getting your knickers in a twist."

"It could have been poisonous," said Keenan, glaring as his weapon's beam swept the darkness.

Franco held out his hands. "But hey, it wasn't, right? We're cool and fine and dandy. Just a bit of leftover oxygen, down here in the..."

"Understand?" snapped Keenan.

"Eh?"

Pippa and Keenan had joined Franco. Their lights swept the ancient cylinders. There were perhaps a hundred, about thirty of them portable and small enough to carry.

"Why," said Pippa, by way of explanation, "do they need oxygen in a morgue?"

"Good point," said Franco. "Come on! Let's go."

They moved further down the huge space, boots tramping small white tiles, until they came to a wall, a titanic metal wall filled with the horizontal drawers traditionally used for the storage of the deceased. Combat K stopped, eyes staring up, and up, and along the huge wall of battered, rusting metal.

"Don't like this," said Franco, slowly.

Pippa took a step back. "Me too. I'm getting a bad feeling."

"Another test?" snarled Keenan.

"A bad, bad feeling," muttered Franco.

Their lights swept along the wall, along the rusted dented drawers. It was finally Pippa who asked the question they'd all been considering.

"Do you think they're... full?"

"I bloody hope not!" snorted Franco. "I had enough shit with zombies and shit during that bloody Biohell outbreak!" He laughed, although it was a very weak laugh accompanied by a very weak grin. "Same shit couldn't happen again, right? Lightning doesn't strike twice, an' all that? Night of the mooching dead, an' all that?" He laughed again. Nobody else did.

They walked along the banks of drawers, hundreds upon hundreds, dented and battered, the lights from their guns sweeping tiny pools of yellow against rust. Franco gulped, a few times, and couldn't bring himself to point out that nobody had answered his question.

"I mean," said Franco, jabbering a little now as trace elements of fear and angst and worry threaded through his brain like a maggot cocktail of last night's drugs, "we went through all that shit before, down on The City, with all those damn and bloody bugger zombies turning all foul on us and hunting us through the streets, and things like that can't happen more than once, oh no, not to serious hero fodder like ourselves. It left me quite traumatised, it did. In need of some serious counselling."

"Is that why you humped one?" said Pippa, gun sweeping along a low barrage of corpse drawers.

"No-*oooo*," said Franco, and gave a little cough. "Actually, you'll find that Mel, actually, wasn't actually technically a zombie, *noo*, she was actually, technically, a deviated super-soldier. So I didn't *hump* a zombie, did I? Actually."

"It looked like the same puddle of slime to me," said Pippa.

"And that puddle of slime happens to be dead," said Franco, teeth clenched tight.

Pippa stopped. She placed a hand on his arm. She smiled, a kind smile, which looked crooked, unreal, plastic, wrong on Pippa's face. She wasn't used to being nice; being nice was something other people did.

"I'm sorry, Franco," she said.

"That's OK," grumbled Franco. "I kinda feel she's better off dead. I remember watching her watching herself. In the mirror, y'know? She didn't realise I could see her crying, remembering how she used to be, all slim and lithesome and sexy.

But she did. She remembered, deviated monster or no, and it hurt her, it burned her deep, like a knife through her soul, through her humanity. If I got changed into a zombie, I think I'd rather be dead."

"Well, I'm always here to pull the trigger, sweetie," smiled Pippa.

Franco looked into her cold, grey eyes. "I know that," he said, without any trace of humour.

"I found something."

Keenan halted up ahead, his gun poised, light fixed on a huge machine, easily twenty feet in height. It was metal, gently degraded, patched with rust. It had a squat base, solid, heavy-looking, and from the base rose a mechanical arm the width of a man with several hydraulic junctions. At its end sat a huge disk, with four wide, flat light bulbs glaring grey in Keenan's gun-light.

"An operating light?" said Pippa.

"Nah," said Franco. "That's a CANKER XRD Analytical X-RAY Residual Gamma Stress Analyser. It uses NDT, or non-destructive short-wave electromagnetic gamma rays, to examine the volumes of specimen, or specimens, or more precisely, bones or tissue, inside a hospital environ of course, and produces a radiograph of any particular subject, showing changes or otherwise subsequent alterations in thickness highlighting defects (internal and external) and revealing surface or near-surface organic-structural information. The gamma squeezes through any particular gap, even at a sub-atomic level, and can induce DNA alterations via the effects on whole-body gamma irradiation on localised sub-atomic beta-irradiation-induced tissue reactions, thus causing transformation and distortions on said DNA strands and posing possible cancer-causing issues when over-used and abused. Ironically, as well as causing cancer, gamma beams can be used to kill cancer cells, or they used to, before the introduction of that technology we all love-to-hate, namely biomods which attack a cancer from within and have thus negated any need for a CANKER XRD Analytical X-RAY Residual Gamma Stress Analyser in modern medicine."

Franco stopped. Keenan and Pippa were staring at him.

"What?" he said.

"You ingest the fucking manual?" said Pippa.

"Nah," said Franco. "It's a weapon, innit?"

"Meaning?"

"I'm a weapons expert, innit?"

"Meaning?"

"Anything that can be used for explosions, or detonation, or otherwise form a basis for conflagration, I have an avid interest in, thereof. A CANKER XRD Analytical X-RAY Residual Gamma Stress Analyser when used in topical applications with certain chemicals and explosives can cause a certain amount of, shall we say, Big Bang."

"Big Bang," said Pippa.

"Yeah." Franco grinned. "It's an X-RAY machine. And you can turn it into a bomb."

"Sounds good. Only pointless, here."

"They must have decommissioned them," said Keenan. "Dumped them down here. Look," he played his gun-light over the sad collection of rusting specimens. "There must be twenty of them. Like extinct cyborgs."

"All dead," said Pippa.

Keenan shivered. "Come on. We're wasting too much time. Let's get out of this…"

"Morgue?" suggested Pippa.

"It certainly feels that way."

They eased along the far wall, subconsciously edging away from the huge banks of corpse receptacles. Still, their lights splayed nervously over the endless resting places for hospital unfortunates. Drawer after drawer of horizontal coffins, all metal, all grey, all flaked with rust. Combat K felt chilled to the bone. Combat K could smell the death of millennia.

Franco was the first to stop. Somehow, he had edged to the front of the group, beyond their normal subconscious formation, and Keenan almost bumped into the nurse-outfitted ginger squaddie.

Franco held up a hand.

"What is it?" hissed Pippa.

"A… feeling. An itch I can't scratch."

Pippa was just about to retort with an insult, when she too felt the horror of the grave wash over her. She could taste earth, feel worms on her flesh, smell the stench of oiled wood and roses and pity and hear the rattle on the coffin lid. She coughed, and blinked, and there were tears in her eyes. She looked down, and for the briefest of moments her flesh was grey, sagging, infused with the colour of the dead, the perfume stink of the departed.

She screamed and stepped back. Her scream echoed up and down the cavern, booming from the endless banks of metal drawers and seemingly taking on a weird shrieking life of its own, increasing in volume, shrieking and hissing and snarling up and down the vast space, booming from wall to wall to wall, to finally and gradually die out in a dwindling mini-wail of tortured pain and final agony...

"Shit," she breathed.

Somewhere, somewhere deep, there came a grinding sound.

"Don't like that," said Franco, and took a step back. He realised without humour that his back was against the wall. The corpse drawers were reasonably distant, but still far too close for his liking.

"I think we need to run," whispered Pippa.

"Too late," said Keenan.

On the wall where his gun-light shone, a single drawer edged away from the wall. Rusted wheels squeaked on rusted chassis, until the drawer was fully extruded and there came a solid *thud*. The drawer shuddered. Combat K stood, rigid, frozen, guns aimed as one at the simple opening of steel.

She sat up. Franco gasped.

Her legs swung over the side, and she dropped lightly to the ground.

She was ten feet tall, her skin grey and sagging and quite obviously dead. She was a corpse. A walking corpse. Franco's gaze dropped, and worked its way up. She wore a gold ankle-bracelet which stood out fetchingly from mottled grey corpse-flesh. She wore stockings, sexy items, held by suspenders done in a tasteful white. There, the clothing ended, and the corpse/nurse/zombie was naked.

Franco wished she wasn't.

With shuddering jerks Franco's gaze swept up, past the inverted V of grey sagging horror, the limp waxy pubic mound, the wide rolling hips, the generous tyre of blubbery molten dead flesh, to breasts which mocked femininity and a face... ye gods, a face that was straight out of a comedy zombie horror movie, only framed with shocking peroxide-blonde hair and dead cracked bleeding lips painted a fetching, shining, cherry-red.

"A zombie nurse corpse," croaked Franco.

Keenan cocked his weapon.

"She's ten feet tall!" cackled Franco.

Pippa levelled her D5 shotgun, face grim.

"But hey," said Franco, cheering a little, "this

is a test we can win, reet? Three Combat-K über-squaddies against one ten-foot zombie nurse chick? We can *beat* this bitch! We can slap her arse, put her down, show her who's boss."

"Pick up your guns," growled Pippa.

The nurse walked forward, as if all her limbs belonged to different people. She was gangly, despite her fat; disjointed, despite her womanhood, and she leered down at the three little humans, grinning through bad make-up.

"You've come to play, little people?" she slurred, as if drunk. Her head swayed left, then right, as if attached by loose ball-bearings. "You come to my morgue to pay your last respects?" She giggled, coquettishly, and stared down at the Combat-K soldiers, apparently unperturbed by their guns.

"Let's take her," whispered Franco... as more squeaking and grinding noises filled the air. To their horror, hundreds of corpse drawers began to slide from the rusted metal wall. They slid free, squeaking open, and in panic Combat K's gun-lights roved along the wall for as far as the human eye could see... and for as far as the human eye could see the wall began to disgorge corpses, some male, some female, some tall and short and wide and thin and ugly and ugly and ugly and Franco felt a scream welling in his throat because he knew, knew as hundreds of feet with hundreds of toe-tags slapped the tiny white tiles, he knew there were way too many to take out –

"Which way?" snapped Keenan.

Pippa pointed, and they began to run but the corpses moved like a *wave,* moved like a *tide,* two or three hundred flowing across the tiled floor and squatting, hands touching the floor, suddenly motionless and with every set of dead eyes in gradually decomposing faces fixed on Combat K.

"The avatar said this was a test of aggression," said Pippa, motionless, her eyes raking the wall of animated corpses.

"Maybe it was a double bluff," said Keenan.

"I don't think we have a choice," said Pippa.

The wall of dead grey bodies shifted, undulated, like grass in a breeze. And from their midst came the ten foot nurse they'd first seen, with her blonde hair and cherry lips. She approached Combat K, hips moving seductively, and her large naked feet slapped on the tiles and she stopped, ten feet away, swaying. Behind her, hundreds of corpses growled a long, low growl, like a guard dog baring its fangs.

Franco gulped.

Keenan stepped forward, with Pippa at his shoulder. Franco, cowering behind, decided what they really needed right now was a brave rearward guard.

"Let us pass," said Keenan.

"No."

"Why not?"

"None living shall enter."

"We seek VOLOS."

The dead nurse smiled then, and Keenan caught the cunning in her eyes, in her dead eyes, rimed with treacle mascara. "Nobody shall meet with VOLOS. That is the privilege of the dead."

"Why so?"

"I say so, because I am the Morgue Matron, this is my bridge, my passage, my domain."

Keenan lifted his gun. "Then I will kill you."

"You think others have not tried? You think thousands haven't fallen screaming into the void, worms in their hair, ash on their tongues? You petty fucking mortals, I despise you, you, the living, the sane, the arrogant, the superior, I despise you all. You shall die."

She lifted her arm, and smiled.

Her arm dropped.

"Attack!" she screamed... and the corpse-horde surged forward.

Guns screamed, but the corpses were on them...

Keenan discharged his machine gun in a grey twisted face, and brains and skull shards exploded from the back of its head in a shower of gore. He twisted as a savage punch whirred past his face, knuckles scraping his cheek, and rolled, rising in the path of another corpse which lunged at him. He slammed a right straight, dropped and swept the undead's legs away. Hands grasped at him, and something whacked the back of his head. He felt himself go under, and heard a *boom* as a marionette accelerated above him in a tangle of naked green limbs, toe-tag flapping. Pippa was there, and she helped him rise. He'd lost his gun.

"This is chaos!" she screamed, and Keenan nodded, drawing a knife from his boot and stabbing a corpse in the eye. The eyeball popped free to dangle against the creature's cheek, but still it came on, grey spittle raging on lips and Pippa and Keenan kicked apart, Pippa's shotgun blasting a head from shoulders as she back-peddled and looked crazily about. They were a swarm, a horde, an army, and she saw Keenan back away, knife slashing out to open a throat in what should have been a shower of arcing blood, but no blood emerged. The corpse was necrotic; and more importantly, rigor mortis had set in.

*They shouldn't be able to walk!* screamed her brain, as she tossed her D5 to Keenan. He caught the weapon and blew the knees from a corpse, which hit the ground on its face and continued crawling at him. Pippa drew both swords from sheaths behind her pack, and calmed her raging mind as the corpses meandered around her, towards her, arms stretching for her, and she felt herself slip into the *zone* and started to dance, slowly at first, swords a bright silver blur slashing left, right, in arcs, in circles, each yukana forming glittering webs and each stroke cutting free fingers and hands, arms and feet, knees and heads, and with each twirl there came a *thud* and a shudder but Pippa worked the jarring impacts into her dance, turned them into a beat, into a bass rhythm as she moved forward, before Keenan and Franco who were panting, drenched in sweat, faces lacerated from clutching fingers and old black claws...

Pippa moved with grace, a dancer, her face serene, her breathing rhythmic, and before her fell five, ten, twenty of the corpses, forming a waist-high mound over which more grey sagging monsters climbed to leap at her... and now she was retreating, away from the launch-pad of dismembered bodies, and Franco and Keenan moved back with her, boots thudding white tiles, Pippa their defender with her glittering web of lethally sharp yukana blades.

"Head back to the oxygen cylinders!"

"Why?" came Pippa's slow, lazy voice, and her voice was distant, dream-like as the lethal yukana blades whirled and corpses lost limbs and heads.

"Big Bangs!" said Franco, eyes gleaming bright.

They altered course, a tight unit of whirling death amidst a baying moaning crowd of grey-skinned undead. Flat feet slapped white tiles in an urgency to get at Combat K, to rip them apart, to tear the skin from their ripe skulls.

"Nearly there!" panted Franco, and fired off a few rounds over Pippa's shoulder, taking a corpse in the face, exploding skull into a mush of brain-shrapnel.

"What's the plan?" snapped Keenan.

"Watch," said Franco, and whirled, his body tense inside his tight-fitting PVC nurse uniform.

He grabbed an oxygen cylinder, hoisted it over his head, and flung it into the horde of corpses. The cylinder thrummed overhead, through pools of green light, and Franco's Kekra snapped up and he aimed with the eagle-eye of the sniper.

*Crack.* KABOOM! The oxygen cylinder exploded in a rage, and a bloom of fire and metal shrapnel savaged the corpses, slamming perhaps twenty to the ground in a mushed mushy-pea mess.

"Brilliant! I'll throw, you shoot," said Keenan, hoisting a cylinder. He launched the makeshift grenade, and Franco tracked it through the gloom. His gun cracked, and again fire ravaged the corpses. Several caught fire, their dry hair going up in streamers that made Pippa falter in her dance of sword death…

"Again," snapped Franco.

Again Keenan launched an ancient oxygen cylinder, and Franco tracked it with expert eye. He fired, and there came a *ping,* then the cylinder rattled off amongst slapping corpse feet. "It was a dud!" wailed Franco, and glanced behind. So much for his bright idea!

"It's like trying to hold back the ocean with a spade," said Keenan, a sheen of sweat on his battered face, dirt and oil smeared in his skin, but his eyes lizard-cool. Pippa leapt before him, swords hissing and thumping. "There's too many of them! We either need something far more lethal, or we need to find a way out of this shit-hole."

"If only I had my pack!" wailed Franco. "It had blocks of T7 and Tramp8 explosives; it'd make mincemeat of these dead suckers."

"Yeah, but it'd take us with them," said Keenan, coolly, brain ticking like clockwork. "What about that?"

"What?"

"The Leksell gamma-focus – around your hairy neck. Can you attach it to an oxygen cylinder? Will it focus and enhance the blast?"

"No." Franco's eyes gleamed. "I have a much better idea that that. PIPPA! BACK TO THE CANKER XRD ANALYTICAL X-RAY RESIDUAL GAMMA STRESS ANALYSER!"

They started to move, Pippa their shield. But she was tiring now, tiring fast, sweat soaking her, her movements blurring. She was lethal, she was deadly, she was a killer – however, she was ultimately human.

"You said the CANKER XRD can be used as a big bomb? That's no good," snapped Keenan, loosing off more rounds. Corpses slapped to the floor, to be trampled by their uncaring comrades. "It'll detonate us, as well. We'll never escape the blast. And if we run, we take the corpses with us."

"No no no," said Franco, rubbing his eyes. "Watch! And learn from the greatest detonations expert the Quad-Gal has ever known! They don't call me Franco 'Triple Bang' Haggis for nothing, y'know!"

They reached the huge X-RAY machine, and Franco ripped the Leksell gamma-focus from around his neck. He clambered up the front of the machine like a monkey on speed and, hanging from the huge head with its four flat circles, he screwed the Leksell into the centre, then gave it a pat.

He dropped to the ground, ran around the back of the CANKER, and leapt up onto the control plate. He looked like some dirty ginger big-gun operator, only wielding medical equipment instead of a weapon in his greasy hairy hands. He tugged on several levers, and there came a high-tension *whine*. The CANKER jerked, and the mechanical arm whirred into life with Franco at the controls. It moved, jerking, and aimed at the crowd of corpses...

He winked at Keenan, and hit the switch.

In the chamber, there came another, massive whine, and all the green lights went out leaving the vast space in a total, chilly darkness. A smell of ozone washed over Combat K. And the CANKER machine singularly failed to deliver its payload...

"Great," snapped Keenan, face contorted in the glow of his gun-light. "You're damn right they don't call you Franco 'Triple Bang' fucking Haggis for nothing, mate. They should call you Franco 'Limp Dick' Haggis, or maybe Franco 'Can't Get It Up' Haggis the complete dickhead!"

Franco jumped down from the useless CANKER X-RAY machine. He held up a hand. "Whoa, brother! Just needs more battery power!" He ran to another CANKER, this one in a greater state of rust and degeneration; he kicked open a dented panel, and pulled out what looked to Keenan suspiciously like a set of red and black jump leads, which he spooled across the floor to the first machine...

Pippa stumbled back, to stand with chest heaving beside Keenan and the CANKER XRD Analytical X-RAY Residual Gamma Stress Analyser. "I hope you've got a good plan," she wheezed, "because I'm all out of juice." Both yukanas touched the floor, and scratched the white tiles. Pippa was totally exhausted.

The corpses had fallen back, and were reforming lines with their ten-foot leader at the centre. Many were grinning, and they knew Combat-K were tiring fast; were finished, in fact. Eyes watched Franco clamber up onto the CANKER with interest, but no fear. After all, what damage could an X-RAY machine do? It took photographs of bones, right?

Again, Franco fired the Analyser with a *thump* and swung it down low, aiming at the corpses. They roared then, a sour ancient dead roar emerging from rotting stumps of smashed teeth as grey fingers flexed and gleaming eyes focused on the living... the living, soon to be dead.

"Duck!" screamed Franco, and hit the detonation button as he swung the Analyser from left to right in a quick, savage movement of mechanical joints. The CANKER whined, but did not fire, made no machine-gun rattles, no booms of explosion, just emitted a silent and deadly beam of concentrated gamma rays…

Before them, a line of a hundred corpses were sliced in two in a rapid and vaguely diagonal acceleration. Flesh slapped the tiles, corpse halves slapped the tiles and Franco, like a madman on a crazy gun-turret, lined the CANKER up again as the second row of dazed and confused corpses stared in confusion at their massacred comrades… again the machine *whined* as Franco slammed it along their ranks, and the wide-field surgical *gamma-knife* cut through another hundred corpses and left their coagulated remains slopping across the white tiles…

The rest turned and ran for it, toe-tags slapping all the way back to the safety of their drawers. All except –

The leader. The ten-foot nurse.

She grinned, through cherry lipstick. And leapt… Pippa launched herself forward, ducking a swipe of talons and ramming her first sword through the creature's heart. The Matron of the Morgue shuddered, then laughed a cold corpse laugh and reached down for Pippa, who sidestepped, the second yukana whistling as it cut free her head.

The headless corpse hit the tiles, and Pippa stood on her sternum as she pulled free the first weapon without a word.

"I don't get it," said Keenan, breathing deeply, face weary, exhaustion mastering him. "It's a fucking X-RAY machine. What did you do to it?"

"It was developed for surgery," said Franco, leaping down and picking up his Kekra quad-barrel machine pistols. "It's called gamma-knife surgery, where intense and multiple concentrated beams of gamma rays, the most dangerous form of radiation in the Quad-Gal, are directed on a single spot. The beams are aimed from different angles to form an infinitesimal point of impact. This fucker could cut through a planet crust." He beamed, and winked. "Not bad for a simple cheese-eating squaddie, eh lad?"

Keenan laughed, and whacked him on the back. "Not bad, mate. Not bad at all."

"So now to VOLOS?" said Pippa.

"Yeah." Keenan's eyes hardened. "Now on... to VOLOS."

They squelched through dismembered corpses, with only the lights on their guns for guidance. It took another forty minutes to cross the Morgue, and every minute was a nerve-jangling experience as they waited for yet another, second wave of undead to attack and rip off their heads. But it never came; the corpses had returned to their sanctuary; to their peace; to their rest.

The door, when they found it, was small, fashioned from a single piece of mineral, a black slab like a coffin lid. Keenan stopped, seeing the door but hearing a tiny clattering noise behind. Combat K turned, in an agony of fear, and from the blackness, the stygian gloom, creeping into the edges of their gun-lights, emerged...

First, a *buzz*, as tiny insects flickered around the dancing beams of light. Pippa hissed, lifting her yukana swords in defence, for these were Morphs: the insects created from tiny hypodermic needles, from back at the hospital where she and Betezh had been stung, and taken prisoner. They flickered, swooping and whining like mosquitoes on bad acid. But even as they jittered, from the black came more enemies... nurses, tottering on legs made from hypodermics, crutches, scalpels, their peroxide hair curled, their lips bright and red, teeth snarling... there were doctors and surgeons, many with their own internal organs hanging on strings and chains, and each bearing medical weapons of exaggerated proportions... there were patients, squaddie patients, many with three legs or five arms, cam-cream on their faces, their green backless gowns flapping forlornly in the damp dour gloom of the Morgue. There were patients in straightjackets, gibbering and drooling and grinning, and yet more nurses with bags and pans for heads, eyes slopping around in colostomy sack faeces... there were Cryo Medics with thick black masks and ice-throwers, their breathing coming in short rasping bursts, and then flickers of blue shot through the darkness accompanied with the *buzz* and *spark* of the cackling battery-mouthed Convulsers. More nurses came, some on fire, the flames lighting up the darkness like torches and revealing *revealing a huge and endless rolling wave of bodies, of twisted mutated medical deviations of every possible size and description...* across the floor jumped and crawled babies, their wails squawking out as sick drooled and little black eyes fixed on Combat-K and thousands and thousands of medical staff, hospital staff, they all filled the Morgue from end to end as they advanced on Combat-K with a singular purpose...

"What shall we do?" squealed Franco, like a girl.

A roar went up, a roar so loud it deafened Combat K.

"*Be calm, my son,*" said Father Callaghan inside Franco's head. His Temple Pill throbbed. "*Use the core of your Wisdom, my son.*"

At last! thought Franco. He's earned his $19.99! Reaching into his mouth, Franco clicked free the two tiny WiT bombs, armed the dets, and hurled them into the fast accelerating medical ranks... the *boom* was incredible, and a couple of hundred medical bodies shot up and out, nurses and doctors, babies and mutations all spinning into a powerful tornado flurry of merged and mashed limbs and faces, and Combat-K turned, sprinted, and heaved through the coffin-lid doorway, leaping through into a smooth tunnel beyond where walls gleamed with tiny crystals and veins sparkling through stone.

The door slammed behind them. There came a savage *thud,* and the door began to shake as Keenan coolly threw three huge bolts into position.

"How long will it hold them?" Pippa's voice was small, her face ashen.

"Let's move," said Keenan, shrugging, and Combat-K moved forward, onwards, ever down… with muffled distant booms and shrieks and clatters and squeals and shouts and squawks following from The Morgue.

THE END OF the tunnel glowed with a bright black light, so bright Combat-K had to shield their eyes on approach. They stepped out onto a ledge, perhaps six feet wide, where the avatar of VOLOS waited, in silence, hands clasped before him.

Holding hands protectively before faces, they tried to look into the vast edifice before them, but could not. It was black, but not black. It was every colour and it was no colour; it was every colour not yet invented, every colour never before witnessed by human eyes, and thus incomprehensible, even to a relatively advanced mammalian brain.

"Welcome," said VOLOS. "Although you have led the hordes to my core."

Franco poked Keenan with his gun, and Keenan stepped forward, almost reluctantly. He knew; here was something so powerful, so strange, so alien, that what could three simple soldiers with machine guns possibly hope to achieve? They could never kill VOLOS. All they could do was talk. But would he be willing to listen?

"Why did you try to kill us?"

"I did not." The voice was soft, lilting, almost musical. It came, seemingly, direct to the brain, without involving complex organic audiometric equipment. It was neither too loud nor too quiet, and had no sexual attachment. It was just a voice, a beautiful voice, a powerful voice.

"Well we weren't playing a game back there," snarled Keenan. "You put us through your pointless tests to see if we were worthy to meet you, face to face. Well, we're here. We're pissed, and we want to see you, fucker!"

"You look upon me," said VOLOS. "Your eyes cannot properly interpret what you see. However, let me explain a little. I am not a creature, a lifeform, as you would understand it. I, VOLOS, am the planet."

There came a stunned silence.

"Like, as in the *whole* planet?" splurted Franco. "That's damn bloody impossible! How can you be a bloody big buggering planet?"

"My head and heart are the core of the world," said VOLOS, and the voice seemed now more gentle, more intuitive as it linked to Combat K's brain-patterns. "The mantle is my flesh, my muscle, and the crust is my skin. My veins are the faults that run through the rock, the magma that flows through the billions of channels in my flesh; earthquakes are my shudders, my pain, and the sun warms my face every day for eternity."

Combat K were silent. Stunned. Confused.

"Impossible!" persisted Franco, clutching his Kekras to his chest like a small child holding a stuffed teddy. "Nothing so big can live!"

"Fool," said VOLOS, and only now did they perceive a hint of human emotion, of frustration, of annoyance, of *anger*. "What is life? What deserves the right to be called life? I think, I feel, I construct, I create, I destroy. I am not flesh and blood as you consider life; however, you stand here conversing with me, deep down near my heart and soul and mind, and it causes me great pain to converse with you, to focus everything on such a narrow spot."

"Why not use the avatar?" said Keenan. "Why go to all this trouble to bring us here?"

"I have a problem," said VOLOS, choosing words with care. "And I would ask for your help. But we must be swift, for even now the twisted medical hordes are marshalling their strength. I can only keep them at bay for so long."

"Then why try to kill us?" snapped Keenan, losing his temper. "Since we landed, you've thrown every fucking thing you can at us! From deviant nurses and doctors and patients, with their twisted medical technology and fucked-up genetics, to earthquakes and cryo-soldiers, battles between armies of deviant mutations, and even down to your pathetic tests of mercy and savagery, twisting our minds and fucking with our brains... this has been a damn hard exercise in survival, VOLOS, for somebody who simply wanted our help. You're fucking lucky we got here at all. And we've... lost friends along the way." Keenan was scowling, into the weird black light, not bothering to shade his eyes now as he felt the pulse of alien blood in his veins and felt the heat of the Dark Flame glowing in his heart.

"I have lost control," admitted VOLOS, and they felt a huge *pulse* of sorrow emanate from the world. It eased through them, like treacle through honey, and they felt his, or *its*, incredible sadness. "Once, a million years ago, I was strong. I was powerful. But with every passing second I grow weak. Yes, once I watched as the junks were created, even helped the suckling Leviathan create his army; but the Junkala were a plaything to me, that is all, and I wished to supply a twisted lesson to a proud and arrogant alien race who Leviathan wished to educate. The Junkala were cultured, and beautiful; yes. But they had designs on conquering the Galaxy, on invading, to create a vast and powerful Empire! Their arrogance was awesome to behold. You met Elana, yes?"

"I did," said Keenan, voice low.

"She has the facts twisted. She said they were like gods... and that Leviathan created me, VOLOS, to watch over them. Such a petty misguided angle of view; to be so narrow, so channelled. I knew Leviathan, yes. But I am far older than Leviathan. I saw his birth, and if you help me, I will watch his death."

Keenan swallowed, and glanced at Pippa.

"So all the nurses and doctors running wild on the surface – you do not control them?" she said.

"No. They follow their own deviated paths. Yes, I was instrumental in setting them on the road to their twisted medical civilisation; it is what I do. I plant a seed, but whether that seed grows into a bright beautiful flower, or a savage, suffocating, killing weed, I do not decide. I allow the chaos of nature that privilege." VOLOS laughed. "The great irony is that my power is all but gone. I am a shadow, a wisp of smoke, a decimation. The tests you went through to reach me – they were not *my* tests. They were created by the medical deviations, to stop any such as you reaching my Core. I am sorry you suffered so much pain on your journey here. It was never my intention."

"I thought we'd ignite the proto-matter and blast you to High Heaven, and then the loonies would have their world back," laughed Franco. "They'd all twist back into normality, and it'd be all fine and dandy. After all, Keenan here promised Lunatrick a new world…"

"No!" said VOLOS, and they felt the world shake, a trillion tremors running through every fault and line and lode. "Lunatrick is a dark spirit, he would have you transfer him to another, clean, new planet... so he could expand the corruption. You have to help me, Keenan. You have to help me grow strong."

"You are a machine?" said Keenan, remembering his conversation with the Junkala King.

VOLOS laughed then. "I have seen and heard your conversation, aeons past. Again, the Junkala had great arrogance. They imprisoned me! With machines! I was never truly imprisoned, but they restricted my energy, used ancient magic to stem my control. I am not a machine god, there is nothing mechanical about me. Yes, I am different physiologically, my blood is magma, my nerves are crystals; the Junkala, their history is as corrupt as their central nervous systems. I admit, I did not stand in the way of their deviation... but now, now I can start to put these things right."

"Why would you do that?" said Pippa.

"I have tasted humility," said VOLOS. "It is quite a thing to live in fear. Quite a thing to spend a million years growing ever more weak, watching those on your skin twist and corrupt and begin to understand you, to hunt you, to torture you. On your way here you saw the great machines they built, for burrowing under the ground. They were excavating me, searching out my Core. The creatures of Sick World want nothing more than to corrupt their Master." He laughed, a long sad laugh, like the extinction of comets. "If you help me, Keenan, if you help me I will save your friends, I will send them back to the surface where they can connect with the DropShip and leave this place…"

"And?" Keenan's eyes were bright.

"I will give you the key to unlocking the junks. You cannot fight their pestilence, Keenan. They are too strong. Instead, you must change them back again. Make them whole again, make them good and clean, make them pure, without a need to spread their toxic filth. I can do this. I can tell you where Leviathan hid the Soul of their Race. It is locked away in a Photon Shield. You can use it, spread it through the junks like a virus through software; and slowly, they will revert from poison."

"That's a strong bartering tool," said Keenan, warily. "What do you want of me?"

"You must give yourself to me."

There was silence. Keenan was frowning. "You wish me to die?"

"No. I wish you to *merge* with my Core. I need your Dark Flame, Keenan. I need the blood given to you by Emerald, by the *Kahirrim*. But you must give freely, or it will burn me, pollute my essence. I cannot force you. Will you do this, Keenan? Will you help me, help all the races of the Quad-Gal survive the junks?"

"No!" shouted Pippa. "You cannot ask this of him!" She turned to Keenan, grabbed him, shook him. "He's lying, VOLOS is lying, how do you know he tells the truth? How do you know he won't betray us, send us on a wild-goose chase? It's bollocks, Keenan, it's a lie!"

"There's something else," said Keenan, looking back to VOLOS. He was calm now. Serene. He could picture his little girls, in his mind, his Rachel, his Ally, and their deaths were a bitter pill under his tongue and in his throat and he realised; he was tired of life, tired of the fight, and all he wanted was to be reunited with his children. With his dead children...

"I can help you stop Leviathan," whispered VOLOS.

The avatar stepped forward, and in pale white hands it held a small envelope.

"Inside are instructions on how to halt Leviathan, how to build the machines used to imprison him... the machines that broke down, the machines you helped to... destroy. Combat K. You can put right that which you broke. You can save the Quad-Gal... and more. Protect it for another million years."

A hushed silence fell.

Pippa shook Keenan, harder now, and tears were coursing down her cheeks. Keenan lifted his hand, and made a strange gesture; from the black walls long green tubes emerged, like the wavering tendrils of creeping vines, and they slowly wound around Franco and Pippa. Pippa started to kick and struggle, but within a second she was held tight and lifted easily from the ground.

"You will send them back to the surface? With Betezh, and Olga, and Snake?"

"Yes," said VOLOS.

"I agree," said Keenan, face devoid of emotion.

"No!" screamed Pippa, as the avatar moved forward and handed the envelope to Franco. He clutched it tight, and tears stained his cheeks, ran down into his ginger goatee. "You don't have to do this, man," he snarled. "Keenan! Look at me! There are other ways to solve this problem! You don't have to die!"

"I won't be dying," said Keenan, gently. "I understand. Emerald gave me that gift. And I know VOLOS will not betray me; he will not betray *us*. This is our answer, Franco, our cure, Pippa. Don't be sad. This is a fine day, I assure you." His voice was melancholy and as Franco and Pippa were dragged backwards, upwards, to be deposited in tiny capsules and shot up through rock and stone and metal, they saw the last images of Keenan stepping forward, off the ledge, suspended, and then sucked down into the raging blinding black fire to be gone, and merged, and assimilated into the Core that was VOLOS.

THE SUN EASED over the horizon, fingers of orange pushing away the green light of a dying moon. Heat flooded Sick World, and despite the snow, the remainder of Combat-K were warmed as they sat, on rocks, staring bleakly out across the rugged landscape.

Franco clutched the small envelope tightly, and rubbed at his nose occasionally, lost in thought. Betezh and Olga had built a fire near the Giga-Buggy and, using utensils and ingredients from the vehicle store, were cooking a pot of stew over the flames. Snake was locked by Snapwire to the Buggy's rail, his face dour, expression unreadable. He would await court martial and trial by Quad-Gal when they lifted from the planet.

And Pippa... Pippa sat a short way off, alone, a gentle breeze ruffling her hair. She had ceased crying, and her face had the rosy after-glow of sorrow, her eyes a hard edge of bad intent. She glanced up, as Cam emerged, weaving across the snow, and halted amidst the camp with a spinning shower of blue lights.

"What happened?" came his tinny voice.

Franco explained, in a low, quiet monotone, everything that had occurred since the Silglace and their crash. Cam listened in silence, spinning, all lights now gone from his battered casing. When Franco had finished, Cam simply sat, unmoving, in the cool winter breeze.

Pippa moved over, and sat close to Franco, leaning in to him, sharing his warmth. He reached around her, squeezed her, and for the first time in his life made no sexual innuendo, no lame jokes.

Sadness ran like molten lead through his veins, melancholy through his mind. With regards dirty jokes; well, he simply no longer had it in him.

"I can't believe he's gone," said Pippa, eventually.

"No," said Franco.

"I loved him," said Pippa.

"Me too."

"He's at peace, now."

"With his little girls."

"Yeah." She smiled at that.

"Have you looked at the envelope?"

"Not yet." Franco opened it, for once fumbling with clumsy fingers normally used to setting the delicate det. cords on bombs. He pulled free a digital sheet; they asked Cam to translate.

"It's very simple," said Cam, for once without his bouncy humour. "There are co-ordinates, and a very simple set of instructions. You seek… the Junkala Soul. The Soul of their Race, taken by Leviathan and used to deviate their genetics. With this, you can re-infect them, as with a computer code virus, only on an organic level. You can make the junks good with a disease they once lost; you can stop the war, and the death."

Franco nodded.

"I haven't got the heart," said Pippa.

"What, you'd let the Quad-Gal die?" snarled Franco suddenly, feeling a surge of mad anger and they both leapt to their feet, guns out, aimed at one another's heads. Pippa's eyes were hard, cold, grey, filled with hate. Franco crumbled first, and lowered his Kekra.

"I'm sorry, Pippa," he said, miserably.

Pippa melted. She sighed, and sat down, re-holstering the D5 alongside her yukana swords. "Me too, Franco. You know I'd never harm you."

"Oh yeah?"

She stared at him. Hard. "Yes," she said, voice in cold stone. "I've lost one member of Combat K. I don't need to lose another."

"You must go to the Ganger World," said Cam, his AI voice soft.

"That's a bad place," said Franco.

"A dangerous place," agreed Pippa.

At that moment, they heard a distant rumbling, a grind, a slamming of steel on the hard-packed earth. From snow-heavy conifers there came a trembling, a crashing, breaking of branches and boles of trees; and then, like a vision from an esoteric metal nightmare, the digger lurched from the tree-line and ground its way through the snow and rocks, and basically anything that stood in its path.

Combat K watched the vehicle approach, then settle down with a sigh and a hiss of steam. A hatch opened, and Miller screamed as he was launched head-first into a deep snowdrift, where his legs kicked in a modestly comical fashion. Betezh moved over to him, dragged him out, rapped him on the head with a stew-ladle, and tied him up alongside Snake, who growled at the treatment. *Nobody* deserved to be locked up with a Health and Safety Inspector. Except, in fact, maybe a traffic warden.

"Mel!" bellowed Franco, and ran towards the digger.

Mel clambered down, and picked Franco up in an embrace that showed, despite the beatings, despite the screaming, despite the *divorce*, there was still love there. Olga looked on in disapproval, and stirred her stew, a woman cuckolded.

Franco looked around, beaming, elated that his true love, his true *zombie love*, was still alive. But there was no Keenan. No Keenan to make wise-ass cracks about taking her to the vets, being a *bitch*, or having her jabs done.

Franco let out another deep sigh, a sigh of disbelief, and of resignation. He moved back to Pippa whilst Mel disappeared to sort out her severe personal hygiene problems.

"I miss him already," he said.

"Yeah."

"Although he was a sarcastic bastard."

"That was our Keenan."

"So, what we gonna do now?" Franco peered around. "And where's that dumb mutt bloody dog, Sax, got to?"

"He trundled off across the snow going *ticka ticka ticka*, and muttering 'ruff' and 'borrocks', to pick up the damn DropShip so we can get our arses off this diseased and depressing ball of shit."

"Can he fly?" frowned Franco.

"Yeah," said Pippa, and smiled. "He showed me his license. He also told me about saving your dumb ass, on that collapsing snow cliff. He's one cute little metal doggie friend, y'know? Except for that wig. It's a bad wig."

"He's an acquired taste," muttered Franco. "Only I haven't acquired him yet."

Betezh brought them a bowl of stew and, reluctantly, Franco and Pippa sat alone, eating not tasting, and remembering Keenan. Only when Franco was dipping his third slice of sausage into the stew, did he repeat, voice little more than a whisper, "So, Pippa, what we gonna do now?" It was the voice of a small child.

Pippa looked at him, and drew her yukana sword. She angled the blade so that an esoteric blue glow from the snow flashed along the terrible, deadly weapon. "We're going to the gangers," she said, and smiled without humour, grey eyes bleak. "We're going to stop the junks."

## ACKNOWLEDGEMENTS

Thank you to the inhabitants of SICK WORLD, for making themselves so easy to write. Kisses to Sonia, for modelling the, erm, nurses, uniforms, and big hugs to my mad and bad little boys for making life so entertaining. Thanks must also go to th3 m1ss1ng for their esoteric musical soundtrack, and to various friends and colleagues for fine test reading duties. Thanks also to Ian Graham... for liking the babies.

Finally, a big hearty sausage to all at SOLARIS, especially for that time when they got drunk and dressed up in PVC and, erm, taught me about the dark side of the medical profession.

## ABOUT THE AUTHOR

**Andy Remic** is a British writer with a love of extreme sports, kickass bikes and sword fighting. Once a member of an elite Combat-K squad, he has since retired from military service and works as an underground rebel fighting bureaucratic oppression wherever he finds it. He does not condone the use of biomods, and urges human- and alien-kind to rebel against the market-oppression of nihilistic mega-corporations.

*Hardcore* is his seventh novel.

You can discover more about Andy Remic at *www.andyremic.com*.